DAVID KIRBY

Upper East Bride

OTHER BOOKS BY DAVID KIRBY

Evidence of Harm

Animal Factory

Death at SeaWorld

When They Come For You

COVER DESIGN BY CAROLINA BUZIO

First edition

This book was professionally typeset on Reedsy.
Find out more at reedsy.com

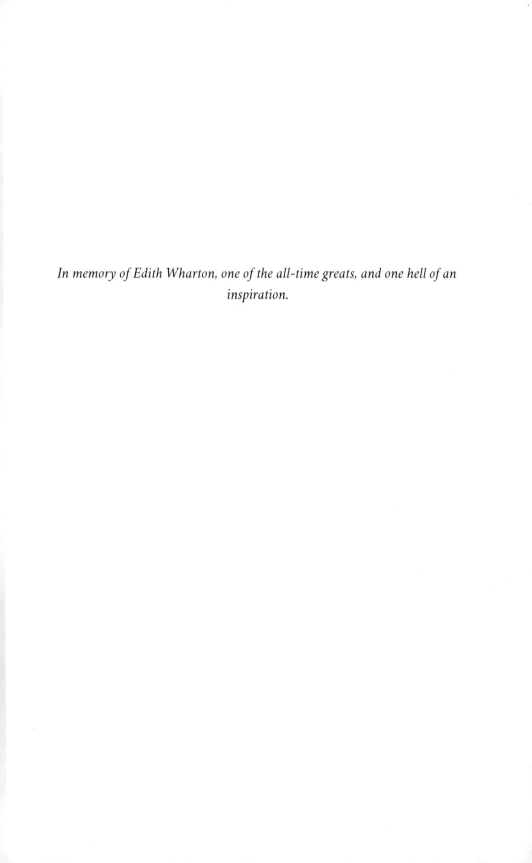

In memory of Edith Wharton, one of the all-time greats, and one hell of an inspiration.

Contents

Preface

NEW YORK POST

"The Gleaner" with Jamal Dix – September 8, 2018

"Rags to Riches at Saint Thomas Church"

It was one of those fairy tale weddings-of-the-century that makes New York go gaga.

Speaking of Gaga, she actually showed up, proof of the nuclear charisma of the media-darling groom, that gorgeous venture-capitalist, philanthropist, and most-eligible bachelor, Rexford James Bainbridge, III, 29, better known in the columns as "Sexy Rexy."

For weeks, he had entreated the star to attend, with flowery tweets, use of his villa in Mallorca (chez Jagger is right next door, *he reminded her) and a parade of strategically publicized donations to her favorite charities.*

And here she was, stepping out of a modest Lincoln Town Car, at 53rd and 5th, stopping for the pulsating pool of paparazzi outside the carved limestone façade of Saint Thomas Church, New York's Gothic Revival temple of High Episcopalian riches and rectitude.

Sadly, for Gaga, the late-summer heat was not her friend. Her pancetta leggings, though radiantly matched with a tunic woven entirely from crushed abalone shells and shredded Three Musketeers wrappers, began to wilt.

As far as The Gleaner *could tell, nobody cared. Not even a somewhat greasy Gaga, nor any number of Vanity-Fair-worthy denizens of Gotham and beyond — the cable news anchors with their dazzling teeth, the towering NBA ballers, the A-minus or, more often, B-minus Listers imported from The Coast, minor Royal Family members, Liza, Martha or Regis — could yank the limelight away from the Cinderella bride, young Megan O'Malley, 24, of Ypsilanti, Michigan.*

The aspiring journalist, utterly outside her middle-class league, was about to step down the aisle and smack into that ridiculously rarified world of private hedge funds, insider real estate schemes, offshore bank accounts, exorbitantly priced charity balls, Hamptons mansions, Swedish au pairs, last-minute charter jets and Fifth Avenue penthouses replete with panic rooms that define 21st Century uber-rich life in our fair city.

"I don't really see how the poor dear is going to pull it off," whispered Wanda Covington, that ex-pat Londoner and Type-A socialite whose sharp-tongued wit has been known to land her in more hot water than a rock lobster at Le Bernardin. "Heaven knows, we tried to help. But when it comes to this whole Pygmalion thing, she's a bit, well, daft, *isn't she? I mean, you can take the girl out of Walmart, but…"*

As The Gleaner *has reported previously, this was a production crying out for producers, and some of the most celebrated (for better or worse) socialites of the Upper East Side — friends, neighbors and assorted orbs in Sexy Rexy's solar system — leapt at the chance. But it wasn't easy.*

"The bride is sauntering into our little milieu on rather wobbly terroir,*"*

one of the Matrons, who insisted on anonymity, solemnly confided. "And when you've never summered in East Hampton or attended a polo match, when you don't even know a fish knife from a butter knife, what else can you do but accessorize, and lavishly so?"

But pish-posh. With her striking figure, porcelain-and-rose-dust complexion, sweep of raven hair and speckled violet-gray eyes, many have invariably drawn comparisons to Liz Taylor. Sadly though, given Megan's proletarian provenance, some of the snider members of Rex's circle have quietly taken to calling her "Liz Trailer."

The bridal party arrived in a white limousine carrying Megan, along with her mother, Maureen O'Malley of Greater Detroit, younger brother Todd and his boyfriend, Juan Carlos Bautista Santa Maria. It was their first big wedding, first limo ride and first time seeing actual rich people. When they pulled up, photographers rushed the car, demanding pics.

I peeked inside: The occupants looked petrified, like four trapped otters being dropped off at SeaWorld.

The great oaken doors swung open, the organ began wailing, and the bride entered the church. Megan took a deep breath as 500 faces turned around to stare at her, most of them smiling, some smirking like bored, grumpy goats.

Standing by the Rector, Canon Arthur M. Chadwick, was Rexford, this generation's John-John Kennedy. He looked delicious with his combed-back jet-black hair, charcoal-colored eyes, cheekbones for days, a buff but not too buff build, and perfect posture to match his custom-made Dolce & Gabbana tux.

Nearby stood Thaddeus M. Pepper, MD, the best man and our sceptered isle's somewhat uppity and most talked about Freudian Psychiatrist, revered for his magical prescription pad. Next to him stood a line of handsome young groomsmen, mostly from the "investment community." On the other side, rather conspicuously alone, was Megan's bridesmaid, her high-school buddy Brigit Tenpenny. Behind them on risers perched a battery of very white altar boys and, above them, not-so-white gospel-choir members from the Brooklyn Tabernacle.

The ceremony, mercifully brief and slightly uplifting, ended with the sober admonishment of the Canon that marriage was "not to be entered into unadvisedly or lightly, but reverently. Will all of you witnessing these promises do all in your power to uphold these two persons in their marriage?"

"We will," almost everyone said, including many who had no intention of doing anything remotely like that.

Now pronounced (rich) man and (unbelievably lucky) wife, the newlyweds walked back up the aisle to cheers, tears, applause and, it did not escape The Gleaner's notice, more than a smattering of crossed arms and pursed lips.

It was time for some serious soiree-going at Le Cirque, followed by a flight to Bora Bora, where the happy couple will spend two weeks at Halle Berry's "little place" by a secluded lagoon.

As they left, strangers gathered on the sidewalk commenced some raucous cheering (it was rumored they were hired by a mysterious downtown PR outfit but that has not been confirmed). The paparazzi popped. Two white peace doves were released into the sky. They were, it was noted with much fanfare in the gilded wedding program, former members of the Holy Vatican Flock, which had thrived at St. Peter's Basilica until one chilly morning in January 2014, when Pope Francis and two small children released a pair of the birds, who were promptly eviscerated by a seagull and crow before the mortified faithful.

And then something dreadful happened.

Just as they were climbing into the vintage Bentley, with UK plates, the sound of shouting and women wailing broke out near the church doors. I saw Megan turn around to look, only to see armed federal agents with the words "I.C.E." emblazoned on their uniforms grabbing two of Rex's terrified maids and slapping them in handcuffs.

"They can't do that!" Megan cried out. "Aren't they here legally?"

Rex paused. "I'm not really sure," I heard him grumble. "We'll have to sort this out when we return." Whatever the circumstances, and regardless of the maids' immigration status, bride and groom knew, of course, that someone had turned in their staff. And today, of all days.

But who? And why?

Chapter 1

Leaving, On A JetBlue Plane

A year ago, back in 2017, if anyone had told Megan O'Malley she'd move to New York and get swept off her feet by a handsome young multimillionaire, she would have told them to go jump in Lake Erie.

But then her best friend from Ypsilanti, Brigit, fell in love with a guy from Brooklyn and moved off to the great big city, where she'd found an administrative assistant position at the *New York Post*. Megan, though insanely proud of her friend, could not expel that distinct whiff of envy puffing around her mind. Megan's dream in life was to be a journalist, a professional and successful one, with major-media bylines and a passel of awards hanging on her office wall. And if that meant moving to New York, then even better.

And now, on this frigid Michigan morning in January, Megan was preparing to leave: Brigit had landed her an interview with New York's – and thus the nation's – preeminent gossip columnist, her boss Jamal Dix. And even though digging up dirt on Manhattan socialites and celebrities was hardly her dream job (that would be senior political reporter at, say, *The New York Times*), it was a humble start. An open door is, after all, an open door. Besides, most of her journalistic experience had come from her school paper at the University of Michigan in nearby Ann Arbor.

Megan was blasted with the aroma of burning bacon and crappy coffee wafting from the kitchen downstairs. Though she'd been back at her mom's for seven months after graduation - arriving jobless, penniless and with three loads of laundry – she was still startled by the fake-maple sizzle of Smithfield and the bitter urgency of Maxwell House.

A stunning beauty with long chocolate hair, violet-gray eyes and a diminutive but alluring 5-foot-6 frame, Megan rose like a lazy salamander crawling from a sun-warmed mud puddle. Wrapping herself in the frayed 100-thread-count sheet, she stumbled down the hallway toward the upstairs bathroom in her mother's creaky, rented clapboard house.

The bathroom was bolted. "Goddamn it Todd," Megan said, slapping the hollow door with her palm. "Haven't you pleasured yourself *enough* already? It's only nine."

A bilious fart, followed by silence, issued from behind the door.

"Breakfast!" Her mom yelled, so loudly Megan was sure everyone could hear it in downtown Detroit.

"Coming! But can you *please* tell your son to get out of the bathroom? Jeez. How many craps can someone take in one morning?"

"I don't take them," the voice said. "I leave them."

Sometimes Megan hated her little brother. This was one of them. Swearing under her breath, she ran downstairs to her mom's bathroom, to pee and grab a shower.

The plane to New York was leaving that afternoon. Only nuclear war, or the surprise return of her ex-boyfriend Ray, who unceremoniously dumped her during junior year, might keep Megan from getting on it. Even the sight of her AWOL dad sauntering through the door would not have deterred Megan. Her father, Drake, a burly, shaggy-haired mechanic with a lazy eye and dicey temper, ditched them when she was thirteen, only occasionally checking on his kids' well-being after filing for a quickie divorce in Ensenada. Megan missed him; Todd refused to speak to him.

The family huddled in silence over breakfast. Maureen, their 47-year-old mom, a generously proportioned, auburn-haired former beauty fighting long-term debt and the laws of gravity, poked at her eggs, eyeing the kids warily.

"So," she said finally, a pained expression etched on her face, which looked older and wearier beneath the unforgiving florescent overheads. "In the same week I learn my son's gay, my beautiful daughter goes off to live a life of decadence among the media whores in New York…" she paused, then spit out the final word like an olive pit…"*City*." Megan and Todd exchanged glances. "What am I to tell Father Quinn? He practically *raised* you two."

"Mom, stop." It was Todd. Tall but still somehow impish, the 21-year-old with buttery brown eyes, smooth skin and wavy ginger-colored hair, was even more obstinate than his sister. "Father Quinn tried to raise a lot more than *that*, if you know what I mean. I think he'll understand about me, you know, liking boys and all."

Megan smiled at her kid brother. Yes, he was a jerk. But he was also brave and honest. Megan, as an aspiring journalist, appreciated such qualities. Few gay kids in Ypsilanti, after all, came out to friends and family, even in this allegedly enlightened *Schitt's Creek* America.

"Hey Meg," Todd asked, "when you move to Manhattan and get all rich and famous and stuff, can you help set me up with my catering business?"

"Sure Toddie. We'll plan a hostile takeover of Martha Stewart's test kitchens, and then you can saute until the cows come home. Hell, you can saute the cows *as* they come home."

Later, they piled into Maureen's '96 Saturn for the 15-minute ride to Detroit airport. Megan wondered if she would miss this place as they drove through the quiet, frozen streets. Ypsilanti, or "Ypsi" as the locals called it ("Let's get tipsy in Ypsi!" Megan and her friends use to say), is not exactly the prettiest of places in the best of months. In January, it gives the word "dreary" a mournful ring.

At the airport, they climbed from the warm cocoon of the car to say goodbye. Icy tassels of fog billowed about their heads as they made small-talk in the thick winter air.

"I really hope you get this job," Todd said. "No wait, I *know* you will get this job."

Megan found herself endeared to her bratty kid brother more than ever. She would miss this little asshole. She and her mom struggled against tears, hugging goodbye. Todd stood by tentatively, unsure whether to witness the tender farewell, or check out the adorable Latino curbside-attendant helping a middle-aged couple grapple with their luggage.

Once through security and in her cramped seat, Megan pondered her brave new future. She was destined to hit the big time, she was certain, just like those other Michiganders, Madonna Ciccone, Marshall Mathers and Michael Moore. Like most writers, thoughts of fame haunted her dreams. But she intended to use the power that comes with it to make the world better – to expose injustices, right wrongs and give a voice to the voiceless, hope to the hopeless.

Megan had followed that dream all through college, where she was a rising reporter at *The Michigan Daily*, covering everything from the serious ("Campus Rapist Nabbed at Sorority Party"), to the sublime ("Katy Perry to Don Giant Panda Suit During Commencement.") By the end of junior year, Megan was a leading candidate for the paper's Editor-in-Chief position. Her job interview, with senior faculty advisor Trip Gottley (she always called him "Skip Yachtly," for his pompous insouciance) had gone well, at first.

And then Yachtly, without a word, reached across the desk and gently cupped his right hand under her supple left breast. "Tell me how much you want it, Megan," he slithered.

"Trip!" She swatted him away like a gnat. "I mean, Mr. Gottley! Is this how I'm supposed to get this job?'

He turned the color of farmed salmon and ordered Megan out. "You little… You wanted this position so much. And now the whole thing is out the window."

Megan leapt up, raced out the door and across the newsroom, shame and disgust suffocating her like methane gas. She ran into the humid June air, salty tears melding with beads of sweat. Megan grabbed her cell. She wanted to call Todd. But instead dialed her boyfriend Ray, the unsettlingly ambitious journalism student who'd managed to wrangle a weekly column out of Gottley on, of all things, *ethics.*

She told him what happened.

"Listen, I'm pretty tight with Gottley. I'll have a word."

A word? Megan was dumfounded. What did that even *mean*? Even worse, Ray had urged her, practically commanded her, not to report the assault. It would ruin her career, he said. She hung up on him. The next day, she met with her academic advisor, a 40-something, overfed professor named Delano Blanchard, and told him everything. What she didn't know, however, was that Delano and Gottley were allies and strip-club buddies, sworn to help each other achieve tenure, no matter what.

"Oh my," Delano frowned after Megan told him. "Professor Gottley is one of the most selfless, respected, no, *revered* members of our faculty. If you were to bring these salacious charges into the public realm, I hate to think what ugliness would arise."

"Bring it into the public realm?" Megan had asked, incredulity flooding her face. "Isn't that what journalists are supposed to, you know, *do*?"

Delano tossed Megan a murderous look, warning her, "Don't do this. You won't win. It's his word against...*yours*. I for one don't believe it. Nobody else will either."

A week later, Ray left Megan, on the same day that her newspaper contract was not picked up for her senior year.

Just before takeoff, Megan's Android went *bling!* A message from Todd, whose cheap-ass Blackberry (how many times had she *begged* him to upgrade, and didn't those things go out with the fax machine?) had gotten the letter "T" stuck in a tiny droplet of epoxy when he was trying to repair something.

Miss you already. It have been wonderful wih mom. Much love for being my Megs, odd

On the airporter bus from Newark to Port Authority, Megan thought of the wonders that lay ahead. She had never seen the ocean. The beach, (Coney Island she imagined), was on her NYC-things-to-do list, even before the Statue of Liberty.

The traffic was sick, made up, Megan assumed, of Jersey kids heading out for a liquored-up night in the restaurants, bars and expensive nightclubs of Manhattan. She even saw a red Ferrari, belonging to a mafia Capo, she decided, snapping a photo and texting it to Todd.

Todd and Mom, Megan thought, an unexpected thump lodging in her throat. They suddenly felt so distant, back there in ice-covered Michigan. Fighting back an actual tear, Megan realized she missed her family already.

The tollbooth line moved with the lack of urgency of an old man walking in the park with nowhere to go. Horns blared, tempers flared. Megan looked up and saw, beyond the chaos, the towering city shimmering like Royal Family jewels, a jagged string of pulsating lights set against a dense, black winter sky. Megan punched something onto her Twitter account, and its 27 followers: *Big Apple, get ready cuz here I come! If you don't hear from me, please know that I died a happy camper*

Outside the bus terminal, a light snow had developed and Megan, heading into it with her luggage, yanked the faux-fur collar on her cloth coat around her neck. People walked past in a mighty hurry, shivering and bitching about the cold, even though it was 33 degrees, practically springtime for Michigan. Some of the snippets of conversation she caught were epic New York.

"Don't worry," one stressed-out looking young man in a Burberry trench-coat said to his female colleague, also wrapped in waterproof khaki and plaid-lined comfort. "They don't make as much money as we do."

"OK *good*," the woman said, as if this were the only thing in the universe that mattered.

She glanced at Brigit's address: 2194 5th Avenue, 6-W. So glamorous sounding. But Megan did not fully grasp that Fifth Avenue is a very long street. Its far-northern reaches, where Brigit and her boyfriend Bill lived, was uptown, 133rd Street, far from the glittering wealth to the south. People further down the avenue liked to joke that it was colder, way up there in the northern climes of Manhattan. It was also poorer. But it was all Fifth Avenue, as far as Megan was concerned. And Fifth Avenue meant *style*.

There wasn't a whole lot of style to be seen when Megan, exhausted with a case of what she called the "travel ickies," descended the stairs from the elevated platform at 125 Street, unsure which way was Fifth Avenue. She approached a kind-looking middle-aged woman.

"Excuse me? Can you tell me which way is Fifth?" Megan asked with her sincere Midwestern civility. Suddenly the nice lady didn't look so nice.

"What do I look like? A tour guide?" the woman shot back.

Megan was so taken aback she was unsure what to say. "Um, no. But is Fifth Avenue this way?" she asked, pointing west.

"Five dollars."

"What?"

"Five dollars. And I tell you."

"Listen lady, I probably have less money than you do. Five dollars. Give me a fucking break," she said, startled at her own profanity. If this is what life is like in New York, I think I can handle it, she thought.

She pulled up the map on her phone and made her way to Brigit's dull brick building with its crumbling mortar, corroded iron cornice, and phalanx of Direct-TV dishes. Megan regarded it with trepidation. She rang the bell.

"Jose? Is that you?" A guy's voice, sounding desperate, echoed from above.

"No! It's me, Megan! From Ypsilanti?"

"Oh," the voice said, deflated. "I thought you were the pot guy. Hold on."

Megan wasn't sure what to "hold on" for. She looked up. It was a guy with a shaggy goatee and glazed look in his eyes.

"Yo, Megan!" he shouted. "Catch!"

Megan peered up into the blurry glare of snowflakes and streetlights. And then, *tinkle, tankle, CLANK.* A metallic object struck her forehead before falling to the ground. A tiny drop of warm blood trickled to her mouth. "What the hell?" Megan cried. "Ouch!"

"You okay?" the male voice called back. "Did you get the keys?"

Those were *keys*? Don't these people have buzzers, like on *Seinfeld*?

Megan scavenged around in the dirty snow, searching for the keys. It took a minute of kicking the slush before hearing their jingle. There were so many of them. This was, like, a *pound* of keys.

She let herself into the hallway, which smelled of boiled chicken and cat pee, and began the five-story climb. Sore and bloody, she wanted a hot shower, a cold beer, a bandage, and a nice nap.

"Megs!" her old pal Brigit greeted her. "OH-EM-GEE!" it's so great to see you!" As Megan would soon learn, her childhood friend had picked up the rather annoying habit of spelling out abbreviations that people put in texts. "BEE-TEE-DOUBLE-YOU," she liked to say, or her current favorite, "DOUBLE-YOU-TEE-EFF?

"Bridge!" Megan cried, unaware of the paper-thin walls. "How the hell are you?"

Brigit put a finger to her lips, ushered in her friend and introduced her to Boo-Boo, her Irish terrier, and Bill, her cute but lazy pothead boyfriend.

"Hungry?" asked Bill, a sort-of sexy guy in his late twenties, with shaggy, sandy hair, the slightest paunch, and warm brown eyes.

"Actually, I am," Megan said, her stomach growling after a day of travel.

"Coolest of beans," Bill said. "We have leftovers from the Polish-Korean food truck. Brigit, why don't you heat up some of those kimchee kielbasas?" And then to Megan, "You wanna bong hit? Last of the good stuff. It's why I'm waiting for Jose."

It took a while for Megan to take all this in. What was kimchee? She knew what a bong hit was (Todd loved marijuana) but also knew that stuff made her paranoid. "No thanks, I'm good," she managed a smile. "But I wouldn't mind a beer."

"Of course!" Brigit went to the fridge. "And a Band-aid. Anything for our weary sojourner. How was the trip? How's the family? How the hell is Ypsilanti?"

"Long. Fine. And duller than ever," Megan said, beginning to unwind. "Toddie says 'yo' and my mom says 'thanks.' She's right, Bridge, I couldn't have done this without you."

"Billy boy was part of the decision too, weren't you sweetie?"

"Boom," Bill said with a boyish grin, before hitting on some truly stinky weed. When he exhaled, the room filled with sticky smoke. It burned Megan's eyes.

"Um. Can we open a window?" Megan asked.

"It's fucking snowing outside!" Bill laughed, earnestly, not meanly. "I mean, jeeze. What's a little second-hand weed? Isn't your brother a big pothead?"

Brigit opened the window. "I'll show you to your luxurious little futon in the corner," she said. "Believe it or not, you paying three hundred a month for such splendor is a bargain."

After showering and some first-aid, Megan joined her friends in the living room for dinner on the sofa. The kimchee-kielbasa was blisteringly spicy. She gulped down a cold beer as Bill surfed the channels on TV.

"Ooh! Stop there. I wanna see this," Brigit said. It was the local news, featuring live coverage from one of those hyper-swank charity balls that rich people were always buying outrageously priced tickets for. This one, "Pop Against Poverty at The Pierre," was a sea of bejeweled women in Oscar de la Renta and men in fitted Ralph Lauren tuxedos, all rocking out to Taylor Swift.

"What do you want to watch these bloated oligarchs for?" Bill whined. "They're the most boring people in town."

"They're also my bread-and-butter," Brigit said. "And part of my job description."

Megan heaved a dreamy sigh and pointed at a gorgeous young man, seated with perfect posture at a prime table near the podium, sporting dark eyes, black hair and a smile that radiated power, self-confidence, and the slightest hint of haughty. "Who in sweet Jesus is that one?" she asked. "Some Broadway heartthrob I've never heard of?"

"Oh him." Brigit said with a jaded look. "That's Sexy Rexy. He's not an actor. *Per se.*"

"Sexy who?"

"Rexford Bainbridge, III. The best-looking, best-dressed, richest, single-straight-guy in the entire city. Venture capitalist. Hedge funder. Big-time philanthropist. Always in the papers. Half the debutantes on the East Side have been trying to land him – or at least bed him – for years."

"I can see why," Megan said. "He's so pretty, it hurts. Are you sure he's not gay?"

"Not entirely. There is talk. But there's always talk with these types. I tend to doubt it."

"And who are those women he's with?"

"The one on the left is Beverly Gansevoort-Stein. Big-time society gal, Rex's downstairs neighbor, pompous shrew. The other one, Mrs. Silverhair, is Wanda Covington, Beverly's British sidekick. They're a packaged deal, as inseparable as they are insufferable."

"Welcome to Gotham City," Bill said.

Just before bed, Megan asked Brigit about the interview with Jamal Dix. "I haven't asked him yet. But I will," she said.

Megan felt sick. "Brigit, the whole reason I came here was because of this interview. What gives? I left everything behind for this, and you didn't even arrange it? Damn."

Brigit grew defensive and, Megan thought, a bit snotty, for a fact-checker at the *Post*. "You left *everything*?" she said. "What everything? Your mom, who clawed her way to the middle? Or your brother, who's stuck in Ypsilanti with a cheap spatula and a caterer's dream? Come on Megan. You didn't leave shit behind." She softened after seeing the dejection on Megan's face. "I've been crazy busy. But I'll get you that interview, I swear."

"I hope so," Megan said. "If I don't get that job, how am I supposed to survive here?"

"I will call him first thing tomorrow. I'm not going to let this city chew you up and spit you out, Megs. That happens too many times to too many nice people. And you are nice people. Now, nighty-night."

Chapter 2

1080 Fifth

"**C**arlotta! Carlotta! *DON-day ESS-tahs?*"

Beverly Gansevoort-Stein didn't know much Spanish, but she did know how to summon a maid, sort of, when needed. She had several to choose from. Most seemed to come from El Salvador, which Beverly had taken to calling "El Silverdor" in front of her friends because "those people will rob you like raccoons if you don't watch them every *momento*."

"Carlottta!" she called again. Silence. "Juanita! Lupita! *Somebody?*"

A young woman with a warm, caramel-colored face, Mezzo-American eyes and long black ponytail peeked timidly around the corner of the light-filled master bedroom.

"Yes, Missus?"

Beverly regarded her employee, in classic black-dress and white-apron garb

14

she herself had designed, much to her friends' derision. "Juanita?"

"Margarita," the pretty young woman corrected her.

"Where's Juanita?"

"She was fired. On Tuesday."

"What about Carlotta? Where is *she?*"

"Cuscatancingo."

"I beg your pardon?"

"Back home. In El Salvador. ICE took her away last week."

"Why doesn't anyone ever *tell* me these things?"

"I don't know. Maybe they are afraid. Of you."

A long pause. Beverly's worried brow signaled distress. "Margarita. Did Mr. Dexter ever have you sign any, you know, *papers*, before you started in my employ?"

"In your what?"

"When we hired you into this house." Beverly's voice grew stern and businesslike. "Did Mr. Dexter ask you to sign…" she slowed down, as if Margarita were an imbecile, "a…non…diss…CLOSE…zure…agree…ment?"

"No ma'am. I did not sign."

"That's what I feared." Beverly frowned. "Run down to my office. In the top left desk-drawer you'll find a stack of forms. Bring me one. And a pen. A Mont Blanc, preferably."

Margarita scurried off, making her way down an endless hallway, past pointless rooms. The *Señora* had recently converted her "Scrapbooking Room," for instance, into a "Facebooking Room," in a transparent go at keeping up with the times.

Damn. My whole village could live in this fucking room, Margarita thought as she peered through the door, more in awe than bitterness. She and her family had fled their home in the middle of the night a few years back, after local gang-leaders threatened to slaughter them all if her brother, Juanito, did not join their murderous ranks. After a long, grueling journey north, they were denied asylum by immigration officials at the Arizona border. With no money for a coyote, they decided to try their luck far out in the desert, where there was no fencing. It took them four days to hike up over the scorched mountains and down to Tucson. Margarita's littlest brother, Manuel, did not make it.

She grabbed her phone, took a photo, and posted a quick tweet to her friends, Latina maids working up and down the East Side: *Mi nueva jefa es una loca pendeja rica viviendo en la quinta. Aqui esta su "cuarto de Facebook" Que demonios deberia hacer?#lascriadas* (My new boss is a crazy rich asshole living on Fifth. Here is her "Facebooking room" What the hell should I do? #themaids)

Upstairs, Beverly prowled around her cavernous chambers, peering under furniture as though she had lost an earring, then rummaging through her cherished "every day" walk-in closet – her "couture closet" was at the opposite end, near the sitting area, a tedious design flaw that picked away at Beverly's pride.

Sulking at not finding what she sought, Beverly moved about the bedroom, well-appointed in cream, bone, and "plaster of Paris," and looked out at her dazzling terrace near the top of 1080 Fifth, a 1961 white ceramic-tile affair on the corner of East 87th that must have seemed quite sleek and glamorous during the Kennedy years, but now, truth be told, was considered by people from better houses to be *un peu gauche.* One practically expected Lisa Douglas from *Green Acres* to come ambling out the front door en-route to "Da stores!" and "Times Squaihr!"

Still, the interior of her glorious two-story, seven-bedroom, six-bath apartment was vast, marbled, and undeniably spectacular. Beverly's real-estate friends assured her the place could easily fetch "in the high seventeens," though Beverly insisted she would never part from her beloved home for anything under twenty million.

Wrapping herself in a peach-and-purple silk robe that Issey Miyake had personally selected for her when she last visited Japan, for tsunami relief, Beverly stepped out onto her delightfully askew aerie perched high atop 1080 like a wealthy crane's nest. The commanding view was the Beluga caviar on the water cracker. One could take in the winding snail-shell of the Guggenheim, just below, and look down one's nose at its snaking lines of tourists. Heading south, the elegant neo-Gothic spires of the Pierre and Sherry Netherlander rose like sentinels of the über-rich.

Now shivering, the Manhattan society doyenne – she was on the boards of so many foundations, guilds and charities she needed a full-time staffer just to keep up with the use of her name – returned inside and gingerly closed the priceless antique French doors (discovered in "one of Paris's better *arrondissements*," she told everyone), shutting the winter outside.

Madame sat at her vanity and regarded herself in the mirror. For 68, all in all, she was holding things together not too shabbily. Still, another trip to the clinic in Sao Paulo might be advisable before summer in the Hamptons. "Thank *God* for Brazil," she said to no one.

Beverly tap-tapped her iPad awake and looked at her schedule. "Pilates with Jean-Paul at 9:30. Okay, I can do that," she said, flicking her finger upwards on the screen. "Meeting with accountants at 10:30, aroma-and-oxygen therapy at noon. Fine." Then she saw it. "Staff planning meeting for the Pampers Luncheon on Thursday." She sighed. "Holy mother of Zion."

Beverly had a way of mixing her religious metaphors. Decades earlier, she had married Herbert Hirsch Stein, of the fabulously wealthy real estate family, at a splendid flower-filled wedding in Bridgehampton in 1968. *The Times* itself had pronounced it "one of the most lavish, if not unattractive, wedding ceremonies of the Vietnam-War era, so far."

Two decades later Herbie died, of shock they say, around lunchtime, halfway through Black Monday, the calamitous '87 stock crash. His last words, reportedly: "You fucked me Reagan. I'll never vote Republican again." Overnight, Beverly Gansevoort-Stein became the 13th-wealthiest woman in the city, according to an ill-advised and controversially titled story in *Paper* Magazine, "Which Gotham Bitches Have All the Riches?"

Madame's riches, born of Herbie's uncanny knack for turning tenement sites into luxury condos, were underwriting the lavish luncheon in the Formal Dining Room on Thursday. Written invitations had been hand-delivered on engraved linen cards that the house manager, Mr. Dexter, had "hand-selected" himself. The guest list included some of Beverly's best friends, family and neighbors, a smattering of media types, plus a few executives from the Third Avenue offices of Proctor & Gamble, the conservative Cincinnati-based makers of Pampers brand disposable diapers.

Beverly and some of her chums were setting up a charity, partly because one of their inner circle, the self-absorbed Jacqueline Farquharson, suddenly had a lot of unexpected free time. She had recently but quietly (thank God) resigned her board seat at the Spanish Harlem School for Boys when it was discovered she harbored an unacceptable affinity for Spanish school boys from Harlem. Her defense, "well, they looked 18 to *me*," just didn't wash. The petite Presbyterian with long blondish hair (shade depending on season) impossibly white teeth and impeccably tailored wardrobe was out the door that same day. Everyone agreed to keep the scandal hush-hush "for the sake of the *muchachos*."

The idea, establishing a home for single moms with young children and nowhere to turn was, in fact, Jacqueline's. She was the not-quite trophy wife of a top New York hedge fund bull shark, Jonathan Farquharson who, at sixty-eight, was sixteen years older. "Jackie" (only a few were permitted to call her that) also went to Sao Paulo often, so frequently, in fact, it was said she was quietly shopping around for a little condo in the Jardims district.

Jackie bristled with unbridled energy, which many thought explained her affection for financiers nearly twice her age and, as recently revealed in court documents, Puerto Rican cocaine dealers half her age. Far too easily bored, Beverly thought, the fidgety and rash Mrs. Farquharson was constantly needing something to *do*.

Somewhere beneath her overblown self-esteem and blind self-promotion, Jackie had a soft spot. She'd been quite moved, she told the ladies, by stories from - let's call them her young suitors from the *barrio* - about their own mothers' struggles to raise them alone, or friends who were single new moms, or pregnant.

"Some are truly teetering on homelessness," Jackie said, with more concern and urgency than Beverly had ever observed in her before. Beverly, no outward fan of the poverty-stricken, was moved.

Thursday's luncheon had somehow slipped Beverly's mind. She thought it was next week. Her social calendar was that full. Things got confused. She made a note to hire someone to manage it.

Every little thing, of course, had to be *grand.* Thank God for Mr. Dexter. He and Chef had specially ordered Westcott Bay oysters flown in from the San Juan Islands. A slab of fresh Kobe beef was confirmed aboard Japan Airlines flight 27 from Tokyo, and Black Forest ramps were on their way from greenhouses just outside Baden-Baden. The wine would be Opus One, the champagne Dom Perignon. "Cristal is so tacky," Beverly had scolded Mr. Dexter the first time he suggested it. "It's for Beyonce, not society people. Honestly Dexter, I assumed you would know that."

"Missus?" It was Margarita, non-disclosure form and Mont Blanc in hand.

Beverly asked the maid, who would now hold one of the privileged "upstairs" titles, to sign the paper. She explained that Margarita could never, ever, say or write anything about anything she witnessed going on in the house, under penalty of civil litigation and, in her case, possible deportation.

Margarita hesitated a moment. "May I have a minute to read this?" she asked.

"Yes."

"Do you have a copy in Spanish?"

"No.".

"Can I have my attorney review this?"

Beverly huffed like a Bette Davis drag queen. "Dear God. Why does a housekeeper need an attorney?"

"Um...immigration?" Margarita said with a slightly hostile look.

"Do you want to keep this job or not? Either you sign, or you walk."

"Give me the pen," Margarita said, suddenly sheepish, but with a look of defiance burning in her dark eyes. Beverly softened. "That's a good girl," she purred. Margarita signed the form, which Beverly snatched away and tucked under her jewelry box.

"Now," she said. "Where the hell is Walter Mitty?"

Margarita's brow knitted in bewilderment. "Who?" she said. "Mr. Kitty?"

"Walter Mitty! Dear God, didn't you even read that agreement? He's my ferret, for Chrissake! They're terribly illegal in New York. The authorities would snatch him away from me in a flash. And now he's gone missing, the little bastard."

Margarita was in the weeds. "Ferret? Mitty? I don't understand these words."

Beverly exhaled a puff of exasperation and grabbed her iPad, Googling the word for "ferret" in Spanish, then displaying an image for Margarita to see. "FAIR-rut," she said. *"Hoo-RON-Nay"*

"Okay," Margarita replied at last. "I'll go look for him. I tell nobody."

"You *can't* tell anybody, Margarita. You just signed the paper. Have you forgotten already?" She put on a brighter face. "Now *vamos.* We have a luncheon to plan."

Suddenly, the iPad belted out "Turandot's" *Nessun Dorma*, her preferred ringtone. *"Nessun Dorma! Tu pure, o, Principessa, nella tua fredda stanza,"* she sang along in Italian. ("Nobody shall sleep! Even you, o Princess, in your cold room"). Beverly adored Puccini. Those words haunted her.

When she looked at the caller ID, her *own* room grew cold. Her heart practically halted.

It was Stroganoff, the impossibly overbearing, permanently crabby Russian and self-made millionaire, previously of Brighton Beach, out in the far reaches of Brooklyn. Known as Little Odessa, Brighton was "lousy with sullen Slavic mobsters who kick around in dreadful black-leather coats," Wanda had once explained to Beverly. "They hang out in argument-filled cafes that smell of tobacco and cabbage, with no English on the menu. If you don't speak Russian, you don't eat."

Alexi Ivonovich Stroganoff was an imposing hulk of a man in his late 50s, with deep-set blackish eyes and a perpetual stubble, who, among other more illicit activities, made his first million from a small chain of bathhouse/dining halls in Coney Island, where Russian immigrants of every shape and size pay twenty-five bucks to be whipped silly with eucalyptus branches in a steam rooms by chiseled, pouting youths with white towels around their waists, before gorging on borscht, boiled beef, fried potato chunks and copious shots of Stoli, all to blaring Eastern-Euro rock videos of buxom blondes and scowling gangsters holding assault rifles.

Beverly shivered with tension. This was the last person she wanted to hear from, on the last day she would want to hear from him. Better not to answer, she thought. Not before pilates. Whatever it is, it's not good. The call went to voicemail and five operatic notes announced a new message. She stared at the device for what seemed like an hour, afraid to even touch the thing.

Beverly, who was not stupid, especially when it came to money, had started growing suspicious of Alexi about a year ago. Just little things, like when she noticed him wearing the same suits repeatedly, or the time he waited for her to pick up the tab one day after lunch at Jean-Georges.

In recent years, Alexi had risen to become one of the most talked-about, coveted financial advisors on the East Coast. He could take a million and have you near one-point-five in a year. His celebrated investment acumen and uncanny ability to predict the next hot thing, it was said in the wealthiest wards, was a sure thing. Everyone had money tied up in Stroganoff. Rexford, from upstairs, had put in perhaps tens of millions, according to the rumor mill, a good chunk of his fortune. Beverly's late husband had put in about two million, and now the account was worth at least three times that amount. Beverly, having grown suspicious of Alexi, had recently invited him up to 1080, and pounced.

"I want to see the financials," she had demanded. "You know, the books. The ones you've been cooking."

"I don't work like that," he replied, gruff as a polar bear. "Your money's safe. Trust me. Everybody does."

"Mr. Stroganoff, I neither like you, nor do I find any reason to trust you. My husband invested two million dollars with your firm, and my most recent statement indicates it is now worth more than six. That's very impressive. I wish to cash out."

Alexi had turned the color of rubies and stammered in semi-broken English. He rattled off some kind of hedge-fund mumbo jumbo about delayed derivatives and reporting periods and banking errors caused by red tape and bumbling clerks.

"I want it all, Mr. Stroganoff, *now*," Beverly had said with deadly determination. "I should think you'd be able to wire a deposit today. If you can't, I'll be forced to presume you are running some kind of Ponzi scheme, in which case I will inform all my friends who have invested with you, beginning with my neighbor Rexford. I fear he has overextended himself with you."

"No informing," Alexi had growled. "You get money. No worries."

"I'm not the one who should be worried," Beverly warned him. "I'll inform a lot more than my friends. I'll inform the SEC. And the FBI."

Just yesterday, six business days later, Stroganoff finally scrounged together the money. Beverly cringed to think what he had done to procure the funds, but once they safely cleared in her account, in a day or two, she would blow the whistle on this Russian rapscallion. It was potentially a risky move, she knew. Rumors had connected him to a few shadowy figures allegedly aligned with the bloodthirsty Russian mafia. "Those people are positively ruthless," as Wanda put it. "They have no ruth."

And that's why Beverly had let *Nessun Dorma* play on. A half-hour later, Dexter knocked at the bedroom door. "Mr. Stroganoff is here," he said. "He insists on seeing you. I tried to send him away, but he won't leave." Beverly, petrified but determined, went down to the reception area to speak with him.

"You should answer my calls," Stroganoff said. "You have your money. Now to be shutting up. You will not tell. I know this. I know this because my father was…" he paused and then hit the next word hard, "*there…* In 1960s. Same as you. We have pictures. Full dossier. My guys have copies, ready for dispersal. If you talk."

Blood pounded in Beverly's skull and her vision darkened. She wanted to throw up. Nobody alive was supposed to know about this. If such intelligence, kept so well hidden all these decades, ever got out, it would not just change her life, it would blow it to smithereens.

Stroganoff, sickeningly, was not finished. "If that won't stop you," he added grimly, "maybe you like nice visit to bottom of Sheepshead Bay."

Chapter 3

A Helluva Town

"How much money do you have?"

It was Brigit, "just asking" and eager to help her friend, who was "flipping out like Pop Tarts from a toaster," as Bill put it. Megan excavated bits of clothing from her backpack like a terrier rips guts from a gopher. But everything kept coming up "no."

"I thought I had the perfect outfit for today, but it all looks so gray, wrinkly and sad," Megan said, worried about getting a second-hand buzz from Bill's 9AM bong ritual, potentially causing her to blow the interview. That might send her back to Michigan on the cheap Chinese bus, back to the dreariness, and her mom, who would get all *schadenfreude* and everything over the whole "New York fiasco." No way was that happening. "That reminds me! I have the rent," Megan said, grabbing her wallet from a side pocket. "Here."

"Thanks. How much does that leave you?"

"Enough."

How *much*, Megs?

"Well…about a hundred-twenty. But only until I get my first paycheck, from the paper." Brigit suppressed a nervous grin. "Bridge, I gotta buy something. Any suggestions for a girl on a budget?"

"You've heard of H&M?" Megan nodded. "Good. Put on something warm and let's go. Not much time before your interview."

Brigit kissed Bill's forehead and led Megan out the door, down the rickety stairs and into the winter air. The sky was a gray mass, like a CAT scan positive for brain cancer. A steady cold raged in from the East River. Brigit covered her ears and cried, "Jesus, Mary and Joseph! I'm getting an ice cream headache out here!"

Megan was shocked by her friend's wimpiness. "Bridge, c'mon. You've forgotten what cold *is*. We used to wear shorts and tank tops in this kind of weather."

"Yeah, and we used to be ass-crack crazy, too."

They walked to the station in wind-blown silence. Megan looked around for signs of the crazy lady who had demanded five bucks, but decided the poor soul had either found a place to sleep, or was discovered frozen in a gutter somewhere, one ungloved middle finger pointing straight up at God.

On the way downtown aboard the packed 4 Train, Brigit debriefed Megan about the job interview with Dix. "First of all, no jokes about his last name, no matter how funny, and I've heard some killer ones," she began. "In fact, no funny stuff at all. He's not the happiest camper in the Jellystone Park of life. Secondly, drop names like a B-52 drops cluster bombs. Big names, and bigger names. Celebs you've seen, celebs you've seen in rehab, celebs you dated, whatever bullshit it takes to impress this man. Fill him in on your latest dinner with Jake Gyllenhaal, say, or cocktails with his sister Maggie, who lives in Park Slope and buys extra-firm tofu, cold-pressed flaxseed oil and organic Bolivian kale chips at the Food Coop, as you just *happen* to know. He'll eat that shit up."

"But it's not true!"

"Well, she really does shop there. The rest of it? Who knows? But we're *The Post,* Megs. You know. Bullshit R Us?"

"I really didn't expect to enter the field of journalism on a sack of lies. It goes against everything I learned in school."

"*School?*" Brigit said it loudly enough to draw the surly attention of bleary-eyed commuters packed into the subway car like lambs to the morning slaughter. "You're in New York now. The only education that matters here is a degree from the University of Balls and Bullshit, with a major in Ambition and a minor in Attitude. If you truly believe your own PR, you can talk your way into anything here. Just ask Donald Trump."

"But I don't have any PR."

"We'll think something up. We still have an hour."

They got off at East 58th Street and walked over to Fifth, engulfed by smartly dressed New Yorkers scurrying about to advance their careers. "Is everyone here so good looking?" Megan asked.

"Of course," Brigit said. "That's why the rents are so high."

Suddenly, Megan grabbed her friend's arm and shook it like a ragdoll. "Oh my God, *look!*" she cried. "It's the Plaza. Hi Eloise! And there's the entrance to Central Park, isn't it? And right down there is 57th Street, where Carnegie Hall is. And, holy shit!" she pointed down Fifth and into the raw sky. "You can see the Empire State!"

"Megan. Honey. Get a grip," Brigit said, using a two-palms-down gesture, telling her friend to lower the volume. "We're not the Out-of-Towners here. No oohing and ahhing, please. And no touristy gawking at buildings either. Don't even look *up* at them. New Yorkers never do."

"Then why even live here?"

"Because you can get condoms, Claritin and kosher-vegan delivered at two in the morning. And you never need a car."

Megan was appalled. "But, why live in this city and never look up? It's crazy."

"Those who look up trip and break their necks," Brigit adopted an air of jaded authority. "Real New Yorkers look straight ahead, without making eye contact. Which would explain all the sunglasses, even on the darkest days. Like Anna Wintour."

"Funny you should mention her," Megan said, smiling once again but still unhappy about the "get a grip" lecture. "I was thinking of sending my resume to Vogue, just for shits. They publish serious journalism, sometimes, at three bucks a word! Condé Nast sounds so dreamy and, well, plush. I hear you could never leave the cafeteria, and be perfectly happy."

"And what would you wear to your interview? H&M might work at *The Post*, but at Cunty Nasty? They would halt you at security and frog-march you back out to the West Side Highway." Brigit gently elbowed Megan and pointed at the cut-rate Swedish department store, just ahead. "We're here. Thank you, Stockholm, for the blessings we're about to receive."

28

It didn't take long to find something decent: a cream-colored chiffon blouse and conservative-looking blue pencil skirt with dark pinstripes. Twelve minutes and $37.90 later, the jittery job applicant was ready for her closeup with Dix.

After Megan changed, Brigit grabbed her hand and they hurried out onto the windswept avenue and bustled over to the News Corp building, home to Rupert Murdoch's *Fox News* and the equally right-wing *New York Post*. Located in a forgettable beige high-rise at 6th and 52nd, it stood just across from NBC, at Rock Center, and its lefty cousin, MSNBC.

They entered the lobby at 1211 Avenue of the Americas, a street called that by exactly no one in New York. It was always just Sixth. The Pan-American name never caught on, just like no one called the Queensboro the "Ed Koch Bridge." Renaming, Brigit said, was "stupid."

Brigit flashed her ID and told Megan to show hers to security. "The only photo ID I have is at your place. I didn't know I needed ID to enter an office building. Isn't that kind of, oh I don't know, Orwellian?"

Brigit smiled. "It's a 9/11 thing. I can vouch for you *this* time. But you need to carry ID if you're gonna stay. You're not in Kansas anymore, Toto."

They walked to the elevators that led to the *Post's* floors. Sean Hannity walked in before the door closed. *My God!* Megan mouthed to her friend. When Hannity got off, Megan burst out laughing. "I can't believe we were in the same elevator as the overfed frat boy from hell!"

Brigit looked alarmed and put a finger to her lips. "Megan, honey! Yes, this is as Republican as it comes, but ya gotta play the game. Many staffers here are progressive enough. It's Murdoch, management, and the TV 'talent' that are the bat-shitters. So check your politics at the door, babe. Now, let's meet my boss."

The elevator opened at the 36th, onto a ragged jangle of motion and noise. The newsroom stretched the whole floor, with phones ringing and people buzzing down long alleyways of cubicles, staffed by young, mostly white worker bees, heads down, fingers click-clicking away at keyboards, shouting questions into their headsets over the din.

"Nancy Pelosi's grandson is a *what?*" one guy said. "Get me some un-doctored pics and a witness, and we can talk."

"You know," another reporter said, shaking her head, "We're not ready for another piece on people who want Miley Cyrus to run for Senate. Thanks."

"Get *out!*" a third squealed. "Fire at a gay S&M club? And now it's covered in a pool of molten latex? Damn. My boss'll have a field day with that headline."

Megan was dazzled and disgusted. It was a far cry from her serene Midwestern paper. This whole place oozed toughness, competition and cynicism. You could smell the ambition, mixed with the scent of morning deli coffee, egg-and-cheese breakfast sandwiches and crippling insecurity. These co-workers weren't friends; they were gladiators, hacking their way up the chain of command, waiting impatiently to get noticed.

They walked toward a private office, halfway down the floor. The custom-made carved ebony sign on the closed walnut door said simply, in all-caps, *DIX*. Brigit set her purse and coat on the desk in the cubicle just outside, and knocked lightly.

"Jamal?" She pinned an ear to the door. "It's Brigit. Your 10:30's here."

"Come!" a man's voice rumbled, rather too grandly, Megan thought.

"Who is this guy?" she whispered to Brigit. "Captain Piccard?"

30

"He wishes," Brigit laughed. "He's more like Dr. Smith on *Lost in Space*. If you want, you can still run, Will Robinson."

"Bridge, this is Megan you're talking to. No turning back. I'm ready to play. With Dix."

Brigit growled under her breath. "Okay, but make one little penis joke and you're toast."

"It's little?" Megan couldn't help herself. "Are *all* the Dix in this newsroom small?

Brigit lost control. She burst into a spritz of laughter just as she opened the door. Jamal looked up and sighed. "Another good joke at the water cooler, Brigit?" he asked, in a tone that begged "spare me."

"The usual childish gossip. But some of the guys here do get *a little cocky*."

Megan bit her lip until it hurt. Damn you Brigit, she thought.

Jamal Dix cut a striking figure, even sitting down. A handsome, gay African-American man, he was dressed in a violet velvet blazer with a saffron-colored silk button-down and plum-and-mustard bowtie that only he, in all reality, could pull off. Dogged in his reporting and positively fearless, he didn't give "a flying fig" about exposing the foibles, bad behavior, beyond-conspicuous consumption, adultery and especially backstabbing, (something at which was unsurpassed in facilitating), of the richest, most famous and most ridiculous folks in town.

He was feared, from the boardrooms of Wall Street to the dressing rooms of Broadway. He had the power to make or break: a trendy martini bar; a start-up sneaker brand; a closeted bishop; a skirt-chasing congressman. He wielded much clout with his trademark, half-bitchy prose, which most New

Yorkers either loved or hated. Non-controversial he was not.

Jamal looked at Megan with a forced grin and extended his right arm, palm up, like a benevolent dictator. The gesture was understood: You want to do this, you come over to me.

At least he didn't roll his eyes, Megan thought.

"This is Megan, Jamal. My friend from back home," Brigit said, now all business. "Be nice. It's her first full day in New York, and she's rather fond of her head. Don't bite it off?"

"I'll make my own dining choices. Thank you."

"I'll leave you two alone," Brigit turned and walked out, leaving the door halfway open, just in case.

Jamal, without looking up from Megan's resume and clips, waved for her to sit down on the hard chair opposite his desk. She waited patiently, hands folded, like a youngster at church. She strained to detect anything that might betray Jamal's thoughts, but his face was pure poker. A clock ticked. Megan looked out the window. Just across the street was another nondescript beige high-rise, where she could see people working on the 36th floor.

It was a parallel office universe, and it mesmerized Megan. *That* 36th floor was so different from this one. Only 100 feet away, it was light-years apart. Those people looked so poised, elegant, and serious. A certain intellectual tranquility seemed to permeate the place. It was studious, with lots of potted palms and orchids, and important-looking plaques on wood-paneled walls. Megan fancied it as some award-winning architectural magazine, or a vital yet unsung foundation working to bring about social justice and world peace.

Then she noticed a young, exquisitely tailored Asian woman staring straight out the window and back at them. She was looking directly into Jamal's office, directly, it seemed, into Megan's eyes. Megan looked away quickly, unsure of the etiquette in such brave new surroundings, these crammed-together workplaces in the sky. It all seemed so *Jetsons*.

Jamal's voice rattled her back to the task at hand: Getting a job.

"Food," he grumbled.

"I beg your pardon, Mr. Dix?"

"You write a lot about food. I don't do food. And it's Jamal," he smiled a tiny smile, but a real one. It actually startled Megan. "Please. I'm not that much older than you."

"Alright then, *Jamal*," Megan said, mannerly as a Mormon. "Yes, I did write about food because I was on the 'Student Life' beat and, as you're aware, students and food are like, you know, Tom Hanks and his wife. You can't separate them."

"That's pretty good. What kind of celebrity writing you got?"

"Well," Megan was beginning to stumble. "Well, there's… there's the Katy Perry piece I did when she spoke in Ann Arbor. It's right there!" she pointed at the file folder on his surprisingly messy desk, "in my clips."

"Ah yes, the Panda suit," Jamal responded, his voice devoid of impression. "You know, I thought *Gawker* did a really great job with that story. Yours? A little too, well, collegey, if you know what I mean."

"It's a college paper, Jamal." Megan was getting annoyed. Brigit was right. Her boss was pompous. And an ass. He was a pompass.

"Anyway, I wrote about a whole bunch of stuff, back in Michigan. I think my versatility speaks for itself." She glanced at the office of eternal serenity across the street: the young woman had vanished.

Jamal regarded her intently. "Michigan. Good college. Maybe you should return and go to J-School?"

"Excuse me?" Two more years studying for a journalism degree seemed absurd, unthinkable. She was ready to begin her career now. "I don't think I need J-school. I'm ready. I have *clips*."

Jamal handed her the folder, unsmiling, but not nasty. "You need more. And you need a fuckload more experience before you walk in that door and expect me to offer you work." Megan looked tortured. A *fuckload*, she thought. What is that? Some kind of Manhattan measuring cup? "Oh come on, now, Megan, it's not that bad, You didn't really expect me to just *hire* you."

"Yes Jamal. I did." Megan felt about five inches tall. "That's what I was hoping, at least."

"Well, as I am sure you've deduced, that's not happening." An unexpected look of mercy crossed his face. "This is a tough business in a tough town. Sorry I busted your balls…I mean, you know what I mean."

"I'm fully aware of my testicular shortcomings. What I need is a way to make a living, preferably through writing. You know, what I was trained for."

Jamal softened more. "Listen. We have a blog on our website, and some of the content is generated by freelancers. You gotta find the stories and you gotta bring back the receipts. No bold faces? No publication. But get me a good column item, something about supermodels on molly splashing in a fountain, or Lindsay Lohan going pee-pee in a dark corner somewhere, and we can talk. The pay is crap, but it'll get more reads than the entire student body at your college."

Megan lit up like a lava lamp. A big break, on her first day in town. God I love this city, she thought. "That sounds wonderful, Jamal!" she answered. "When do I...? How do I...?"

"Pitch me five ideas, maybe I'll assign one. *Maybe.* On spec of course. And remember, the hours are revolting. These people we cover, if they're not staying up until all hours, they're usually not worth writing about. The most amusing antics happen after four, when the clubs close."

To Megan, it all just sounded like work, good work that involved glamour, intrigue and an actual paycheck. "How crap is the fee?"

"Fifty cents a word. Typical blog runs about 500 words. You do the math."

"That's two-hundred-and-fifty dollars!"

"Yes, but it's a fuckload of work, and it's not like I'm gonna assign you one every other day," Jamal brought her back to earth. "Even if I did, you'd still starve to death."

"But I need money now."

"We pay 20 days after publication. If you ran downstairs and saw Bob Saggett dry-humping John Stamos on the sidewalk, you wouldn't get a dime until then."

He saw her disappointment. "You know how to wait tables?"

"Of course. I did it in college."

"Good. I have a friend who runs a nice restaurant uptown, Roberto

Delmonico."

"The guy on the Food Network? I love him!"

"The very same." Jamal took a Post-It note from a glass dispenser and scribbled something down. "Take this and head up to Caffe Piazza San Marco, on Madison and 84th, and show it to Delmonico. He owes me an embarrassingly large favor. You'll be working the dinner shift by tonight. And believe me, the tips are crazy. I know because our accounting people have been ragging on me about it. I spend there like a runaway Amish kid in a titty bar."

"I don't know what to say. An offer of freelance work and a hot lead on a job. Thank you Jamal. I think I like you."

"At least someone does. And remember, that's *possible* freelance work. No promises. Now, tell Brigit to come in. I got a tip that Lindsey Graham hired Elton John's personal masseur and, boy, do I have questions."

"I thought this was a Republican paper."

"It is. But sex sells. And weird gay Republican sex sells big. Now, off with you. Go *be* somebody."

Megan fairly skipped out of the office to Brigit's cluttered workstation and grinned. "You *got* something, Megs?"

"Well, kinda. He offered me freelance work for the website, on spec. But he also gave me a great tip for a waiting job, at a place owned by Roberto Delmonico!"

"Piazza San Marco. Goodnight nurse. He sends all the pretty girls there."

"Can I write up my waitress resume at your desk? Jamal needs to talk to you

36

anyway, about some dicks."

Megan banged out her resume, printed it, and headed up to Madison Avenue, the world's most lavish thoroughfare of boutiques, some without price tags. If you have to ask, stay on the sidewalk and gawk through the windows, like all the other great unwashed.

Piazza San Marco had been around since Rexford Bainbridge was in diapers. It was one of those comically overpriced Eastside Italians where a "free-range" chicken breast sautéed with "Greek fennel and Venetian clams" went for forty-five bucks. Everyone ate there, but no one really liked it. Megan walked in, yellow sticky in hand, in search of Delmonico.

The first person she encountered was a tall, lanky, twenty-something busboy with thick dark hair, curly as a lamb, trimmed goatee, and dreamy eyes the color of charcoal. He was a babe, Italian-American for sure. "Hi. Is Mr. Delmonico around?" she asked.

"Sure," cutie-pie said in a deep voice. "He's around. *And* he's my uncle." He flashed her a platinum smile. "I'm Tony. Can I tell him why such a beautiful girl is here?"

Megan hated the sexist remark, but played along. "Yes please, Tony. Tell him the beautiful *woman* is here about a position slinging pasta in this fine establishment."

Whatever kompromat that Jamal held over Delmonico, it clearly had gotten the job done. As he predicted, or better, preordained, Megan began work that night, guided by a seasoned waitress named Silvie DuBois, a large, stern woman from Haiti who trained all the new girls recommended by Delmonico's buddies. She was tough and by the book, in that post-colonial Caribbean way, but warm and forgiving when needed. She never, ever wanted to go back to Port-au-Prince.

Megan was jittery but determined. Most of her experience waiting tables had been at an IHOP in Ann Arbor, where hungover freshmen stumbled in every morning, yelping for coffee, waffles and extra bacon. She spent the afternoon back at Brigit's, trying to memorize the menu, Bongload Bill's second-hand reefer smoke notwithstanding. Now, it was showtime.

Megan approached her first table, with Silvie standing discreetly behind. Seated right before her was Sexy Rexy himself, his cocky smile both off-putting and alluring, and the two ladies she saw him on the news with: the pompous one with lots of work, and the beautiful upper-class Brit, the likes of which made most Americans wilt with intimidation.

Megan's Midwestern impulse wanted to say "Hey, everybody!" but she checked it. "Good *evening*," she said instead, unsmiling and deep, sounding far too sullen for the occasion.

"Mr. Hitchcock, I presume?" Rex asked with a leering grin. "If so, color me *spellbound*."

Holy moley, Megan thought, Brigit was right on the money. This guy has hump-'n-dump written all over his flirty face. She was torn between smiling at the cheesy joke or tossing water in his face. What a sexy jerk, she thought.

"Rexford! Really! Such brute manners," the American woman, Beverly, said. "What would your mother say?" And then to Megan, "Sorry dear. He's never been good with the help."

The *help*? Megan thought, realizing that class warfare, New York style, was alive and kicking.

"Well at least we know he's not a poof," Wanda mumbled. "Or so it would appear."

Rexford said something inaudible and stared at the Brit, who stared at the menu. Megan decided this was shaping up to be a troublesome table. And it was only her first. Her instincts quickly proved correct.

"My dear," Wanda asked with a slightly haughty note, raising her head with a wee tilt. "These so-called baby lamb chops are new. Are they *really* baby?" The question nauseated Megan, a mostly vegetarian. She turned to make sure Silvie was just out of earshot over the rising banter in the dining room. She leaned over to whisper.

"They're practically fetal."

Wanda shoved the menu back at the waitress, nodded her head, and turned away with a look of pained boredom. Rex laughed so hard he had to hold his stomach. Megan liked that. "And for you, sir?" she asked. "Fetal as well?" He flashed a brilliant smile, his dark eyes like a fawn's, his perfect teeth like sun-bleached shells collected on a Mediterranean beach. If this is what all the single guys in New York look like, even the cads, she thought, I'm never going to leave.

"Yes. Fetal. And, I'm not *sir*," he said, charm smeared across his face like buttercream. "I'm Rex. And you?"

"Me?" Megan was flummoxed. The continued flirting was too much. "I'm Megan. I'll be your server tonight."

"God how I tire of that word, 'server,'" Wanda said. "Why can't we go back to the old terms, like footman and lady's maid?"

Beverly looked at Megan. "So then, *server*. What are you serving, for specials? You do know, don't you?" Tension settled over the table like a bad day on Wall Street. Silvie, four paces back, sensed something was amiss. Megan had to act. "*Panzanella*," she said, unsmiling. "The special appetizer is a savory *panzanella* bread salad with roasted peppers, tomatoes, cucumbers and onions."

Wanda pouted. "How perfectly dreadful. Beverly dear, we really must have a little chat with Mr. Delmonico. It's a slippery slope, you know, from bread salad to, well, *Chef Boyardee*."

Megan ignored Wanda which, she noticed, elicited an admiring nod from Rex. "Our special pasta tonight is spinach ricotta ravioli *Firenze* in browned butter and sage, for $44.50."

This time, Beverly winced. "God, not more Tuscan food. Browned butter and *sage*? It takes me straight back to the nineties. You know, all Princess Diana and sundried tomatoes."

"Oh please, Beverly, spare us," Rex said. "You were on your knees asking me to escort you to Tuscany, until St. Kitts became the shiny new object of your distraction."

Megan was amused, but she pushed on. What a nutty gaggle, she thought, one big bowl of Fruit Loops. *"Lombatina di Vitella alla Griglia* is our main-course special, a grilled veal chop with olive oil, lemon and pecorino." She spoke with all the faux grandeur she could muster. "It's 52.50."

Beverly looked pale, unhappy. "I'll have the tortellini *en brodo*, with prosciutto and fiddleheads. Put the sautéed porcini on the side."

Megan had never heard of that dish. With a look that suggested half-panic, she said, "I...I don't believe that's on the menu, ma'am."

"Precisely,"

"But, who does that?" Megan asked with enough ah-shucks sincerity to be excused.

Beverly looked at Megan as if she'd just caught fire. "Who orders off the menu? The Aga Khan, that's who. Hillary Clinton. Bill Gates. *Me.*" A look of clarity crossed Beverly's face.

"Say, you're fresh off the bus, aren't you? When did you arrive? Yesterday?"

Megan blushed with tension. Was she really that much of an obvious out-of-towner, as Brigit had said? "Yes, actually. Ma'am. Only it was JetBlue. Does it show?"

"Like white shorts after Labor Day," Wanda said. "But that's okay, sweetie. This town takes time. Now, two fetal chops and some tortellini *in brodo,* if you can remember all that. Off you go."

Rex sat up straight and glowered at Wanda. "Must you always play the role of bitch-on-a-baguette when it comes to the wait staff?" He gazed up at Megan and smiled. "Look at this young woman. She's a perfectly pleasant person, from out there in the hinterland. She's new to town and probably a tad nervous. We're not exactly the nicest customers. Now, if there's any slack left in that hole where your heart used to be, can you cut a bit for…?" He looked at Megan with inquiring eyebrows.

"Megan. As I said before."

"Yes. Let's all cut some slack for Megan, shall we ladies?" Silvie approached to inquire if everything was alright. Wanda was about to spew some of her famous venom about the service, but Rex intervened. "We could not be more delighted. Your server Megan is most helpful, and really very charming." Beverly scowled. Wanda let out an audible harrumph.

"And what about wine for this evening?" Megan asked. "Would the gentleman like to select, or one of the ladies?" Rex took charge, ordering up a saucy little Burgundy, for $495.

Megan excused herself from the nut-basket table and walked across the enormous dining room, thick with expensive perfume and loud, endless chatter about stock prices, media mergers and townhouse sales. The steamy kitchen suddenly seemed like a welcome refuge. She placed the orders with the line cook.

"So. How are the rich and infamous treating you?" someone behind her said. "Sullenly?"

It was Tony, the busboy and nephew of the owner. "That guy Rex is alright, but those two women are among our most, um, *bemusing* customers. Their self-regard is breathtaking. One-percenters to the nth degree."

"Are they actually human, or just vestiges?"

"Good question. Beverly is some society lady who thinks she can buy respect. My uncle Jack is her personal chef. The English one is Wanda something or other fancy-schmancy. No one likes her. But she does know how to tip." A bell rang. "Looks like you're up. Bring those *amuse bouches* to Sexy Rexy and the lunatic ladies, and give them my regards."

At night's end, Megan sorted through checks. So far, her tip share amounted to $229. She had never earned so much in eight hours. Then she came across the final check, from table twelve: those two loony ladies and that rich, handsome lout. Their bill cleared $800. Megan almost fell over when she saw the forty-percent tip.

Then she spotted a business card, from "Rexford J. Bainbridge, III - Private Investor." On the back, a few drunken words were scrawled.

Hey Megan! Call me? Let's have fun xo

Chapter 4

The Isle of Coney

Megan stared out the window of Brigit's apartment at the dull morning sky and endless rows of brick tenements rising above pawn shops, bullet-proof liquor stores, greasy "Chinese/Spanish" take-out places and dingy corner delis called *bodegas* that smelled of floor-cleaner and cat litter. Megan missed Michigan, she was shocked to realize, and she terribly missed her crazy little family.

She walked over to her futon in the living room and folded it on its frame back into a loveseat, then went into the kitchen to make coffee. Brigit was already up, though Bill was still asleep, blissfully lost in the peculiar dreams of a compulsive cannabis consumer. Brigit was working overtime and it had been a couple of days since they had a chance to catch up.

"So how's the restaurant?" Brigit asked. "Good tips?"

"Amazing. I had no idea New Yorkers were so generous. And one New Yorker in particular."

Brigit laughed. "Oh really? And what do we mean by that? C'mon...*tell.*"

"You're not going to believe this. My first night, I waited on Sexy Rexy himself. He flirted with me, I swear, and then left me forty percent, on a $800 check! Can you believe it?"

"Not bad," Brigit said, not as impressed as Megan had expected. "I've heard of bigger."

"And he left me his card. He wants to go out with me, I think."

"Megan, I warned you about that guy. Please, be careful."

"What's the worst that could happen? He buys me some jewelry? Oh the humanity! So, what else can you tell me about him, other than being a drop-dead gorgeous schmuck?"

Brigit explained all about the over-the-top penthouse at 87th and Fifth, the famous taste in clothes, the It Girls he dated, the polo ponies and outrageously priced summer rentals in Sag Harbor and the family villa in Mallorca. Rex was the only child of high-society parents, the sole heir to their fortune, which ostensibly came from importing maple syrup from Canada (Bainbridge Brand Maple had been extremely popular in the 60's and 70's) but, much like with the Kennedy family, most people believed the real money had come from rum-running in the 20's.

"So, what happened to his parents?" Megan asked.

As she boiled water for more coffee, Brigit walked her friend through the entire Lake Lucerne affair. It had been "mega news" in New York, she said.

"They flew off to Switzerland on an impromptu ski trip a few years back, and stopped in the village of Küssnacht, on Lake Lucerne, for a late lunch and some kirsch. It was the day before Christmas," Brigit began.

The two had stumbled upon a welcoming little *fonduerestaurant,* with lit candles in the windows and a roaring fireplace in the back, where the joyous couple spent the next three hours supping, unaware that their fondues were filled with as much kirsch as their snifters.

"Eyewitnesses said they toddled out of the cafe and into the snow, lurching like sailors on leave, singing *O Holy Night* in really bad German and way off key," Brigit continued. "As it turns out, the village has this huge procession on that evening, the *Klausjagen,* with about 1,500 marchers. The Bainbridges got in their rented BMW, hoping to reach Gstaad by midnight, where they'd leased a chalet. Anyway, Bainbridge lost control of the car just as the parade was moving past. He plowed into the procession. It was a calamity, the likes of which Küssnacht had never seen before."

The car had first rammed into old St. Nicholas himself, who was walking with four attendants in black robes handing out pastries to merry-makers. The silver Beemer continued barreling down the road, ramming into men with tubas and trombones, cowbells and cow horns, all of which went flying into the crowds, bruising and lacerating many. Finally, the car tore through a section of men wearing giant bishops' hats with colored tissue paper resembling stained-glass windows, illuminated from within by flickering candles. The hats, some of them seven feet high, exploded into flames as the panicked men ran about in circles, setting fire to a pile of straw and a row of parked Vespas, which exploded like bomblets and spread their flames to nearby buildings. Half of Küssnacht burned to the snowy ground. Thirty-seven people were severely injured.

"My goodness," Megan gasped. "How awful. What happened then?"

"The chase. Hundreds of enraged men in lederhosen and tights approached the car and began banging on the windows with dented brass instruments, shouting in Swiss-German. The couple panicked and took off, turned left down a side street, and plunged directly into Lake Lucerne."

Apparently, the good people of Küssnacht were in no particular rush to pluck the rich Americans from the fabled lake. Their car began taking on water, and within minutes they were dead of hypothermia.

"Even then, no one wanted to fish them out. Their village was a smoldering ruin, so I guess I can't blame them," Brigit said with a shrug. "Eventually Rex had to contract a company from Italy to come in and retrieve his parents."

Megan felt a sudden pang of empathy for the raffish rich boy. Even though his parents were responsible for an outrageous catastrophe, they were still his parents. And they were dead. Rex became more than a handsome asshole to her. He morphed into a human, with pains of his own, despite all the buffers that millions of dollars can afford. Rex was lonely, Megan thought. Lots of New Yorkers were.

"I'm going to call him," she said, surprising even herself.

"Okay mate, go for it. But be prepared for heartbreak. Listen, I gotta get ready for work. Let's eat together tonight. There's a new Belizean place I want to try, Belmopan Spice. My treat: fish patties, garlic collards, rice and peas. Date?"

Megan nodded uncertainly. As Brigit went to change, Megan wondered what she would do with the day ahead of her. She wasn't scheduled to work for another two nights. She picked up a copy of *Time Out NY* on the counter and instinctively turned to the free-events section. Holy Moses, she thought, this city sure does keep itself busy.

There was the "Jewish Women's Prayer-and-Drum Circle" at the 92 Street Y at 10:30, a reading by "Authors You Thought Were Dead," at an indie bookstore on Lexington at 11:00, "Bagels, a Walking Tour" with the Lower East Side Lox & Schmear Working Group at noon, a kimchi pickling demonstration in Little Korea with the poorly thought-out title "Put Spicy Cabbage Up Yourself!" at 3:30, a legal clinic for pedestrians bowled over by food-delivery bicycles and mothers with strollers at 4:30, an early-evening "mix, mingle and nibble" for Nigerian lesbians over 40, at the Chelsea Hotel at 6:00, a book launch by right-wing zealot and noted homophobe Cody McCoy, hosted by Tucker Carlson, on McCoy's new title, *Guns, Gays, and God: Yes; No; and Yes,* at Hooters on 56th Street, at 7:00, (extra security provided), and a reading by Alec Baldwin at Barnes & Noble Union Square, from his new book, *Why I'm Such an Asshole, and other Excuses,* also at 7:00.

So much "diversity," yet none of it really appealed. Megan looked out the kitchen window. The overcast had thinned to reveal a low sun. It was one of those warmish late-January days that give New Yorkers some hope. "Spring will come, my friend," they might say at such times. "It's like Fashion Week: Nothing can stop it."

Megan could hear Bongload Bill stirring in the bedroom just behind the thin kitchen drywall. He and Brigit were bickering...again. Megan liked Bill alright, she supposed, but Brigit could and should do better. Then again, Brigit had said the same thing about Megan's ex Ray, before he ditched her, and his soul, in exchange for promotion at the school paper.

BooBoo sniffed Megan's shins, looking like he needed to relieve himself. "I gotta get out of here," she said to no one but the potted fern by the window. "I think this is my beach day." Moments later, after conferring with Brigit on the best route to Coney Island, Megan set out to see the ocean for the first time.

The sun was even brighter now, although a cold relentless wind raced down the avenue. A frantic siren wailed a block away. Megan made her way to the now-familiar elevated station like an old pro and headed downtown to connect with the D Train for the long, rumbling journey out to Coney Island. It seemed to take forever, but Megan didn't mind. After Prospect Park in Brooklyn, the train went "elevated," and she got to look out over the rowhouses and pocket parks, the jammed shopping avenues and forgotten backstreets, the wards of Orthodox Jews, Mexicans and Central Americans, Russians and Eastern Europeans, Arabs, West Indians and the occasional vestiges of old-school Irish-Italian-Germans. Synagogues, mosques and Protestant, Catholic and Eastern Orthodox churches punctuated the low-rise skyline. No one on board seemed to be speaking anything remotely close to English. Megan might as well have been heading to the Sea of Okhotsk.

The train limped into the final station, Coney Island/Stillwell Avenue, as the conductor announced their destination in utterly undecipherable gibberish, double-mangled through the aging PA system. No one seemed to notice, but Megan was scandalized. My God, she thought, even in Detroit you can understand the transit announcements.

There was not much going on in ramshackle Coney Island on a winter morning. Virtually everything except Nathan's Famous was shut down. Megan gravitated there and ordered some cheese-fries. She knew about Nathan's from their Fourth of July hotdog-eating contests, but the idea of meat at this hour made her want to puke. Megan took her taters and Diet Coke along the dirty, silent streets until she hit the white, rickety Cyclone, the ancient wooden roller coaster that's scary simply for seeming to be in perpetual disrepair, then turned right toward the concrete-gray Atlantic.

Up on the boardwalk, Megan could look out across the wind-frothed sea to Staten Island and New Jersey, though she had no idea what they were. It was colder here, and she huddled her arms around herself as she descended the stairs and onto the sand. She picked up speed, practically running the rest of the way to the roiling water. It smelled of fish and freedom and places with faraway names. Megan was entranced – there was nothing like this on Lake Erie. She spent nearly an hour watching the surf, the play of light against a cold silvery sea, the bravura of seabirds plunging into the jerky brine, occasionally emerging with squirming smelt in their determined beaks.

"Hellooo OCEAN!" Megan roared over the waves, "so nice to meet you, at last." She pulled out her Android, snapped a few quick shots, and posted them to Twitter with the caption, *Atlantic or Bust! Here I am, on the Island of Coney.*

Megan took several deep breaths through her nose, exhilarated by the positive ions rushing in on the salt air. She closed her eyes, thought about her great fortune, and gave silent thanks to God.

"You want to stand here and freeze to death?" It was a deep voice, coming from just behind her, and it wrenched Megan from her trance. She turned to find an outsized man growling with a thick Slavic accent. "What are you? Lunatic? Who goes to beach in January? Come," he grabbed her arm, "I take you to nice place. Very warm. Good soup. Clean towels."

Clean *towels*? Megan's mind was racing. This unsmiling thug with the broken English scared the bejesus out of her. White slavery, she thought; the international sex trade. I'll be kidnapped and shunted off on the next flight to Uzbekistan. Panic ensued. She had seconds to think this through. "Who are you?" she shouted, grabbing her phone and showing him she was dialing 911. "What do you want?"

The man snatched her phone and dropped it. "I am Yuri," he hissed, snarling. "And you know what I want." He grabbed her arm and grinned, revealing two missing teeth.

Megan screamed and jammed her right knee directly into his groin. Yuri moaned, much more softly than she would have imagined, fell to his knees in the cold sand, and toppled onto his side. "You bitch!" he sobbed in agony. "I won't forget. I find you. Make you pay."

Megan scooped up her phone and dashed like an Olympic sprinter toward the boardwalk, looking back every few seconds at Yuri. He pulled himself up, brushed off the sand and, for a moment, stood there glaring at her escape.

Then he came after her.

Megan felt as though she were trapped in one of those nightmares where, no matter how fast your feet move, they carry you nowhere. Yuri was now right behind her. She could hear his heavy breathing, his cursing in some unknowable tongue. As she ran toward the boardwalk, Megan saw the blue flash of a uniform, just yards ahead. She stopped, laughed, and knelt in the sand.

"Fuck you Yuri!" she cried back at the man, who had also halted upon seeing the NYPD officer. "Thanks for ruining my first trip to the beach."

The cop rushed to the sand to make sure she was alright, as Yuri ran to the boardwalk and down a side street. "You want me to go after him?" he asked. "Did he hurt you miss?"

Megan didn't know what to say. She felt scared and weirdly violated, though the cop's presence was comforting. "That's alright," she stammered. "I'm okay. I think I'll just go home now."

The trip on the D Train seemed even longer going back than coming down. Megan shuddered to think what could have happened with that Soviet-era goon on the beach, if not for the cop. She broke down in tears. Ypsilanti – comfy, cozy and relatively safe - was calling, hard.

Megan returned to Brigit's apartment, where it was warm, quiet, and mercifully empty. She put water on for tea, drew a bath, and turned on the television.

What the hell, Megan said to herself. Why not give ol' Sexy Rexy a call? She went to her backpack, found his business card and dialed the number. It went straight into voicemail.

"Hey," the outgoing message began "It's Rex. So, maybe I want to talk to you... but maybe I don't. We'll find out." Before the beep, there were tasks. "For more options, press pound," an Alexa-like voice said. Megan laughed. Had *anyone* in the history of wireless communications ever pressed pound for "more options?" There was more. "To mark your message as interesting, press one. For a text of your message sent to your I-Phone, press two. To calculate the odds of this person returning your call, press three. To gripe about the government, press four. *Para espanol, marque el cinco.* To hang up, simply hang up."

Megan waited for the beep. "Hello, Mr. Bainbridge. I mean, Rexford? I mean, Rex?" God she felt stupid already. "It's Megan O'Malley, from Piazza San Marco? I found your card and your little...*message* on it. I hope you remember what it said. I accept. I'll text you soon."

Chapter 5

Power Luncheon

Although everyone had liked Jacqueline Farquharson's idea about a shelter for single moms, nobody would like her proposed name for it. Even so, she was determined to have her way, through pure stubbornness and wearing down the others with a cleverly timed second round of remarkably dry Martinis, one afternoon at her place, down on 77th Street.

"I've *got* it!" she had cried out of the ether, though nobody had a clue what she was jabbering on about. "The name!"

"And that would be?" Beverly asked, attempting without much success to raise a tipsy eyebrow.

"The Little House of Booboos!" Jackie flashed the smile of a girl who just woke up to find herself in the Barbie department at FAO Schwartz. "Get it? Boo Boos are cute. But they're also, well, you know…"

Puzzled silence ensued. The ladies grabbed their martini glasses (up, with lemon rinds, Moldavian vodka, and, for some reason, granite pebbles, which was the trend that season), sipping hard. Jackie waited. "Well?" she asked, oblivious to the body language around her.

Only Wanda Covington, the unfiltered Brit who "couldn't give a flying fuck to Jesus" what anybody thought about her, spoke up.

"Dear *God*," she said with a piercing look that could wither a Buckingham Palace guard. "That's quite possibly the *stoopidest* idea that's slithered from your tiny cranium to date." Then, shifting into the passive-aggressive mode that made her feared and famous up and down Manhattan, she asked, "You're not really the sort of girl who would have a successful career lecturing at Oxford, *are* you dear?"

With her long, fabulous coat of silver-white hair, perfect nose and aristocratic jawline that kept her English teeth in a state of perpetual clenching, Wanda was the prettiest, and by far smartest of the bunch, and they hated her for it. Being fully aware of this only made Wanda want to belong to the catty little club even more, for spite, she reasoned, if nothing else.

Wanda knew absolutely everybody but had few friends. She'd never wanted to come to New York. Allegedly born into money so old it creaked, she had been busy preparing a prestigious art academy in Kensington for all those rich, bored London wives with nothing better to do than sleep with each other's husbands. An accomplished water colorist herself, she retained the UK's best teachers, and even found the perfect place, on Sheffield Terrace.

But Wanda's husband Trevor, the highly sought-after venture-capital wizard, had been lured to a position over here, going on seven years now, to manage holdings of The Blackstone Group, including SeaWorld.

Beverly knew that Wanda's ambitions had been trampled by those of her husband. She also knew that Wanda knew that Trevor had been spotted around town with a tall, empty-faced trainer with a perky ponytail and blinding smile, Veronica Clark, "visiting" from Orlando.

Wanda was, when Beverly thought about it, a sad sack. Tough as tungsten on the outside, she was brittle as Baccarat on the inside. Too bad the jaded lady from Great Britain could never, *ever* allow herself to let it show. Beverly needed Wanda more than she realized. In the meantime, she was resigned to comfort herself in the firm knowledge that she was richer than the witty Brit or, for that matter, anyone else in their group.

Jackie, like she usually did, ignored Wanda. "What about you guys?" she asked anxiously, still clueless about the clearly unanimous disapprobation.

Martha Bradbury, tall, thin, light brunette and pretty in a TV sort of way, and widely regarded as "the nice one" both inside and outside the cadre, played the usual role of applying a soothing verbal-balm onto sore nerves and over-demanding egos. Widowed a few years back, Martha had inherited her husband Chuck's lucrative cannabis plantation in Boulder, cashed in and moved to Fifth Avenue, down in the 50's, *below* the park and thus not quite worthy of the same exalted status as the others. Not one to call attention to herself, Martha was known in the tabloids as the "Mysterious Hemp Widow of the West." Beverly had taken pity on this slightly lower-caste parvenu and invited her into the fold. She liked Martha, even though she was sweet, which in New York, of course, meant useless. With both kids far away at college, these alleged friends were the center of Martha's world.

"I think what Wanda is trying to say…" Martha mustered all she could to aim a nasty face at Wanda, but was just too nice a person. Her contorted expression looked more resting Bozo than bitch. Wanda guffawed. "What I am *sure* she is trying to say is that it's a great start, a wonderful kernel of an idea," Martha pressed on, her innate smile bouncing back like memory foam. "It just needs a little…tweaking."

54

"That's not what I'm saying at *all*, Martha." The impatience in Wanda's voice was thick as Devonshire cream. "It's utter bollocks and it should be tossed into the rubbish bin of bad ideas at once. Bloody hell. You may as well call it 'Jackie's Shelter for the Knocked-Up.'"

Jackie stared blankly, tilting her head like a confused puppy.

"*Hello?*" Wanda went in for the kill. "Your elevator doesn't really stop at the higher floors, does it sweetie?"

"Leave her alone." Beverly found herself interjecting in a rare bout of sympathy for Jackie's struggle with the real world. An unfamiliar wave of diplomatic largesse washed over her. "Ladies, what we have here is an *issue*. And we can resolve it, like the cultured adults we are. Now, as I see things, we have a great idea," she gave a grudging nod to Jacqueline. "Thank you, Jackie. But we don't, I'm afraid, have the perfect name, just yet. I propose something more simple and straightforward."

"Such as?" Wanda asked.

"Well, it occurred to me that when we go sailing off Mustique, on Richard Branson's yacht, for example (Beverly was never above dropping names, Wanda thought, like so many pebbles in a martini glass) and a storm brews up, the captain always cries, 'To safe harbor! To safe harbor!' Then we usually haul into some little protected cove and have cocktails, all cozy, as Chef prepares *lagostine-a-la-Normandie,* or whatnot. It's really quite charming."

"You're losing us, dear," Wanda said.

"Well, *we* are offering a safe harbor from the storm to these poor young women, though without the brandied-and-creamed lobster, I should think. They can have tacos and tap-water and be perfectly content, from what I hear." Beverly glanced at Jackie, who pouted and looked away. "How about calling it, simply, 'Safe Harbor House?'"

Jackie sat motionless. But then her pout melted and she burst into a grin. "I like it!" she said, leaping back into the circle like a jump-rope player. "Can we call it *Jackie's* Safe Harbor House?"

"No," Beverly ruled, the wave of diplomacy having receded from the shore of self-interest. "That's so silly. Who would give us money?"

"Can we put a 'u' in the word 'harbor?'" Wanda asked, knowing full well the answer.

Beverly turned to Wanda, her famous "in your dreams" look fully intact.

"Well, *I'm* not sold," said the final holdout.

It was Jenna, naturally, the youngest, newest, most stubborn and dumbest member of the sorority. Jenna Forsythe came from good enough stock, shipping and charter airline people, mostly, perfectly respectable. But her wing of the family had fallen on hard times lately, with rising fuel costs and all. At 38, Jenna, to her own horror and those around her, "took the option," as she he euphemistically put it, of moving back into her parents' coop all the way over on, God forbid, *Second* Avenue, amid the noisy pickup lounges and stupidly named yuppie hangouts that reek of single-malt and mid-priced Italian cologne purchased, most likely, at Bloomingdale's.

Jenna preferred "moody" music, certified organic food and, it was rumored, three-ways with male twins. She was arguably a real looker, of medium height, with emerald-green eyes and honey-colored hair - often pulled so tightly into a ponytail, she looked like she was giving herself a slow-motion face lift. With her ample curves and two generous dollops of presumably enhanced *décolletage*, Jenna drove most men wild - "even the gays," as Beverly observed. In her eyes, Jenna had always been a combative, entitled, "I'll-hold-my-breath-until-I-get-my-pony!" sort of soul who simply never grew out of her overly provisioned upbringing.

A few years back, Jenna had married a sexy third baseman for the Mets, a rather lackluster ballplayer named Vinny Delle Donne. Jenna had told absolutely everyone, including the *New York Post's* Jamal Dix, that for their honeymoon, he was taking her, "Down to France for two weeks." Dix, seeking comment about the geographically challenged quote, turned to the acerbic Brit Wanda Covington, who did not disappoint.

"That's our Jenna," Jamal quoted her. "It's not like she doesn't try. But her IQ sort of matches her waistline, no? I mean, the poor dear couldn't find France on a *map* of France."

The blessed union lasted all of 18 months, no children, and Jenna immediately recouped her maiden name. Delle Donne, a swarthy, swaggering brute, turned out to live up to his name, which translates from the Italian as "Of the Ladies." He complained to locker-room reporters, after a divorce that was "sticky" (his words) and "overly publicized" (Beverly's words), that Jenna was "too high maintenance for too much of the day."

Bringing this moody little Forsythe number from the gossip columns into their inner circle had been the rash idea of Jackie, of course. Beverly should've vetoed the plan in the bud, she rued. But everyone else seemed to like Jenna. She was so "gritty" and "ambitious.".

That aside, Jenna was overruled, and "Safe Harbor House" was born.

Beverly instructed Mr. Dexter to look at a number of properties uptown, way uptown, that could be purchased and renovated at reasonable cost and converted into a single-room-occupancy shelter for young moms and their penniless babies. Each lady in the rich circle committed to twenty-five grand. They would need much more.

That's where the "Pampers people," as Beverly called them, came in.

It was the admittedly genius idea of chipper Martha to attract corporate cash through cross-promotional "feel-good-about-feeling-good" opportunities, as she said, ones that made companies look human and humans look charitable, with crates of free diapers thrown in. "It's a win-win," she told the ladies.

Beverly realized that trafficking in disposable diapers conflicted with her work for the Sierra Club (NRDC was too left, World Wildlife Foundation too right), but she compartmentalized such uncomfortable particulars, keeping them away from each other through exaggerated force of will and an early cocktail hour.

Beverly had cast a proud gaze on her budding protégé Martha. Even Wanda was impressed. "I bloody *love* it," she said. "They get the touchy-feely publicity, we get the money, and the up-the-duff mums get free nappies for their future felons."

"They might not be felons tomorrow," Martha said softly, "if we help them out today."

And now, the luncheon was upon her. Time to be one of the most famous hostesses of the avenue, again, Beverly thought. She reviewed the guest list glaring from her iPad. "Just look at this fresh hell." Beverly adored Dorothy Parker and referenced her just a bit too much, most people said behind her back.

In addition to Wanda, Martha, Jackie, the unfortunate Jenna and the Pampers people, engraved linen cards had also been couriered to Brent Ashby, one of the most boring directors of the New York Stock Exchange, Celia Bergstrom, the impossibly chic, overly opinionated editor of the fashion and culture magazine, *Wow!* (how Beverly loathed that exclamation), Chester Mansfield, deputy managing editor at *The Times*, a "nondescript but necessary evil," as Wanda called him, and his down-market counterpart Jamal Dix, the infamously bombastic gossip columnist at the *Post,* not above the bribing of chambermaids and sorting of garbage to get a salacious scoop. Still, with just one well-placed mention, everyone knew, Dix could sell a hundred-plus tickets to any upscale fete, Hoe-Down for Hemophilia, say, at fifteen hundred a pop. He could come in handy raising big bucks for Safe Harbor House, (which the ladies had wisely decided not to call by its acronym: SHH).

There were three more affirmatives on the list. Rexford James Bainbridge RSVP'd that he would be "honored" to attend luncheon, along with his (uninvited, Beverly frowned) college mate, Thaddeus M. Pepper, MD, PhD. Finally, there was Hillary Stein, Beverly's daughter. A struggling jewelry designer (though dividends from her trust fund kept things fat and happy) she did not live in a "dingy Greenwich Village warren," as her mother imagined, but a pricey 2,300-square-foot loft at Essex and East Houston. Jennifer Aniston kept a place downstairs and Diana Ross lived around the corner. Slumming, it was not.

Still, Beverly imagined nothing but the worst in regards to her only child's lifestyle, way "down there" in the far reaches below 14th Street, the soiled bowels of the city. She refused to visit, and now Hillary was returning the disfavor. She would agree to appear tableside, but not in person.

Yes, Hillary Stein Skyped in meals with her mom.

Beverly heaved a deep Hollywood-ish sigh as she finished reading the list. "It's like luncheon with *The Munsters,*"she said, suddenly cracking herself up. "At least the Kobe's on the plane."

Meanwhile, downstairs, Phillip Harmsworth Dexter was having a devilish day. Frankly, he was quickly tiring of America, and especially the people who populate its purple mountains' majesty. The "terribly British" house manager, as most people referred to him, was weary of the devious backstabbing, the hilarious pretension, the utter lack of compassion of these crass parvenus. The fourth generation of "gentlemen's gentlemen," Dexter was still not quite accustomed to serving a lady (such as she was) of the house.

But after three taxing years, he was getting into the swing of it, he thought. He learned, for example, that gushing over a rich American's wealth, power or status won big points, thus greasing the arduous wheels of "service," at which he excelled beyond comparison, and with the utmost discretion. His famed sycophancy had even earned him a few holidays on St. Barts, at Beverly Gansevoort-Stein's yoga instructor's villa.

Manhattan was by no means the glorious isle of civility he had left behind. Dexter grimaced as he contemplated his challenging New York day to come. Another fine charity luncheon, he growled to himself. How lovely for us. More drooling snobs who wouldn't know a proper dessert knife if it stabbed them in the back, which, given this crowd, was entirely possible.

"Mister Dexter? The Kobeef is here." It was Margarita, announcing the arrival of the Japanese delicacy, via air freight. It roused him from his sour reverie. "Yes, fine, thank you Margarita," he said. "But that's Kobe beef, not Kobeef."

"Whatever. At one-hundred-fifty a pound plus airfare, it better be *muy buena.*

"I have every confidence it will be." Dexter's expression was particularly dour. He was not pleased with Margarita this morning. By the time she'd reached the kitchen, Maria Eugenia, the middle aged, rather plump head maid from San Salvador and Dexter's right-hand henchwoman, had already shucked the San Juans. "Now please, run along," he told Margarita. "Surely you have something to dust, somewhere?"

The maid muttered to herself as she left the enormous, bleach-white, exquisitely outfitted and overstocked kitchen, now humming with activity in anticipation of *El Lonche Grande* as the servants sarcastically called it on

Twitter.

"*Idiota ingles*," she said under her breath.

"I heard that!" Dexter called back, perhaps more triumphantly than he intended. "*Yo hablo espanol, senorita.* He turned to Maria Eugenia. "Where in the blazes is Chef?"

"Right here, Dex!" said a short, 40-something guy with droopy brown eyes, unshaven face and growing belly, emerging from the walk-in with a bushel of fresh ramps, marked *Hergestellt in Deutschland/* MADE IN GERMANY. "It's time to give these babies a bath, before I proceed and butcher up all that Kobe like Freddy Kreuger."

Chef's real name was Jack Gillespie, a good-old Irish boy who came from Flushing, Queens "before all the Orientals moved in," as he put it, without racial animosity, but clueless as to how offensive it was. Jack looked and spoke like an old-school NYC cabbie. Uncouth and unschooled, his only true education came from the pricey Caffé Piazza San Marco, where his brother-in-law, Roberto DelMonico, offered to pay his tuition at ICE, the Institute of Culinary Education, Peter Kump's palace of gastronomical miracles down on West 23rd, steps from Fifth Avenue in the trendy, bistro-jammed Flatiron District.

"That place is awesome. They pop out award-winning chefs like a rabbit pops out offspring," Jack had joked at one of several pained interviews with Dexter. "Of course, that's before you lightly braise it in a raspberry-balsamic reduction, served on a bed of wilted wild frisee and warm lardons. From Brittany."

Dexter had glared at him for what seemed like decades before saying, simply, "How very droll, Mr. Gillespie." He was not fond of Chef, it was clear, an emotion that two years of working together had only intensified. There was no getting used to this *cretin*, Dexter fretted. Most of the hiring and firing were his duties. But Gillespie had come so highly recommended from Beverly's buddies on the Board at ICE, she insisted that Dexter interview and re-interview "that nice Irish man from Queens." Once she tasted his cooking, that was it. He was *that* talented; diction and appearance be damned. Jack became Chef and, as Madame made abundantly clear to Dexter, Chef he would remain, until she said otherwise.

"You fuck with him," she told Dexter late one night after one too many Martinis, in a rare display of salty idioms in front of the help, "And I'll have your balls for brunch. *Avec le sauce béarnaise. Comprenez vous??*" She moved in very close, as if she really meant it.

"Yes Madame," Dexter had said, discretely turning his nose away from the vapors that spewed from her vodka-soaked mouth. "Perfectly."

The English house manager regarded the frumpy Irish-American cook and frowned. "Chef, I've told you repeatedly that I do not appreciate being called 'Dex.' It's neither my name nor my nickname, nor does it even make sense," he said, stiff upper lip intact. "You may call me 'Mr. Dexter,' or simply 'Dexter,' if you like. If you insist, I suppose 'Philip' would be congenial but professional enough. But you must never call me 'Phil.'"

"Oh really, *Phil?*" Jack growled with the most exaggerated wise-guy voice he could summon. "Well I don't like bein' called friggin' 'Chef,' neither. Okay? My name is Jack. But you don't go around hearin' me whining about it all tha time. Sheesh, it's like eggshells with you people."

It was going to be a complicated morning. Why in the *devil* didn't I take that position in Bristol, Dexter thought, when I had the chance?

Things "backstage," as Madame Gansevoort-Stein liked to call the kitchen and adjacent service areas, did not get better as Dexter's morning wore painfully on. The staff was not only unusually surly today, a few of them were caught speaking Spanish in a "public area," something that was *totalmente prohibido,* as Dexter learned to say. He would have to think of some appropriate discipline later.

Even worse, the peach-hued lilies Dexter had ordered, specially flown in from Asuncion, turned out to be a garish shade of bright *salmon*, which Madame instantly rejected, insisting they would clash with the dark-green silk curtains in the formal dining room – a walnut-paneled vault with seven picture windows looking out over the park and beyond. Someone had to run out to get more flowers. Dexter sent Maria Eugenia.

Meanwhile, the ramps had gone "wimpy," Chef complained, two bottles of Dom Perignon were corked and undrinkable, and the linen company had yet to make its delivery. Then again, Dexter knew, those linens, hand-dyed and stitched by elderly nuns in Dusseldorf with ample time on their hands, had been carefully selected to harmonize exactly with the Paraguayan lilies. And now? No lilies, but no German linens either. What was the big deal? Dexter laughed giddily at his own self-imposed predicament, and life.

Dexter felt one of his heads coming on. There was only one remedy. He walked down the long hall to his quarters and swallowed two pills, alprazolam, better known as Xanax, an increasingly common occurrence during work hours, though he'd never taken more than one tablet, the maximum dosage. If the entire household was going to melt down before his eyes, then he wanted a nice buttery-soft landing pad to ease into the apocalypse. He grabbed a third, highly inadvisable tranquilizer and slipped it into the breast pocket of his deep-slate Brooks Brothers blazer.

I could very well find myself in great need of this later, he thought.

Dexter never bothered to read his med's warnings on that thin piece of paper with the tiny printing. Huge mistake, he would later discover. "Do not drink alcohol while taking Xanax," it warned. "This medicine will add to the effects of alcohol."

Back upstairs, Beverly looked at the time. Guests would start arriving in an hour. It was time to prep. She called for Margarita to draw the bath and lay out her pre-specified cosmetics and hair products. There was a list, printed out and shoved under Margarita's door by God-knows-who. *Ese pinche británico,* (that damn Brit) the maid imagined.

Beverly inspected Margarita's handiwork, checking the cosmetics against her copy of "The List." She tested the bathtub with a digital thermometer. It was eight degrees too warm. She just hated it when staff got the bathwater wrong. "When will that stupid girl learn? It will take *minutes* to cool down to my requested temperature," Beverly said out loud. But there wasn't time. "Oh, what's eight degrees? It won't poach me."

There was a giggle from just outside the bathroom. It was Margarita, standing near the doorway bearing fresh, fluffy towels and thinking to herself: First-world problems, lady, first-world problems. Beverly looked scornfully at her maid. "The bathwater was unacceptably scalding today." She held up the thermometer. "*Moo-choh call-EN-tay.*" Margarita gestured with the towels as a peace offering. "Put those down, then get out of here," Beverly said, before adding, with exasperation more than anger, "*por favor.*"

Apres-bath, Beverly applied her lotions and potions, oils and creams, East Asian herbal packs and Southern European tonics. Next came her makeup, by Guerlain, which she thought gave her a youthful allure. That, and the fact that her selections were very, very expensive, informed her purchase.

As for what to wear, Beverly had personally taken a cab all the way down to Bergdorf's at 58th and Fifth to "pick out a little something" (usually a small team managed her acquisitions). After driving the saleslady to the point of contemplating self-immolation, she settled on a Donna Karan sleeveless cashmere "cozy," with draped shawl collar and cascading front.

At 1:02 the first bell rang. "Margarita!" Beverly shouted, as predicted. "Door!" Beverly went downstairs to find three of the girls: Wanda, Martha and Jackie, in various combinations of Lauren, Gucci, Chanel and Ferragamo, with some Bulgari and Kate Spade thrown around the sides for kicks. They smelled, collectively, like an English rose garden blooming amid wild juniper and cinnamon trees.

"Jenna couldn't make it." It was Martha, looking sheepish, as if Beverly would take it out on her personally. "I don't know why. She just said to send her regrets."

Beverly harrumphed. "Regrets?" she said, raising a perfectly-plucked eyebrow. "I sent that girl an engraved invitation three weeks out? And after all my planning and all my hard work, she cancels at the last minute with nothing more than her *regrets*? Does she have any idea how strenuous it is to design a proper seating chart? Does she? How charming Jackie's little friend is turning out to be."

"Don't try to blame this on me." Jackie said. "And you can lose the drama. It's just lunch."

"It's *luncheon!* A damn important one, too, about…diapers and things."

"*Problemas del primer mundo,*" Margarita whispered to Isabel, the tiny, mousy maid standing next to her. Isabel, sweet as a sugar-coated churro, was the only Mexican on staff. Margarita had quickly come to confide in her.

"Yep. First world problems," Isabel repeated in English. "Their little rules, games and arguments are so stupid. It's like we're living in *Game of Thrones*, except it has been remade as a comedy."

Martha stepped in to calm things down. "It's okay. Ladies, please! The P&G people will be here any minute and we don't want them to see us arguing like baboons. Jenna is a little, well, flakey, we all know that." Jackie issued a snort of mild protest. "Well she *is* Jackie, so let's just deal with it. Beverly, maybe I can help you with seating rearrangements. Where's your chart?"

Beverly was touched by the offer. "Margarita! The chart! Where's the damn chart?" When the maid returned with the requested object, Beverly and Martha retired to a quiet corner of the formal dining room and conferred in two Queen Anne chairs upholstered in the same dark-green silk that had clashed so irreconcilably with the Paraguayan lilies.

The bell rang again. "Margarita! The door!" The shrillness echoed from the dining room, where Beverly and Martha were shuffling around place cards like chess pieces. Dexter, feeling so light and loopy now, ditched them to go swallow the third pill, washed down with an embracing snifter of cognac.

Again, the bell. Before Beverly could yelp, Margarita cut her off. "I know," she said. *"Dee* door." It was Brent Ashby, the boring stock director in his boring, battleship gray suit, arriving with the considerably less boring Celia Bergstrom, editor of *Wow!*, who did look smashing - though perhaps trying a bit too hard, both Beverly and Wanda later judged. Gorgeous Celia, from a prominent family in Barbados, with her mixed-race complexion, high forehead and lilting accent, invariably drew comparisons to Rhianna.

Air kisses ensued and Tyrolean sparkling water was proffered by the small brigade of maids standing by, looking for signs of parchment.

Next at the door was Chester Mansfield, the short, stocky editor from *The Times*, dressed as one would expect, in khaki trousers and blue button-down shirt, most likely from The Men's Warehouse, and a tweed jacket with, (were those *really?*) leather patches at the elbows. When Beverly saw him, she hurried into the reception area.

66

"Chester darling! Lovely to see you," Beverly turned her cheek for him to kiss. "It's not a party until *The Times* shows up!" The powerful editor was not impressed. He knew why he had been invited. Let's see what the P&G folks are going to do first, he thought, before I decide to assign anything. We never guarantee coverage, she knows that.

Next to arrive was the *Post's* Jamal Dix, in magenta pants, cobalt-blue blousy shirt, no tie and a canary-yellow jacket adorned with stencils of the little blue Twitter bird, with white ruffles at the cuffs. Margarita did a double take over his unorthodox looks, tempted to ask if he was "on the list," though she knew that was way above her station.

Then came the Pampers people, Vanessa Yoon, a startlingly beautiful Korean-American and the senior product manager, commanding in a ruby-red Prada business suit, with jet-black hair in a tight bun and tea-colored eyes, and two members of her staff, Ralph Karloff, a middle-aged, utterly forgettable Senior VP of Marketing at the company's "personal hygiene division," and Rick McConnell, an attractive youth with a pale complexion, thick ginger hair and robin's-egg eyes, who looked about twelve. His title, if mentioned at all, nobody could remember. Beverly wondered if perhaps the Pampers people had sent an *intern* over for luncheon. On the other hand, the kid looked innocently cute in his slightly-too-large Jones New York suit, Beverly mused, correctly pegging him as a Macy's shopper.

Lastly, as if by design, came Rexford, even though he had the least distance to travel – one floor – along with his friend Thaddeus Pepper. They were both casual and striking: Rexy, tall, handsome and rich-looking in a sleek black Dolce & Gabbana suit with white shirt open at the collar and French cuffs with fire-opal links, and Thad, a medium-built dark-blond man of Scandinavian stock with delicate features and bedroom-blue eyes. He was dressed in a sapphire Hugo Boss with a pumpkin silk shirt and, daringly, deep purple tie. Rex's loafers were black Bottega Veneta, Thad's were "seedling" from Bruno Magli. Their footwear alone was staggering, each costing more than four months of Margarita's salary.

Yeah right, Beverly laughed to herself. These guys are most definitely *not* homosexual.

"Luncheon is served." It was Dexter, enriching his tipsy accent with just a smidgen of *Downton Abbey* nasal snobbishness, in misguided hope of impressing the diaper brigade. "I do hope every person here enjoys the meal as much as we enjoyed pr'preparing it." The drugs and cognac were really starting to drive. "Chef works so hard. We love Chef. We love his bloody arse so *very* fucking much."

Beverly visibly heaved. "Dexter! Are you quite alright?"

"Oh yesh ma'am," he slurred, a dopey grin on his face.

Wanda was not fooled. "Bullocks! He most certainly is *not* alright. He looks stoned as an old coot. Utterly legless, if you ask me."

"Thank you both, dear English friends, for illuminating us on this subject, which I believe is about to change. At once," Beverly said. This whole thread had disaster scribbled all over it. "Dexter, tell Chef we're ready to eat. And maybe go sit down a while. You look pale."

"Yeshth, Madame," Dexter said, weaving back toward the kitchen. As everyone took their seats and the maids served the San Juans and poured the champagne, Beverly's IT guy, Bill (she had no idea what his last name was), fixed an I-Pad to a seated, frightfully dressed manikin's face, wheeled it to the table, pressed some buttons and, *whamo*, in Skyped Hillary. The result was surreal: a talking head atop a stiff body, dressed as a prostitute.

"Hello mother," Hillary said. "Hello everyone." The Pampers people looked perplexed. Beverly jumped in to explain. "This is my daughter Hillary, who couldn't join us in person, so we set a place for her at the table, represented by this… dummy. Hillary, these are the nice people from Procter & Gamble who want to help us with the shelter for single mommies. Isn't that lovely?"

"Heartwarming, *mother*." Hillary's tone, dripping with odium, sounded eerily like Christina Crawford.

Vanessa, the product manager, tried to chirp her way out of the awkwardness. "Hillary, you must be very far away to miss such a great meal with your mom. Where are you now?"

"Essex," said the disembodied head on the screen.

"Oh I love Essex! Are you in Thirstable, by any chance, near the English coast?"

"No. Essex Street. Near Katz's delicatessen."

"But then why….?"

"Long story," Wanda said. "Terribly unimportant."

Beverly offered a flimsy explanation. "My daughter doesn't like to trek this far uptown. She says it gives her vertigo."

"I see," Vanessa said, glancing at her colleagues with a look that said, *why are we here, again?* "I think we have a product for that, don't we Rick?" Little Ricky, the kid in the Jones suit, whipped out a phone and tapped away as if his career depended on it, which it probably did. Within seconds, he was grinning like a well-trained spider monkey.

"Yes! Yes we do, Ms. Yoon!" he declared, pleased as peach pie. "Our pharma division makes a great steroid for it. Should I have samples messengered over today?"

"That won't be necessary," Hillary said. "I'll just stay below Fourteenth Street, thanks." A long pause. "Mother, what do you have me dressed in today? JC Penney? H and crappy M?" There was no answer. "I have a right to know! What am I wearing?" Hillary was now near tears. "Someone show me right now! Where's Dexter? I wanna see me!"

"Dexter's not here, sweetie," Wanda said. "He's, um, resting."

"Wanda? Is that you? What does mother have me in?"

Wanda looked for guidance to Beverly, who mouthed the word 'no,' and shook her head vigorously. "I'm afraid I can't do that right now, sweetie," Wanda answered, looking scornfully at the garish rags draping the dummy. "But I can say that you look quite…"

"Very cute, Hillary!" It was Martha, moving in for the block; another effort at soothing.

"Who said that?" Hillary demanded. "Was that Martha? Oh God. If she thinks I'm cute, then I must look dreadful." A miffed Martha got up and stalked off to the powder room, where she remained for a conspicuous duration. The three media reps, the two metrosexuals, the dull Stock Exchange guy, and especially the Pampers people, were without words. It was all just so weird.

Beverly called Margarita,whispering in her ear: "Get that Bill guy down here, pronto."

Rex decided to take a stab at civil conversation. "Hillary," he said to the manikin. "I have a friend here with me. I'm sure you remember him. You two went to Nightingale Bamford together," he said, mentioning the highly prestigious prep school just up the street. "His name is Thaddeus Pepper.

Jackie, can you swing Hillary around so she can see Thad?"

"Hi Hillary," Thad said. "Long time, no, um, *see?*"

"Thad? Thad Pepper? Aren't you the guy who ran around school trying to get all the kids to tell you about their dreams?"

"That's me! Glad you remember." They spoke over each other as if on cheap cell phones.

Thad: "You were so *cool.*" Hillary: "You were so *creepy.*"

"Thad has a successful psychotherapy practice now, in Chelsea," Rex told the iPad. Of course it's in Chelsea, Beverly thought. It's Gay Grand Central down there. "And he got his MD from NYU."

"So," Hillary interjected, "that would make him *Dr. Pepper?*"

"I prefer 'Thaddeus Pepper, MD.'"

Wanda fought down a spit-take of her Dom Perignon and howled. "No way mate! From now on, you'll most definitely remain, forever, Dr. Pepper."

Hillary switched subjects, but not in the best of ways. "So, tell me Rex. Is it true that you and Thad are doing the nasty, like they say? Because I know people who would drop major coin to live-stream *that* shit."

"Hillary Stein! You cut that filth out this instant!" a mortified Beverly exclaimed. Bill the IT guy entered the Formal Dining Room. Beverly glanced at him with desperate gratitude, nodded at the manikin, and made a cutting motion across her throat.

"I saw that mom!" Hilary cried. "What are you guys up to? Bill? You're not going to unplug me again, like that time when…?"

Blip! Bill pushed a button and the screen, mercifully, went black. The garishly dressed manikin sat in silence, looking like a dejected drag queen after a hard night on Christopher Street.

"Well," Wanda said at last, piercing the uneasy hush. "That went over like a house of kittens on fire."

Beverly looked drained of life. She glanced around the solid oak dining table desperately trying to read faces, especially the diaper faces. "I do apologize for my daughter's behavior," she said. "Her insolence gets the best of her at times, I'm afraid." The P&G people said not to worry about it, but clearly they didn't mean it. Rex and Dr. Pepper looked, well, not amused.

As if cued by the angels above, medallions of Kobe arrived just in time, borne on the arms of Central American women after being perfectly scalloped and served under a Burgundy-peppercorn glaze, with chevre-mashed turnips and braised ramps, magically de-wimped.

It was an exceedingly silent course. The food was delectable.

The maids came in to clear. Just one more round to go, coffee, cognac, dessert and petit fours, Beverly thought, closing her eyes as if in prayer, and this whole mess will be over. She was desperate to get the P&G executives out of her home before lord knows what other cringe-worthy moment might befall her.

Rushing dessert, regrettably, was at odds with her basic design for a winning major-donor luncheon. Sweets and cognac were the portion of the meal that Beverly liked to privately call "the interview." Today, to create the congeniality needed, Beverly and Chef had settled on candle-warmed snifters of Courvoisier L'Esprit (at $2,300 per hand-cut Lalique-crystal bottle: they meant business), crème brûlée with imported Portuguese lavender and sea salt crystals harvested from the Danish island of Læsø, and bone-china demitasses of rich espresso from Beverly's "little artisanal shade-coffee plantation down in Costa Rica."

The well-tested formula usually went thusly: As the cognac warmed everyone's throats and minds, Beverly would casually begin talking about the mission of Project A, with whatever selected media were invited who cover Subject B, and then masterfully bringing major donor(s) C into the conversation, subliminally infusing them with a sense of pre-owned "ownership" on the issue.

"Once they see that *The Times* is interested," Beverly had assured her girlfriends, with the confidence of a seasoned pro, "those Pampers people will be lining up to write checks." But the diaper folks were still looking a bit baffled and more than a tad concerned, despite the artisanal coffee and Danish salt, "flown in just for this luncheon," Beverly had been sure to mention (it was on her neatly printed card of "Things To Say Today," tucked under the rim of her late-19th Century Spode plate).

Sensing doom, Beverly decided to engage the reporters immediately, even before the petit-fours arrived on extravagant silver trays said to be from the Romanovs. There was no time for throat-clearing: The jittery hostess dove right in, lest another wretched calamity be unleashed upon her by the wrathful Gods of Contemporary Formal Dining.

Subtlety went out the imported Italian windows. "Chester, I haven't seen your paper writing much lately about companies that fund wonderful projects, such as shelters for unwed mothers. Why is that? When did *The Times* stop caring about poor children?"

Chester Mansfield was impressed with the framing of the question, a twist on the old joke of asking a politician, "When did you stop beating your wife?"

Of course we haven't "stopped caring" about the issue, he thought. But when was the last time we covered it? Back when people actually gave a damn about the poor? This Beverly gal does her homework, but I'm not going to step into her shit.

After all, Chester held the cards.

"Funny you should mention that," he said, wiping a swirl of lavender from his mouth. "We were just talking about that the other day. It's been a while since we looked into it."

Beverly's heart raced with triumph. *Bon Travail!* she told herself. She was going to get Mansfield to deliver, right out of the gate. The other ladies looked up from their dessert, eyes blinking.

"But we discovered that teen pregnancy has fallen dramatically in recent years, and it's just not that much of a story anymore."

Beverly looked crushed. The *Times* editor looked smug. Vanessa Yoon looked at her watch.

"On the other hand, the fact that the issue has dropped off *our* radar, and thus that of the national media…" he said with a pompous, self-satisfied chuckle, causing Jamal to whisper into Celia's right ear, "These *Times* people are such arrogant fuckwads, don'tcha think?"

"Go on," Beverly said, hope returning like a hungry collie who's been wandering from home for days. "On the *other* hand…?"

"Well, we actually do think it's time for an update on the issue."

"Brah-VAH!" Wanda said, moving to high-five Beverly, then checking herself. "Well that is lovely news, Mr. Mansfield." She promptly reverted to proper

English businesswoman mode, for the cause. "We would be so excited to hear what you have planned."

Brent looked directly at Beverly. He knew this would bulldoze her. "There's a new home being developed right now, downtown by the harbor. Interesting story. It's sited in a building that was washed clean by Sandy. And get this, they have enough space left over to be reserved for refugees from other storms, when needed."

"How interesting," Vanessa Yoon said, smiling for the first time in at least an hour. "The place is like a safe harbor?"

Beverly felt a cold steel blade plunging through her chest, she was sure of it.

"Exactly," Chester said. "The foundation has even lined up a few B-listers to support the project," he paused and looked derisively at Celia. This was her beat, after all. "Celine Dion, the Olsen Twins, Khloe Kardashian, Snooki…"

"*Snooki*!?" Wanda roared. "Hah! They should call her Snacky, if you ask me."

"No one did, dear," Beverly said.

"Which foundation is doing this? There are so many out there," Little Ricky said, in what Beverly read as a veiled insult to her efforts. Snot-nosed little shit, she thought. You're not that cute after all. And your cheap suit is way too big.

"Well, Rick, funny you should ask. It's a group that P&G has supported in the past. The Vogue Foundation for Better Futures, VFBF, chaired by Ms. Wintour herself."

Everyone took deep breaths: the Pampers people with excitement; the society ladies with unbridled horror.

"Well, fuck me with a rusty tire iron," Wanda snarled, tossing down her napkin. "Not that *stoopid* slut again."

Anna Wintour was Wanda and Beverly's personal arch-nemesis. It cemented their friendship. Their disdain stretched thick, all the way down to The World Trade Center, where "that woman" held court ensconced from the world somewhere high up in that perfectly hideous edifice, with its snaking black town cars idling out front, polluting, waiting for fashion editors and art directors to be whisked out to JFK, or uptown to Per Se, or wherever, for dinner.

None of the ladies could abide Wintour. "I can't say it, but it rhymes with 'cunt,'" Wanda had once remarked about the all-powerful fashion arbiter, known for wearing dark glasses indoors and "a hairstyle that hasn't changed since LBJ was President," as Wanda put it. Wintour, the subject of some American derision for her icy, regal demeanor, "is giving us Brits a bad name," Wanda had said. "We need all the warm-fuzzy PR we can scare up over here in the States. But it's always the same: One step forward, two Annas back."

Even sweet Martha had once spoken unkind words about Wintour, and she liked positively everybody. "I think her taste in fashion," she said with more resolve than she knew she had, "well, it's just stupid. It's ugly, and I don't get it at all."

Rex glanced over at his downstairs neighbor Beverly, who now took on the sorry, semi-flaccid form of an inflatable air dancer at a carwash, with a slowly dying pump. Her arms appeared to wither under all that Donna Karen cashmere. Rex realized he had known this legendary lady his entire life. Beverly and Bernie Stein had already moved into the building when he was born. His parents used to attend the Opera and try expensive new restaurants with them. Some nights, he was allowed to come downstairs and watch projector movies in the "Cinema Room" with Hillary, who was odd and ornery even back then. Rex harbored fond memories of this "little apartment downstairs," as his mother, no stranger to smugness herself, used to say, before that terrible evening at Lake Lucerne.

There were still two other journalists in the room. Rex went in for the save. "What about you, Dix old boy?" He smiled at Jamal. "I'm sure you have an abiding interest in young, single moms?" Beverly, despite her deflation, offered Rex a look of exhausted gratitude.

Jamal Dix was ready to oblige, and to make that *Times* jerk look like the fuckwad he was. "Sure Rex! I can do something on the page regularly, as the project proceeds. If they have a big kick-off gala, which I'm sure they will, we can plug the hell out of it." Then, turning to the Pampers people, he added. "We'll promote the underwriters as well, of course."

Suddenly, it seemed, Safe Harbor House was back in the ballgame.

"You'd do that for us, Jamal?" Jackie asked, after pouting basically since the San Juans were served. "Wow! I'll have to start reading the *Post*!"

Awkward laughter ensued as Jamal's smile vanished.

"Good one, Jackie." It was Wanda, of course. "Open mouth, insert Jimmy-Choo. And you were taught etiquette *where*, dear? On a canal barge?"

Rex spoke up again. "I read the *Post* every day, especially Jamal's column," he said, ingratiating himself, as usual, to just about everyone, especially those with a byline. "Even when I'm mentioned, unflatteringly."

"I read it too," Celia said. "We get lots of trend-story ideas from the zany items in your column. Say Jamal, maybe we could do some coordinated coverage of… what's the name?"

"Safe Harbor House," Beverly said, glaring at Mansfield. "Shelter from the storm."

Finally, snifters were drained and lavender-streaked plates cleared. It was time to end this.

Looking back on the misadventure that was lunch, things could have gone worse, Beverly reckoned, trying hard to buck herself up. Jamal's hail-Mary pass did help pivot the conversation, and hopefully the Pampers people's interest, back toward Safe Harbor. What a nice, if grotesquely attired young man, she thought.

A thunderous crash rippled down the hallway and into the room. Beverly leapt from her chair and ran out to look. It was Dexter, who had tripped while carrying snifters and what was left of the cognac on a now-dented Romanov tray. The glasses were in shards, but the Courvoisier's Lalique bottle emerged unbroken. Dexter grabbed it, somehow yanked himself up, and waddled across the crushed snifters and directly into the room, before a gobsmacked Madame could do anything to stop him.

"More Kwah-vah-SEE-yay, anybody?" he wailed merrily, tilting around the table. "Who wants schum? How 'bout you, dove?" Dexter leered at Vanessa. He edged toward her chair and tripped again. The hand-cut Lalique bottle somersaulted toward the long oak table and smashed into a solid-brass candelabra, shattering the crystal into tiny shards and knocking over the candles, in turn setting fire to the tablecloth. Wanda, the smart one, snuffed the flames out with leftover Opus One and a fistful of Læsø salt, emptied from the small Xing Dynasty jade bowl near her plate.

"Ow!" Someone said. "*OWWW!*"

It was Little Ricky, whimpering and holding his left eye shut. "Something went in my eye! I think it was a sliver from the bottle." Everyone sat, too stunned by these developments to respond. There was no sound, save for

Dexter, who was giggling again. Only kind Martha had the presence of mind to get up, walk over to Rick, and help. "Let's get you into that bathroom there and see if we can't wash it out with water," she said like a school nurse.

Well, Beverly mused bitterly, we can kiss *those* diaper checks goodbye.

Wanda put her hand on Beverly's shoulder and said quietly, in her Wanda way, "I suspect you tried as best as one possibly could do in such a flea circus. Didn't you, sweetie?"

Beverly wanted to go upstairs and cry. "I utterly give up" should have been the final item on her "Things to Say Today" card.

And then, "AAAAAAIIIIIIIIHHHHHHHH!" This second cry, unlike Little Ricky's snivel, was a deeply disturbing, gut-piercing scream.

Dexter? No, it was Vanessa, scrambling atop her chair and teetering in terror. "What on God's earth was *that?*" she trembled. "Something bit me! Something just came up under the table and bit my ankle!" Vanessa grabbed a German nun-napkin and dabbed her leg. "Look at this!" she said, displaying the now-ruined linen. "Blood!"

The executive looked down at the carnival of ruins strewn about her: The unstable hostess and her daffy friends, that whack-a-doodle butler, the bizarrely clothed manikin that once served as a daughter, the charred, soaked and salted tablecloth, those overdressed gay guys "Sexy Rexy and Dr. Pepper," the three feckless reporters, that boring Stock Exchange man who'd barely spoken and now looked peptic, the linen napkin soiled with her own blood, and poor Rick, in the bathroom rinsing a Lalique shard from his cornea.

"What kind of shit show are you people running here?" she said. "We are a *family* company!"

Just then - Beverly was certain no one had seen it, except maybe Margarita, which was okay because she signed the paper - from the corner of her eye, there was a flash of gray and white, shooting like a torpedo from under the table to behind the silk curtains that had clashed with the salmon lilies of Asunción.

The haggard hostess, defeated, bedraggled and under a death threat from the Russian mob, still managed to raise a feeble smile. At least, she thought, I have found my Walter Mitty.

Chapter 6

Not Very Luncheony

Megan could not believe she had been in the city for nearly two weeks. Life here was hard, but endlessly fascinating. No one, she thought, has time to be bored in New York. But back in Ypsilanti, the news was getting harder to bear. Megan's mom Maureen, a customer service rep for the local cable company, had just seen her hours cut radically. She was already working part-time, thirty-five hours per week, so the company could avoid covering her health insurance. But now, with Obamacare, firms were obliged to cover all employees working just thirty hours or more. Maureen was cut to twenty-five hours, the equivalent of losing a weekly paycheck each month.

The company cited "efficiency measures" and "pressure from stockholders," but she knew it was cutting her hours to skirt Obamacare. "I voted for that man, twice, and look what happens," she had said to her son, her voice strained, her eyes wet. "We're in trouble. I got rent to cover, car payments, insurance, *you.* Losing $700 a month is gonna kill us. You gotta get a job."

Todd didn't take time to blink. He went to his computer, jumped on Craigslist and saw that the Airport Marriott was hiring a prep cook. He grabbed the keys to her Saturn and sped to the hotel and a brighter future, chopping red peppers and parsley for $9.95 an hour.

Todd started the next day, which is when he met his future husband, Carlitos, a new bellboy at the hotel. It was the same cute guy he had ogled at the airport, the day Megan left.

At sixteen, Carlitos' parents had booted him from their house in a small village outside Puebla, after someone caught him making out with a neighbor boy. He spent the next six months hiding out alone in Tepito, Mexico City's filthy and dangerous flea-market district, sleeping in roach-covered flophouses and selling batteries, gum and occasionally himself to stay alive. But then he heard that an armed gang from the village, relatives of the boy he kissed, was in town, looking for him.

Eventually, Carlitos made it to the States and received asylum. He wanted to become a professional cook. Todd was amazed. "Me too!" he said. "Maybe one day you can help me run my catering company, as soon as I can save up the money to get started."

Megan couldn't have been prouder of her kid brother, stepping up to the plate like that. A sharp pang of guilt stabbed at her conscience. She called him. "As soon as I can, I'll start sending money. I need more hours at the restaurant – I only have three shifts right now. But tell mom when things pick up, there will be checks."

When she hung up, there was a bling! on the phone. It was a text. From Rexford Bainbridge.

> *Megan! Sorry I did not call back. It's been crazy busy. Listen, please*
> *come with me to lunch, at my downstairs neighbor Beverly's place? You*

met her at San Marco. I promise to keep her in check. Thursday at 1. 1080 5th. Pls say yes?

"You're going *where?*" Brigit had said when she found out, her mouth suggesting humor but her eyes betraying a "what in the fuck were you thinking?" horror. "Beverly Gansevoort-Stein is widely regarded as the most obnoxious creature on Upper Fifth. And the competition is very stiff. I'll need to brush off the frost from your shoulders when you get home. Does she know you're coming?"

"I don't know."

"Hah! Oh my God that's rich. She could not possibly know. She would've nixed the idea right then. You, my friend, are crashing M'Lady's luncheon."

"It's not 'crashing' if you were invited."

"What in the world are you going to wear?"

Megan had not even thought about that. It didn't occur to her that a luncheon on Fifth Avenue was not quite the same as pasta and salad at Applebee's back in Ypsilanti. Brigit regarded her friend for a moment. "You got nothin', right?"

"Nada."

"C'mon." She grabbed Megan's hand. "We're going back to H&M." They returned home two hours later, with a light turquoise calf-length dress in "softly draped jersey" with narrow straps and flared skirt, satin slingbacks and a signature H&M "black coat," short, straight-cut with welt front pockets. It looked like an old-fashioned artist's smock. A poor artist's smock. Still, Megan liked the whole look, even if she couldn't really afford it.

"I never thought it would cost more than a hundred bucks to go somewhere for lunch," she sighed. "A *free* lunch."

Brigit laughed. "Don't fret, you're getting off easy. I imagine the other women Rex has brought over there were not, exactly, how shall I say? *Pret-a-porter* girls?"

"Thanks Bridge. That makes me feel so much better."

"Wear it off-the-rack, sister." Brigit chuckled. "And wear it proud."

Meanwhile, back in Beverly Gansevoort-Stein's world, things were more or less normal, even though Dexter had been sent "on sabbatical" to Betty Ford, and was still in Rancho Mirage. Plans were proceeding to renovate and refurbish an old tenement building uptown for Safe Harbor, even without the largess of Proctor & Gamble, which had still not made a decision. Walter Mitty had been secured and restrained in Beverly's massive bedroom. And best of all, there'd been no more threatening messages from Alexi Stroganoff.

She looked at her calendar: 1:00 pm, lunch with Rexford. It was to be a fairly simple affair, served in the study by Margarita and Maria Eugenia. Chef would to start them off with a scallop bisque and toasted pork-belly relish, followed by a warm spinach salad with caramelized grapefruit, toasted pecans and candied pansies, and then roasted quail stuffed with duck pate, currants, and, in chef's little nod toward irony, hard-boiled quail eggs.

Rex showed up bearing a pot of rare leopard orchids from Vanuatu and a big smile. Margarita let him in, took his Ermenegildo Zegna coat and led him into the study. Maria Eugenia walked in soon after with a chilled bottle of pink prosecco, vinted in extremely limited editions at Madame's favorite little *azienda vincula* in eastern Umbria.

Beverly greeted her neighbor with air kisses and floating wafts of Channel. "I'm so glad you're here," she said. "We haven't lunched privately in ages.

What's new?"

"Couldn't be better. The China deal is coming along, despite that unfortunate setback with the plutonium-contaminated fish. The partnership between Bainbridge Associates and the Central Bank of Malta is almost done. I'm going to date the waitress at Piazza San Marco. And I'm executive producing a new Hulu series about lepers who are recruited by the CIA to spread disease. It's a comedy."

"What?" Beverly cried so loudly that Margarita burst into the study, almost in tears, certain she had done something wrong.

"A comedy. I know, it's a bit *outre,* but it IS Hulu."

"I'm not talking about Hulu. What *is* that anyway, some kind of retro pupu-platter? Is that what the cool kids are ordering these days? Now, you said you are going to date whom, exactly?"

"Megan. Her name is Megan. She served you tortellini *en brodo.*"

"I know what she served me, but what do you suppose she is going to serve you? Gold dug up on a silver platter, if you ask me. Never date the help. You know that."

"And you know what I already told you, Beverly: A waitress is not 'the help.'"

"Balderdash!"

"Balderdash? What is this, the Coolidge Era? So, I'm dating a waitress. So what? She's gorgeous, she's funny, she's smart and she doesn't seem the type who would take shit from me, which I kinda, you know, *need.*"

"What you need is a fierce blow to the nether regions. You've simply lost your mind."

"No. I haven't. I'm tired of the sycophantic socialites on training wheels, the tipsy trust fund bimbos, the insatiable It-Girls prowling the Hamptons before their 15 minutes are up. I want to know what it's like to date somebody real."

"Well," Beverly sighed, as if she had been holding her breath since the final episode of *Friends*. "It doesn't get any more (air quotes) *real* than a waitress, my dear. But just you wait until the tabloids get word of this. Jamal Dix, for one, will eat you for Sunday brunch."

"Jamal Dix can suck my...."

"Rexford Bainbridge! Language! In my house." The pause that ensued was so pregnant, it could have given birth to quintuplets. Finally, sounding rather gloomy and sad, Beverly asked, "So, when's your first date?"

The doorbell rang. Rex flashed one of his impish, please-don't-be-cross grins. "Oh no. Oh dear God *no*. How could you? We don't even have an extra setting. And Chef will be furious. Are you purposely trying to sabotage my perfectly good day? I won't forgive you."

"Yes, you will."

"Watch me. I won't."

"How can I watch you *not* do something?"

Out in the hall, Megan could hear the sound of voices rising. Whatever it was, it didn't sound very *luncheony*. Oh sweet baby Jesus on the half-shell, she thought, what have I gotten myself into? She took a deep breath, smelled the dozen pink carnations she'd picked up at the Korean deli on her corner, crossed herself, and rang the bell again.

"Margarita!" she heard someone bellow, presumably M'Lady. "Get the damn door!"

Margarita let the unexpected visitor in and led her to the study. Megan entered the room, smiled at Rex, and did an awkward little curtsey-cum-bow toward Beverly. She froze, unsure what to do, where to sit, where to put the carnations. Then she noticed: just two place settings. Brigit had been right.

"Rex. Did you not let Mrs. Gansevoort-Stein know I was coming?"

"Of course he didn't, my child," Beverly said, with barely disguised miff. "But that is what we adore about our Rexford. He's the *maître des surprises!* And please, call me Beverly. It's so nice to meet you. Oh, but what am I saying ? I already did. At dinner. Only, you were standing, and we weren't."

"She's still standing," Rex said.

"Well, where are my manners? Margarita! Another chair, and a place setting. And make sure that Chef has enough scallop bisque and quail for the, um, *three* of us."

As Megan waited for seating, pondering the very idea of scallop bisque and quail for lunch, she presented her hostess with the carnations. "I brought these for you, ma'am. I hope you like them."

"Well bless your little heart! That was so very thoughtful. What *are* they?"

"Carnations."

"And those are….?"

"Flowers, Bev," Rex said. "They're pink. For you. Perhaps you should thank Megan."

"Well I do thank her! These are so…so…*exotic*. Are they from Luxembourg?"

"No. New Jersey, I think." Megan tried to look pleasant. My God, she thought. How many courses is this lunch going to have? I want to go home and get fetal.

After an uncomfortable stretch of time, with Megan just standing there with her stupid flowers, Margarita finally appeared to set another place. She took the flowers and threw a discreet "what do I do?" look at her boss, who just as discreetly nodded toward the kitchen, where the carnations were duly disposed of.

Lunch proceeded apace, despite atmospheric tension so thick you could send it through a paper shredder. After the first course had been served – with a private, rather cheeky note from Chef that berated Beverly for the embarrassing little portions he was forced to plate – things seemed to settle into a banal truce.

As Margarita presented the warm spinach and pecan salad and sprinkled candied pansies on everyone's plates, Beverly said, arching a brow, "So, my dear…."

"Her name is Megan, Beverly."

"Right. Megan, my dear. What is it that you do, aside from hauling tortellini at San Marco?"

"I'm a journalist," Megan said, smiling with pride.

"You don't say? Have you ever written for anything that *I* would read?"

"What do you read?"

"*The Times. The Journal. Vanity Fair.*"

"Then no. I wrote for my college paper, and I have contributed some pieces here and there, online mostly. I even won an award, of sorts, once."

"Wow! Tell us," Rex interjected.

"I wrote a blog about sexual harassment for *Mother Jones.*"

"Mother who?" Beverly asked.

"It's a communist thing," Rex said. "You wouldn't understand."

"It's not, Rex. It's democratic socialism. Like Sweden."

"And what did you say to Sweden, dear?"

"I wrote about the time my college advisor wanted to sleep with me if I wanted to get an academic appointment."

Rex looked at his date with unmasked respect, a hint of awe. "I think the 'Me Too' movement was one of the best things to ever happen to this country."

"You do? Because that's not what I'd expect to hear from a New York City playboy."

"I learned from women I've dated. Their stories rocked me to the core. The abuse – physical and emotional – that they had to endure really stuck with me. And I got involved."

"That's just amazing. How?"

"I know people. People who have worked with people. Using my media contacts, I helped bring some of these jerks down. Matt Lauer, Charlie Rose, and that creep Weinstein."

Now Megan was the one looking at her date in awe. How could someone be so rich, so good looking, and such a hero? She sipped some prosecco as Rex added, "And now we're gunning for Trump."

Megan jerked. The bubbly got caught in her throat and she expelled it through her nose and mouth, causing a clangorous *swoosh*! And a big wet mess. Beverly looked like she had just seen a cockroach.

"I am so sorry! That really took me by surprise," Megan pleaded to her hostess.

"We'll just pretend it didn't happen, dear. Margarita! Get in here please?"

Megan looked sheepishly at Rex. He smiled. "Megan can be forgiven. That was a biggie."

"I know! I mean, Trump? Really? That's fucking amazing." Megan instantly realized this was not proper luncheon-table talk, and she turned to Beverly once again, begging for mercy. "Oops I am so sorry. That just came out."

"Like the prosecco?"

"Yes." And then quietly she added, "darn." Megan took a deep breath and turned toward her date. "Anyway, Rex, I really admire you."

"We'll see how long that lasts," Beverly said. "Now, Megan, Rex told me where you come from. I'm so sorry. But, why did you come to New York?"

"To find a real writing job. I have a friend at the *New York Post*. She is trying to help me."

"So you want to scribble dishy trash about my wealthy friends in that gossip rag."

"No! I want to do real stories, about issues that affect real people."

"We're real people."

"No, Beverly," Rex said. "We're not." Megan was beginning to like Rexford Bainbridge, III even more.

"Well, I suppose not everyone can start out at the *Times*. I wish you luck, dear," Beverly said, almost as if she meant it. "Rex? You have pull in the yellow press. You must know people. Columnists and others of that ilk. Why don't you make a few calls?"

Rex looked at his date. "I think that should be up to Megan. I would never presume to help someone without their asking. Especially a woman. It's kinda, you know, sexist."

"How very *woke* of you," Beverly said.

"And where, pray tell, did you learn that expression?"

"I watch Trevor Noah. Sometimes. I'm not as unhip as you might think, you know."

Rex turned to Megan. "Would you like me to make some calls? Because I could."

Of course she did. Megan nodded and grinned. Then, so impulsively she couldn't believe she was even doing it, she leapt from her chair, ran over to Rex, and planted a big, long kiss on his chiseled left cheek. Beverly rolled her eyes conspicuously. Megan noticed, but didn't really care. "That's great of you, Rex, gosh. How can I ever thank you?"

"By going out with me again?" The look on his face was part sad-puppy dog and part sexually charged brahman bull. Megan swooned, much to her own mortification. She literally blushed.

"Well, at this point, I…I think that's a given." And then, summoning a lascivious smirk of her own, she added, "Can't wait for our *third* date."

Beverly howled. "Good grief! You young people and your preposterous lack of subtlety. Why don't I just lend you one of my bedrooms, right now? Margarita can make one up."

"That won't be necessary," Megan said as she walked back to her seat, a triumphant grin aimed squarely at the overbearing hostess. "We'll find a place."

Silence ensued, save for the buses and cabs out on the avenue. The tick-tock of a grandfather clock became deafeningly loud.

"Where on earth is that damn quail?" Beverly asked, finally. "Margarita!"

There was no answer. She summoned the maid again, hollering like a country auctioneer. "Well, I guess I'll just have to go check on it myself," she said, folding her napkin and slapping it on the table. After Beverly sauntered off in her self-imposed huff, Rex turned to his date. "Well?" he asked.

"I don't think she likes me."

"Good."

"Good? How so?"

"Because if she liked you, I mean, come on. What kind of endorsement is that? What matters is...."

"Yes?"

"What matters is that I like you. I really do. I *like* like you, Megan O'Malley."

Megan giggled. It was the only response that came to her. It sounded so high school.

"And that's funny, because?"

"It just is. I mean, you're a handsome, rich, if it's ok to say that, I don't know...
"

"It's fine. Please proceed."

"...successful member of the Manhattan elite."

"And?"

"And I'm just this lowly girl from Michigan with few prospects other than serving outrageously priced Italian to the smug glitterati of the world. It's funny, that's all. Don't you think so?"

"Not really. I think it's great. I've met a brilliant, gorgeous, charming young woman with enough balls to rattle Mrs. Gansevoort-Stein. I consider that a blessing. Besides, you are hardly lowly. And you won't be serving pasta much longer. One way or the other."

Megan was not sure what that last line meant. Either he would help her find serious work, or...? She put it out of her mind. Instead she said, "Anyway, your friend's quite a handful."

Rex laughed. "Higher maintenance than the George Washington Bridge with more baggage than Terminal Four at JFK. But I've known her all my life. Played with her daughter. She's like a nutty old auntie to me."

"Well," Megan said. "You got the nutty part right."

Rex looked at Megan longingly, and then an unmistakable seriousness engulfed his face. He leaned over toward her. "You know, the two of us dating will make the columns. Are you okay with that?"

"What if I'm not?"

"Unless you're prepared to go out with me in a burka, I'm afraid that resistance is not an option."

"Don't worry," Megan smiled. "I'll deal. I deal with all kinds of stuff. You have no idea."

"No, I suppose I don't."

Voices arose from backstage. Though they could not make out the actual words, Rex and Megan heard Madame barking, and a man with a Queens accent shouting back even more ferociously.

"Well, that can't be pretty," he said.

"What do we do?"

"We wait. The quail, I assure you, will come."

Almost on cue, Margarita entered the salon bearing the fulsome main course, followed by a beet-red Beverly, who, preposterously, was trying to look pleasant and unruffled. "I do apologize, my dears, sometimes chef just doesn't follow my meal schedule to the letter. It's unbearable, really. I'd let him go, but he's so damn talented, I don't dare."

"I know his nephew!" Megan said, hoping to effervesce the waters. "His name is Tony. He's a busboy at San Marco. Cool guy."

"How nice," Beverly said. "Rather irrelevant. But nice."

"Beverly. Stop. It. Now," Rex warned. "Megan is my guest."

"Well, technically, she's *my* guest.

"Even more reason to knock it off."

"Very well. So, what pleasantries shall we discuss over the main course? Hmmm? Megan, do you have any suggestions?"

Megan wanted to say, Yeah, let's talk about what the hell time this miserable affair is over. But common sense prevailed. "The quail is delicious," she said. "Where's it from?"

"From a farm, of course."

The rest of lunch went pretty much in that fashion. When it was over, there were more air kisses and handed out coats.

"Thank you so much for everything," Megan said. "I hope we can meet again some time."

Beverly stared at her. "I have a feeling," she said with a barely perceptible sigh, "that we shall. Ta-ta!" Then they were out the door and in the hall. Megan exhaled deeply.

"She has that effect on everybody." Rex took her hand as they approached the elevator. "You'll get used to it."

"I don't possibly see how. But if you say so."

They exited the modern white-marble lobby into a blustery gray day on Fifth. It smelled like it was going to snow. "Where are you going now?" Rex asked.

"Home. I'm gonna walk, it's not that far."

"May I join you?"

Megan froze. How could she have Rex see the hardscrabble existence she was living?

"Well, maybe part of the way." They crossed over to the park side and began walking north, with the ice-spotted Reservoir looming behind barren winter elms and oaks. It began to lightly snow. Rex took Megan's hand again. It was warm and surprisingly strong.

They passed a small playground, with a sign on the gate that caught Megan's eye. It was a black-and-white stencil of a terrier, holding a cigar and a cocktail, while scooting on a skateboard, all surrounded by that international red circle-and-slash symbol of "NO."

"Look at that!" Megan said. "That dog looks like a lot of fun. I want that dog."

"Forget that," Rex chuckled. "I want to *be* that dog."

Megan was still busting up when, just ahead, a young man in a business suit and expensive overcoat strolled briskly toward them, typing furiously on his phone. Oblivious to his personal trajectory, he slammed smack into a street sign, banging his head with an audible *thwump*.

"And to think," Megan said. "They call those *smartphones*."

Megan waited for Rex to chuckle. Instead, he gently dropped her hand and went to see if the guy was okay. He was. It made Megan feel smaller than her bank account. "That was very nice of you, Rex. I don't know what came over me. It seemed funny in the moment. Dang, I can be a dolt sometimes."

"Don't beat yourself up. It *was* kind of funny. Very Monty Python."

"I *love* Monty Python! Do you want to know why?"

"Yes I want to know why! I want to know as much as I can about you. Everything. What do you like to do? What do you read? What's your favorite kind of pizza?

"That's quite a list for a first date."

"As long as this is not the only date, then okay."

Megan began telling the gorgeous millionaire her life story, her dreams and desires, her setbacks and defeats, her taste in art and literature, and her love of Monty Python lines such as, "I'm not dead yet! I'm getting bettah!"

At 90th Street, they sat on a bench under the gathering flurries and kept chatting like old pals. Rex opened up about being rich and single in New York, and the gay rumors. "They're not true," he said.

"I know that. I can tell. Besides, I wouldn't waste my time. But just to be sure…" She turned his face with her hand and placed her lips on his. They were cool as cream, hot as dynamite.

Eventually, Rex continued talking, telling Megan about his parents' horrible accident, about his rich friends, good, bad and downright diabolical, and more about his work in the MeToo movement.

Megan looked at her phone. It was almost five and she had to be at work by six. Three hours had elapsed and she had barely noticed, much like the snow that had dusted them. "I gotta fly! I have to get ready for work."

"You need to go home and change? You don't have time to walk there. Can I get you a cab?"

Megan regarded him for a moment. "If you mean hail one, of course. If you mean pay for one, I can handle it."

"Are you sure?"

"Quite."

Rex threw his hand in the air, whistled loudly, and within a minute a taxi pulled up. He gallantly opened the door, placed his arm formally across his stomach, and bowed. "Your chariot awaits, fair maiden. To whisk you away to Oso Bucco and other untold pleasures." They kissed briefly and Megan got in, realizing she had never been in a cab before. She lowered the window.

"So," Rex said. "When's next time?"

"You tell me. I'm off for the next few days."

"Great, text me your address and I'll pick you up tomorrow at seven for dinner. Okay?

"Sure. But just one thing. I don't have anything to wear to a fancy restaurant."

"Don't worry. We'll go somewhere casual, as far from the Socialite Belt as possible. Deal?"

"*So* deal."

Chapter 7

Somewhere in Bushwick

At seven sharp, Rex texted saying he would be downstairs in five. Megan looked at Brigit, then in the mirror, then back at Brigit. She was wearing her interview outfit, only now dolled up with a good dose of makeup, some borrowed costume jewelry, with her raven hair pulled up into a silky, elegant bun, very Grace Kelly, revealing the gentle curve of her neck.

"Well?" Megan asked.

"Honey, no one can pull off discount clothing better. You look ravishing. Doesn't she look ravishing, Bill?"

Bill looked up from his reality police show, *You Are SO Busted: Atlanta*, and smiled. "She does. I feel like a stoner gazing at a bacon double-cheeseburger at two in the morning."

Megan laughed at the stupid joke, but Brigit threw her boyfriend a stern

"ESS-TEE-EFF-YOU, Bill."

"Bridge? Are you going to keep doing that?"

"Doing what?"

"You know, that whole acronym thing. It's kind of, well, weird."

"Oh, *is* it now? And since when are acronyms weird? People say EFF-WHY-EYE, right? They say AY-ESS-AY-PEE. They say CEE-EYE-AY! I'm just trying to enrich the language, is all."

"Then, God save us," Bill laughed. "And the Queen too, for good measure."

"Megan," Brigit said, flatly ignoring him, "don't you have, like, a hot date or something?"

Megan glanced at the time. "Right. Gotta motor."

"GEE-GEE-AITCH-KAY!" Megan shot her a look that was half puzzled, half annoyed.

"Go get him killer!"

"OK, that's not weird, that's just stupid." Megan grinned broadly, blew kisses to her flat-mates and rushed out the door, practically tripping as she hurried down the stairs.

Megan was expecting to see an ultra-stretch limo like those on *The Real Housewives of Beverly Hills*, but Rex was in the backseat of a rather modest Buick Enclave town car. The driver, she noticed, didn't even have a cap, as she also expected. She was relieved. Rex threw open the door and Megan climbed in.

101

They kissed hello. Soon after they drove off, they stared at each other, giggled, and started making out. Megan gently pushed Rex away and pointed her eyes toward the chauffeur.

"Oh, don't worry about Dimitri," Rex said. "He's been my driver since tenth grade. There's little he hasn't seen – and he is a paragon of discretion. Dimitri, this is my date for the evening, Ms. Megan O'Malley. Am I not a lucky guy?"

"Yes boss. Very nice lady," Dimitri said. "Like rose in winter."

His Slavic accent was thick, like under cooked red cabbage. Megan pegged him for a Russian and she immediately thought of that thug in Coney Island, Yuri, who had tried to drag her away. She closed her eyes and shuddered until the awful memory passed.

"Where are you from, Dimitri?" Megan finally said.

"Crimea. I am Ukrainian. If I lived there now, I'd be Russian. I'd rather be rat freezing in reservoir in Central Park than Russian. Fuckers."

"I totally understand. They can be a bit....*rude.*"

"Yes. Rude like rattlesnake. Boss, where are we going?"

Rex handed Dimitri a small piece of paper. "Here, punch this into the GPS. One place we are *not* going, is back down Fifth Avenue."

Megan looked at Rex and laughed. "Well that really narrows it down. So, where *are* we going, oh man of mystery?"

"A little hipster place I've wanted to try."

"Really, why?"

"Because no one can get in there."

"What do you mean?"

"They take reservations once a month for twenty minutes at 6AM on a Monday. I had to call in many chits to get a table."

"You shouldn't have gone to the trouble. I'm more of a soup-and-salad type. And I'm not even sure what a hipster is. If something's hip, I'm usually a hundred miles away."

"If it makes you feel better, they're faux-hipsters," Rex said. "Bored trust-fund kids, mostly, who sleep in million-dollar co-ops in Williamsburg, kicking around in knit caps and plaid, hanging in cafes, moaning about their manuscripts."

"I'm not sure I could identify with that."

"Exactly. They write their own jokes. But they do know how to ferret out some of the ultra-coolest spots, with the foodiest of all foods, before the place is no longer hot anymore and everyone moves on, usually after about six months or so. The trendies are *peu loyal*. I suspect the same fate is in store for Blood Sport."

"What? That's the name of the place?"

"Yep. They feature wild animals you would never think of eating. Bear, beaver, ostrich, hippo. Hey Dimitri, maybe we can bring you out a doggie bag?" Rex broke into a grin, and an overblown Russian accent. "And for tonight's specials, we have *moose and squirrel!*"

Megan could not help but laugh, even though she wanted to throw up at the impending cave-man menu. "I'm not that much of a meat eater," she said sheepishly.

"Oh shit! I am *so* sorry. I had no idea." He looked at her. "So why did you eat the quail yesterday? And why didn't you tell me this in the park? I mean, Monty Python is a good segue into vegetarianism, with all those cows being catapulted over castle walls and all."

"Well, I am not a vegetable Nazi. I'll eat fish or fowl on occasion, like yesterday. But I try to avoid things that remember their mother. It's not that big a deal. Still, I think I'll skippo on the hippo."

"Sure baby." Megan, once again, melted. He was too great. "And don't worry, I bet they have soup and salad."

"And if they don't?"

"Then we'll order off the menu. Like Beverly. Even if they have to go out and buy some damn veggies on the corner."

Megan felt breezy as they crossed the Triboro Bridge and got on the Brooklyn-Queens Expressway heading south to Bushwick, just a few years ago a rat- and blight-ridden war zone, but now arguably the hippest, artiest, and, yes, foodiest, neighborhood in the metropolis. Looking out at a light-spangled Manhattan across the East River, and Rex's amazing profile in between (and his wonderful smell: what *was* that?) she had completely put Russian rapists and barbecued bear out of her mind. She rested her hand on Rex's. He turned to her and smiled. Megan was warm with contentment.

They made out again, the entire rest of the way to Blood Sport.

It was one of those places with no name out front – a shopworn one-story brick affair that probably had once been an Italian-bread bakery or Chinese dry-cleaning facility. The outside was oppressively ugly, the inside positively mobbed.

They entered to find young people with blasé expressions hanging about, waiting for a table. Rex said he was going to speak with the "host" – an unsmiling, gangly youth of about 20, with a face carved into permanent pique, dressed in green denim overalls and red long-sleeved waffle shirt, with a scraggly goatee and strawberry blond hair pulled up into the tiniest man-bun Megan had ever seen.

"I don't get it," she whispered to Rex. "I mean, if you're going to be hip, be hip all the way. That little marble on his head looks ridiculous."

Rex laughed. "Maybe he doesn't want to be made fun of a big bun. You know, he's a wimpy hipster."

"That would make him a wimpster," Megan said to Rex's delight, as he approached the podium. "Hello. We have a reservation for," he looked at his watch, "well, right now, actually."

"Name?" Wimpster said, not looking up from his table chart.

"Bainbridge. Party of two. We'd like to be seated, please."

"Oh, *would* you now?" The sullen youth looked up. "Isn't that special? Have a seat. I'll come find you."

Megan looked around. "But there's nowhere to sit here."

"And that's supposed to resonate with me, because….? You know, stand-up desks are all the rage now. Very ergonomic."

"Look buddy," Rex said, with the first flash of anger Megan had seen, "we have a reservation. It was not easy to get. We want to be seated. Now."

"Well Katie bar the door. Here come the friggin' Manhattanites." Wimpster smirked. "I suppose now you're going to flash me a Benjamin and think it'll work? Because that shit is *so* played."

"No," Rex answered, whipping out his phone. "But I do happen to have the owner's number right here. Shall we call your boss, a client of mine who owes me a great deal, and inquire as to the delay?"

The guy glared at them both in silence. "Fine. I'll get your table ready. We'll put you in the overbearing financier section, is that ok?" He signaled a young woman standing nearby. "Breckenridge, will you show these kind people to their table?"

They entered the main dining area. It looked like Bungalow Bill's living room. Megan took in the unsettling milieu with both horror and wonder: The animal skins draping the walls, the hanging stuffed-zebra heads, more taxidermy on the floor, hunting rifles and wolf traps strung from the ceiling, and a rusty, flickering kerosene lantern at every table.

The place was raucous: a cacophony of chatter, laughter and assorted drunken yelps. Dinner conversation would not be easy.

"Would you like something to drink?" Rex shouted.

"What?"

"A drink. Would you like one?"

Megan nodded, perhaps a bit too enthusiastically. Rex tried to get the attention of Breckenridge, who was standing at a nearby table, giggling and gossiping with some customers. He shot a crooked index finger into the air, like Bernie Sanders asking for time at a political debate. She looked around, saw him, and returned to her chatter. "It's going to be a long night," he said.

"I'm sorry."

"Don't worry, it'll give us more time to talk. I have questions."

"Oh really? Well fire away, because I always have answers."

"I was just curious. If you don't mind. What is it, exactly, that you, um, *do?*"

Rex laughed. "People have been trying to figure that one out for years. Basically, I'm an entrepreneur. I dabble. I *really* like to dabble."

"In what?"

"Hedge funds. Tech start-ups. Media ventures. Offshore banks. Stuff like that. But that's just the business side of me. I also run a foundation dedicated to environmental conservation, wildlife protection, saving the oceans."

"Wow. I should've Googled you more. But why're we in a place that serves wildlife?"

"None of these animals are from endangered species. I checked. And, they don't serve any marine mammals. Besides, hunting wild animals is a lot more eco-friendly than raising cows, pigs and chickens in factory farms that pollute the air and foul the waters with, well, shit."

Megan hadn't thought of that. She looked around the room at all the young people and their overblown self-satisfaction. Could they really be that happy? Some of the laughs seemed too forced, the smiles a bit too fixed. And then, she made precious eye contact with the waitress.

"Breckenridge!" she yelled over the din. "Can we get some drinks here please?"

The waitress turned and walked away. But just as Megan was about to concede defeat, Breckenridge returned with two menus and a notepad.

"I'd like a double Tito's martini, up, with olives please. And make it dirty," Megan said. Rex looked impressed.

"That's a very New Yorkey thing to order."

"I know. I practiced it. There's an app for that."

Rex laughed and ordered the same. They peered down at their menus. All the main dishes were made of wild game: Broiled hippo steaks with wild boar chorizo and sour cherries; seared filet of beaver breast with a Roquefort-bacon sauce; deep-fried ostrich nuggets with a poblano remoulade; molasses-glazed BBQ bear ribs with kale slaw and fries, and all kinds of offal, far too disgusting to even read the details.

"Yum," Megan said, "gazelle ribeye poached in port wine and its own blood."

Rex noticed her face. "Again, I am so sorry. I thought this place would be cool. Would you like to go?"

"No, not really. I'm sure I'll find something. They have a nice salad, and some of these appetizers look edible."

"You mean the broiled water-buffalo balls with Mendoza-style chimichurri? Or maybe the fried jellyfish chips? They come with a chipotle and shark-liver oil mayo, you know."

"I see an ostrich egg and chevre omelet here, for two. Maybe we could start with that?"

Breckenridge approached the table, a martini in each hand. "I'll be back in a minute for your order," she announced, without making eye contact.

Thirty minutes later, they were still waiting. Rex was growing annoyed, and rightly so, Megan thought. This was ridiculous. And then she noticed the restaurant's phone number on the menu. She whipped out her Android and dialed.

"Hello? Do you have delivery? Wonderful. I'd like the ostrich-egg omelet and the wild spinach-dandelion salad, but hold the Newfoundland goose chitlins, please."

Rex regarded his date, gaping in utter astonishment.

"And for you, dear?" Megan asked. "What'll it be?" Rex chose the wood-fired alligator tail with a peach and Jack Daniels *gastrique*, and Megan ordered it.

"The address? One sec." She grabbed a passing busboy and asked politely, "Excuse me. What table is this?"

"Seventeen," the kid said.

"Table seventeen. Near the stuffed antelope."

"You," Rex said, "have become such a New Yorker already."

"It's just a dose of Midwestern common sense. And manners. I wouldn't want to raise my voice at Breckenridge or Mr. Wimpster in front of all their little friends. It might hurt their *feewings*. Besides, we'd never get any food."

The dishes began arriving quickly. They spent the next two hours laughing and chatting, occasionally holding hands across the table, and making those stupid googly eyes that young couples sometimes make, much to the nausea of those around them. Megan thought this was the best date she had ever been on. And she was beginning to suspect that, maybe, Rex felt the same.

Over dessert (nearly all of it, thankfully, crafted without animal byproducts), Megan asked Rex a question.

"Honey? Can I call you that, 'honey?'" Rex nodded with gusto. "Um, can I post a tweet?"

"About what?"

"About this crazy place. About us. My 27 followers would really love it." Rex nodded again. Megan began snapping photos of the overdone dining room. "Let's do an obnoxious selfie!" she said, the Tito's now doing most of the talking.

"Get over here, then."

Megan obliged. Soon they were snapping photo after photo, mugging, smiling, kissing. Megan posted the pics to her account, and added, *On my second date with the amazing Rex. In Brooklyn, no less! BROOKLYN! Can you believe it?*

It took them a while to realize that another flash had been going off. Not just their own.

Megan and Rex looked in the direction of the lights. There, at the bar, they saw Jamal Dix, iPhone in hand, smirking like a devil doll. He got up and approached their table.

"Rex Bainbridge!" Jamal said with unfettered glee. "How lovely to see you again after that most *unusual* luncheon the other day."

"Hi Jamal," Rex answered flatly. "What are you doing here?"

"I just had to come. If this place had any more buzz, it would be passed out on its own post-industrial concrete floor. And that sort of thing pretty much defines my job description."

"I thought you didn't *do* food, Jamal," Megan said, a bit more snarky than she intended, but still, it hit the mark.

"You two know each other?"

"Why yes," Jamal said. "Ms. O'Malley came in to see me. For a job interview."

Rex turned to Megan. "You didn't tell me that!"

"You didn't ask." Megan smiled softly.

"And I know *so* much about this young lady. I have her resume, her clips – such as they are."

"Dix? What are you up to?" Rex said.

"What do you think? Simply everyone is fascinated by the dating rituals of Gotham's most, um, *intriguing* bachelor. I think that a waitress – from Ypsilanti, of all places – would be of the utmost interest to my readers. Don't you, Sexy Rexy?"

"You little piece of shit."

"Rex?" Megan asked, looking a bit pained. "Are you ashamed to be seen with me? Is that why you took me all the way out here?

"No! Of course not. I don't give a damn who sees us."

"Well that's reassuring. I think."

"I'm not the least bit worried about what this little weasel is going to write about *me* – sorry Jamal, but everyone says so – I'm worried about what he's going to write about you."

"How chivalrous," Jamal said. "May I quote you on that, Rex?"

"Get out of my face."

"Very well. I'll have to get my hippo steak to go, because, damn, do I have a column to write." He turned around and walked back to his drink at the bar.

"I'm so sorry," Rex said. He looked genuinely crushed.

"Don't be. He was actually kind of nice when I met him. I don't think he will trash me. Too much."

"No, he won't. He'll let others do the trashing for him. That's his M.O. It's not going to be pretty, I'm afraid. Everyone reads that poison-pen column. I mean *everyone*."

"Fine, then. Perhaps my fifteen minutes have arrived sooner than I anticipated."

"That's brave, really. But what happens if we keep dating? At this point, do you even want to?"

"Hell to the yes!" Megan laughed, almost as loud as the gaggle of hipsters sitting nearby.

Rex smiled and leaned over to kiss her cheek. "Great, are you free tomorrow?"

Megan nodded. "Where to this time, Staten Island?"

"Somewhere a bit farther afield. I know an awesome seafood restaurant with the freshest fish in the world. You *will* eat seafood, yes?" Megan nodded. "Afterwards, we can go for a nice swim."

"Where? It's 20 degrees outside!"

"Anguilla."

"Antigua?"

"Anguilla."

"Not familiar."

"Exactly. Few people are. It's paradise, with one of the most exclusive hotels on the planet. They only have eight rooms, each with its own butler and chambermaid."

"That sounds a bit extreme."

"Well, I believe they have a Holiday Inn Express, somewhere near the airport, if you prefer that. You even get waffles. For free."

Megan feigned a dramatic sigh. "No. For the greater good, I shall go with Plan A."

"Now, the big question – do I book one room, or two?"

"They only have eight rooms, let's not be piggy. Plus, I think we can share a butler and a chambermaid, and still survive, somehow. But we're going all that way for one night?"

"How about two?"

"How about three? I can get off work."

"Got a passport? Technically, we're going to the UK, you know."

"Yep, we used to go drinking in Canada all the time."

"Perfect. I'll pick you up tomorrow at two."

"Deal!"

"*So* deal!" Rex laughed.

Chapter 8

Safe Harbor

On the day that Megan and Rex went on their second date, Beverly Gansevoort-Stein had risen from her $100,000 bed and hollered for the maid. "Yes, Missus?" Margarita asked, poking her head in the door.

"I'll be taking my coffee upstairs today, please. Oh, and do feed Walter Mitty. He's looking a bit scraggly."

"But he scares me."

"Really? As much as *I* do?"

"OK," Margarita said, with half sheepishness, half veiled aggression. "I will feed him."

"And," Madame added with a huff, "today you will draw my bath exactly to the specifications specified. Ninety-seven. Hot water is just ruinous for my complexion. Now, run along. Double latte."

It was going to be a good day, she thought. In fact, the past few days had been quite good, indeed. To begin with, Dexter was back from rehab, thank God. He had gained some poundage, fleshing him out a bit and making him look almost handsome. Beverly had always considered him "just a tad on the spindly side."

Dexter seemed calm, if not resigned to his fate – back at *that* house. But he took great comfort in retrieving the reins, especially backstage, and most especially in the kitchen, where chef had ingratiated himself to Madame in his absence to the point of practically taking over the place. Thank goodness for Maria Eugenia, Dexter told himself. His majordomo had kept Chef in his station, and kept Dexter informed of all Chef's assorted misdemeanors, which Dexter had determined to address at the soonest possibility. Beverly, oblivious to all the politics, was just relieved to have her House Manager back.

In fact, Madame was feeling so peaceful and magnanimous, she actually considered trying to help out Jackie, who'd been droning on about her latest distraction, opening an upscale restaurant that sourced everything from local, sustainable producers in Jersey, Long Island and the Hudson Valley, peddling the stuff at hilariously marked-up prices. But the capital estimates were coming in much higher than she expected. Jackie was "a bit short" on funds, she said. She was now pressing Beverly to round up some investors, Rex Bainbridge, say, if not open her own checkbook and be done with it. (No way in frozen hell was *that* happening, Beverly had told herself.) Jackie was desperate. She'd just found the perfect place, on West 46th's revered Restaurant Row, no less. She'd even registered a DBA under the name "Green Acres." She needed cash *now*.

Beverly jotted it down on her list of "things to think about." Meanwhile, she relished the enormous progress the ladies were making on Safe Harbor House.

Astonishingly, the Pampers people had actually come through in the end, despite the "rather sketchy pitch luncheon," as Beverly had called it, though Wanda would henceforth refer to it as, "that rodent-gnawed catastrophe of biblical proportions."

The blatant snub to Anna Wintour's foundation would not, of course, go unavenged. As soon as Procter & Gamble made the big announcement – at Safe Harbor itself, in front of a decent number of reporters, including, as promised, Jamal Dix – *Vogue* stealthily let it be known that it was going to prepare a "hard-look, mega-profile" of the goings on of Upper East Side society and its Grande Dames. The message was clear: Anna was gunning for Beverly and Wanda.

"Fine, let that wench publish whatever she bloody hell wants," Wanda had told Beverly when they read about it in (where else?) Dix's column. "For fuck's sake, what's she going to say? That we have razor-sharp tongues and wildly extravagant tastes? Every social climber in New York knows that. Where's the *news*, darling? There is little we have said or done that hasn't made its way into one gossip column or another."

Beverly had hardly been reassured by Wanda's poo-pooing of the situation at hand. What if the *Vogue* reporters found out about her *history*? After all, Stroganoff clearly knew. And so, to deflect such terrors, she ridiculed her friend's fearless English moxie - and uncharacteristic optimism - by labeling Wanda, quite cleverly she thought, "Pollyanna Wintour." The nickname drove Wanda to apoplexy, which of course only spurred Beverly to deploy it as often as possible.

But now, safe and cozy in her grand and oh-so-well-appointed boudoir, Beverly thought about good things.

The launch had exceeded all expectations of the five ladies – Beverly, Wanda, Martha, Jackie and the insufferable Jenna. A Deputy Mayor showed up, along with the city Housing Commissioner, the local City Councilwoman, and a few odd Assembly members and State Senators. Beverly had appointed herself MC – to the grudging acceptance of everyone else – and felt she had done a bang-up job of introducing the new center and each of the speakers.

P&G had agreed to an initial annual donation of $500,000, to help outfit and staff a day-care area, with trained attendants, allowing the mothers to go out and find work while the babysitters changed the name-brand diapers. It was an "adorable" room, everyone concurred, painted pale yellow with white trim, and a giant-daisy mural on one wall, all of it bathed in exuberant natural light and littered with toys, musical instruments and little plastic rocking horses. There were even eight kid-friendly computer stations in one corner.

For the photo-op, P&G's Vanessa Yoon held up one of those comically large foam-board checks and the Deputy Mayor and Commissioner instinctively moved in on the action. So did Beverly. Upon seeing this, the other four board members rushed to the front and stood for the photo which, when it appeared the next day, showed them smiling like schoolgirls at the prom, with the glaring exception of Beverly, who looked like she had just swallowed Drano.

But no matter. The free publicity was priceless, the Pampers people were over the moon, and Anna Wintour could just suck on sour cheese, which is what she always looked like anyway, Beverly told herself.

And now, today, the Board of Directors, along with a gaggle of attorneys, accountants, PR people and assorted marketing and social-media gurus, would hold their first meeting, at Safe Harbor, over chilled sea-urchin consommé, escallop of Tasmanian lamb with Macedonian chanterelles, Moroccan chickpeas and a jaunty champagne-elderberry sauce, paired with an uplifting grilled hearts-of-romaine Caesar, with roasted peppers and madrona-smoked capon, procured from an *edition limitée* farm in Aix-en-Provence co-owned by Gina Lollobrigida, a "distant acquaintance" of

Beverly's.

Beverly took a deep breath and scowled. There were so many *things* on the agenda, aside from the board members' self-important bitch-fest that would surely arise like yeasty dough in a brioche recipe.

There was, for one, the communal kitchen. Did they really need Jenna's idea of granite countertops and stainless-steel appliances, which, as Wanda had asserted, would be "thankfully one day become shit-out-of-fashion?" Should they hire cooks to make meals for their "guests?" — a term they settled upon because it sounded more "Ritz-Carlton," than "clients," as Jackie suggested. And if so, who would pay for it?

What would we do, Beverly thought, without the most meticulous consultants in the city?"

Margarita returned with coffee and *The Times* and went to run the bath. "Remember...!" Beverly said.

"Yes, Missus. I know. *Complexion.*"

After her bath, Madame had breakfast *en chambre* as she read the paper and sipped her own Costa Rican latte. "Damn, that's good," she said. "If I weren't rich, I'd sell this stuff."

The morning was slated to be mostly uneventful: a staff meeting headed by Dexter, who was berating positively everyone for the "sloppy hell" into which the house had descended during his absence; a private tutorial in origami by Master Folder Ashiro Akiyama from Yokohama; and catching up on her correspondence, in the Facebooking Room, which Beverly dictated into a vintage Dictaphone that could have been used by Rob Petrie, sent out for transcription, and then posted in linen envelopes with an embossed *BGS* on the flap.

A bit after noon, Beverly picked up the house phone. "Mr. Dexter, have Driver retrieve the car and meet me downstairs in five," she said. After locating Walter Mitty under the bed, caging him and blowing him a kiss, she headed out.

The board meeting did not begin auspiciously. Jenna arrived late, cold and moody. Jackie looked like she'd been out partying with sailors all night (and who knew, maybe she had), Wanda appeared bored and resentful, as if she would rather be at her own execution. Even Martha seemed fraught and fidgety.

Their antics, while unwelcomed at this particular juncture, were certainly nothing new. What positively slew Beverly was luncheon. The lamb was slightly overcooked, Gina Lollabrigida's capons were conspicuously salty, and the Caesar had "positively limpified" by the time it arrived, as Beverly would later scold Chef.

Finally, the meeting began in earnest. Beverly presided as Board Chair, a position she had not obtained without a minor challenge. A week prior, while the ladies were lunching at Elaine's, Martha floated the idea that Jackie should be chair, what with her unfortunate departure from that *other* charity and all. "She has the know-how," Martha said, "and now, she has the time."

"I deserve this," Jackie chimed in, chin jutted firmly but comically out. Her apostle Jenna, of course, concurred.

Everyone knew that Beverly would hear nothing of it, but she wisely left it to Wanda to deliver the *coup-de-grace*. "Jackie," Wanda said, pulling a twenty from her handbag. "There's a little Clue Shop down on the corner. Why don't you go buy yourself one?"

"Fuck you, Wanda," Jackie said, loud enough for other patrons to turn and stare. She lowered her voice. "Are you saying I'm not qualified for this position?"

"Qualified!?" Wanda laughed. "You're not qualified to chair a four-person book club, with three of the members being stuffed animals."

"Well," Beverly said, looking around the table. "I'm glad that's settled."

Now, today, taking in the outsized walnut conference table, Beverly couldn't help but notice that the accountants were dry as burlap, the lawyers surly as feral cats, and the PR and marketing people thoroughly uninspired. But they slogged through it: The endless stream of "logistics" required for such an operation. Chief among them: what kind of full-time staff were required?

"You'll need," one of the three-piece lawyers spoke up, "an executive director, two assistant directors, a client-intake director, a director of communications, a building manager, a housekeeper, a mental health practitioner, a pediatric nurse, an on-call doctor, plus five day-care providers, a kitchen staff of three, about four administrative assistants, and a laundress or two."

"That's *all?*" Wanda asked, her face bunched into sardonic disbelief.

"Yes," said a portly lawyer with bald head, trim goatee and fussy demeanor. "You can outsource the IT, legal counsel, security, accounting, cleaning crew. And the like."

"It's the *and the like* part that will sink us like a German U-Boat," Wanda snapped. "We might as well call ourselves 'Lusitania House,' for fuck's sake."

"Wanda! Manners," Beverly heaved. "These people are here to help us. Pro Bono."

"Yeah, Wanda," Jackie said. "Don't crap where you eat."

Everyone could hear Beverly gritting her teeth, interrupted by the soothing voice of Martha. "Approximately how much will this all cost? Can you give us a ballpark?" The room fell silent as the accountants punched numbers into their calculators.

"With mortgage and insurance, about $2.3 million a year," one said, as the others nodded.

"Where on *earth* are we going to get that kind of money!?" Jackie said. "I've been trying to start a restaurant. Farm to table, you know, locally sourced." Beverly winced and Wanda let out a barely audible, "Oh sweet Jesus, here she goes again about her Brussels sprouts." Jackie pressed on. "I'm trying to raise far less than that, and it's been, well, *hard*."

"At least you're getting the diapers for free!" a young PR woman with pulled-back hair and plastered-on smile offered.

"It *is* a terribly large sum of money," Beverly said. Much more than we had bargained for. How much cash do we have right now?"

About $600,000.

"Well, ladies," Beverly said, trying but failing to look like a fearless leader, "we have our work cut out then, don't we?"

The talk naturally turned to fundraising. The PR and Marketing people offered all the usual boilerplate stuff: direct mail, major donors, foundations and corporations, government grants, online appeals, PSAs, celebrity endorsements, and, of course, a battery of high-priced, high-profile galas throughout the social season.

"It's so daunting," Beverly said.

"*Daunting?*" Wanda scoffed. "Trying to talk your way into 11 Madison Park on a Friday without reservations is 'daunting.' This is suicidal. And not in some cool Sylvia Plath way. We're going down."

"But we've already made our big announcement," Martha warned. "There's no turning back now."

"I suppose you're right," Wanda sighed. "Can you imagine the kerfuffle were we to fail? We'd become a laughing stock, from which Jean-Georges would make bisque and deliver it to Wintour's coven, high up in their tower, already plotting and drooling over our irrevocable demise. I'm in."

And then Jenna, who had remained remarkably, and wisely, quiet, raised her hand.

"Really, Jenna." Wanda said. "Just blurt it out, like you always do. Good grief, this is a board meeting and you *are* a board member, not some pupil at Miss Twyla Pennyfarthing's Finishing School for Girls. What the hell is it?"

"I didn't know the rules. Sorry," Jenna said. "It's just that…"

"Just, what, sweetie? Do you need to pee-pee?"

"No, Wanda! It's not that. I have an…*idea*."

"Oh good God, another tiny fragment of jetsam ejecting from that minuscule mind."

"Wanda!" Beverly growled. "Hear the board member out. Remember, Robert's Rules and all that. Now please, Jenna. Proceed," she said in a manner that made her feel highly judicious and serenely selfless.

"Well, I was just thinking, on those rare occasions when I don't helicopter out to the Hamptons, I see these Adopt-A-Highway signs, where people pay to sponsor one mile. I think Jerry Seinfeld has one. And Shakira!"

"And?" Wanda asked.

"And I thought, why can't we do that? We all know wealthy people. We ask each of them to 'adopt' a single mom and their kids, based on the annual average cost of taking care of our guests. Each year, they could renew, and we could send them cute little adoption papers. Plus, we can furnish them with photos, videos, even arrange personal visits."

The room fell silent again. Beverly looked around, trying to gauge someone's, anyone's response. "I think it's brilliant," said Bradley Bacon, one of the lead PR people from the pro-bono team, on loan from the prominent Ogilvy firm, which bills itself as "an award-winning integrated creative network that makes brands matter."

"You do? *Really?* Jenna emitted a squeal of delight and cast a look of deep shade at Wanda. "It means a lot to me. I mean, *us.*" Martha and Jackie smiled. Wanda looked as if embalmed.

"It adds a personal connection," Bacon said, "an intimate touch one doesn't often see in high-profile charity work. That said, we should make the adoption fee fairly reasonable, so we can reach out to more people other than the crazy rich. I'll put together a working group among ourselves. We'll make this happen."

"And," Beverly added, begrudgingly, "the Pampers people will be happy. Good on you, Jenna. You saved the day."

"Yes, Jenna," Wanda, still dumbstruck, managed to say. "You're a regular little Mighty Mouse. Aren't you, dear?"

Chapter 9

Anguilla

Megan woke up with an Excedrin headache. It felt as though the entire cast of Cirque du Soleil had dismounted onto her cranium overnight, then pirouetted through her mouth in their silk stockings.

No matter, she had to drag herself off the futon. There was shopping to do. She didn't even have a bathing suit. By now, she had a modest stash from her tips. She could afford a new bikini, some lingerie, a flouncy floral print cover-up, maybe a fun beach read.

She went into the kitchen. Brigit was seated at the table at her laptop, gawking.

"Hello? What are you reading with such absorption, Bridge?"

"OH-EM-EFF-GEE!"

"What is it?"

"You."

"What do you mean?" And then, in her hungover daze, Megan remembered: The flashing camera lights; the menacing grin of Jamal. "Is it Dix? Did he write something?"

"Let me make you some very strong coffee, because you're gonna need it."

Bill, up uncharacteristically early, was in the living room watching *It Happened Last Night... In Gotham.*

Megan sat down, throbbing head in hands, slightly rejuvenated by the wafting scent of Italian roast. She could hear the TV, but only make out a few words: *Bushwick. Hippo. Michigan.* And then, *Sexy Rexy.*

"Oh my God!" She sprang from the table into the living room. "What is this?"

"Your dinner date seems to have made... well, it's a big friggin' deal."

Megan looked at the screen. She and Rex were flirting and taking selfies.

"The unlikely couple were spotted at a bizarre eatery called *Blood Sport*, in Bushwick," the anchor reported, as if delivering a grave dispatch from Afghanistan. "Yes, the millionaire bachelor is courting a waitress. From Ypsilanti. If Hollywood isn't on line two yet."

"Jamal," Megan said. "That rat bastard."

"Megs!" It was Brigit. "Get in here. You've got to read this."

Megan went in, took a deep breath, grabbed the Post, and plopped down to read.

126

—————————————————————

THE GLEANER
By Jamal Dix – January 16, 2018

"A Not-So-Blind Item"

What bachelor extraordinaire-about-town was spotted last night in Brooklyn with a member of the (gasp!) teeming proletariat? The Gleaner knows, because he was there. And he is only too eager to share.

I sojourned all the way out to Bushwick, hardly a characteristic venue for me, as you know, to see what all the fuss was about over this new restaurant, Blood Sport. It's one of those bistros that attract the hopelessly trendy by being positively grotesque: They only serve wild game. You know, hippo, bear, springbok. That sort of thing. But once I learned that Zac Efron had been spotted there, chowing down with Chloe Sevigny (honestly campers, what was that all about?) I simply had to go have a look-see for myself.

And here is what I saw.

I had bellied up to the bar for some very adult beverages while awaiting a table. As I am wont to do, I surveyed the crowd. Intensely. One never knows what interesting things one might discover a-la this technique. Last night, it paid off handsomely.

I spied with my little eye none other than Rexford Bainbridge, III, seated at a dark table near a stuffed gazelle (I believe), making goo-goo eyes across from one Megan O'Malley, of Ypsilanti, Michigan.

Yes, Ypsilanti.

So, who is this Megan O'Malley? It's a perfectly appropriate question, to which I just so happen to have the answer. You see, young Megan came to my office recently, hat in hand, begging for a job at The Post. *She was so Midwestern-modest, yet somehow cheeky at the same time, I didn't quite know what to make of her.*

Now, don't get me wrong. Ms. O'Malley seems to be a perfectly lovely young woman, and she's unquestionably gorgeous in that way that makes even my gay brothers buckle. But — and if you know me, you know there is always a but — she is a waitress.

That's right. Perhaps New York's most sought-after bachelor, that King of the Columns, Sexy Rexy, is dating a waitress, or "server" as I believe they prefer to be called. You can catch her most evenings wielding overpriced Italian at Piazza San Marco, on Madison.

Ms. O'Malley arrived in our fair city just a few weeks ago. One wonders if she is ready for the splash she is about to make. Well, get out your slickers, dear readers, because The Gleaner *believes this one could be downright tidal.*

I have it on good authority that, just the day before, Rex had asked Megan to join him – uninvited, a cardinal sin – to lunch at the Fifth Avenue home of his downstairs neighbor Beverly Gansevoort-Stein, that gal-about-town who never seems to age, despite her age. It did not, I learned, go swimmingly. For one, the young unknown brought the Grande Dame carnations. Carnations! *The befuddled hostess had no idea what they were.*

Predictably, lips are already wagging up and down the East Side.

"It's one thing to go slumming in Bushwick," one woman familiar with the situation told me. "It's quite another to go slumming in Bushwick with a waitress. *Isn't it?"*

"He's doing this purely for shock value," sniffed another source. "Rexford craves the attention. He simply needs to be in the papers. And what better way to achieve that than to date scandalously below one's position? I give it a week before he moves on. I mean, what's he going to do? Marry the girl? She would bring him down to her level, not the other way around. Of that, I can assure you."

As for young Megan's future in journalism, I cannot be all too sanguine, having reviewed her "experience" in the field. Among the binder full of clips she delivered to me, mostly from the University of Michigan's school paper, The Michigan Daily, *highlights included such masterful works as, "Restroom Renovations Nearly Completed at The Office of New Student Programs," or "Sorority Members Stage Protest at Library*

Over Cell-Phone Ban," or the all-important "UM Students Flock To New Applebee's For (Get This!) Apple Pie."
Now, just imagine what the lowlights were like.
So no, my friends, I'm afraid that, if our dear Rex insists on continuing with this most unlikely of courtships, he will still be dating a waitress, I mean, server, for quite the foreseeable future.

Megan looked up, her face a knot of anger. "Your boss is a prick."

"I know. I'm sorry. But he was right about one thing: This *is* tidal."

Megan went for her phone, to call her mom. But the thing kept going *bling!*

"What's that?"

"Some kind of notification," Brigit said. "Twitter or something."

Megan looked. She now had 877 followers. The phone rang. It was Rex.

"Hi," Megan said flatly.

"You saw it."

"They saw it on Pluto, Rex."

"Oh baby, I would do anything to have this *not* happen."

Megan softened. "Don't worry. In retribution, I shall flog you with conch-shells on the sands of Anguilla."

"You still want to go?"

"I'll need a break from the paparazzi. And no, I cannot believe I just said that."

"Yay!" Brigit said. "Anguilla, baby!"

"I'll see you at one," Rex purred. "Bring a swimsuit. And a tankful of *passion*."

"Roger that, and roger that other thing."

Rex and Dimitri arrived on time. The drive to JFK, on the moribund Long Island "Expressway," seemed interminable. They finally pulled up to Terminal 7, British Airways.

"What?" Megan said, "No private jet?"

Rex laughed. "As an NRDC board member, it's not advisable."

The cavernous terminal was jammed with self-important looking people, many, Megan surmised, casting about for an upgrade. Near security, Rex spotted a small murder of photographers, waiting for some celeb to catch a flight.

"Shit."

"What is it, Rex?"

"Those guys. With cameras. I don't know who they're waiting for, but I have a sneaking feeling that my travel agent tipped them off. Again."

"What do we do?"

"Come with me," Rex took her hand and whisked them into the serene privacy of the BA First Class Lounge.

Megan had never seen anything so fantastical. Amid the plush beige-and-brown sofas and matching coffee tables, the understated artwork, the serene lounge music wafting through the lily-scented air, and the racks of newspapers from a dozen world capitals, there was also a vast spread of food. She surveyed the scones and clotted Devon triple cream. She took in the smoked salmon with crème fraiche and chives, watermelon-mint salad, braised artichoke hearts, and every description of mini quiches, seafood pasties, Roquefort croquettes and other yummy-gooey-warm things. The open bar alone, with its VSOP brandies, aged cognacs and vintage Bordeaux – was staggering.

"This, we don't have in Ypsilanti," she marveled.

After appetizers and beverages, a hostess called their flight in a posh accent. At the TSA Pre-Check line, the paparazzi spotted them. Rex had been right: The ambush was for them.

The flashes were blinding.

Rex and Megan bowed their heads like common criminals and hurried through the checkpoint. "Megan! Megan! Over here!" the photographers shouted. "Megan, how's it feel to be New York's newest gold-digger?"

They rushed toward the gate. "Well," Rex said. "Methinks the jiggeth is uppeth. Now they'll know where we're going. The island will be crawling with those losers."

They settled into their brushed leather seats. Megan perused the inflight magazine ("Why Madagascar Is A Great Investment Opportunity Now. Seriously!" was one headline), while Rex made business calls, in Mandarin, before they pushed back.

"You speak Chinese?"

"Marginally, Enough to flatter them, and move things along."

A prim, middle-aged flight attendant (she could have been Wanda, born with considerably less luck) approached with a tray. "Sparkling water? Mango juice? Champagne?"

"Champagne please!" Megan reached for the glass. "How much do I owe you?"

Rex and the attendant exchanged knowing glances. "First time, I suppose?" she asked. Rex smiled and nodded. Megan felt like an underclass slug.

The flight over the white-capped Atlantic was smooth, the food and wine "scrumptious," as Rex declared, prompting Megan to second-guess that gay thing, if only briefly. The conversation was airy and cheerful, as would be expected on a deluxe winter's escape.

After landing they were relieved to find themselves at peace. No cameras. Outside, a driver leaning on a black BMW held aloft a sign saying "Mr. Watson."

"That's ours," Rex said.

"Mr. Watson?"

"After the media frenzy this morning, do you think I was going to have it say 'Rexford Bainbridge, III?'"

Megan stared at him. "How do you live like this?"

"One adjusts. One just *does*. Hopefully, you will too."

"So, I'm going to have to?"

"If we keep going out. Which I hope we will. Like I said, either that, or a burka."

The ride to the hotel, Anguilla Reef, passed palm-fringed shores and aquamarine waters, interrupted now and then by quaint settlements.

Then they heard the motorcycles: five of them, cameras looped around the riders' necks. Megan's heart sank. Rex blared at the driver.

"Did you tip them off?

"No sir! I don't even know who you are."

"Then who did?"

"Our dispatcher, maybe? She's putting three kids through parochial school."

"So it's okay, then, to invade our privacy."

"Rex. We'll make ourselves invisible," Megan said. "Somehow."

They pulled up to the lobby, an open-air, thatched-roof affair with views beyond the infinity pool to the shimmering sea. It was all potted palms, cobalt-glazed vases brimming with hibiscus and hushed chatter among the formal staff and richly casual guests.

The motorcycles roared up as their luggage was unloaded by a bellboy in a British colonial outfit. Yelling and flashes began immediately. Two massive guards, arms folded, blocked their entrance to the lobby. The couple ducked safely inside where the manager, looking up from his paperwork, scurried over to greet the VIPs.

"My name is Bixby," he said in a crisp London accent. "We shall take every measure to keep these animals at bay. Please, let me show you to your room, personally."

Their "room" was the two-story "Brandywine Cottage," a gabled, bougainvillea-covered Queen Anne with four tastefully appointed bedrooms, a professional chef's kitchen and massive living room opening out onto the veranda, with its secluded whirlpool and expansive sea views. Bixby introduced them to Blakely, their private butler, and Maude, the housekeeper, both of them island natives with smiling eyes and Caribbean lilts.

"Shall Maude prepare supper for you in the cottage, or should I reserve a table at the poolside dining grotto?" Bixby asked.

Megan shrugged. "Who cares? Look at this place. It's paradise. I could eat on the floor."

"The grotto," Rex said, slipping the bellboy some pounds. "Thanks."

They showered and changed. Megan lavished herself in the European hair-and-skin products lining the shelves. She slipped into the breezy Annie Clost dress she had bought, and some open-toed sandals on loan from Brigit. She emerged feeling like a queen and smelling of honeysuckle. Rex was at the wet-bar, pouring brandy. She had never felt so happy in her life.

"Is there WiFi?" she asked. I'd like to tweet something."

"So we can have 20 *more* paparazzi waiting outside? Megan, you gotta start thinking about these things. Every columnist from LA to New York is following your social media now."

"I didn't think of that," Megan said, feeling stupid. "This is all so new. And kinda creepy."

Rex set the snifters down on the white marble bar and approached her. He threw his arms around her and gently rocked her.

"I'm sorry I got you into all of this. But I really wanted to go out with you."

"Just give me time to adjust, that's all."

"Take all the time you need."

Megan looked at her Twitter account: 3,463 followers.

They walked out onto the verandah and gazed at the rosy throes of dusk. Then they headed downstairs, across the elegantly lit, palm-and-fern-filled grounds, to dinner. Only two other couples were in the grotto, lending an air of privacy. There was no menu. The Anguillan chef had prepared a special five-course meal, each course matched with the perfect wine.

They began with croquettes of snapper, followed by conch-shell bisque laced with a hint of yellow curry, crab-and-scallop salad with wilted greens and blood orange *gastrique*, wood-flamed mahi-mahi in a chardonnay-shallot reduction, and a decadent banana coconut crème pie made with enough rum to inebriate half the island. It was too much. They asked for the pie to be wrapped up.

Over espresso, Megan asked Rex about his work for the Me Too movement. "More big names coming down the pike, I hope?"

"If I told you, I'd have to drown you in the infinity pool. Which, by definition, means they would never find you."

Megan laughed loudly enough to draw scowls from a middle-aged couple across the grotto. "Sorry," she whispered. "We'll try to keep it down." A more serious look crossed her face. "Rex, I haven't told you this. I haven't told anybody, but I was almost raped."

"*What?* When?"

"I think I was. A guy grabbed me on the beach at Coney Island and tried to drag me away."

"My God. Did he hurt you?"

Megan told him about Yuri, about her terror on the lonely beach, and the cop sent from heaven to rescue her. "I feel horrible about it now," she said. "I should've helped the police catch him. Instead, I just went home."

"It's not too late. I'm going to find that son of a bitch, and I'm going to make him pay."

"No!" Megan protested. "He could be dangerous. He sure looked it. We should let it go."

"Fuck that. I know lots of people down there. My investment manager, Stroganoff, lives there. He knows everybody, and he knows the Russian mob. Don't worry. This Yuri will be handled appropriately."

"Will they kill him?"

"I hope not. But he needs to learn a lesson. When we get back, I'll set up a meeting with Stroganoff and you can provide him with a description of this creep. He'll keep your name out of it."

Megan reluctantly agreed. "But I can't believe his name is Stroganoff," she said. "My mom used to make that all the time."

They walked out to the cliff, where the quarter-moon and warm breeze caressed them like a nursing mother. Both tipsy, they fell into a passionate kiss.

Shouting and flashing rose up from the beach below. The photographers had staked out the place, and waited.

Rex cursed at them. But Megan laughed loudly. "They want a show? Fine. Let's give 'em a show." She grabbed Rex again and kissed him hard, then glowered down at the cameras. "That should satisfy them for one night," she said. "Now. Rex, please hand me the pie."

He looked at her curiously, but obliged. Megan unwrapped the slices, and hurled chunks down like medieval molten lead tossed by defenders of a Crusader castle onto the aggressors below.

"Hey!" one of them shouted. "You fucked up my camera!"

"Good!" Megan shouted back. "But don't worry. It's chock-full of rum. Just lick it off, and you'll feel much better."

Rex regarded Megan with a look of utmost respect — and astonishment. "Wow wee!" he laughed. "Crème pie! No one I ever dated thought of doing *that*!"

She grabbed his hand and led him back to Brandywine Cottage, where they made crazy love like college kids until a kaleidoscope of birds began chirping at dawn.

They slept until eleven. Megan got up to make coffee when she saw Maude in the kitchen, already getting some ready. Megan couldn't tell if the housekeeper disapproved of their sleeping arrangements or not, but she brushed it off.

"Breakfast will be served on the verandah." It was said formally, colonially. Yep, she was judgmental all right. "Of course," Megan replied. "Thank you. So much, Maude."

Breakfast was poached eggs and swordfish cakes with Béarnaise sauce, on a bed of caramelized leeks and yellow squash, with fragrant pumpkin fritters on the side. After they finished, Rex whipped out his phone and began making business calls.

"You're not going to do that all day, are you?" she inquired.

"Babe. How do you think I can pay for things like this?"

Slightly miffed, but slightly ashamed of feeling that way, (he did have a point) Megan went to the bedroom to fetch her old Canon, with extra-long lens, leftover from her student-paper days. She started snapping photos of the sea.

Suddenly, a small pod of bottlenose dolphins, maybe eight of them, swam across the viewfinder. They were moving fast, with determination.

"Wow! Look Rex. Dolphins."

Rex peered up, annoyed. "Yes darling," he said. "They have them here."

As Rex went back to his business call, Megan shot images of the racing pod, leaping from the water every few feet like agile acrobats. And then she heard the roaring of speedboats. About 50 yards behind them, three inflatables crewed by men in black chased the dolphins up the coast. Megan shot them, too.

"Oh my God!" she cried.

Rex looked up at the ocean and glowered. "I gotta call you back," he said.

"What's this?" What's going on?" Megan asked.

"Poachers. Actually, kidnappers. They're rounding them up to sell to those 'swim with' monstrosities they have down here. We've spent a lot of time fighting this at the Animal Welfare Institute. I'm on the board there, too."

"What can we do?"

"Keep photographing."

"But they're almost out of sight!"

"Let's follow them."

"How?"

"In the Jeep. In the garage downstairs."

"What? The Jeep? We have a Jeep? What are you, a *magician*? Why didn't you tell me?"

"C'mon," Rex said smiling.

"Exactly how much did you spend on this place?" Megan asked, running after him.

"You don't want to know. But it looks like it's paying off. Let's go!"

They climbed into a gleaming new Land Rover, keys in the ignition, tank pre-filled, and headed out in the direction of the boats.

As soon as they left, three motorcycles appeared from nowhere and chased after them.

They raced up the west shore of the island, with Megan using her long lens as a telescope. Nothing. And then, as they rounded a bend, she spotted the boats pulling into a secluded cove, hidden from the road by trees and a low cliff.

"That's them! Rex, pull over here and let's walk out to the edge."

They made their way through thick underbrush until they reached the rim, followed by the photographers. The view was horrifying. The men had driven the animals into the cove, then surrounded them with a "purse seine" net, where the trapped dolphins began flailing about in terror. In addition to the black-clad crew members, there were five other men who had arrived in several trucks. Megan began snapping photos.

"Yep," Rex said. "Kidnappers."

"But why don't the dolphins just jump over the net?"

"No one knows for sure. They just don't."

"This is horrible! I'm going down there to find out what they're up to."

"Are you insane? These are international criminals!"

"I'm just going to play the dumb-but-curious American tourist, who happened to stroll along the beach. Don't worry." She headed down a narrow path to the cove and casually sauntered over to the men.

"G'morning!" Megan cried as she approached them. They regarded her with hostile alarm.

"What are you doing here?" a crew member asked gruffly.

Megan flashed him a disarming Midwestern smile. "Oh, I was just out for a walk when I came across this lovely little beach. What's up with the dolphins?

Are they okay?"

"Actually, no," another man said. "This pod is, um, *struggling*. They can't find enough food to eat. We're from the Royal Marine Mammal Protection Fund. We're going to bring them back to our rehab center, feed them, and then release them into more suitable waters."

Megan looked at the other men on the beach. One had a small decal on his shirt that said "St. Kitts Swim With The Dolphins," Another had the words "Dolphin Adventure – Tortola" on the back of his shirt. A third's read "Anguilla Dolphin Express."

Clearly, they were buyers. "These guys don't look like animal protection professionals to me," Megan said. "So…"

A crew member, the leader, Megan surmised, approached her, discreetly lifting his shirt to reveal a small pistol tucked into his shorts. "You ask too many questions," he said.

Rex, up on the cliff and nearing panic, noticed the paparazzi shooting film. "I'm actually glad to see you jackasses," he said. "Please record everything." He heaved a massive sigh of relief as Megan turned around and swiftly walked toward the cliff. "Quick!" Rex called to the photogs. "Get behind those trees! They can't see any of us up here! Please!" To his amazement, they obliged.

When Megan climbed back up, she saw Rex hiding and ran over to him. They hugged.

"Call the police," she said. Rex looked up the number, and dialed.

Within minutes, two squad cars, lights flashing, arrived along with a truck marked "Anguilla Wildlife Protection." The ringleader threw his gun into the water. Rex and Megan, (now taking photos again), watched as the men put their hands on their heads and, one-by-one, were handcuffed and taken away. The wildlife protection people swam out to the net and opened it. The elated animals fled their confinement and headed out to sea.

"We did it!" Megan laughed.

"No, sweetie. You did it. I am beyond proud."

"Rex, this is a *story*. I want to write an article about it."

"Great!" Rex grinned. "I know people at *Outside Magazine.* This is perfect for them. Want me to contact them?"

"Well, duh!" Megan laughed again. "But first, let's head over to the police station, and then the wildlife protection office, so I can do some interviews. I wonder if the cops will let me speak with any of the prisoners."

"Highly unlikely," Rex said. "And highly inadvisable."

Rex drove them to the station, where he patiently waited while Megan interviewed the constable, and then to the wildlife protection office, where he did the same. They returned late and exhausted. Maude served a light supper of grilled tuna with pineapple chutney and a tomato-lemon risotto, out on the verandah.

Megan's phone began blinging like mad. "Twitter," she said, looking at the device. "My God, I'm up to 9,766 followers now."

"That means the paparazzi photos are out. You're a star babe. Let's Google you."

It was positively everywhere. "Yank Lass Saves Doomed Dolphins," The UK's *Sun* reported. "American Tourist Risks Life To Take On Poachers," said the

Miami Herald, along with a closeup photo of the gun in the man's shorts. The *New York Daily News* took a local angle, with a headline that blared, "Sexy Rexy's Gal Pal Waitress – Heroine Of The High Seas!"

Rex's phone rang. Megan frowned. "Oh geez, not another business call."

"Um, I think it's for you." Rex handed her the phone. Megan looked at it: JAMAL DIX – NY POST. She pressed the talk button. "Yes, Jamal?" she said, with a world-weary sigh. "What? An exclusive? Well that *is* flattering. But I'm afraid I can't do that. Why not? Because I'm going to be writing about it myself. So, sorry, but no scoop for you." A pause. "Well I'm sorry you feel that way. Okay, buh-bye."

"Well?"

"He's not pleased. He said I would live to regret it."

"Oh Jesus."

"Not to worry," Megan laughed. "I have dealt with plenty of Dix in my time."

That night, they had sex that was even hotter, if possible, than the first time. Only now, they fell asleep long before the birds woke them up, which is when they decided: No more leaving the compound for the rest of the trip.

The last two days were heaven.

Arriving at the Anguilla airport, they saw three times as many photographers, and a local TV crew. "Oh what the hell," Megan said. "Let's give 'em what they want. One last time." They held hands and posed, smiling brightly.

"Miss O'Malley!" the TV reporter shouted, shoving a mic in Megan's face. "How do you feel about saving those dolphins?"

"I think it's just wonderful," she replied. "It shows what ordinary citizens can achieve, if they put their mind to it. Now, as for Anguilla Dolphin Express. I think it's a disgrace that such a lovely island should have such a criminal enterprise. Shame on them. I hope they get shut down."

The reporter gasped. "But, that's a major tourist attraction, a driver of our local economy!"

"It's a driver of cruelty and inhumanity. C'mon Rex, let's go."

Landing at JFK, Megan braced for the worst. "There will be paparazzi?"

"Tons. But don't worry. I arranged for VIP deplaning service. We get off first and into a car. No fuss, no muss, no flashing lights."

Sure enough, a British Airways Jaguar waiting by the gate whisked them to a secluded building where an immigration officer stamped their passports. Dimitri was waiting to take them back to Manhattan. Rex dropped Megan off and headed home. She looked up at the tenement building, with its crumbling cornice and dirty windows. She climbed the cat-pee stairs and entered Brigit's apartment. No one was there. They must have gone out.

It was kind of depressing to be back, frankly. The culture shock was unavoidable: Not just the transition from tranquil Anguilla to noisy East Harlem, but from the lap of luxury straight back to the gritty grips of working-class life.

Chapter 10

Courtship

They couldn't stay away from each other.

Rex wanted to go out each night that Megan wasn't working. But Megan knew: she simply did not have the wardrobe to keep up. Rex, of course, knew it too. He called Celia Bergstrom, his editor friend at *Wow!*

"I know you have tons of clothes left over from all those fashion shoots that the staff takes home with them," he said. "Why don't you invite Megan over, and then give her what she wants?"

"Why don't you just *buy* her what she wants?"

"I would. But she would never go for that. You know, Michigan proud. In fact, don't even tell her I asked you. She'd be mortified."

"Of course. I'd be happy to do it. In fact, this will be fun. Like a project!"

"Celia," Rex said dryly, "she's my girlfriend. Not Eliza Doolittle."

Celia invited Megan to lunch, and to tour the offices and photo studios, but didn't mention the clothes. She wanted the offer to look like spur-of-the-moment. Megan, meanwhile, thought she might be offered some freelance work.

She didn't walk away with an assignment, but, after much insistence from Celia, left with six new dresses, eight pairs of trousers, six leggings, ten blouses, four jackets, six pairs of shoes, a handbag and several belts, courtesy of Prada, Givenchy, Marc Jacobs, Stella McCartney, Dolce & Gabbana, Chloe, Kate Spade and Jimmy Choo. Megan, who looked stunning in all of it, could barely cram the clothes into the Uber ride home.

With her clothing deficit resolved, Megan threw herself into dating life. Rex took her absolutely everywhere that rich people gather — Broadway premieres, a private Met suite at *Don Giovani*, exclusive openings at swank Chelsea galleries, a cancer gala in the grand Egyptian Temple of Dendur at the Metropolitan Museum, a polo match in Westchester, brunch at Gracie Mansion with the Mayor, and so many meals so lavish that Megan determined to save up for a gym membership.

For a while, every time they went out, the paparazzi followed and the gossipers gossiped. They were constantly seen in the papers, galavanting around town. But, not unlike the outrages of Donald Trump's tweets, over time everyone got used to it. Public interest in the couple waned a bit, much to their relief. Megan's twitter account stopped blinging so damn much with new followers.

Reaction to the courtship inside Rex's social circle was mixed, to put it optimally. Some treated her with respect and kindness, most notably Martha Bradbury, "the nice one," and of course, Celia, who not only took Megan under her fashionable wing, but offered a battery of etiquette tips for navigating high society.

146

"Always arrive ten minutes early," Celia counseled. "Those who arrive late will resent you, but it's worth it. And never ask anyone what they do for a living. You might as well ask them how much money they make." Other pointers included: Laugh at every joke (but not too hard) no matter how insipid it is; unless you know them well, address doctors, elected officials, judges and clergy by their title; and if there is a celebrity, asking for autographs or selfies is an unforgivable faux pas. In fact, selfies period are way off the table.

"Be extra careful with air kisses," Celia added. "They are *always* done right cheek to right cheek. However, if the person is European, expect to hit both cheeks. And vice versa. And no matter what, take every precaution to ensure there's no lip or skin contact. That's eminently frowned upon."

There was even more: Don't speak with your hands. It makes you look inarticulate, and you will be taken for a Sicilian peasant. Always say "excuse me" and not "pardon," which is only used by service staff; or "sorry," because "most people are not really sorry, most of the time." In the same vein, the term *bon appetit* was thoroughly passé. "Only poseurs say that. Stick to 'I hope you enjoy your meal.'"

Rules for dining and entertaining were equally onerous: "Never take more than one passed canape at a time," Celia warned. "Wait for the hostess to lift her fork before eating. Always pass food from left to right. Scoop your meal away from you, not toward you, but never let anyone hear you scrape your plate. If your food is too hot, whatever you do, don't blow on it, and always taste it before adding salt or pepper. As for wine glasses, hold white wine by the stem and red wine cupped in your hands. And, if you need to use the ladies', for God's sake don't announce it. Simply say 'please excuse me,' because, let's face it, no one wants to picture what you're doing in there."

Even napkins, Megan was astounded to learn, came with their own rules. "The first thing you do when you sit down is to gently unfold it – *never* shake it open - and put it in your lap. Always wait for the host or hostess to unfold their napkin before you do. The napkin should remain in your lap unless you need to get up from the table."

Celia continued. "If you must get up, neatly fold the napkin, with the crease facing you, and set it next to your plate. No wadding, and no leaving it on your chair. And do not, whatever you do, wipe anything but the corners of your mouth." Finally, when the meal is finished, one should neatly fold their napkin in half and leave it on the left side of the plate, she said. "It must *never* look twisted or crumpled."

Megan was an agile pupil and quick study. Her manners were becoming quite acceptable, if not precisely impeccable. But that hardly made things right with the rest of the crowd. Rex's male friends, including Thaddeus Pepper, the pompous psychiatrist and Rex's longtime pal-about-town (Celia warned Megan that, in this case, calling him "Dr. Pepper" was most inadvisable) positively ogled Megan the first time they met.

It happened at Minnewaska Mountain House, upstate, where they went with Thad and his current squeeze, Patricia Schweinsteiger, on a weekend "double date" at the enormous and extravagant Victorian manor with its award-winning spa, private lake and, to keep out the riff-raff, $50 entry fee for non-guests, even if they were having dinner in the $300 per-person Main Dining Room, which *The Times* had recently dubbed a "destination" restaurant, whatever that meant.

They arrived for lunch, a buffet feast of Hudson Valley delicacies. Rex and Patricia, a rather uptight, petite young woman with cropped yellow hair and a slight facial tick, got up from the table to get dessert, leaving Megan and Thad, who were stuffed, alone at the table. Thad turned to Megan with a look that said nothing short of "I'd really love to fuck you." She was shocked – and disgusted.

"What are you looking at?" Megan said, sounding a bit like Madonna at the start of *Vogue*.

"Your eyes. Your hair. Your... rest of you. My buddy Rex really lucked out, didn't he? Even if you are a waitress."

Megan wanted to hurl the honey-mustard crudité dip that remained in a small bowl at him, but reckoned that surely would be on Celia's list of "things that are frowned upon."

"Does Rex know you do this?"

"Do what?"

"Flirt with his girlfriends. And, really, really badly. I might add."

"No. He doesn't."

"And what about Patricia?"

"Her? Oh, she's cool with it. I wouldn't date someone who wasn't."

"Well I'm not cool with it. Look. I'm not going to say anything to Rex. But only if you, Doctor, promise to keep your wandering eyes – and claws – off of me. *Capiche*?" He seemed to get the message.

But it was Beverly and Wanda who were most daunting. And openly hostile. Rex begged them to play nice, to little avail.

"It's not like we're going to be murderous on her, or anything," Wanda huffed at the request. "But you cannot possibly expect us to *like* her. We certainly have no intention of letting her into our little group. Unless she wants to serve lunch."

"You're a blustering bag, Mrs. Covington," Rex had replied. "But you knew that already."

Wanda laughed. "You think that hurts my feelings? Rexford, If I had any fucks left to give, I would've put them up for adoption. But I'm afraid Mother Hubbard's fuck cupboard is perfectly bare."

One evening, Safe Harbor had its grand opening party, with 150 attendees invited to tour the building, meet the new "guests" and staff, and mingle with each other among the cocktail tables, flowing with Veuve Clicquot *Grande Dame*, iced seafood bar, carved New South Wales lamb, "Venetian Table" groaning with luscious desserts and the obligatory jazz trio in the corner.

Rex and Megan, who turned heads in her vintage Givenchy printed short-sleeve A-line dress and truss of dark hair pulled into an elegant wavy up-do, arrived on time. Beverly greeted them in the lobby.

"Hello Rex," she said, completely ignoring Megan. "How good of you to come."

"Beverly, you know Megan. Why don't you say hello?"

The matron turned to the gorgeous young woman. "No carnations this time?"

Inside, Jackie and Jenna pounced on the couple. "Rexy! How glorious to see you!" Jackie cooed. "And this must be the young waitress we've heard so much about." She turned to Megan and held out her hand. "You're the patron saint of dolphins, *n'est pas?*"

Megan shook Jackie's hand and grinned. "That's me. And you are...?"

"I am Mrs. Jacqueline Farquharson. But you can call me 'Jackie.' It's more, how shall we say? Proletarian."

"And I'm Jenna!" Jenna said, grinning in a lame effort at comity that made Jackie furious. "You know, it's nice to see Rex going out with someone so, well, *humble*. I think it's very important for the classes to mix, don't you?"

"How very Dickensian of you," Rex said.

Megan adopted a country-bumpkin accent while glaring at Jenna. "Well, as us poor folk are always a-sayin', it's not what's in your bank account that matters, it's what's in your heart. Assuming you have one."

Jenna scowled. Jackie huffed. Rex chuckled. "The city's best surgeons have been looking, but so far...*nada*."

Wanda approached the little group. Megan recognized her from the restaurant. "Rex, darling!" she said, holding out her hand for him to kiss. "And I remember Megan. You've become quite the little celeb around here, haven't you?"

Megan blushed. "Well, I wouldn't go that far."

"Rex, we simply must go back to Piazza San Marco soon. The service there is so, well, *interesting*. Now, Megan dear, come sit with me and tell me absolutely every little thing about you. I suppose I have five minutes to spare."

Megan looked at Rex, who discreetly shook his head.

"Maybe next time," Megan said. "It would be a pleasure to get to know you, too. You're English, right?"

"Yes. Does it show?"

Megan nodded. "Like jellied eels with kidney pie and mash."

"Such a witty girl! Rex, this one is almost a keeper, isn't she?"

"Wanda, what did we discuss?"

"Oh right. I'm to be on my best behavior. But to be honest, I don't trust myself. Lovely to finally get to know you a wee bit, Megan. That is, without an order pad in your hand."

As Wanda turned, Megan muttered under her breath, "If only I could say the same." Wanda pretended not to hear, but the look she flashed at Rex told another story.

"Where the hell does *she* live?" Megan asked. "At the corner of Diabolical Drive and the Passive-Aggressive Highway?"

"God, I love you!" It came from absolutely nowhere and Megan was stunned.

"You do? Really?"

"You just played hardball with some of the most egregious bullies in New York, and dispatched them one-by-one to their pathetic little corners. So, yes. Really."

"But aren't they your friends?"

Rex didn't answer. Finally, he said, again, "God I love you."

The days wore on. When not waiting tables, or being waited upon, Megan finished up her dolphin article. Rex not only set her up with *Outside Magazine* (online, but still), he used his contacts in the marine-mammal community to get interviews with leading scientists and conservationists, including Dr. Naomi Rose, of the Animal Welfare Institute, and Dr. Lori Marino, Director of the Whale Sanctuary Project.

Megan's article detailed not only the events of that day, but skillfully transitioned into a scathing manifesto against the entire marine-mammal industry. It went big, receiving nearly fifty thousand likes. Megan not only got $500, but her Twitter followers began to mount anew.

Megan occasionally stayed at Rex's place. The first time he took her there, after front-row seats at an Ariana Grande concert at the Garden and late dinner at Rosa Mexicano, she almost died. It made Beverly's place look like a shack.

It was exactly what one would expect from a $22 million dollar, 18-room penthouse bachelor pad, Megan thought.

To begin with, it was endless – an entire top floor of gleaming white marble, light-filled windows and wrap-around terraces. It took nearly an hour for Rex to give her the grand tour through the myriad bedroom suites, the luxurious parlors, sitting rooms, game room, formal dining room, cinema room, his enormous office suite with its bank of computer screens flashing stock, bond and foreign-currency quotes from around the world ("This is where the magic happens," he told her) and a kitchen almost as big as her house in Michigan. The artwork was priceless, the décor restrained and masculine.

And those views, especially to the west, with Central Park and its enormous reservoir spreading out below.

Megan got to know the staff, including the French chef, Madame Dominique Duchamp, Ramon, Rex's dashing butler, who hailed from Montevideo, and the housekeepers, Carlotta, the plump but pretty head maid, from Oaxaca, and Lorna and Lupe, from the same village outside Puebla. When they were introduced, the three women regarded Megan with thinly veiled disdain, as if they didn't approve of her, as if she weren't good enough for their boss.

My God, she thought, even the maids around here are snobs. Megan put on a brave smile. *"Buenas tardes! Como estan?"*

¿Habla *español?"* Carlotta asked in amazement. *"Los gringos no hablan español!"*

"Un poco," Megan replied, explaining that she'd studied Spanish in school, and always wanted to visit Mexico. She hoped she could practice with them, she added, to which the maids exchanged looks that said: what choice do we really have? Megan knew it would take time to win over their trust. Actual affection might be too much to ask.

Meanwhile, their sex life just kept getting better. Rex loved oral sex. And not just getting it. Megan, who obliged him on both counts, confided in Brigit that, "his dick is really big. But it's not gag-worthy, so I'm good."

One sunny morning in April, (had Megan really been in New York for more than three months?) while eating breakfast on the west terrace, Megan began tapping on her phone.

"More tweets?" Rex asked.

"Nope. I'm looking for an apartment. A studio. But the only thing I can afford is in central Jersey. How long do you think that commute would be?"

"Megan, honey," Rex said, gently grabbing her hand. "You're not renting anything."

"Oh, so I'm supposed to live out my days on Brigit's futon, with Bongload Bill stinking up the place? I don't think so."

"Of course not. What you are supposed to do, *I* think, is move in here with me."

Megan was flabbergasted. It came out of nowhere, just like the "love" remark.

"I don't know what to say."

"Say yes? Pretty please?"

"I need to think about it.".

"There's just one thing," Rex said with a serious look. Megan raised an eyebrow.

"I'd like you to quit your job."

"What? Why?"

"To begin with, you won't need the money."

"And that would make me…? A kept woman? I think I'm too old for a sugar daddy."

"It would give you more time to pursue what you love. Journalism." Megan pictured life without Bolognese sauce staining her shirt. "And, it has the added benefit of not being the brunt of so many jokes. About you."

"Me? There are jokes? Like what?"

"I don't want to say."

"Oh c'mon! I can handle it."

"Okay, like, 'How many Megans does it take to screw in a lightbulb? Two. One to marry rich, and one to bring the veal picatta.'"

"That's not even funny."

"Some of my friends are not the wittiest bulbs in the chandelier of life."

"What else?"

"Some of them call you 'Liz Trailer.'"

"OK, that *is* kind of funny."

Megan took two weeks before making her decision whether to move in, and ditch Piazza San Marco.

"Yes," she told him. "Oh, and I love you too."

When she broke the news to Brigit, her friend almost fainted. "That's incredible!" she cried. And then, more solemnly: "So, I guess we'll never see you again. Except in the columns."

"Bridge, I'm gonna be just down Fifth Avenue. I'm not moving to Mars, you know."

"You might as well be. It's less than a mile, but it's five million light years away."

Megan laughed. "Tell you what. We'll have Richard Branson send over a rocket to pick you up. He's pals with Rex."

Once settled in, Megan began to learn the ropes of running a household – managing the staff, stocking the right kinds of food, wine and spirits, ordering flowers, arranging meals, planning dinners. Celia often came over to dish out advice, which her protégé genuinely appreciated.

One morning, Megan stepped into the cavernous tufa-lined shower, got dressed and went out into the hall. She found Rex in the salon. The table was set for breakfast – for three.

"Someone's coming?" she asked.

"Yeah, that guy I told you about. Stroganoff. The Russian. He just called and I asked him over. I hope you don't mind."

Megan said it was fine. The doorbell rang. Lupe let the guest in and led him into the study.

Alexi Stroganoff was a gruffly enormous bear of a man, with scorching blue eyes, receding gray hairline, a few acne scars and a perma-scowl look. (Rex later told Megan it was his "resting dick face"). His Men's Warehouse suit seemed a bit timeworn and rumpled for an investment manager, as though he had been sleeping in his car.

"*Dobroye utro,*" he grumbled. "Good morning. So, you have problem?"

"Yes. Please, sit down." Ramon came in bearing coffee and French pastries, followed by Bonita with three plates of *oeufs en cocotte* and a multicolored *salade de fruits tropicaux.*

"So, tell me," Alexi said. "What I can do for you."

Megan told him about Yuri. She described his face, hair, clothes, and approximate age, height and weight as Rex looked on anxiously. "Can you help us?" he asked.

"*Da.* Of course. People like him give us bad name. Leave it to me."

"But please! Don't mention my name!" Megan pleaded. "He scares me."

"Perhaps. But me, he doesn't scare. I look at this as *problem*, not crisis."

The couple thanked him profusely. A few days later, Alexi came by the penthouse with a photograph. "Is this him?" he asked Megan, who gasped and nodded. "Good. Then I have news. Yuri is no more." Megan was mortified. "So they *did* off him? Oh my God."

"*Nyet,*" he answered. "Nothing like that. Let's just say his visa was, how you say? Revoked. He should be back in Volgodrad by now."

"That's great!" Rex cried. "What do I owe you, buddy?"

"This one," Alexi said, smiling at Megan, "is on house."

Chapter 11

"La Gran Cena"

"**D**id you get one too?" It was Beverly, on the phone with Wanda, staring at a most unusual invitation. It was a hand-stenciled card, emblazoned with an image of the Mexican flag, a Mariachi band, and a steaming platter of enchiladas. Inside were the words: *"Bienvenidos*! Please come to our Mexican Fiesta! Casa de Rex y Megan. *Hasta luego*, baby!"

"I did," Wanda huffed. "What on God's wretched earth was she thinking? Megan's big debut on the society stage, and she opts for Taco Tuesday."

"Well, are you going?"

"Is the Queen German? I want to see that poseur crash and burn into her own salsa verde."

Beverly sighed. "Yes, I suppose that could be entertaining. And I really don't have an excuse. Rex is a friend, despite his current unfortunate *situation*. See you then, then?"

"Yes. I shall have my makeup girl paint a nice unibrow on me, and I'll go as Frida Kahlo. Perhaps you could go as Diego, dear."

"That's very witty, Wanda."

A few days later, upstairs in the penthouse, Megan was frazzled by nerves and logistics. Could they really seat 30 people in the dining room? In what order should they all be seated? Does one use formal china for Mexican food? Were there any acceptable Mexican wines, or should they just have Coronas with lime wedges? And most importantly, who could cook an exquisite south-of-the-border meal?

And then it came to her. Carlitos, and Todd, of course. She would ask Rex to fly them in to cater the occasion. After he agreed, she called her little brother.

"Todd! I have a gig for you."

"What? Where?"

"Here. We're having a Mexican fiesta and I thought you and Carlitos would be the perfect caterers. Surely he has some old *familia* recipes?"

"He's genius. You have no idea. But, how do we get there? Where will we stay?

"Rex. And Rex. Leave the details to me. Can you do it?"

"*Sí!*"

"Great. It's two weeks from Saturday. Why don't you guys come that Thursday? And let me know what your fee will be."

"Fee? Megs, we'd do this for free."

"No way, little brother. I have a budget. How about two thousand, plus expenses?"

"Seriously?"

"Trust me, in this world, that's bargain basement," Megan said. Then she heard Todd softly whimpering.

"Toddie? What is it?"

"I'm just so grateful. We really need this money. Mom had her hours cut again. And I lost my job."

"What? Why?"

"Apparently, Trump's promised American Miracle did not make its way to Detroit Airport. The hotel's occupancy rate is sinking like an anvil. Thank God Carlitos still has his job. He moved in with us and helps out with food and stuff."

"Oh my God," Megan gasped, looking around guiltily at the fabulous splendor of her own surroundings. "I had no idea."

"It gets worse. We're behind on the rent, and the landlord is getting all itchy, like he does."

"Then, let's make it three thousand. And I'll skim some more off the budget for you guys, somehow. I'm not sure how, but I'll make it work."

"I love you Megan. So does mom. And, all is not lost. I have a job interview with a catering firm. I'm going to learn the ropes so we can start our own company. Meanwhile, we'll put together a menu for your fiesta."

"Great. And Todd? Give mommy a big old kiss for me."

Megan put the phone down and hugged herself, fighting back tears. But there was work ahead. Celia was due any minute, to advise about menu, décor, music, flowers and the all-important seating chart.

Megan pulled herself up and went into the kitchen to check on lunch, which she had asked Ramon to serve on the north terrace, with its cedar table and shady grape arbor. When Celia arrived, Megan grabbed the iPad that Rex had bought for her birthday and led her outside.

"I have news," Celia said. "The Mayor and his wife. They're coming."

"Holy shit on a soda cracker. You're a miracle worker."

"I promised them a major spread in the magazine. You owe me, sister."

After a light lunch of chilled cucumber soup, *salade Nicoise* and lemonade, they got to work.

"So?" Celia asked. "Flowers?"

"All I could think of were poinsettias. But it's not Christmas. I know marigolds are popular in Mexico, but I've learned they are considered pedestrian. Like carnations."

Celia suggested a topical mix of birds-of-paradise in tall vases, set amid pink hibiscus, white orchids and ferns.

"Done," Megan said, typing up the list. "What about music? Mariachis? Or is that too much muchness?"

"The latter. I suggest a single guitarist playing traditional Mexican folk music, and a vocalist. I could ask my friend Enrique. He knows all of those songs. If you invite him to dinner, he might be persuaded to serenade us afterwards."

"Great! Enrique who?"

"Iglesias," Celia said, as Megan almost choked on an olive. "He's a sweetheart. Plus, he owes me a favor. Most people do."

"He's gorgeous, in every way! But he's not Mexican."

"No, but he got his start in Mexico, and knows a lot of the famous ballads."

"Can you get him?"

"I rarely fail in these matters."

They turned to the seating chart. Yes, there were rules for that, too.

"If the number of guests is a multiple of four, you and Rex cannot be seated at the head of the table opposite each other," Celia explained. "If that's the case, then the male guest of honor, the Mayor, sits at the head, with you and Rex sitting to his left."

"I'm expecting thirty."

"Not a multiple of four, so you two sit at the head of each side."

Meanwhile, distinguished guests were to be assigned according to their social rank. "If the second-most important guest is female, she goes to the left of Rex, and if it's a male, he sits to your left. From there, you seat people according to status, but always alternate between men and women. Let's get to work. Show me the list."

Megan pulled it up on the screen, and Celia broke into a smile.

"I see you have the Mexican Consul General. That's brilliant. And Anderson Cooper. Good get. 'Plus-one.' so he must have a new boyfriend. And Brooke Shields? Okay, very classy."

"Where do I put them?"

"De Blasio sits to your left, and his wife Chirlane to Rex's left. The second most-important male guest, the Consul General, sits to your right, and his wife to the right of Rex. And then, in descending order, you sit Anderson and his beau, just not together, followed by Enrique and Brooke. The only other real VIP you have here is Chester Mansfield, from *The Times*."

"And the rest?"

"You seat them, also in descending order, with the most prominent guests closer to each end and the rest sort of mashed up in the middle. So, I would humbly start with myself, if you don't mind?"

"Of course Celia."

"Fine. Continuing down the list, I would say Jamal Dix, because you don't want to piss off *that* queen. He's such a big girl. I'll bet he spends his 'me' time pulling the heads off his dollies." She looked at the screen. "Next, this Stroganoff character, because he has everyone's money. After that, Rex's friends, Thaddeus Pepper and, oh dear, what happened to Patricia?"

"Apparently, she wasn't as, um, *progressive* as he'd assumed," Megan laughed. "He's dating a model now. Betty-Ann something or other. I'm sorry, but God I loathe him."

"Don't be sorry. Everyone does," Celia smiled. "They're just too afraid of losing access to his prescriptive creativity."

Celia looked at the rest of the list. "These folks, these society ladies all go in the middle – the overbearing Beverly, the atrocious Wanda and her dullard husband Trevor, troubled Jackie and her befuddled Jonathan, sweet little Martha. And finally, that twatwaffle, Jenna Forsythe. I understand why you had to invite her, but *damn.*"

"I know, a necessary evil. That leaves two more."

"Brigit and Bill? Who are they?"

"She's my high school friend, the reason I'm in New York. She works for Jamal. Bill is her boyfriend. I'm not even sure what he does, except smoke weed. He's a huge stoner."

Celia flashed her a look that said *really?*

"I had to. They'd be crushed if I didn't."

"Very well. Plus, you know what they say. The bigger the stoner, the better the boner. Okay! We're done. Now, what about food?"

"Hold on." Megan checked her email. "It's here. My brother and his boyfriend just sent the menu. I'm flying them in to cater the dinner."

"How lovely! What are they proposing?"

"For passed appetizers, mini chile rellenos stuffed with smoked gruyere in a poblano-cream dipping sauce, wood-fired chile-lime prawns on sugarcane skewers, and little medallions of beef, served warm in a chipotle, raspberry and blue-cheese glaze."

"That," Celia said, "sounds extraordinary. And the first course?"

"Papaya-mango salad with grilled scallops in honey-roasted jalapeno strips and bacon."

"Not bad. And the main?"

"Let's see. Hmmmm."

"What, hmmm?"

"It says chicken cooked in Coca-Cola."

"You're joking."

"Nope. Says it right here. One sec, let me look it up." Megan banged away at her computer. "What do you know? It's considered a delicacy in Mexico. And all the young trendies are getting into up here."

"What's in it?"

"Chicken, Coca-Cola, ground chile, ketchup and onions."

"How dreadful! Megan, you simply cannot."

"I think it's cool. And I'll bet you a gillion dollars that nobody at that table will ever have tried it."

"And for good reason. Are you sure?"

"Positive."

"OK, suit yourself. But if you think the dogs of society howl only in Elton

John songs, you're in for a rude awakening."

"Maybe. But they'll be talking about it, and me, for years to come. What more could a fledgling hostess want?"

Thursday before the dinner, Megan asked Rex if he could send Dimitri to LaGuardia to pick up the boys. The reunion was as joyous as it was raucous, causing several on staff to peek around doorways to see what the fuss was about. They saw two handsome young men, clearly out of their pond amid such luxury.

"Damn, sis. You *live* here?" Todd marveled. "This place is bigger than our school. And that view! Oh my God! Carlitos! Come here! We aren't in Ypsi anymore."

Megan was elated to see her brother, and his new partner. They seemed so happy together. She showed them to a guest room, with its private bath and little balcony, facing south toward the Guggenheim. An ice bucket with champagne was on the table, with two glasses, some strawberries and other assorted goodies.

"Make yourselves at home, have a shower, and then I'll show you around the kitchen and introduce you to the staff."

"Where's Rex?" Todd asked.

"I really don't know." Megan gave a light scowl. "He should've been home by now. But he always has these business thingies going on, and they seem to run late a lot. He'll be here for dinner. It's at eight. When you're ready, I'll show you the kitchen."

When Todd and Carlitos walked into the kitchen, they looked like holy pilgrims glimpsing Our Lady of Fatima for the first time. They were, literally, speechless.

"So?" Megan asked. "Will this do?"

"Yes," Carlitos said. "We'll get by."

"Good. After you meet the staff and describe the help you'll need, we can order the food. It will all be delivered tomorrow."

Eight o'clock came and went. But no Rexford. "Fuck it," Megan announced. "Let's eat. Lupe can keep some warm for him." As they were finishing dessert, Rex walked in the dining room, looking ragged and sweaty.

"We waited. But then we got hungry," Megan said. "Your dinner's being kept warm. Where have you been?"

"Shitty day. Long story," Rex grumbled, walking past them toward the kitchen.

"Rex! Come back and say hello to my brother and Carlitos! Jeez, what's wrong with you?"

Rex stopped, turned around and said, not unpleasantly, "Hi fellas. Welcome to New York."

"And?"

Rex shot a blank stare at Megan, who mouthed the words "thank you" to him.

"Oh right, right. Thanks guys, for doing this. Megan is very excited. It's her first big dinner party, and I know she could use the moral support. Some of my friends are, well, not very easy to stomach." And then he left the room.

"He seems nice," Carlitos said.

"I've met grizzly bears that were friendlier," Todd frowned and turned to Megan. "Is everything okay?"

"I think so. It's a New York thing. When they don't feel like it, they neither chit, nor chat. I'm sorry. He's probably tired. He'll be better tomorrow."

Finally, the big night arrived. Todd and Carlitos had been working their magic for two days, assisted by the able hands of the Mexican maids. Madame Duchamp had wisely taken the time off. The feast was ready.

At around 7:30, the guitarist arrived and the maids went to change into the outfits Megan had chosen: matching white cotton peasant dresses embroidered in a peacock floral pattern with red lace mantillas covering their heads. None were happy about it.

Rex agreed. "They look like the Holy Sisters of Our Lady of Perpetual Salsa," he said. "In Acapulco."

"It's atmospheric," Megan explained. "Are you going to be like this all night? Because, we've been working really hard. Try to be a little more *suavecito*. Please?"

Rex relaxed, smiled, and kissed her. "Sorry. I'm a bit tense. Aren't you?"

"Like Mike Pence at a drag show."

At eight sharp, the doorbell rang. Megan signaled for the guitarist to begin strumming and went to answer.

"*Boo-WAY-nahs no-chays!*" It was Beverly, arriving with Wanda, unibrow, shawl and all, and Trevor, in a navy business suit. "You remember my partner in crime, Wanda Covington. And this is her husband Trevor."

"How do you do?" Megan said. "Please come in. What would you like to drink?" She nodded at Ramon, stationed at the bar with several bottles of Patron tequila, limes, ice and salt. "Margarita?"

"Good God no," Wanda sniffed. "I mean, where are we? Club Med Cozumel?"

"Well, Bonita over there has sparkling water, from Tehuacan."

"From where?" Beverly said. "It sounds like an Aztec venereal disease."

Wanda roared. "Good one Bev!" And then to Megan, "You do have wine, yes, sweetie?"

"Lupe has it. Lupe? We couldn't find a really great Mexican wine, so I ordered this lovely limited-edition Malbec, from Mendoza, Argentina.

"That's thousands of miles from Mexico. But you get a B-plus for effort," Wanda said, grabbing a glass from the Holy Sister. Megan looked at Rex, who was standing nearby.

"Ladies, please. Don't make this any harder than it is on Megan."

"Whatever do you mean, Rexford?" Wanda scanned the room. "You must admit, it looks," she sniffed the air, "and *smells* like a Chilis. I mean, how hard could that be to pull off?"

Megan smiled formally "I do hope you enjoy yourself, Mrs. Covington. That is, if you have ever learned how. But I sense the jury's still out on that one." Rex suppressed a laugh.

As the guitarist played, the nuns passed around *antojitos,* and the drinks flowed like water in the East River, guests continued arriving. Megan greeted each of them personally at the door, a stunning breach of protocol, but she wasn't giving any more damns around these people. Etiquette, like wealth itself, has its limits.

She air-kissed everyone with panache: The Mayor and his wife, the Consul General and his wife, Anderson Cooper and his "plus one," Gregorio, a doe-eyed young man from Palermo, Enrique and Brooke, who arrived together, the singer in an all-white cotton Mexican peasant outfit with a jaunty red bandana around his neck, Ms. Shields in a fetching sapphire-blue Donna Karan, with pearl necklace and matching earrings, her hair pulled back into a tidy bun.

When Dr. Pepper arrived with his date, Betty-Ann Babcock, the redheaded, sultry, stunning young model, Megan hesitated before any air kisses. Thaddeus grabbed her by the waist, very close to her butt, pulled her tight and planted a big wet kiss on her cheek. Betty-Ann, Megan noticed, was too distracted ogling the VIPs to see it. "Get your greasy paws off me," she whispered sternly into his ear. "*Now.*"

"You know you want it."

Megan pushed him away. "Holy shit, Thad. I don't know what your spirit animal is, but I'm pretty sure it has rabies."

Thad laughed nervously. "Honey?" he said to the model, who turned her head with a look that begged, please don't bore me now. "Come meet our hostess, Rex's most recent acquisition, the delightful Megan...?"

"O'Malley. It was on the invitation. Can I get you anything to drink?"

"Nothing with alcohol," Betty-Ann pouted. "We have a, um, *pact.*"

"We have sodas. Let me ask Lupe to fetch you something. Is Dr. Pepper okay?" Megan turned and walked away, fighting the temptation to watch the steam tooting from the good doctor's ears.

Next at bat: Jamal Dix. "Good evening, Jamal," Megan greeted him with a pleasant if somewhat forced smile. "I hope you're hungry. We're fresh out of hippo, but I'm sure you'll find something to your liking."

"How nice, *Dolphin Lady*," he said. "I saw your piece. A bit quotidian, if you ask me."

"I'm not aware that anyone did, Jamal."

"Not really my cup of tea."

Megan glared at him. "You know what, Jamal? Fuck you. And fuck your tea."

He laughed. "That's pretty good!"

"I know. I heard it on *Curb Your Enthusiasm*. I've been waiting years for the right time to use it. So, thank you. Here," she grabbed an appetizer from a passing silver platter, "keep yourself busy with some skewered shrimp. We're serving it well-chilled, like your soul."

Wow, Megan thought as she went to check on dinner. I'm getting pretty good at this. And then it struck her: She had officially become a New Yorker.

When Brigit and Bill arrived, one could have scraped their jaws off the Persian-carpeted floor with a spatula. They stared at the plush surroundings and all the very fine people. They looked up in disbelief at the 15-foot high ceilings with their crown molding and Italianate plaster bas reliefs.

"Bridge?" Megan said. "Remember my first day in New York, when we were on Fifth Avenue? New Yorkers never gawk, you said."

Brigit palmed her forehead. "Of course. For a minute there I thought we had left New York and gone to Mar-a-Lago. Where that stuff is expected."

"That's not funny," Megan said. And then, "Okay, it's a little funny. Now, come have some Patron margaritas. You can put your jackets in the cloakroom."

"You have a *cloakroom*!?" Brigit and Bill exclaimed in unison.

"Of course," Megan giggled, her head slightly turned, her nose pointed firmly skyward in feigned snobbery. "Doesn't everybody?"

One of the last guests to arrive was Alexi Stroganoff. Megan couldn't be sure, but he seemed to have a thing for her. Very well, she thought. Play along. He did something *nice*. The two of them sat down on a corner settee and gossiped for a while, as Megan giggled with the big old Russian. He was actually, against all odds, charming. Perhaps they could become friends, and allies, one day.

Todd came out and discreetly informed his sister that dinner was ready. Megan rapped a spoon on a wineglass. *"La gran cena* is served! You'll find place-cards on the table." As guests moved into the dining room, Megan spotted Jenna, alone in the salon, pouting like a seven-year-old who was just told she couldn't get a bunny.

"Jenna? Aren't you joining us?"

"I have to think about it."

"What on earth is there to think about? Come. *Please.*"

"I don't like where you sat me. Right there in the middle. I want to switch. With Beverly. Why is *she* so close to the VIPs?"

"Because she's older, smarter, and, I hate to say, more charming. Not by much, but enough. Besides, there's no way in hell that she'd switch. So your petulance is moot."

Jenna huffed, got up and slouched her way into the dining room and her third-class place setting.

As the nuns brought out the first course, Mayor Bill De Blasio ceremoniously stood up and offered a gallant toast to the host and hostess. This was followed by the Mexican Consul General, who unfurled a proclamation on a piece of parchment festooned with green-and-red ribbons affixed with a wax seal. It was signed by the Mexican President in tribute to Rex's *"servicio heroico"* to the Monarch butterfly preserve in Michoacan.

Then the table fell into itchy silence. Mercifully, it was soon broken by Anderson Cooper, telling some off-color jokes about the bathroom habits of Wolf Blitzer.

The patter resumed to a respectable level, punctuated by intermittent expressions of "Mmmm!" and "Oh my Lord, this is good." Carlitos and Todd were winning the evening.

And then the main course arrived. Megan looked around apprehensively as everyone dug in.

"Excelente!" said the Consul General.

"One of the best chicken dishes I've ever had the pleasure to try," Jamal pronounced.

Even Beverly and Wanda were shoveling it down with relish. "Megan, darling, what is this? I must admit, it's as delectable as it is unusual," Beverly said.

"Chicken," Megan said. "Cooked in Coca Cola."

Anderson Cooper guffawed and clapped his hands. Jenna pouted in that famous way of hers. Brooke discreetly set her fork down. Wanda heaved, brought her napkin to her mouth and spit the food out. "What? You couldn't find any taquitos down at the Mobil station? Good God, it's like Paula Deen meets Colonel Sanders."

"I think it's fabulous," Enrique Iglesias said.

"I love it, too." It was Celia, coming to her new friend's defense. "I was skeptical, to be sure. But I think it's brilliant."

Over dessert – papaya soufflé with a Kahlúa, tequila and lime sauce – Rex and Megan stood up to speak. "We are honored to have each of you here," Megan said. "Mayor de Blasio, thank you for the kind words. Señor Consul General, *gracias, y bienvenidos a nuestra casa.*"

Most, though not all the guests, fell into a round of polite applause.

"Good grief," Wanda muttered, just loud enough to be heard. "She actually pulled it off. Beverly, be a darling and go look out the window. I suspect that pigs must be floating down the avenue by now."

Megan introduced the chefs and thanked the staff by name, like a rising starlet at the Oscars.

"And now, dear friends, we have a very special treat. The fabulous Enrique Iglesias has graciously agreed to sing for us. Mr. Iglesias, I believe you have the floor."

His songs, bittersweet and soulful, transfixed the room. When he finished, Rex got up, walked over and whispered in his ear. "Oh my gosh, yes!" the crooner said. "With pleasure." And then he belted out a romantic rendition of *Bésame Mucho*:

"*Bésame, bésame mucho. Como si fuera esta noche la última vez,*" ("Kiss me, kiss me much. As if tonight were the last time.")

The guests cheered. Rex called Megan to his side. She looked perplexed. This wasn't in the playbook.

"What is it?" she whispered to him gently, and then almost fell over when he got down on one knee and opened a small blue velvet box marked "Tiffany & Co." It was the biggest diamond she had ever seen.

"Oh, my God. Rex."

"I don't care what God thinks. What do *you* think?"

There was an excruciating pause as the guests stared in anticipation: some in hope, others in near panic.

"I think…I think…Why, I think yes!"

Many guests were verging on tears. Brooke and Anderson swooned as the young couple kissed. The Mayor said, "Hear, hear!" The Consul General cried, "*Estupendo!*" Jamal Dix got out his pad and began scribbling furiously.

"Good for you!" Martha said. "Good for both of you."

"OH-EM-GEE!" Brigit squealed, loud enough to be heard over on the West Side.

But the ladies, minus Martha, were visibly not amused. "What the fucking fuck?" Wanda said. Beverly rolled her eyes so intensely her irises virtually disappeared into two globes of white. "Rex. Are you quite sure about this?"

"I'm sure as Captain Sully landing his plane in the Hudson, Beverly. I'm in love, and I want everyone here to witness it."

Todd, now hugging Carlitos, shouted, "Way to go, sis! Way to land the big enchilada."

Thaddeus, meanwhile, looked apoplectic. "Rex. Dude. Have you thought this one through, buddy? Cuz, maybe you need to think a bit more."

"You know what, Dr. Pepper?" It was Carlitos.

"What, *muchacho?*"

"Oh no," Carlitos wagged his finger in Pepper's face. A lot. "You do not speak to me that way."

"Oh, really? And I'm supposed to care what you think...because?"

"Because Megan is family. And now, so is Rexford."

"Oh, spare me. No one cares. And don't speak to *me* like that. I have an PhD from MIT!"

"Is that so?" Carlitos asked, bending over to show off his perfectly rounded behind. "Well I have an A.S.S. from G.O.D. And you don't hear me going on about it."

Thad scowled. The ladies gasped. Brigit and Bill giggled. The Mayor looked at Jamal hoping to keep all of this out of the paper.

There was silence. Finally, Anderson's date said, "Well, it's true. He does."

Chapter 12

Day Of Reckoning

THE GLEANER
By Jamal Dix – May 12, 2018

"Ole! Sexy Rexy Takes a Most Unexpected Plunge"

Hell did not exactly freeze over last night, but it damn well could have.

It was as shocking as it was laughable, like a Donald Trump tweet flushed from the White House at three in the morning.

You see, I happened to be invited to the home of Our Town's most intriguing bachelor, Rexford Bainbridge, III. Billed as a "Mexican Fiesta," the food was extraordinarily passable, the guest list solid: Mayor de Blasio and his wife, Chirlane McCray, the Consul General of Mexico and his esposa, with Brooke Shields, Anderson Cooper (and his sultry Sicilian beau-of-the-moment), and the still-gorgeous Enrique Iglesias rounding

178

*out the MVP list, the latter who belted out honey-voiced renditions of
several south-of-the-border ballads.*

*Despite the Cinco de Mayo décor and over-the-top outfits of the help
(they looked like extras in Madonna's "Isla Bonita" video), the evening
went smoothly – enough.*

*That is, until Rex took a knee after Enrique crooned "Bésame Mucho"
and put a ring on it.*

*That's right, dear readers, Rexford Bainbridge, III proposed to his waitress
girlfriend, one Megan O'Malley, of Ypsilanti, Michigan. One cannot
help but imagine what his venerable parents, who perished in that most
regrettable accident on Lake Geneva, would have thought.*

*"If there is Xanax in the afterlife, they now have a permanent prescription,"
noted Brit socialite Wanda Covington, whose comment about pigs floating
down Fifth Avenue did not go unnoticed à la table.*

*No release of any nuptualistic details just yet, but you can rest assured
that The Gleaner will be thoroughly on top of this breaking bit of news.*

*Until then, thoughts and prayers for the cardiovascular health of Rex's
upper-crust friends, some of whom appeared to go into congestive heart
failure upon digesting such news.*

There, as they say, goes the neighborhood.

Beverly crumpled up the newspaper and tossed it. This whole thing,
she told herself, is one massive fuckburger. There was a knock on
the door. It was Dexter.

"Madame, there is a package for you."

"What is it?"

"It's from Mr. Stroganoff."

Beverly unwrapped the parcel. Inside was a dead rat, with a note that said, "Here is a reminder. This is what happens to rodents who squeal."

Beverly shuddered, her once-perfect morning shattered into a thousand little shards. "Dexter," she asked, "Do you think I'm a bitch?"

Dexter brushed some lint off his lapel. "Only at breakfast, Madame, and then only before your latte. Otherwise, certainly *not*."

"Very well. Please make a note to staff that Mr. Stroganoff is no longer welcome in this household."

"Yes, ma'am. Duly noted."

Disturbing as the Stroganoff situation was, Beverly was ecstatic that she'd rescued her own assets. In fact, she was feeling so giddy and flush about it all, she had an unforeseen flash of benevolence. I'm *am* going to loan Jackie the money for her silly restaurant, she thought. It's not that I *want* to help. It's that I can. And that will forge the strategic alliance I need to rid our clique of that human tragedy, Jenna, forever.

Wanda called. "About last night. Jesus fuck."

Beverly exhaled. "I wish I could think of a more apropos adjective than 'dreadful,' but I'm afraid that's the best I can do at this hour."

"I can do better," Wanda said. "'Shit-bucket,' maybe. Or 'draggle-tailed guttersnipe.'"

"Whatever you wish to label her, it all means the same thing."

"What are you getting at, darling? I suspect it's not felicitous."

"It means we must take that creature under our wings," Beverly said. "Rex will demand nothing less. We are to become her collective Henry Higgins. We'll have to teach her not only how to walk and talk and act like a regular *laidy*, but how to throw a halfway decent party. And how to do charity like one of us, unfathomable as that may sound. And don't even get me started on the wedding plans."

"So, if I'm to understand you correctly, we're dragging young Megan through Socialite Boot Camp?"

"*Oui.* Even if kicking-and-screaming. *Je suis desole.*"

"But where do we begin? I mean, our work is not even cut out for us. It's still in its primordial ooze stage."

"Well, get out your latex gloves. We've got work to do. I'll arrange a little tea at my place. Tomorrow at three. Are you free?"

"Tragically, yes."

"Fine. I'll tell the girls. And I'll have Dexter carry an invitation upstairs. See you then, Dr. Higgins." Now feeling as righteous as a Pilgrim, Beverly dialed up Jackie, to announce her offer of help.

"Oh, my goodness, Beverly!" Jackie cried. "Seriously?"

"Seriously. But I do ask for ten percent."

"You mean, like, interest?"

"No. Of the business. I'll have one of my attorneys draw up the papers. Deal?" Dead silence.

"Jackie? Do we have a deal?"

"Yes…We do. But…."

"But what?"

"You *never* come into my kitchen, and you have no say over the menu. For ten percent, you can choose the flowers."

"And the wine list."

"Yes, the wine list. Fuck, Beverly."

"Good. Now, make a note to be here at my place tomorrow at three. We're having tea with Megan O'Malley. It's time for us to show that bumpkin how things are done properly around here."

"But I have a meeting with my chef!"

"Your chef can wait. Otherwise, so can my check."

"Fine," Jackie said. "See you then."

Upstairs, Megan's morning was off to an emotional start. She read Jamal's column, fantasizing about the slowest way to kill him. She recalled Alexi, in their little chit-chat, speaking about growing up with "rats the size of cats" in his family's flat outside Moscow. "We ground glass and rolled it into cheese. It was only way."

There was another development. Five days had passed since she should have had her period. The doorbell rang. Ramon stepped out on the terrace. "Message for you, *señorita*." Megan opened the lilac-scented linen paper and read the impeccable cursive.

> *Megan, I hope that you might join us downstairs for tea tomorrow, at three. We all have so much to discuss, and we're only here to help. See you then?*
>
> *Best,*
>
> *Beverly*
>
> *P.S.: The mini chile rellenos were better than what one might have anticipated! Well done, darling.*

"What the actual fuck?" Megan said aloud. She picked up the phone and called Brigit.

"Hello? Is this Mrs. Lovey Thurston Millionaire the Third?"

"Shut up, Brigit. I've been summoned to the High Court. Downstairs."

"Oh brother. What for?"

"I suspect the good ladies are plotting to school me in the finer points of pretentious pettiness."

"Bring a notebook and pen, and jot down every dippity-do socialite rule they try to ram down your throat."

"And then?"

"You publish it. *The Intelligencer* column adores that stuff.

"I'm not sure," Megan said. "But seriously, should I go? Do I *have* to?"

"No," Brigit said. "And yes. Wear something tasteful and bring really expensive flowers."

Megan arrived, ten minutes early, carrying an elegant green ceramic vase with fragrant stephanotis and English scented roses. Maria Eugenia opened the door and led Megan into the Great Room. "May I take these from you?" she asked, reaching for the vase.

"No." Megan smiled softly. "These babies aren't going in any kitchen. Thanks."

Beverly and Wanda were at the table. "Megan! Sit down." Beverly smiled.

"Thanks. I brought you these; a bit more suitable than carnations," Megan said, channeling the haughty-but-nice falsetto of her new world. She placed them on the table.

"Isn't that thoughtful?" Beverly chirped. "Wanda, don't you think that was thoughtful?" The Brit shrugged.

"You know something Wanda?" Megan said. "I'd probably like you, if you were somebody else."

"Oh. The Midwestern gloves are off, I see," Wanda replied. "So much for Michigan Nice."

"That's Minnesota Nice."

"I rest my case."

Megan drew a breath. "Listen, I'm sorry. I'm just a little nervous about this tea thing."

"And intimidated, I hope?" Wanda asked.

Megan glared. "Look. We're going to have to live with each other. We're trapped together like steerage passengers on the Titanic."

"Bite your tongue!" Beverly said.

"It's a metaphor. Anyway, I know you want to be helpful. And I *need* advice, God knows."

"So. Truce?" Beverly asked. Megan nodded. The doorbell rang. "Margareeta! Maria Eugenia? Dexter?" No response.

"Would you like me to get the door?" Megan asked.

"No, that's fine, thank you; I'm perfectly capable," Beverly said as she rose.

"Well that's a first." Wanda said. "At least she's good for something."

"I see we have things in common."

Wanda smirked. "Megan, I can tell that Rex adores you. I've never seen him so happy."

"Thank you. That's very kind."

"Kindness is not entirely alien to me. Look, I know I can be a monster. And I've unleashed more than my fair share of vitriol on you. For that, I apologize."

Megan did not see that one coming. "I don't know what to say, except, apology accepted. God knows I've gotten a few barbs into you, as well."

The sound of greetings and air kisses coming from Jenna, Jackie and Martha, who arrived as a unit, echoed from out in the hall. They entered the Great Room and chose their seats.

"No place-cards," Jenna said, staring at Megan. "Nice touch, Beverly."

"Let's tea, and let's chat," Beverly announced with a forced smile.

"So," Megan said. "You want to talk to me."

"I think the better way to put it is, '*confer* with you.'" Martha ventured. "Right, everyone?"

"Yes," Beverly said. "Let's confer." The ladies nodded in agreement. "I think we should start with the most important. The three C's."

"And what are those?" Megan asked.

"Clothes, clout and clicks," Beverly said.

"Cliques? Like groupies?"

"No. The number of followers you get on social media. Now, beginning with clothes. One can have style without taste. First and foremost, one must display a sense of timelessness and grace. Style is all good, but it's hardly the equivalent of taste."

"What's the difference?"

"Style is what your friend Celia has been handing down to you. Taste is not something that's been yanked off the rack after a fashion shoot. I think, we all think, that some of the outfits you've been given are a bit, well, *outré*. We must strive to be more understated."

"Well Michigan is, like, the most understated state in the country."

"Wonderful!" Beverly said, clapping her hands. "Grey, black, charcoal, bone and cement. Those are the preferred colors right now. We call it 'austere luxury.' Pale rust or a subtly refined burnt sienna might also suffice."

Steaming Earl Grey tea, warm rosemary scones, Dungeness crab puffs and boysenberry-apricot tartlets with Devon cream were served by Margarita.

"Now. On clout," Wanda said, in a way that established this as her particular bailiwick.

"What about it?" Megan asked.

"You're going to have it. By the yacht-load. And clout does no one any good if one doesn't shove it in other people's faces."

"How dreadful."

"No. It's quite fun, actually. Like *The Hunger Games*, only your quiver is filled with status, not arrows."

"Your first task is to make lists so you can keep track of the pecking order, in which you will land not too far from the top," Jackie interrupted, sending Wanda into a fit of disbelief, which Jackie, naturally, ignored. "I think the *Wall Street Journal* put it best: 'Make A-Lists, and B-Lists, and lists of people who could never make the lists.'"

"It will come in handy," Jenna chimed in, "for your spats!"

"My spats?"

"Of course," Jenna went on. "Big ones, that make the papers. You gotta cultivate high-profile foes. Without them, you can't have spats. And without spats, you can't assert your clout. It's quite simple. Everyone does it."

"I don't," Martha said, looking uncomfortable.

"And that's what makes you so perennially and endearingly B-list, my dear," Wanda said.

"You know what? Fuck you, Wanda," Martha blurted out, to a round of audible gasps.

"What the HELL was that?" Wanda asked.

"A spat. I'm not incapable. I clawed my way to the B-List and I'm defending my status."

"Whoa!" Wanda roared. "Who knew your inner child was such a little bitch?"

"Let's keep moving, shall we?" Beverly said. "Megan, you must choose your spats with great care, with someone equal to or slightly above your ranking. One never starts spats with one's inferiors."

"Consider Beverly and me," Wanda said. "We've been feuding with Anna Wintour since the Clinton Administration."

"Over what?"

"No one remembers. But that's not the point. The point is to keep the damn thing going."

"How?" Megan asked. "This all makes no sense."

"A well-placed barb on Instagram is helpful," Jackie suggested. "Anything about a major wardrobe faux pas, a drunken display at a dinner party, and of course, infidelity. Nothing says spat like exposing an affair."

"You can also feed searing little scraps of gossip to the columns," Wanda suggested. "In that regard, as I assume you have surmised by now, Jamal Dix is a particularly useful tool."

"The item, of course, must be placed in a way that your rival knows exactly who did it," Beverly advised with experienced self-confidence.

"I have no feuds," Megan said.

"Then we must create one!" Beverly said. "We have dibs on Anna, of course. I suggest someone a bit less venomous. How about Kim Kardashian?"

"Why would I attack her?"

"Because it's easy, dear," Wanda said. "You know: fish, meet barrel."

"I don't know. I'll think about it."

"Good," Beverly said. "Now, displays of clout are also *de rigueur* when you go out in public. Those snot-nosed salespeople at Bergdorf's, for instance, are prime targets. Not a word need be spoken. Just a flash of indignation across your face. One that unmistakably screams, 'You *do* know who I am, don't you?'"

"Mind you, restaurants take a particular kind of exertion," Jackie said. "You want to get on the good side of every maître d', and you don't achieve that through cattiness, but gifts. Only, not cash."

"I find Cartier watches to be effective," Wanda said. "It worked with those two oafish bouncers stationed outside the Polo Bar. And I hear they turned away Emily Blunt! But not me. If I'm craving a cheeseburger, even at 8 p.m. on a Saturday, I just waltz right in."

My God, Megan thought. These women are nutter butters. I can't wait to tell Brigit.

"Now. Let's move on to social media," Beverly said.

"Well, I have a Twitter account, and maybe close to 12,000 followers."

"Twitter? Are you joking?" Wanda laughed. "Twitter is for kooks, Christians and Canadians. We all use Instagram. Except for old Beverly here. She still insists on Facebook."

"It serves me well, thank you very much."

"So does your surgeon in São Paulo, sweetie."

"But what do I post about?" Megan asked.

"Photos," Jackie said. "Lots of lovely photos."

"Of what?"

"It doesn't matter," Wanda cut in. "You can post about your bloody chairs, for fuck's sake, and people will eat it up. Your latest sartorial acquisitions. A picture of you with Michael Bloomberg at the Opera Guild. Like that. As long as it's fabulous, it gets Instagrammed."

"It's all about playing with the fantasies of the riff raff," Jenna said. "I mean, Gwyneth has positively mastered the art."

"Instagram is also essential for promoting your side businesses," Martha advised.

"My what?"

"We all have one, dear, and we plug the hell out of them on social media," Wanda said. "I, for one, buy jewelry at barn-sale prices from down-and-out socialites and sell it to the finer auction houses. It's a win-win-win. Jackie, of course, is opening her little organic eatery. Even Martha has gotten in on the game. She has her own line of pet clothing, woven from 800-thread-count Egyptian cotton. The little cat bonnets are all the rage now."

"And you, Jenna?" Megan asked.

"My life coach told me I've yet to find my niche," she said glumly. "And he's Tibetan, so…"

"What about Beverly?"

"I am my own business, dear."

"But I have a business, too," Megan said. "I'm a freelance journalist."

"The media is not considered respectable in our circles. You might as well operate a urinal factory," Wanda said.

"But I saw you fawning all over Anderson Cooper at our place," Megan said.

"Well, he's cute. And he's on television. Of course I was. But scribbling little nothings for those eco-blogs of yours is not going to cut the Dijon." Megan marveled that, just fifteen minutes earlier, she had actually felt a pang of camaraderie with Wanda.

"Speaking of media, have you settled on a publicist?" Beverly asked.

Megan was dumbfounded. "What for?"

The ladies exchanged knowing smiles. "It all comes back to clout," Beverly said. "Nothing can multiply status more exponentially than good P.R."

"For now, if you like, I can lend you mine. Claudia Bing," Wanda said. "She's a bloody wizard, that one. She dines with all the big TV bookers. And then there are the magazines. Claudia can help you land the right one, for your first cover."

"Cover?"

"Of course," Wanda said matter-of-factly. "Your wedding is most cover-worthy. I was thinking *Town & Country*, but we might want to go a bit, for lack of a better term, down-market. Only for the wider reach. *Glamour*, say. If we insist on Annie Leibovitz."

"A few other things about the press," Jackie cautioned. "One, 'off-the-record' means bupkus. If you don't want to be quoted, shutteth thy moutheth. Trust me on that one." Wanda let loose a knowing snort. "Two," Jackie went on, "No nude photos. And for God's sake, no sex videos. Those girls have the social longevity of a gnat."

"Well said!" Wanda cheered. "Just ask Jenna how all that worked out for her."

"Wanda? I thought we had agreed that that never actually *happened*."

"Did we?" Wanda asked with feigned innocence. "Must've been a Freudian slip. From Kmart. You know, like the one you *weren't* wearing."

"Third," Jackie pressed on, desperate not to lose the floor. "At red carpet arrivals, the Tonys, say, or the Met Gala, always stop for the paparazzi. Even if they're not certain you *are* somebody, they'll shoot your picture just in case."

Beverly glanced at her agenda. "That leaves just two pressing items, and we're done. First, your charity. What's it going to be? I was thinking dolphins, maybe, given your little adventure down in Anguilla. Everyone loves dolphins."

"I'm not sure," Wanda said. "*The Cove* was so long ago. People move on. I hear that orangutans are quite in vogue now. How do you feel about the great apes, Megan? I suspect they might be right in your wheelhouse."

"Actually," Megan said, "I plan to work with all of you. At Safe Harbor House." Silence fell on the afternoon tea like a radioactive shroud of doom.

"Plan?" Jackie finally asked. "What plan?" Megan looked puzzled.

"What Jacqueline means, is that you don't need a plan," Beverly sniffed. "You need an invitation."

"Well?" Megan asked.

"We'll take it under advisement at our next board meeting," Beverly said, looking the color of fire-pit ashes. "We'll get back to you."

"I was thinking I'd like to be your volunteer coordinator," Megan pressed on. "As a volunteer, of course. I've given it a lot of thought. I could bring in students from Pratt to teach the kids about art. We could have nutritionists do cooking demos of affordable but healthy meals for the moms, maybe have a computer clinic for them, even teach them code. And much more." Megan looked around the table.

"I love it!" It was the nice one. "Megan, you're hired."

"Martha!" Beverly protested. "Protocol! Board meeting! Robert's Rules!"

"Oh jeepers. Fuck Robert," Martha said, sending Wanda into a hysterical squeal.

"Two F-bombs at one tea!" Wanda said. "If I didn't know better, I'd swear you had died and come back as Ricky Gervais."

"It's a cute idea, I suppose." Beverly retook control of the table. And then she added, all businesslike, "Like I said, Megan, we'll get back to you."

"Wasn't there one more item?" Megan asked.

"Oh, right, the little matter of your wedding. When? Where? Who? And by 'who,' I don't mean guests. The worthy know who they are, and invitations they shall receive. We'll see to that, right, ladies?" Megan frowned as the others nodded like bobbleheads on the dashboard of a car speeding down a pothole-filled road. "I mean the wedding director, dress designer, chef, florist, and hair and makeup people, just for starters."

"Well," Megan said, taking a deep breath. "I don't really know about that. Except I think the wedding will be sooner rather than later."

"And what makes you say that, dear?"

Megan knew the answer. Before heading down to this clown-car of a high tea, she took a pregnancy test. The proverbial rabbit had died. Megan was stunned: she was taking birth control. But a quick Google revealed that the pill is 99% effective, and, "people aren't perfect and it's easy to forget or miss pills," according to Planned Parenthood. "So in reality the pill is about 91% effective."

Oops.

Megan didn't have a chance to tell Rex yet, but she knew he would want to tie the knot ASAP. "I'm pretty sure Rex will want it that way," is all she said.

"So, when were you thinking?" Martha asked.

"Early September. Right after Labor Day. When everyone's back in town."

"Megan. That gives us just three months to plan," Beverly sighed.

"Well? Make it so, commander," Megan said. "Rex and I will contact venues tomorrow. We'll have a date set soon."

"So, ladies," Beverly pronounced, "This calls for another meeting."

"More than one," Wanda sighed. "Let's have the first one at my place. How about next Tuesday for lunch?" The socialites looked at their phones and nodded. "Brill! Megan, would you like to join us?"

"Not really. But I will. Can I bring Celia?"

"Must you?" Beverly looked pained.

"Yes. Yes, I must, Beverly. See what I did there? I exerted clout. And I liked it." Megan looked around. Only Martha had broken into a smile. "I'll show myself out. Thanks for tea. It was swell. Except, Beverly, the rosemary scones were a touch too garlicky, don't you think, dear?"

Chapter 13

(Pre)Nuptials

Megan returned to the penthouse feeling spent. Todd and Carlitos were sitting in the lounge, also looking glum. "What's the matter?" she asked. "You look like Cher just died."

"I didn't get the job. With the catering company."

"I'm so sorry, Toddie. But there will be others, I'm sure. Chin up."

"Mom is beside herself."

"We'll figure something out. After all, I'm marrying a multimillionaire, right?"

"It's his money. Not yours. And certainly not ours."

Megan had not actually thought about that. The notion of being Mrs. Rexford Bainbridge III was less than 24 hours old. "I'll do anything I can to help. Now, it's your last day here. And we have much to celebrate. Your dinner, for one, was a triumph. And I'm engaged. And there's one other bit of news."

"You got hired at the *Post?*"

"Hardly! You'll have to wait 'til dinner. Why don't you sad lads take in a museum? How about the Whitney? Dinner's at eight."

Megan wanted the perfect meal to go with announcing a pregnancy. She went to confer with Madame Duchamp. "Tell me," she said, "What's Rex's favorite meal?"

Duchamp set the ladle into a pot of lobster consomme. *"Canard a l'orange* with white asparagus and sauce hollandaise. And a nice Chardonnay. From Burgundy. We don't serve that oaky California *merde."*

"Wonderful. Can you make that tonight? It's a very special occasion."

"Of course, mademoiselle. And congratulations on the engagement. *C'est très merveilleuse!"*

"Thanks Dominique." Megan leaned in to whisper: "I still can't believe it's real. Also, it scares the crap out of me."

Duchamp laughed. *"Ce n'est pas la mer à boire!"* she said. Megan cocked her head in puzzlement. "We say it all the time in Provence. It means 'It's not as though you have to drink the sea.'"

"I still don't get it. Sorry."

"No, please. We French can seem very obtuse, especially to Americans. Basically, it means things could be much worse."

"You're right. Talk about first-world problems. Being nervous about marrying a millionaire is pretty much at the top of the list."

"But Rex, he's crazy about you! This is so obvious. And compared to *monsieur's* previous companions, you bring a touch of class to this house."

"Really? I don't think the maids feel that way. They don't like me, do they? They don't think I'm good enough."

"Who cares what those silly girls think. They're jealous."

"Jealous?"

"But of course. You get to sleep with him. Them, not so much."

Not so *much*? Maybe something was lost in translation, Megan thought. Or maybe she meant he was boffing them before she showed up?

That evening, Megan decided to serve champagne (for Rex only, no more booze for mommy), Alsatian *charcuterie* and Normandy cheeses on the west terrace, alone with her fiance, to give him the news. Then she would tell the boys and they would all celebrate over duck dinner.

Rex came home and gazed at his fiancée, outside in the rose-and jasmine-scented evening light. She never looked more lovely, he thought, taking in her Hepburnesque little black dress, her hair à la Bacall, swept to one side like a midnight wave. She looks, he thought, she looks like a Manhattanite. "You're gorgeous," he said. "You know that, right? Inside and out."

Megan felt like she was bathing in warm cream. "Last night was magical," she said. "I love you, baby."

"I love you more."

Rex sat down and Ramón appeared with Dom Perignon in a silver bucket and the appetizers. Megan told Rex about the tea party. "It was totes Mad Hatter," she laughed. "Those women have some serious issues. I wonder what they spend more money on, therapy, or plastic surgery?"

Rex laughed. "I can handle one, maybe two at a time, tops. But get all of them together at once and you just want to go home and cry. Still, I'm really glad you went. And I'm glad they want to help with the wedding."

"Can't we elope? I hear Tijuana's lovely this time of year."

"I was thinking something a little closer. Like down the street. At Saint Thomas. My family has ties to that church that go back to its founding. In 1824."

"Well, that really puts the knicker in your bockers, doesn't it?"

"Yeah, the blood. It's inky blue. So…When were you thinking?"

"Right after Labor Day," Megan said, aware there would be another labor day, in February.

"But that's three months away! Honey, these things take time. Saint Thomas is booked a year in advance."

"Well," Megan drew a deep breath. "There's something else that's about three months away, and I think it might impact our plans." Rex stared at her. "The beginnings of a baby bump." Megan beamed, rubbing her belly.

"My God." Rex fought for his breath. "No!"

"No?"

"No, I mean, yes! I mean, oh my God!"

Megan squealed in delight. Rex stood up, lifted her into his arms, and they swung around the terrace like stars in a Sam Goldwyn picture. "These," Rex said, "have been the best two days of my entire life."

"Me, too, baby. Me, too."

"And yes, let's do September. I'll call Canon Chadwick tomorrow. It's not unheard of for someone to cancel the booking in exchange for… compensation."

"Are you sure?"

"Everyone has their price. There are plenty of brides, and their parents, who would happily switch venues in exchange for someone underwriting their wedding."

"That's amazing."

"Ain't money great?"

"Yes. Except for when you don't have any."

"Well," Rex said, "that's never going to happen to you again."

Duchamp came out on the terrace. "*Le dîner est servi!*" After Megan broke the news to Todd and Carlitos, both of them overwhelmed and fighting back tears, they toasted the person-to-be. Dinner was beyond sublime, or as Todd put it, "nuclearly orgasmic."

"One day," Carlitos said, "we will cook like this."

The next morning, after seeing the boys off to LaGuardia, Megan went out for sandwiches with Brigit at a Vietnamese bubble-tea shop on West 47th. "Jamal sends his regards," Brigit grunted. "How many 'fuck-yous' should I bring back with me?"

"Tell Jamal he can eat my *bánh mì*." Megan said, pointing to a photo of the popular Vietnamese sandwich roll on the menu.

Brigit giggled. "You know what they say: If you've seen one asshole, you've seen Jamal."

"Besides," Megan grinned and stuck out her ring finger, "he's not getting married. *I* am!" They squealed like teeny boppers at a Maroon Five concert, prompting a sharp shush of rebuke from the sour-faced middle-aged woman behind the counter.

"Okay, we're going to get 86'd when I tell you *this*," Megan said. "I'm pregnant." This time, they each clasped both hands over their mouths, but screamed like banshees anyway.

"AITCH-EFF-CEE!" Brigit cried.

"Holy fucking crap?" Megan was getting used to her friend's tired game.

"Yes. Does Sexy Rexy know?"

"I told him last night."

"And...?"

"He's flying around in heaven."

Brigit's face took a sudden turn toward the serious. "Megs, what about...?"

"What about what?"

"Money. *Dinero*. Moolah. Benjies. You know, it all belongs to him."

"Yeah, I get it. I don't know, yet. We're going to see his attorney."

"*His* attorney! Shouldn't you have one there, as well?"

"Brigit, we're getting married, not divorced."

"Exactly! Cuz, honey, you gotta frontload that stuff. Expect a prenup, of course."

"Of course."

"And he'll make it ironclad, locked in Fort Knox. With Army snipers on the roof."

"I get it. I don't care."

"And your expenses? This society gig doesn't come cheap. The *accoutrements* alone, my dear!" she added, channeling Beverly's clique.

"I hadn't really thought about that. It's only been two days. Barely."

"Well, most blue-ribbon wives get generous monthly allowances."

"I'm not a prostitute."

"Maybe. But they are. At least the prettier ones. I mean, you think Melania fucks that thing for free?"

Megan crowed. "I assumed Barron was a baster baby. Anyway, Rex is not going to let me go barefoot and hungry. We'll work it out. Besides, I'm still going to pursue my journalism."

"Well, that's great to hear. If you save up real hard, you can buy – oh, I don't know – a dinner saucer."

Megan laughed, adopting the Upper East Side dialect, "but it will be the *finest* saucer, hand crafted from Bruges bone china, glazed by Belgian high masters and fired in a kiln of lotus petals and flamingo feathers."

Brigit laughed. "They have flamingos in Belgium?"

"Imported ones. Yes."

After lunch, Megan headed to the office of Rex's personal attorney, Barton C. Devonshire, Esq., of the uber-WASP and widely feared firm of Devonshire, Cheadle and Atherton, on the 54th floor of a glass-encased skyscraper on Madison in the 40's. The views were staggering. Clearly, this was the vaunted lair of a superpower lawyer. Rex was waiting on the long black-leather Eames sofa by Devonshire's enormous glass-and-chrome desk. It was all very *Bauhaus*, Megan thought.

Coffee was poured and business was immediately gotten down to. In the event of divorce, Rex would retain all of his assets prior to marriage, the lawyer, a handsome but formal man around 50, with salt-and-pepper hair, pale green eyes and just the right number of crow's feet to still look sexy, went on.

Rex's assets – businesses, real estate, art collections, investments, etc. – were estimated at about $100 million. "All of that is off limits, do you understand?" Devonshire said. Megan nodded solemnly as Rex squeezed her hand.

"He's agreed to cover your living expenses, which includes legal counsel. You will also be furnished with two credit cards, and a checkbook, for household items not under purview of the staff, such as food, wine, flowers, clothing and spa treatments, plus travel, entertainment and local transportation. And the wedding, of course. But every expense will be closely examined by the accountants, who are like hungry red-tailed hawks hovering over a pack of plump field-mice. They miss nothing."

Rex looked at his fiancée. "You look like you've had enough. Why don't you go home and think all this over?

Out on the street, it was one of those early-June afternoons when fresh, breezy Canadian air switches place with the stagnant morass from the South. "I hate it when this happens," Brigit had griped at lunch. "Southern air smells like onions, swamp gas and Republicans. These are not good smells."

Megan returned home in a funk, especially after Rex called and said he would be late again, something about protests in Hong Kong. She asked Madame Duchamp to make her a spinach salad and mushroom crepes with gruyere sauce, and went to draw a hot bath to wash away the stress and grime of the humid day. As the water ran, she texted her brother.

> *Hey sweet pea. Just checking in. How's everything with you? Ditto mom and Carlitos?*

The reply was almost instant.

Carlitos and I are okay, Todd wrote, on a new iPhone Megan had managed to buy for him, one with an actually functioning "T" key. *But I'm worried about mom. She rarely gets out of her bathrobe when at home. It's painful to watch.*

Megan felt crushed. While she toyed around with prenups, her family was struggling with rent and grocery bills. She had two options, she figured: Postpone the wedding and go back to Michigan to, somehow, help out; or, ask Rex for a modicum of financial assistance for her beleaguered family. She opted for the latter.

After her bath, Megan sat down for dinner on the west terrace, just as Rex came home. Madame had prepared enough for two and Rex went to join his fiance at the table. He looked tired.

"Long day?"

"Long," Rex said. "So fucking long. I got murdered in the Asian markets. You don't wanna know." He gazed at her softly and said, "Look. I know that meeting was a lot to take in. I'm sorry I had to put you through it. I hope you understand."

"Well, it *was* kind of creepy, if I can say so." Megan took a grateful gulp of well-chilled watermelon juice that Ramon had just served. "But I do understand. You're risking a lot here. This is serious stuff. I guess that money matters always are." Megan paused. "Speaking of money…"

"Yes?"

"Well, it's my family. They're struggling, Rex. Underemployed, short on groceries, facing possible eviction. It's bad."

"And?"

"*And?*" Megan cried in disbelief. "What kind of 'and' did you think I meant? I meant, can you help them out somehow?"

"Like, a loan?"

"I was hoping for better. A gift, perhaps."

"So, let me take stock here. Not only do I have to bankroll *your* life, but your family's life as well? Is that what I'm hearing?"

"Rex. If you don't want to (air quotes) 'bankroll' me, I am perfectly capable of taking care of myself. I just thought you might be able, and even willing, to help my family. I hate to admit I was wrong. But it looks like I was."

Megan pushed back her chair to get up and leave, but Rex took her arm gently and urged her to remain.

"Okay," he said. "How much do they need?"

"I don't know. Maybe five thousand?"

"Fine. I'll cut a check tomorrow."

"As a loan?"

"No. A gift. But this is a one-time-only thing."

That night in bed, Rex wanted to have sex, but Megan resisted. Eventually, she fell into a deep sleep, with bizarre dreams about giving birth to a baby dolphin, in the middle of the desert, then frantically casting about looking for water. She finally came across the Reservoir in Central Park, and gently lowered the creature into the murky waters, where she sat for hours on the grassy shore, gazing at the little miracle. That's when a squad of NYPD officers, led by Yuri, the Russian from Coney Island, and Rex, appeared and arrested her for animal abuse.

Chapter 14

Of Wedding Bells and Revealing Cakes

Wanda Covington woke up late in her twenty-second-floor apartment on Fifth Avenue and 76th. Her husband had long ago left for work, or whatever he did during the day. It was going to be another hot and muggy one, she knew. In her soul, London was calling.

Wanda missed England: the dreary drizzle, the cozy tearooms, the superior curry. She missed all the catty chatter about the Royal Family, and bitching about the French. She missed deep intellect, dry wit, and most of all, genuine class. These Yanks, she thought, were so tedious, scratching about as they did for power and status, in a way the English find unseemly, instead of just enjoying the unfathomable wealth bequeathed to them. But, Wanda realized, these so-called friends of hers were her lifeline to reality. Without them, she most likely would be holed up alone in this giant apartment, for eternity, bingeing on Pimm's Cup with ginger beer and reruns of *Absolutely Fabulous* and *Are You Being Served?*

Wanda Covington felt old.

And now, she thought, I must interact with that deplorable little upstart from Michigan. Will I try to be nice? Of course. Will I succeed? The odds are succinctly against it.

Wanda had two appointments that day with Megan. The first was at Safe Harbor, where they would meet with staff about her latest ideas for volunteer activities, and later, with the other girls, at Vera Wang for some wedding-dress shopping.

The meeting at Safe Harbor went extraordinarily well. Even Wanda was impressed with Megan's proposals, imagination, energy and enthusiasm. Megan brimmed with light and optimism. The staff, visibly thrilled with her ideas, begged her to get started as soon as possible. When it was over, Wanda found herself saying to Megan, "We must have lunch."

"Okay," Megan said, somewhat suspiciously. "When?"

"Why now, of course. Before we go to Vera's. There's plenty of time. My treat. Come along now."

They went to Sylvia's, the famed "Queen of Soul" eatery on Lennox in Harlem, where Wanda insisted they order chicken and waffles. "It's my secret guilty pleasure," she confided. "You must never tell anyone."

"I promise." Megan smiled. "But why not? This food is awesome."

Megan was amazed when Wanda wanted to engage in something bigger than small talk. The Brit asked about her career, her aspirations, and her personal life with Rex.

"I assume you two are doing the rumpy-pumpy, so, he's *not* gay," Wanda said. "I think we can establish that?"

"*Indubitably,*" Megan responded in a faked English accent, cracking herself up. "Tell me, what do you think of his little buddy, Dr. Pepper?"

"That creep gives me the collywobbles."

"The what?"

"A nervous tummy-ache. What an extraordinarily miserable twat he is. And not all that clever. I've met circus animals that were smarter."

"He came on to me. Twice. When Rex wasn't looking."

"I'm not surprised. That loathsome boy was born on the banks of the River Duplicity. I assume you said nothing to Rex."

"Nope."

"Good on you. The last thing you want is two guys cockfighting amongst all those priceless furnishings. And you needn't worry about me. Your little revelation is in the vault, as Seinfeld would say."

"You like *Seinfeld?*"

"Adore."

"Me too. Maybe you're not such an unmitigated bitch after all."

"Don't be too hasty," Wanda said. "I'm not going sugar-coat things. God knows I never do. This little sojourn you are dragging us on will not be fun. By the time it's over, we might all come to loathe it, and each other, like a clunky revival of *Cats.* We'll get through it, thank Jesus-on-a-bun, but we may never get over it."

"Sometimes, it's hard to believe you're for real, Wanda."

"I'm not only real, sweetie, I'm *spectacular.*"

The days and weeks flew by as if the brake pads of time had worn out. Megan's hours were fully consumed by wedding planning, working at Safe Harbor, and prenatal doctor visits. She also carved out time to work on another article. With Rex's help, she had landed an assignment with National Geographic online, about the fledgling Whale and Dolphin Sanctuary Project, including a one-week tour of potential coastal sanctuary sites in the Pacific Northwest and British Columbia. Megan was allowed to bring a photographer, and she asked Brigit, who studied photography in school and knew how to work Megan's camera. Jamal reluctantly gave her the week off.

None of the ladies seemed impressed by the assignment, with the exception of Jenna, who insisted on tagging along. "I've always wanted to see that part of the world!" she said at a working luncheon at Le Cirque, to test drive the wedding menu, (Megan thought the Madagascar boar way too over-the- top, which only made the others insist even harder that it be served). "And I just *adore* whales! They're so…shimmery."

Wanda instantly read the look of mild panic crossing Megan's face. "Jenna. Perhaps Megan could use a brief respite from us hens."

"All of the arrangements have been made," Megan explained. "There's only room for Brigit and me: seaplanes, boats, camping locations."

"*Camping?*"

"Yes," Wanda said. "The kind with sleeping bags and tents, not mumus and mai-tais."

"And bears," Megan added. "Lots of bears."

Jenna frowned. Clearly, she had lost interest. Wanda laid an insincere hand on the pouty woman's shoulder. "It's okay, Jen-Jen. I'm sure you can find something quite shimmery right here at home. You always do."

On a muggy Saturday, Dimitri drove Megan and Brigit to JFK for their flight to Vancouver. Rex had insisted on upgrading them from coach, but Megan refused, saying that "wildlife journalists don't do first class."

It was a magical week, not only to be in such pristine, spectacular surroundings, reporting on an important and fascinating story, but it was pure bliss to be out of the steaming rats' nest that was Manhattan.

They camped right on narrow Johnston Strait, in the stunning upper reaches of Vancouver Island, its staggering green peaks swirled in mist. Amid its bears, eagles, foxes and beavers, the region is also the summertime home to the threatened Northern Resident Killer Whale community. They astounded Megan with their grace and majesty. At night, the stars sparkled like heaven's fireflies.

"How do you put up with it all?" Brigit asked one night in front of a crackling fire.

"With *what* all?"

"You know, the pomp. The circumstance. The napkin rules. The bitches."

Megan laughed. "I really don't know. I wish I were a heavy drinker, cuz I would so take advantage of that."

"But don't you get bored, sometimes?"

"Bored? God no. I have a wonderful life. An amazing fiancé, serious charity work, a career I always dreamt of, a big fat wedding to plan and, oh yeah, a baby on the way."

"How *is* the baby? Do you know the sex yet?"

"A couple more weeks."

"So, who knows you're pregnant?"

"Nobody! Except you, Rex and my family. And I want to keep it that way, until after the wedding."

"Of course."

Mosquitoes buzzed about them like mini B-52s. They were really starting to bite. Brigit snatched a can of repellent from her backpack and, instead of spraying herself, began spraying the mosquitoes.

"What are you doing?"

"It's repellent, right?" Brigit said. "It won't kill them, but this way, they won't be able to stand themselves."

Megan laughed at her friend. But she could also tell that Brigit wanted to ask something. "What is it, Bridge?"

"I was just thinking."

"Oh God. That's never good."

"It's just that…I wonder if you'd…Look. I'm up for a promotion in Jamal's shop. An actual writing job, with the occasional byline."

"That's amazing! But what does it have to do with me?"

"There's competition. People are stabbing each other with ragged, rusty spoons to get this job. I need a scoop. And now, *poof*! You're a scoop."

Megan glared at her friend. "Oh no."

"Please? I've never asked for anything since you got to New York. Jamal is going to find out anyway. You know he is. Why not let me put this one little feather in my pitiful little cap?"

Megan melted. Brigit had done so much for her. She never would have gotten that waitress job, and never would have met Rex, without her pal. "Okay. But only after the wedding."

"Of course."

"And no interviews. I've had it with that cretin. Seriously."

"But he'll need to confirm it."

"I'll have my doctor send him an email."

In the campfire light, Brigit could see worry lines on her friend's face.

"Okay, now what's up with *you*, Megs? I've known you too long to not know that look."

"It's just…well, it's Rex."

"Oh no. What happened?"

"Nothing happened. But I've been noticing some, *things*."

"What things?"

"Well. For one, he's cheap. Like, five-and-dime cheap. I had to beg him to help out my family. I didn't tell you. They're facing eviction. But, I mean, that's loose-change-in-the-sofa to him."

"The more they have, the more they hate to part with it. Or so I've heard."

"And there's other stuff. I mean, he gets so gruff with me sometimes, and for no reason. And he's always working late. Always at some can't-miss meeting or on some international conference call. And there's been some really creepy characters coming over to his home office lately. Ukrainians who never smile. They look like gangsters, I swear. I think something shady might be going on."

"So he's a cheapskate with questionable business partners. Things could be worse."

"They might be. I sometimes wonder if he's cheating."

"Megan O'Malley! You banish that thought right this instant, or I'll banish it for you!"

"You sound like my mother."

"No, seriously. He's crazy about you. I can see it. And you're a zillion times better than those garden-variety trust-fund cadettes he dated and dropped. Money can buy neither smarts nor charm. And you are dripping in both."

Megan smiled softly. "Thanks. I needed to hear that. Even if I don't fully believe it. But I do catch him looking at other women, gorgeous women. A lot. It will only get worse as I get more pregnant."

"Megan. You worry too much. Let's get to sleep. We have whales to watch early tomorrow."

When Megan returned home, the wedding was in full Alpha-Socialite production mode: all those lavish wonders that would soon have the columnists champing to out-gush each other. She barely had time to finish her whale article before the impossibly big day arrived.

There was the showing at Givenchy, in Paris, complete with a photo spread in WWD where Megan and her mentors posed, a bit too stiffly, most people thought, while tippling Taittinger and nibbling canapes before a pouting parade of models. There was the private, after-hours shopping "experience" at Tiffany & Co., where the Good Women of Fifth Avenue positively commanded a highly reluctant Megan not to leave the premises without the tiara of white diamonds accented with nine Fancy Intense Yellow diamonds in 18k gold.

Megan's bridal bouquet, the ladies had decided, was to be a highly curated world tour of extravagantly exotic flora, including Gold of Kinabalu orchids that grow only in one national park in Malaysia, and purple saffron crocuses cultivated exclusively by blind Hindu monks at a monastery on the outskirts of Jaipur.

Hair and makeup involved a four-hour affair conducted, with compliments of the house (in exchange for promotional considerations – including another photo spread, this one in the Sunday *Times*), by leading stylists at Warren-Tricomi salon, conveniently located just blocks up Fifth Avenue at the Plaza Hotel, home to Megan's childhood heroine, Eloise, and her mostly companions.

When it was over, Megan stood on the steps of Saint Thomas Church alongside her dashing groom, posing for pictures and receiving well-wishers. Bells rang, doves soared and Gaga herself gave Megan a giant, if rather oily hug, her pancetta leggings now sweating like an old man at the West Side Y sauna. "Send me the cleaning bill," she whispered.

Just as they were about to head over to La Cirque, ICE officers appeared out of nowhere and slapped handcuffs on two of Rex's maids, Lorna and Lupe, and hauled them away in terror.

Megan knew the maids did not like her, but she still felt terrible. "Rex," she said on the way to the reception, "We need to help them. Someone obviously turned them in. We need to find out who."

"What's the point? We'll get new maids. You can screen them, to make sure they're legal. Now please, don't let this ruin our day."

The flight to Bora Bora lasted longer than an Imperial Chinese opera. Even first-class on Air France could not take the edge off. Megan was exhausted, Rex a bit irritable. By the time they finally arrived at Halle Berry's place, they were both jet-lagged wrecks. Not even Rex was interested in fucking.

Megan swiftly came to adore the atoll, with its serene majesty and coconut palms tilting in the trade winds, and the towering emerald crags of Mt. Pahia and Mt. Otemanu, exotic centerpieces of the dazzling, circular turquoise lagoon.

The remainder of the honeymoon went well enough. There were day trips to out-islands on a catamaran, an authentic Polynesian dinner on torch-lit coral sands, and snorkeling in the color-blasted reefs, teaming with garish fish. Megan positively forbade Rex to conduct any business on the trip, which made him feel, he confessed, "a bit bitchy."

But there was also Chloe, the lovely young Tahitian who cooked meals and looked after the villa. Tall and dark with ample breasts, round facial features, glowing eyes and silky black hair falling down her back, she looked like something out of a Gaugin painting. Even her soft accent was seductive, delicious.

On more than one occasion, Megan caught her new husband staring at Chloe, usually while flashing a boyish grin. It turned her stomach. "So," she said one afternoon over papaya salad and smoked lobster in the shell, served by the gorgeous young woman. "When are you going to wipe that drool off your face?"

"What?"

"Chloe. You like her?"

"Of course! She's lovely. Don't you?

"Yes. But I don't want to fuck her."

Rex's face matched the color of his crustacean. But it revealed more shame than anger. "Megan! Honey! My God, how could you think that? On our honeymoon?"

"So that's a 'no?'" Megan said, softening.

"Of *course*. You're my wife, the mother of my child. I only have eyes for you babe, trust me."

Sure, Megan thought. Trust. But verify.

Things got better after that, and so did the sex, including a raunchy night on the beach under a yellow sliver of moon.

Grabbing a chilled bottle of Cabernet Franc, (for Rex) and a soft blanket, they headed down to a secluded beach. After skinny-dipping in the silky black water, they lay down and began kissing. Suddenly, the loud, mournful wail of a blowing conch shell arose in the distance. This was soon followed by drums, rattles and hypnotic chanting, which washed over them in rising, rhythmic waves of sound.

"What's that?" Megan asked.

"There's a French all-inclusive resort over there, Le Meridien Bora Bora. Must be some sort of Tahitian floor show." He kissed her again and then said, "Wanna get on top tonight?"

She giggled, rose to her knees and then slowly lowered herself onto his massive appendage. They rocked together in increasingly rapid motion, spurned on by the rising volume and intensity of the drums. Lots of couples have sex to music, Megan knew, (Cosmopolitan calls them "boning tunes" and recommends Beyoncé, Nicky Minaj, Nelly and Madonna) but this was ridiculous.

They began moaning and panting heavily. So much so, they didn't notice that the rhythmic noise was not only growing louder, it was getting closer. They were so into it, they didn't even see the torchlight beginning to flicker under the palm fronds. Until it was too late.

The show, it turned out, included a traditional Polynesian wedding procession along the beach. Rex and Megan looked up to see a dozen men and women in vibrant costumes and headdresses made of grass, palms, tropical flowers, mother-of-pearl, seashells, feathers, and coconuts, gyrating and shimmying down the fine, white sand, straight toward them. They were followed by thirty or so boisterous tourists, laughing and chatting *en français.*

Before they knew it, they were engulfed in torchlight. The drumming stopped. The wedding party stared, open mouthed.

"*Mon Dieu!*" A female tourist cried.

"*Qu'est-ce que c'est?*" a man shouted, laughing.

"*Sexe sur la plage!*" some teenage boy cheered. "*J'adore!*"

Everyone started taking photos. Megan and Rex leapt to their feet, fumbling to wrap the blanket around both of them, and then waddled like conjoined penguins back to Halle Berry's villa, where they could still hear the roaring laughter.

The next day they spent entirely in bed, well out of view of Monique, or the outside world. When the time came to leave the exotic atoll, Megan was sad. She would be happy never returning to New York. The morning of their departure, they had one last swim in the lagoon and breakfast on the lanai. As the car was pulling up, Megan Googled the news.

"Oh shit!" she said. Rex looked at her with alarm. She handed him the phone. Some of the tourists had posted images on Instagram. The horny young couple was quickly identified, and now their naked escapade was being gaped at, and wildly shared, from Marseille to Mumbai to Manhattan.

Once back in the unchained chaos of home, Megan threw more of herself into Safe Harbor, introducing new projects in music, art, sewing, cooking, and, she was most proud of, creative writing. The press took note and the charity got boatloads of publicity, and donations. Everyone in town knew about *that night* in the South Pacific, which Wanda called "the hilarious X-rated remake of *From Here To Eternity*," but it only seemed to help.

Beverly, naturally, was getting most of the credit, and good press, for Safe Harbor's glowing success, a growing bone of contention among the board, Wanda in particular. Still, Megan felt needed, and content.

One afternoon, while working at Safe Harbor, Megan called Brigit to give her the green light for telling Jamal about the baby. "You better hurry. Beverly and Wanda know, and they're insisting on a gender reveal-party. They want to invite the media and livestream it on Instagram, as if I were carrying the heir to the throne."

"In a way, you are."

"It's just so vulgar. And self-aggrandizing. It's so damn New York."

"At least the food will be good."

"Of course it will. It always is."

The Big Event was scheduled for late October, at Beverly's place. To sweeten the deal, Martha suggested making it a Safe Harbor fundraiser, with a $1,000-minimum-per-guest, a $5,000 "VIP Reception with the Mother-To-Be," and a casino taking "bets" on the gender, with piles of pink and blue chips for sale at $100 each. When Jackie said all funds should be earmarked for Megan's volunteer program, she had to surrender.

Only Beverly and Wanda knew that the baby was a girl (Rex had accidentally spilled beans), but they admirably kept the secret, as if it were an FBI dossier on suspected domestic terrorists. The fact that Megan was due just six months after her wedding would be noted, the ladies agreed. But so what? This was, after all, 2018.

The "reveal" plan was audacious. It was Jenna's brainchild: Custom order, from one of the finer patisseries, an exact replica of Safe Harbor House made from a massive French-vanilla cake, with a milk-chocolate buttercream façade, little mommies and their babies of piped icing, peering out the windows, and the large chimney, made of miniature pomegranate-candy bricks.

"And?" Wanda asked. "What exactly does this cake do?"

"At the appointed moment," Jenna said, deeply enamored of her own ingenuity, "the chimney will puff out little billows of dyed powdered sugar, either pink or blue, depending." She paused and surveyed the table, anxiously. "So? Whaddya think?"

"I think it's perfectly moronic," Wanda said.

"I think it's messy." Beverly added. "You propose to do *that*? In my Great Room?

Jenna looked like she was going to plotz. As usual, Martha refereed. "Wanda, when brainstorming, there are no stupid ideas, just stupid responses to them." Wanda glowered. Jenna giggled. "I for one think it's cute."

"I do too. And, it would be awesome branding for the charity," Jackie said. "People will love it. What do you think Megan?"

"I hate it. But I didn't want to do this whole stupid party, either. So, okay. For the kids. Speaking of, Jenna, I think we can lose the frosting families in the windows. It's kind of cannibalistic."

"Sure. Whatever you say, *Hula girl*."

"But how will it work?" Megan asked, unruffled. "How will you make the chimney poof!?"

"Don't worry, I've got it all figured out."

"Well, that's unsettling," Wanda said. "But honestly, how? With your degree from The Nutty Professor's School of Pastry Engineering?"

Jenna visibly struggled for a comeback. "You English think you're so damn clever," was the best she could do.

"But we *are*, dear. Plus, science has proven that insults are much more effective when delivered with a British accent. It's a win-win for us, really."

Megan couldn't help laughing. Jenna, glared. "Ooh, burn Jenna!" Megan said.

And then, looking around after a silence: "Oopsie. Hashtag-*awkward*."

"You ungrateful hillbilly," Jenna said. "After all we've done for you. I won't forget this."

Megan's Irish blood roared through her head. "Done *for* me? Or *to* me? Cuz it's beginning to feel like the latter. And, Dr. Smarty McGenius, we don't have very many hills in Michigan."

"Off track!" Beverly said. "Back to business. Jenna, how in God's name will this *work?*"

"Well if you must know…"

"Yes, Jenna. We must. Trust us," Wanda said.

"My cousin Clarence is a high-end electronics manufacturer," Jenna explained authoritatively, trying to upgrade her clout. "I'm sure his lab can come up with something. How hard could it be to blow some sugar from a tube?"

The next morning, Megan and Rex were having breakfast as she debriefed him on the whole cake thing. Ramon brought in the papers. Megan went right for *The Post.*

—————————————

The Gleaner

By Jamal Dix

"Baby Makes Three" – September 30, 2018

And now for my biggest scoop of the Social Season: The population of Millionaire's Row is about to grow. By one. I have it on the best of authorities that Mrs. Rexford Bainbridge, III, known as Megan O'Malley until her recent Grand Nuptials earlier this month at Saint Thomas Church, is expecting a child.

Megan was kind enough to allow her personal physician to confirm the happy news with yours truly. I have come to know the recent arrival to Our Town quite well over the past 10 months, and watched in wonder at her complete transformation from humble Michigan waitress to a leading lady of Manhattan Society. Her premiere dinner party, a Mexican fiesta of the most festive order, is still fondly remembered in certain circles, and no one could argue that her glorious wedding was one of the most splendid in recent memory.

I have gotten my fair share of digs in this column in the past. But not today. I just want to wish the young couple the very best and the greatest of happiness. I bet you didn't see that one coming, did you?

No word yet on the child's gender, but watch this space about forthcoming details of a rumored "gender reveal party." My money is on Mrs. Beverly Gansevoort-Stein, the Bainbridge's inimitable downstairs neighbor, as the most likely hostess of the big fete.

On the morning of the reveal party, Megan had three main items on her agenda: an early sonogram, a midday meeting with a designer recommended by Celia to go over plans for the new nursery, and interviewing maids in the afternoon to replace the deported Lorna and Lupe, despite Rex's failed efforts at pulling bureaucratic strings down in DC, after Megan had begged him to do something.

First, Megan called home to check in. "Howya doin, mom?"

"It depends on the hour. The money Rex sent is going faster than we can replace it. I'm down to 20 hours, and Todd's working part-time at IHOP. Minimum wage for sliding burgers between pancakes. Good times."

"Listen," Megan whispered, looking around for eavesdroppers, "I've been stashing away bits of cash, listing them as miscellaneous expenses. It's not much, but it will help."

"Thanks Megan. I'm going to go see about food stamps today. Yeah, it's that bad."

"What about the church? Don't they have a food pantry?" Maureen said yes. "But we can't be seen there. People will think we're poor, or something."

Leaving the apartment and heading down the elevator, Megan felt like shit. And it wasn't just her soul-crushing morning sickness, which was getting worse. She felt awful for her family. It was all just so unfair: So much wealth on Fifth Ave, so little back home.

If Rex wasn't going to rescue her family (the jerk) then Megan would somehow find a way. As she walked through the lobby, Megan spotted a handsome young doorman standing behind the front desk, who nodded and smiled politely as she passed. He must be new, she thought. And pretty darn cute, to boot.

"You didn't recognize me," he said. "I knew you wouldn't."

Megan stopped, turned, and regarded the guy in his tight-fitting burgundy-colored long coat, with its big brass buttons and gold-trimmed lapels, and an oversized, green military-style hat with red-and-yellow bands and a golden palm leaf, like some kind of hot, young Soviet Commissar. He removed the hat and Megan's eyes went wide.

"Tony?! It's you! I can't believe it!" She ran behind the desk and hugged him.

224

"When did you start working here?"

"First day, ma'am," he said.

Megan laughed. "Ma'am? *Really?*"

"It's in the manual, ma'am."

"Doormen have manuals?"

"Apparently so. The richer the house, the stricter the rules. At least, here, I am allowed to *speak* with the residents without, you know, being spoken to."

"But why did you leave San Marco?"

"Because I got tired of coming home smelling like marinara, and the tips here are way better. I got the gig through my uncle. He works in this building. At Mrs. Gansevoort-Stein's place."

"Ah yes, the famous Chef. He's quite good. Beats me how he can put up with that crotchety old fuckbucket."

Tony flashed his dazzling smile. "And that British butler. Holy mother of hell is he a piece of work."

"All the Brits in New York are, or so it seems. So. Can we still be friends? Can we hang out, like before? Or is that sort of thing frowned upon?"

"Nobody here smiles anyway, so they'll never notice. Besides, I didn't see anything about that in the manual. So as long as I keep calling you ma'am, I guess it's Kosher."

"Even at a bar? I want to take you out for a drink soon. To celebrate your new job."

Tony looked down at Megan's rising belly and arched an eyebrow.

"So…you know," she said.

"Lots of people read Dix's column. Even those who aren't, you know, in it."

"Fucking press."

"Listen to you! Spoken like Donald Trump himself."

"Very funny. Now. What about tomorrow? What time are you off? And don't worry, I'll have a ginger ale."

"Six."

"Perfect. See you then. And Tony, though you do look adorable in that getup, take time to change before we go, okay?"

"Yes ma'am."

"You'd better be careful," she laughed. "I could get used to that 'ma'am'crap."

The visit with the OB/GYN, a Pakistani woman who Megan adored, beside her rather disturbing name, Dr. Makhdoom, went splendidly. "She's healthy as a little oxen." the doctor declared. Megan stared at the fuzzy image on the screen, at the little human forming inside of her. We did this, she thought. Rex and I created this marvel.

Lunch with the nursery designer, Carlisle Calhoun, an imperious imp of a man, with thinning blond hair and an overblown Southern accent that he alone apparently found charming, proved to be less inspiring. "You want me to line the windows with pink *what?*" she asked him.

"Fake fur, Miss Megan," He drawled. "Simply *everyone's* doing fake-fur trim in nurseries this year. Blue or pink, depending. They're calling it the 'New Kitsch.' Don't you just love that?"

"No. And I'm not simply everyone. I'm Mrs. Bainbridge, and my kid's room is going to exude class, not crass."

"Well, bless your little heart." Carlisle flashed a saccharine grin. It went downhill from there. Megan made a note in her calendar to break the news to Celia, and to hunt around for a new designer.

Now exhausted and dreading the party, she sat in the kitchen as Ramon led the housekeeper candidates in, one by one. Megan had gotten word out over Twitter, knowing that every maid within five square miles had a cousin, or sister, or whoever looking for domestic work. But she'd made it exceedingly clear, they had to have working papers. The thought of ICE officers raiding her home gave her the collywombles.

It took almost three hours to slog through it. Of the women who showed up, only two had actual green cards. The rest had excuses, or vague promises of somehow furnishing proof, at some point. Unenthused about going through the tedious process again, she hired the two women on the spot. They each had experience, good references and pleasant enough personalities, though there were a few issues gnawing away at Megan.

The first woman, Paulina, a plump, middle-aged grandmother from Honduras, seemed a bit off, and, frankly, wobbly. First, she knocked over her water glass, and then she fell off her barstool, splat onto the floor.

"*Estas bien?*" Megan asked, helping her up.

"*Si senora. Un poco nerviosa.*" Megan made a mental note to keep Paulina away from the crystal and finer china.

And then there was Gabriela, from Guadalajara. Everything Paulina lacked – looks, grace, youth, good balance – Gabriela had in droves. She's gorgeous, Megan thought, tall and voluptuous. Why isn't she a model or something? Rex, she knew, would heartily approve of this particular hire.

The party at Beverly's was called for seven, with the reveal to take place promptly at 7:40, to be broadcast live on *Entertainment Tonight* and Instagram. Megan had begged for something more local, Eyewitness News 7, for example, but the board was determined to take this national.

"Who knows?" Jackie had argued. "Maybe we can establish Safe Harbors everywhere!

"What a capital idea," Wanda had scoffed. "And which chapter would you like to manage, Boise, or Biloxi?"

Turnout was extraordinary: two hundred people, fifty with VIP tickets. After the journal ads and blue-and-pink betting chips, it was expected to net a half-million (Beverly underwrote the expenses, with tax deductions), plus publicity that would have cost at least a million.

Everyone was there: The happy parents; the matrons and their husbands or dates (Martha raised amused eyebrows when she showed up on the elbow of Chevy Chase, "a friend of my late husband's," she explained); a smattering of local pols; some mid-level celebs like Al Roker; Susan Lucci, Jared Kushner's sister, Nicole, and Caitlin Jenner (Beverly thought that a little gender-bending at her gender-reveal fete was a stroke of sheer genius); gals-about-town; leading hedge-funders; Instagram executives; the Pampers people; and, best of all, the city's top bloggers, photographers and columnists, including Jamal Dix.

Even in Beverly's expansive, two-story quarters, things were a bit tight. But most everyone made do – lubricated by the ample top-shelf open bars and passing trays of champagne.

Milling discretely among the crowd was Martha, handing out "Save The Date" cards to select guests, inviting them to a party – her first soiree ever in town – on New Year's Eve. "Bully for you, dear!" Wanda said when Martha gave her the little postcard, dotted with colorful party hats, noise makers and martini glasses. "And what an ingenious way to upstage young Megan. I love it. Really."

"That wasn't my intention! This way just seemed more efficient."

"Well let me know how *efficient* Mr. Chase turns out to be. I mean, he's plumped up a bit, hasn't he? But it's cute, really. You're thin as a nail. He's round as a zero. When you two stand together, you look like the number ten!"

"Wanda, I want you to turn around, walk away, and never speak to me like that again."

"What? It'd be great for Halloween. Don't you think?"

"Wanda..."

"As you wish. But you still want me at your party, don't you?"

"Yes," Martha said. *"Please?"*

And then the moment arrived. Dexter and Chef wheeled in the enormous cake to waves of oohs, bravos and thunderous clapping. According to the press release's "Talking Points" that a battery of young publicists was handing out to reporters, it was eleven feet tall, took two-hundred-thirty pounds of pastry flour and thirty dozen eggs to make, weighed three hundred pounds, was slathered in thirteen gallons of buttercream, and loaded up with ten pounds of powdered sugar, the color of which was known only by a select few.

Megan had asked the cake artists to drape a last-minute fondant banner over the main door, with the words "SAFE HARBOR HOUSE" stretched across it. "I mean, if we're going to use this little shindig to brand your place," she explained, "then let's brand the crap out of it. Shall we, ladies?" Miffed at the process but grudgingly pleased by the prospects, Beverly chose to let it go. Nope, she restrained herself. Not now. Not today.

Madame summoned as many people as could fit into her Great Room, with others looking on from adjacent hallways and on the grand staircase. Jenna had wanted to herald the reveal, but was promptly overridden by the Board Chair and hostess. "Perhaps, for the next baby, *you* can fork over fifty grand," she had huffed.

The *Entertainment Tonight's* camera lights flashed on. The Instagram people and some 100 guests held their phones aloft. The columnists readied their pens. A hush fell on the room like a lamb's wool comforter. Beverly signaled for Megan and Rex to join her in front of the cake, where they posed for photos, while the other Safe Harbor ladies looked on in their little bubbles of envy. And then, in what she considered a spontaneous stroke of brilliance, Beverly invited P&G's Vanessa Yoon to join them. After all, the Pampers People had snatched up thirty-five VIP tickets.

Martha turned to her date, the portly former star. "You should be up there, too," she said.

"Well, I'm not just going to waltz up there on my own. It wouldn't be polite."

Martha's heart pounded and her face flushed. "I can't believe I'm doing this," she said. "Come on." She grabbed Chevy Chase's hand and guided him through the crowd, until they emerged at the cake and began posing for the cameras. People cheered the bumbling SNL icon with nostalgic relish, even though many of them were not even alive when he was on TV. Beverly cast a homicidal look in Martha's direction.

Chase turned around and gazed up. "My, doesn't that brown icing look exactly like...?" he said. "But so tasty, too!" He plunged two fingers deeply into the buttercream façade, as if eating poi at a luau, and licked the frosting clean. Some thought it rather funny, including Megan. But a large portion of the over-50 crowd were repulsed. Beverly was beyond apoplectic. This whole photo-op thing was getting way out of hand.

"Thank you everyone for coming to my humble abode, and for your marvelous support for our little project!" Beverly said. "You know, there are some fine young mothers and their kids, right now, far up there on Fifth Avenue, who are forever grateful for your generosity. I would have invited some of them, but I'm afraid we were simply too overwhelmed with paid RSVPs!"

Beverly laughed. The chortling that ensued was awkward; the applause noticeably anemic. "And now, my friends, the moment we have so been waiting for!" Beverly placed her thumb on a big cartoonish red START button, to get the thing going. "Rex and Megan, ladies and gentlemen, members of the press, the gender is...!"

Nothing.

"The gender is...!" Beverly was now pummeling the button with her fist. A low rumbling emerged from deep within the dessert. "Ah! There we are! It'll be any second now."

But instead of puffing pink sugar, the cake shook. It roared. Beverly fired a pleading look at Jenna. She scrambled to grab her cousin Clarence, who was flirting with a young female executive from Goldman Sachs. The rumbling grew louder. The chimney refused to belch. Instead, it teetered as if challenged by a 7.5 earthquake. Slabs of pomegranate bricks began to topple free from their sugary mortar.

Beverly sensed danger. "Dexter! Unplug that damn thing at once!" The butler sprinted to the outlet like a lanky, awkward gazelle. But it was too late.

KA-BOOM!

Everyone was smeared in buttercream, to which shards of candy and bite-sized morsels of yellow cake promptly adhered.

And then the wafting powdered sugar began to descend, like a toxic mist in some forgotten Kubrick film. It settled on everything and everyone, coating them in a fine dusting of truly shocking pink, as if the entire Great Room had been magically transformed into a giant box of Peeps Marshmallow Easter Bunnies.

The screams of terror were quickly consumed by utter silence, followed by soft whimpering and subdued swearing over ruined couture.

"Well," Chevy Chase said. "At least we know it's a girl!"

THE GLEANER

"Charity Is Such Dirty Work"

By Jamal Dix – October 28, 2019

Well.

The above paragraph, in its entirety, dear readers, pretty much sums up the whole affair.

I assume you have heard about the... the... let's just call it the Big Party Pooper, by now, or watched it live on Entertainment Tonight *or* Instagram *(until the screen went brown), or have already viewed it, like me, hundreds of times on social media. It is literally impossible to look away, especially the slow-motion version.*

For those of you living far too deeply within your caves to know, last night Fifth Avenue's own Mrs. Beverly Gansevoort-Stein and the good ladies of the charity she chairs, Safe Harbor House – an up-and-coming shelter for single moms – staged an elaborate gender-reveal-party-cum-pricey-fundraiser at her swank park side digs for none other than Manhattan's most anticipated mother-to-be, Megan Bainbridge.

It all began typically enough, with hors d'oeuvres passed by a small armada of maids, chilled champagne, and the soft tinkling of piano keys coming from somewhere, mingling perfectly with the polite chit-chat of the somewhat boldfaced names who packed themselves into the massive apartment for a most original reveal.

And then came the cake, likely the biggest I've ever seen. An exact replica of the shelter building, topped with a red-candy chimney. This chimney, we were soon informed via press release, was the star of the evening.

The whole idea was crafted by Jenna Forsythe, the transportation heiress. Ten full pounds of dyed powdered sugar, blue or pink, depending, were to be gently puffed from the chimney. Instead, the whole dessert exploded, raining down a torrent of cake, buttercream and pink sugar. (It's a girl, in case you hadn't heard).

Aside from the evisceration of certain egos, no one was injured. I asked our accounting people to estimate the bills for cleaning or replacing all that couture, plus damage to the room's opulent interior: about two hundred grand. Who will cover it? Madame Gansevoort-Stein? Homeowners insurance? The company that built the spitball contraption? Or the Safe Harbor charity itself?

Whatever gets worked out, East Side dry cleaners eagerly await the deluge.

Chapter 15

Palace Coup

The Exploding Cake of Fifth Avenue, captured on countless cell phones, became a thing. A really big thing. It was the number-one trending item on Twitter, TikTok and Instagram for nearly three days. A South Korean animation company digitally recreated the entire catastrophe in splattering detail, one gob of frosting at a time, and the video received nearly twelve million views the first day. All the national morning programs featured it widely. Jokes about fuzzy pink Halloween costumes were everywhere.

Beverly reckoned she could never be seen in public for the rest of the decade. According to Dexter, nearly 50 media requests "from London to Singapore and back" had come in for her, which she had told him in advance to decline. The humiliation was so debilitating, Beverly cancelled all appointments for the next three days. Even Walter Mitty, with whom she spent hours playing with yarn, did little to help lift her spirits.

But then, something even bigger happened.

"Have you heard?" Wanda called Beverly to inquire.

"What now? Are we being sued? Audited? Run out of town on a scooter?"

"No. Safe Harbor House is on *fire*."

"Oh Jesus God, no! How? When?"

"Sweetie. Calm down. It's a metaphorical fire. We're hot. In fact, we're positively famous, even outside New York."

"What do you mean?"

"Our publicity, financial and social-media people have been trying to call you for two days, to no avail."

"And?"

"Donations are through the roof! They've never seen anything like it. The cash is coming in faster than we can count it."

"You don't say? I guess I should answer my phone more often."

"That's not all. Our social media followers have quadrupled, and the cable news people simply won't shut up about us. I'm told that Anderson Cooper himself is preparing a segment on the whole thing, not just the detonating dessert, but the need for more charities like ours, and the problem of homeless single mothers in America. Boom, girl! We. Are. Everywhere."

"Why, it's a miracle," Beverly said. "A buttercream miracle."

"It is. Though I suppose now we'll have to thank Jenna for being such a bumbling twit-on-training-wheels. Even so, congrats sweetie. Bye-bye."

Beverly put down the phone and scooped up her contraband ferret, rubbing her face against his flank. "Anderson Cooper! Isn't that marvelous, Mr. Mitty?" And then it hit her. "But wait," she said, still speaking aloud to her pet. "If he's doing this story, he'll have to interview *somebody* from Safe Harbor, won't he, my pumpkin-angel-lamb-pie-face?"

There was zero doubt who that *somebody* would be. Beverly quickly called Megan.

"Yes, Beverly?" she answered gruffly.

"Good day, my dear. I just called to see how you were holding up."

"The fondant is finally out of my hair, if that's what you mean. What do you want?"

"I told you, I just want to make sure everything is okay up there."

"No you don't. Cough it up, Beverly. You know, like a hairball."

"Well, there is just one other little matter," Beverly said. "I need to reach Anderson Cooper. Do you or Rex know how?"

An hour later, Beverly found herself booked to go on the show, live, that evening at 8:30 Eastern. She wisely decided to keep the interview under wraps until shortly before air time, lest the other ladies, consumed with jealousy, tried to storm Time Warner Center and bully their way into the CNN studios.

Beverly had no idea what one wears live on national television, and now she realized she had no one to ask. She decided to err on the side of extravagantly fabulous. Something with *zing*, she told herself. I deserve some zing. That of course meant only one thing: Nieman-Marcus, set deep amid the embarrassingly nouveau riche Hudson Yards and its gleaming, curving glass skyscrapers — Dubai-by-the-River in the booming West Thirties. There was still time to go online, order something, and have it at her door well ahead of showtime.

It did not take long to find it: A shimmery, baby blue Carolina Herrera gown, "in silk taffeta with floral sparkly embroidery." It featured flouncy three-quarter sleeves with tie cuffs, a banded waist, pleated front skirt, A-line silhouette and, for good measure, an extended train back. Beverly thought it the height of elegance, like something that Anderson's mother, Mrs. Vanderbilt, rest her soul, might wear to Opening Night at the Met.

So what if it was $11,990? Beverly loved the way it looked.

Big mistake. Had Wanda been there to confer with her, she would have vetoed the over-the-top outfit with a biting chortle and quick wave of the hand. "It's gorge, but way too much, sweetie!" Wanda might have said, still laughing. "You look like Cinderella's stepsister, heading out to the ball."

Beverly summoned Driver and headed down to Time-Warner. She was escorted up to one of the CNN floors and asked to have a seat in the Green Room, where two other guests awaited their turn: Rudy Giuliani, a man she both knew and reviled, and Nikki Haley, Trump's U.N. Ambassador, a distant acquaintance and, Beverly once remarked in private, "Not that bad, for a Republican Indian…from the South."

Beverly scoffed when asked if she wanted to visit the makeup room. Why, she used the most expensive cosmetics in the world, and tonight had applied them herself. No one was touching this face.

Another big mistake. They don't call it "pancake makeup" for no reason, (the name originally came from "Panavision," but the principle is the same). In front of those glaringly bright studio klieg-lights, one really needs a good dusting, or one will appear too shiny, as if lacquered. Unbeknownst to Beverly, once on camera, she would look even more like a Victorian villainess.

A producer with headset and clipboard came in to fetch Beverly. My God, she thought, suddenly aware that her throat was dry, her heart racing. This is really happening. I'm as nervous as fuck.

They walked into the blinding studio during a commercial break. There was Anderson, all dapper and clean, at his big polymer desk, conferring with a producer. He looked up and saw the Grand Dowager, dressed like, well, *that*, her glinty face ablaze in color, and an overblown, Baby Jane grin.

"Good evening, Beverly," he waved her over. "It's good to see you again. That Mexican dinner was a hoot. Come, have a seat." And then, while she was still just out of earshot, he whispered to the producer, "My mother would never have worn anything like that on television. She hated her you know."

It all went so fast. Before Beverly knew it, Anderson was wrapping up the segment and breaking for a commercial. In her anxious daze, she could barely remember a single question, or answer. She figured she could watch it later somewhere online. Someone would know how. Perhaps that IT fellow, what's-his-name.

As Beverly had anticipated, of course, simply everyone else was watching live, including Megan and Rex, who were curled up on a fluffy sofa in the study. They were both dumbstruck by Beverly's adopted television persona: gracious, soft-spoken and, (could it really be?) a tad humble.

"I am so honored, no, *grateful* to be in the service of so many less-fortunate New Yorkers who need our help," she told Anderson.

"Whoa! What was that?" Megan laughed. "Who stole Beverly and replaced her with Mother Theresa?"

The period of humility did not last long. Anderson returned to what he politely called "Megan Bainbridge's reveal-party malfunction."

"Yes, it was a most unfortunate accident, though no one, thank goodness, was hurt," Beverly smiled. "But, as I like to say…" She looked down, clearly reading from a card, "Every cake has its silver frosting!"

"Hah!" Megan was cracking up now. "She needs crib notes for her own pitiful clichés!"

"It really is the amateur hour," Rex said. "It's hard to watch, but even harder not to."

Further down Fifth, Wanda was spending a typical evening alone (another late business dinner with "some clients in from Panama, don't wait up," Trevor had told her) in front of the TV, watching her alleged chum bask in all the unearned glory, even after her own disaster of a party, which Wanda had taken to calling the "*fiascarade*."

"So what's the silver, um, frosting here?" Anderson Cooper asked.

"Why, publicity, of course!" Beverly giggled like a teenager, making goo-goo eyes at the anchor as if they were the same age and sexual orientation, out behind the backstop. "Let's face it, Anderson. If that cake had not gone kablooey, you never would have invited me on your show, now would you? But, ta-DA!…here I *am*!"

"Oh fucking hell, Bev! This is supposed to be about the kids, you fart-basket cockwomble!" Wanda shouted at the giant screen. "And what in the blazing devil do you have *on*?" She waved her hands wildly, knocking over a Waterford cut-crystal vase on the end table – a 25th anniversary gift from Frederik, Crown Prince of Denmark - and sending it shattering to the floor, calling the attention of Lucia, the head maid.

"Everything okay, Mrs. Wanda?"

"No, everything is *not* okay. Everything is quite not okay."

"Would another brandy help?"

"Of course not. But I'll have one anyway. And can you take care of this shitbasket on the floor, please?" Lucia went to the built-in walnut-and-brass bar to pour the drink.

"Lucia dear, what do you think of our Mrs. Gansevoort-Stein?"

"Oh, I don't think I'm supposed to have an opinion about things like that."

"But you *do* have one."

"Everybody does. The maids, that is. We tweet about her all the time."

"Is that so?" Wanda suddenly wondered what the maids were tweeting about herself. "And, what do they tweet?"

"She's a *reina de control.* A control queen. And, she takes credit for *todo.*"

"Exactly! What a deft observation. I mean, the half-witted old coot just went on national television to brag about an exploding cake, as though she had secretly concocted the whole bloody calamity herself. Which, come to think of it, I wouldn't put past her, if she knew it would land her on C-N-fucking-N."

"Can I share an expression we use back in my village, Mrs. Wanda?" Lucia asked, sweeping up the Waterford remnants.

"I suppose. If you must. Again."

"Don't get jealous. Get even."

"*Me*? Jealous? Of that preposterous poser? In what universe could that possibly occur?"

"Well, I still say get even. It will be fun. You'll see."

The next morning, Wanda was in the breakfast nook when Lucia brought in her poached eggs, wheat toast, sliced papaya and steaming French roast. "I'm taking your advice," Wanda announced, taking a sip. "About getting even."

"How?"

"I'm staging a coup. I'm going to strip Beverly's chairmanship away and keep it, so next time, she can watch *me* on Anderson Cooper."

Lucia, who had over the years absorbed some of Wanda's English phrases by osmosis, grinned and said, "That is *mega,* Mrs. Wanda! And so very bloody clever."

"Why thank you, Lucia! It really is. Isn't it?"

"Oh. I need to tell you. We need an exterminator. I saw mouse poopies in the kitchen, and out in the dining room, too. You want me to call building maintenance?"

"And have it known all over town that we've got rodents? Good God no! This will have to be an inside job. Very hush-hush. You know anybody?"

"Actually, yes. My uncle Juan Carlos. He does lots of places around here, including Mrs. Bradbury's, where my cousin Rosalinda works."

"Well, if he's good enough for Martha, I suppose he'll do for me. If only in a pinch. Is he discreet?"

"Mrs?"

"Does he talk?" Lucia's face was still blank. "Oh Christ on a croissant, girl. Does he snitch!? Does he tattle-tale on his clients?"

"Oh no! He barely speaks English. How could he?"

"Fine. Please have him come over. At once."

With that problem solved, Wanda turned to her plotted coup d'etat. She considered several options, but then decided, why not just go nuclear? It was so much cleaner that way. Wanda had always found that in spats gone by, her private investigator, Broderick Nickelbury, whom she kept on retainer for just such occasions, never failed to produce the desired dirt.

She rang him up. "Hello Brod? Brod, dear, I need a little oppo research done," she said. "On Beverly. Ay-sap. You will? Splendid! You already have a file on her, I know, so that will give you a head start."

Back at 1080, Megan woke up feeling tired, and kind of lonely. She knew so many people, but how many were actually friends? She took mental stock: There was Rex, naturally, her best friend. There was Brigit, and presumably Bill. And Celia, of course. But that was about it. I need more friends, she thought. Girl friends.

And that's when Megan thought of Martha. Yes, she was a bit dull, but she was also sweet, and honorable, and somehow uncorrupted by the murder of crows she flew around with. Megan fired off a text.

Martha, I've been thinking. Throwing a New Year's party is a big deal. You'll need help. Will you let me?

Martha had been thrilled, and the two made it a point to have a lunch meeting every Wednesday between now and the big night, to go over every possible detail, and every possible pitfall. For one, the food would have no moving parts. The first order of business was the caterer. "Who are you going with?" Megan asked as Martha's sole maid, a kind young woman named Rosalinda, brought coffee and pear tarts on a tray. "My brother and his boyfriend are available, you know. And they could use the work."

"I know. And I thought about that. But that annoying Jackie is insisting I hire her chef from Green Acres. It opens in mid-January and she desperately wants the buzz. To turn her down would cause more grief than it's worth. I'm sorry, Megan."

"Oh don't be! Whatever peace you can bring to that nutty little valley of yours, then more power to you."

"Besides, the chef, Charlie O'brien, he's an old friend of Beverly's man, Jackie Gillespie. And he's said to be very good. And ridiculously expensive, I'm afraid. My cash flow is not quite as tidal as the rest of yours."

"Then use your clout," Megan said.

"What clout?"

"You have something she wants. Make her pay for it. Literally. O'brien's monstrous fee, and throw in all the food as well, or no deal. She can write the whole thing off anyway."

"I could *never* do that!"

"That's what I figured. But I could. And I will."

Those hours of female bonding were among the most enjoyable that Megan had spent in her nearly year in the city. The two women, they quickly discovered, shared a mutual affinity for male K-Pop stars, Christopher Guest movies, NPR, Jello shots, Judge Judy, S'mores, Salinger and Hawaiian pizza, among others.

One day Martha rested a gentle hand on Megan's shoulder. "You and I are the only outsiders here in this swish swamp. We understand each other. I married into money, too. *We* are middle America. The real McCoys. They are from another planet."

Megan was touched. "Sometimes I feel like we're ambassadors from Sanityland, on official detail in the Royal Kingdom of Cuckoo Puffs. I mean, the sheer pomposity alone. It would be funny, if it weren't so tragic."

As they grew closer, Megan felt more at ease discussing marital issues with Martha. "When you were pregnant," she asked one day, "did you and your husband still have sex?"

"Come to think of it, no. Not very much. And you?"

"It's been three months. Now, how many horny young men do you think can get by that long without a dose of, you know, something on the side? I doubt that ninety days of wanking, even if it's twice a day, fills the void."

"I can't imagine Rex cheating on you!"

"I can. And I do. Constantly. I only hope that my imagination has gotten the worst of me."

"Why don't you just confront him?"

Megan let loose a bitter laugh. "Yeah right, philanderers never lie. Just ask Bill Clinton about 'that woman.'"

"Then have sex with him."

"I would, if only..." Megan frowned and remained silent for a moment. "Martha," she said at last, "you rarely talk about your husband. I know when he died, but I don't know how."

"It was a freak accident. I don't usually talk about it."

"Of course. But you know, talking can be cathartic. Tell me."

"Well, it was an unusually warm afternoon in mid-September. The clouds that day were feathery, I remember, and the aspens were just beginning to turn gold. I was at the ranch house, going over our books. We had become quite successful by that point. 'The Third Largest Hemp Grower in the Rocky Mountain Region,' it said on our stationery."

"So, what happened?"

"Chuck had gone up to the fields, in the foothills above Boulder. It was harvest season, and he was very hands-on, especially for a CEO."

"And?"

"He was up there with his men, supervising them. Suddenly there was a commotion in an adjacent field. The men began shouting '*Oso! Oso!*'"

"A bear?"

"A big one. It tore straight across the road and into the field where Chuck was, heading right down the same row."

"Holy crap! Did the bear get him?"

"Never had a chance."

"What do you mean?"

"As I said, it was harvest time, and the hemp was reaching eight feet tall. You couldn't see anything between the rows. Chuck took off for his life which, we later learned, is the worst thing that one can do in such a situation. But he didn't know that. He was from West Los Angeles."

"What happened then?"

"Our foreman, Jefferson, the nicest Brazilian man, was operating a harvester in the next row over. A brand-new John Deere. T-Series Combine. Very high tech."

"And?"

"Jefferson did not see Chuck turn the corner, until it was too late. There was very little left of him, I'm told. Though they did find his fraternity ring, dangling on a stripped hemp twig. Fortunately for the others, the noise was so loud, it scared away the bear."

"Oh my God. Martha. I am so sorry. How totally dreadful."

Martha sighed deeply. "I know." And then, almost with a whiff of pride, she added, "A hemp field. A charging bear. And some farm equipment. It was a very Colorado way to go, I suppose. Chuck would have liked that."

A few days later, Wanda Covington got the call she was waiting for. Broderick had not disappointed.

"Holy mother of Marmite! You've really hit pay dirt this time, Brod. I've always wondered why she never talks about the Sixties. I suspected there was some sort of scandalous skeleton in that decade, but I never imagined how, well, radical it was! Well *played*, darling. Messenger me the file, and I'll transfer over your bonus this afternoon."

Next, Wanda dialed Beverly. "Free for tea tomorrow? My place, three-ish?" she said. "I've some *ideas* for the foundation I'd like to run by you. Yes? Gorgeous."

Beverly arrived with macaroons and a potted African violet that was, she mentioned, twice, "exceedingly rare." Swedish gravlax and dill sauce, toasted brioche slices with smoked cashmere-goat butter and lobster clotted cream, and a tastefully arranged plate of huckleberry tartlets were waiting in the Formal Dining Room. Its enormous windows afforded a charming view of the park's Model Boat Pond, typically encircled by the well-fed offspring of the well-off, remotely piloting their miniature skiffs and schooners across the placid waters, as their international flock of au pairs smoked, chatted and gossiped about their bosses nearby.

"So," Beverly asked. "What are these big ideas?"

"The winds of change."

"And which way are these winds blowing?"

"My way. Coming up from the tropics."

"What are you babbling about?"

"Picture this: The Sixties. A young girl swept up in revolutionary fervor. And lust."

"Wanda. Have you gone off your meds again and not told us? Or perhaps you're pitching me a *Lifetime* movie."

"I know, Beverly. I know everything about you."

"My God. You sound like Hannibal Lecter. And his fava beans."

"I believe your little secret is also quite well-known to our Mr. Stroganoff. You know. Regarding Cuba?"

"He told you? Why, that larcenous son of a bitch."

"Hah! No. *He* didn't. And what do you mean by larcenous?"

"Never mind."

"Well, thanks for corroborating my intelligence."

"Intelligence?"

"I have sources. You must know that."

"You're bluffing."

"Am I?" Wanda tossed the file onto the table. Beverly rifled through its contents: official Soviet government cables with Spanish and English translations; phone intercept transcripts from the KGB; piles of receipts from hotels and restaurants in and around Havana; and, most damning, photographs. Lots of grainy black-and-whites of a hot young Beverly - with Fidel.

"Where'd you get this?"

"As if I would tell you."

"What do you want?"

"The chairmanship. Of Safe Harbor House. And its attendant publicity."

"That's ridiculous."

"Funny you should mention ridicule. Imagine the oceans of it that would be heaped upon you if…"

"And to think," Beverly snapped. "This, coming from my best friend."

"*Best* might be a bit of hyperbole. And as you know, in our little world nobody really has friends. Like nations, we only have interests."

A look of uncontrolled panic shadowed Beverly's face. She grabbed the papers and began ripping them to shreds.

"I'm surprised," Wanda said, "that you didn't assume I'd make copies."

"Fine. You win. So. How does this work?"

"At the board meeting, next Tuesday, you shall respectfully tender your resignation as chair, citing the need for new blood. A self-effacing aside about the cake might be appropriate too."

"And then?"

"You throw your unambiguous support behind me, of course."

"Signore Machiavelli would be proud, Wanda, if not envious of your unbridled evil. But how will you convince the others?"

"I only need one. Martha. And that cat will shortly be in the bag."

"Good grief. What mud have you dragged up on *her* with those claws of yours?"

"Enough for some fool-proof electioneering. Ciao."

Wanda hung up and dialed Martha. "Sweetie, my maid Lucia said she had seen a most interesting tweet," she began.

"What do you mean?"

"It seems the *senoritas* spend their free time gossiping. About us. Online. It's quite the conversation."

"I've nothing to be ashamed of."

"I think you might. Word on the *calle* is that you coerced Jackie into paying for your party."

"I did no such thing," Martha said, which, technically, was true.

"Then who did? That wretched waitress?" Silence. "I see. Anyway, I just called to say well done! Devilishly sly. Although, it'd be a pity if anyone found out. In the English-speaking world, that is."

"How *could* you, Wanda? You're, well, you're beneath human rubbish."

"I think the question is, how *couldn't* I? It's just too delish not to share. Unless, that is…"

"Unless what?"

"At the board meeting, and do not tell a soul, Beverly will resign the chairmanship. I am going to run to replace her, with her support, and now with yours, may I presume?" Another long pause. "Dear…?"

"I...I need to think about it," Martha said, sounding clearly shaken.

"Of course you do. You must think about it very hard. Now, see you on Tuesday. Buh-bye!"

The meeting was terse, and brief. Beverly raced through the few items on the agenda, and then dropped her sad little bomb.

"Any new business? No? Well, I have some. I'm stepping down. It's time for new blood, even though we are, I must note again for the minutes, doing very, very well."

"Because of me," Jenna said.

"And brava for you, Jenna!" Wanda blurted out, in a last-ditch effort, Beverly surmised, to win her vote. "As they say, calamity is the mother of publicity."

"What now?" Martha asked.

"According to Robert's Rules, we hold an election," Beverly said, trying not to look as shitty as she felt. "I nominate Wanda Covington. She has the stamina, and may I say, *cojones*, to carry out her duties."

"What kind words! I do hope I can count on your support, Madame Chair."

Jackie cleared her throat. "Yes?" Beverly asked.

"She's not the only one with *cojones*, you know. Besides, I have more experience in foundation work. I nominate me."

Jenna clapped her hands. Wanda's face melted into a puddle of displeasure.

"But Jacqueline," Wanda said. "Unlike your last charity, the boys at *our* home are far too underage, for the most part. Even for you."

"Piss off, you dotard."

"Well then. It seems we're off to the races," Beverly said. "I assume Wanda and Jackie are voting for themselves?" They glowered at each other and nodded. "That makes it one-to-one. As for my vote, it's Wanda. Jenna, not that I need to ask, but Robert has his rules…"

Jenna raised her right hand. "Jackie…Duh."

"And we're back to a draw. The tie-breaking vote would be you, Martha."

Martha cast a fidgety glance around the table. Jackie appeared eerily confident. Jenna put on her pleading puppy-dog face. Wanda, both eyebrows arched like Endora on *Bewitched*, looked like menace itself. Martha had thought about this over several sleepless nights. Jackie did have, for better or worse, more administrational experience. And besides, Martha had learned to loathe Wanda more than fear her. In fact, she hated her fucking guts.

"I cast my vote for…" Martha began, pausing for effect, as if she were in a season finale of *The Bachelorette*, "Mrs. Jacqueline Farquharson."

Collective gasps, a hush, and then riotous squealing from Jackie and Jenna. Wanda shot her trademark "I'll get you for this, my pretty" evil-eye at Martha, who seemed about to cry.

Beverly offered a motion to adjourn. It was adopted unanimously. "Congratulations, Jackie," she managed to say. "I pass the gavel, And I wish you luck. With this bunch, you're going to need all you can muster."

"Thank you, former Madame Chair," Jackie said. "Now, one more vote. How about lunch? To celebrate. Masa. My treat."

Only Jenna raised her hand.

Wanda returned home, fuming like a Nicaraguan volcano. She began plotting her whispering campaign against the traitorous Martha.

But then something crossed her mind. Such a vengeful machination could actually backfire. Everyone liked Martha. They might even take pity on the poor Hemp Widow, just struggling to keep up and throw a decent party. Toss the unfathomably popular Megan Bainbridge into the pudding, and Wanda could well end up as the black-marked villain.

No, Wanda needed some other category of scandal altogether, one far more devastating, something permanent, if possible, to inflict upon Martha. And something that could never be traced back to her.

Against all odds, she found her answer on the pages of the filthy-rich's holiest of bibles, *Town and Country*. According to a brief column item in the front of the book, tucked amid the Gucci and Bulgari ads, there had been reported, much to Wanda's disgust, and delight, a veritable infestation of Manhattan's very best houses with…bedbugs.

Wanda's mind raced in tight circles. She had the ammo. But how to weaponize it? And then it came to her: Juan Carlos, the exterminator. But first, she needed to confer with Brod about the guy's immigration status. He set to work immediately.

"Lucia," Wanda said to her maid the next day, walking into the kitchen. "Could you have your uncle come over right away? I want to make sure that none of those ghastly little mice have staged a comeback. And, there's something else I would very much like to discuss with him. Again, hush-hush, and all that. *Comprende?*"

Just over an hour later, Juan Carlos was at the door. After making the rounds, he pronounced the apartment rodent free.

"Well isn't that lovely?" Wanda said. "Now, Lucia, as I mentioned, I have something to ask your uncle. You will translate, yes?"

"*Si*. Of course."

"Good. Please ask him if he ever treats for bedbugs."

"We have bedbugs? *Ay, dios mio!*"

"Don't be a fool. Of course we don't. Just ask him."

Lucia did, and Wanda watched as he nodded his head.

"He says that lots of people around here have them," Lucia translated. "He won't say who, though everybody else asks him, all the bloody time. He knows how to keep out of trouble."

"Excellent. Now, can he capture some of them, alive? Like, maybe a hundred or so?"

Lucia, completely startled, stared at her boss. Then she asked the question of her uncle, who did the same.

"But why, Mrs. Wanda? We both would like to know."

"I want him to collect them in a small jar from a client's place. Then, on New Year's Eve day, while I take Mrs. Bradbury out for a nice nerve-calming lunch before her party, I want him to go to her apartment and tell your cousin Rosalinda that he is there for a routine inspection. But he mustn't tell her the real reason he's there."

"And what is that? I'm not sure I want to know."

"You're smart enough to figure it out. He releases them, of course. In Mrs. Bradbury's cloakroom."

Juan Carlos did not understand much, but he sensed enough to be worried. *"Esto no es bueno, si?"* he entreated his niece.

"He can't do that! It's wrong! And it will ruin his business if it ever gets out."

"So will deportation," Wanda said with unsurpassed indifference. "I had his immigration status checked. He has no choice."

Lucia nervously explained the predicament to Juan Carlos, who looked petrified, but reluctantly nodded.

"Good," Wanda said. "And Lucia dear, you are not to tweet a peep about this to anybody. Understand? Otherwise, it's ICE-time, baby, for your sweet little *tio* here."

On New Year's Eve morning, Megan, now just more than a month away from her due date, waddled into the car with Dimitri and down to Martha's place. There, she helped receive last-minute deliveries, sort out an entire truckload of exotic blooms with the florist, arrange the champagne in ice buckets, and festooned the place with balloons, streamers and goofy party hats that Martha had deemed "irresistibly adorable." Everything was done except for the food by the time they left for lunch with Wanda and Beverly.

Despite her bloated fatigue, Megan was genuinely excited about a big, festive holiday party. Christmas Eve at the Bainbridge home had been a dark and solemn affair. It was, after all, the third anniversary of Rex's dear parents' demise. The night demanded respect and reflection. Megan could hardly object. In fact, much to her own surprise, she suggested they attend Midnight

Mass, at St. Thomas Church, to pray for their souls. Rex was moved by the offer, like a lost little boy.

Megan was touched by such sentiment, but she was also uneasy. Those Ukrainian goons had been coming around a lot lately. And now, on New Year's Eve, shortly before Martha's party, here they were again, sitting with Rex in his office, yelling and pointing at something on the computer screen. When they looked up and saw her, Rex closed the door.

It didn't help matters that he upstaged her at Martha's, all smashing in his smokey-azure Hugo Boss tux. In contrast, Megan's silver-and-white satin maternity gown made her look like window dressing at some faded-glory resort up in the Catskills.

By the time they arrived, Martha's place was hopping. All the usual suspects were there, though no sign of Chevy Chase. Wanda had slipped in, unnoticed - and coatless.

And what a swell party it was. Martha, it turned out, was an adept hostess. The champers flowed, the exquisite food was devoured as if nobody had eaten all year, laughter and, yes, quite a bit of gaiety, (those boys simply loved Mrs. Bradbury) filled the air. Martha even managed to get a frolicsome conga line going at one point, something not seen on upper Fifth Avenue since MGM musicals had gone out of vogue.

At midnight, after the balloons fell and everyone stole their first kiss of the year, a ten-piece orchestra emerged through the swinging kitchen doors and began tooting out big-band standards, from Nelson Riddle to Cab Calloway. It was Martha's surprise of the evening, (not even Megan knew), and it was an enormous hit.

They could have danced all night, but they didn't. Megan and Rex were the first to leave, around one. By two thirty, the last guests retrieved their coats from Rosalinda in the cloakroom, as an exhausted but triumphant Martha plopped down alone on her salon sofa, and promptly passed out.

———————

"THE GLEANER"

By Jamal Dix – January 3, 2019

"Itchy Itchy; Scratchy Scratchy"

First, Trump's Doral Resort in Miami, and now this.

Some of Gotham's better-known citizens, The Gleaner *knows first-hand, unfortunately, because he is one of them, have woken up these past few days covered in big, red, itchy welts. Are we on the precipice of some alarming new social disease, one might fairly ask? No, for better or worse, we are not.*

It did not take long for all those affected to put two and two together.

"Everyone was at the same place at the same time," as one cortisone-covered courtesan aptly observed. "We were all at Martha Bradbury's apartment. And we all went home with some rather unexpected swag."

Bedbugs.

It happened at an otherwise charmingly festive New Year's Eve celebration on Fifth Avenue in the Mid-Fifties, just steps away, somewhat humor-ously when you think about it, from Trump Tower. Martha Bradbury, as we know, is a member of the revered cult of Mrs. Beverly Gansevoort-Stein, the socialite who will live in eternity for hosting the now-notorious gender-reveal party for Megan Bainbridge last October, at which an oversized cake disgorged its gooey contents upon all the swells gathered for the occasion. (It's a girl, as you may recall).

Martha Bradbury has always remained somewhat of an enigma in Our Town since her arrival here about five years ago from Colorado, where her husband Chuck, a Western hemp tycoon, was tragically killed in a work-related accident. No one seems familiar with the details.

Now, I know Martha. She really is, as they say, "the nice one" in her little group. I truly like her. I believe that most everyone does. Or, that is, did. By my latest count, at least 23 merrymakers went home that night with the little hitch-hikers in tow. My own apartment is choking with the buggers, and I've been forced to decamp to the relative comfort of a suite at the Hudson, pending proper extermination.

The total bill will be astronomical, of course. Not only for all the freezing, fumigation and mountains of laundry that must be purged in boiling baths, but the lawsuits. A handful of civil complaints have already been announced, though I certainly have no intention of doing so. Itch happens.

But pity poor Martha. I have it on good authority that her apartment will be listed today, after a thorough treatment protocol of course (this sort of thing gets around fast in real estate circles) and she has already made arrangements to promptly return to her native Colorado. The Hemp Widow, alas, did not return any of The Gleaner's calls. But I hope we can all wish her a fond adieu and the best of luck in the next, hopefully blood-sucking-free chapter of her life. Despite the curses hurled her way, she deserves nothing less, IMHO.

Of course, everyone was rightly flummoxed at how the famously meticulous Mrs. Bradbury could have conceivably overlooked such a pernicious infestation of her nest. I suspect we shall never know. But there remains another mysterious question to ponder: What sort of unspeakable pox has been cast down upon this celebrated clique of Upper East ladies?"

Chapter 16

The Circle of Wife

After the reveal party hysteria, Megan heroically fought off all attempts by the ladies to throw a lavish baby shower. Besides, she was devastated by the loss of her friend, Martha, who had literally vanished overnight. Megan had no idea how to even contact her, something she desperately wanted to do. Having to move out for four days while the apartment was de-bedbugged was surprisingly difficult, given that they stayed at The Plaza, where Megan spent time in the lobby gazing at Hillary Knight's whimsical portrait of her precocious childhood heroine, Eloise: Just like Megan, with no mother around, and precious few friends. Maybe she should get a pug and a little turtle, she brooded.

The old Megan would have scoffed at such luxuriant self-pity, she knew. But she really just wanted to be home, in her penthouse. Outside her grand-hotel window, the dark January sky hung low in icy gloom. Megan was emotionally and physically spent. Was there such a thing, she wondered, as *pre*-partum depression?

Back at home, on the other hand, Rex was being attentive, enough, though hardly amorous. Megan understood why. Did anyone really want to fuck a zamboni? Much of this final stretch was spent lying down. As the baby kicked her insides with alarming ferocity, Megan passed the daylight hours mostly alone, bingeing on Netflix and waiting for Rex to come home with green pistachio gelato, her latest addiction, which recently had supplanted ultra-spicy kimchi pancakes ordered from Little Korea, on West 35th St. Occasionally, Brigit or Celia stopped by, and even Beverly and Wanda made a date to come over and pay their respects. They arrived with Tony, pushing a luggage cart filled with baby presents.

The gifts. They just didn't stop. Megan had no idea where it would all *go*, even in this enormous palace. The nursery was already brimming with all the luxuries that any newborn millionaire could need. And then it hit her. Although she toyed with the idea of returning a bunch of it and sending the proceeds home, she decided to donate as much of the surplus as possible to the Safe Harbor volunteer program.

The most extravagant and, to Megan, touching present was a silver-and-gold brooch, sent by Stroganoff. The stunning piece of jewelry had arrived with a hand-written card, explaining how it had belonged to his grandmother. It was a Christmas gift, he explained, from her employer, Tsarina Alexandra, "just before the Bolsheviks pumped her full of bullets from their nickel-finished Smith & Wesson Schofield revolvers."

"My Grandmother was very beautiful lady, inside and out," he wrote. "So are you. So will be your daughter. I hope she cherishes it, as I do. All best to you in this crazy world. Alexi."

It heartened Megan, but her cheeriness would not last long. That night, she asked Rex if he would fly her family in for the big day.

"What for?"

"Because I'd really like them to be here. And I can't afford it."

He grimaced as he looked at her. "First class?"

"Of course not. Rex, please? It would mean so much to me."

"The Mexican kid, too?"

"Yes. His name is Carlitos."

"Look. I gave them money. And I told you: that was it. I'll lend you the airfare."

Megan was floored. "Great," she said, frowning. "I'll pay you back out of my allowance."

"You don't have a fucking allowance," he grumbled.

"Exactly."

When Megan's mom and the boys arrived, all giddy with excitement and bearing gifts from Target, the overwhelming wave of love and tears rallied her. She even got out of bed and dressed for the occasion, assisted by young Gabriella, who didn't seem to be sharing in the general festive atmosphere of the house. Megan went to the kitchen to ask Madame Duchamp to prepare her family's favorite dinner: Lasagna with sweet Italian sausage and a nice chopped salad with French dressing. Duchamp had no idea what French dressing was, but promised to do a thorough Google search on the matter.

It was a nice evening. Even Rex was not unpleasant. Maureen, Todd and Carlitos, gulping down their lasagna and celebratory champagne, were beside themselves with content. "So guys," Megan said. "How's it going with the startup plans? Any progress?"

"It's tough out there," Todd said, looking defeated. "Everything costs so much: kitchen rental, equipment, staffing, delivery truck. Hell, even the knives are a fortune."

"And no one will give us a loan," Carlitos frowned. "The banks won't even talk to us, and we don't really know any investors." Maureen looked at Megan, and then ever so discreetly nodded toward Rex.

"Did you hear that, Rex?" Megan said. "Todd and Carlitos want to go into business. A catering company. Isn't that great?"

"You don't say?" Rex asked, smiling but obviously aware of what was coming.

"I do say! And I also say they are damn talented. You know that. Some of your friends are still talking about the Mexican dinner. They loved it. And they don't love anything."

"Perhaps the boys could sit down with you to pick your brilliant brain a little," Maureen suggested.

"Or," Megan cut in, "it might be nice to invest directly in the future well-being of your family, no?"

"We could meet, guys." Rex said, a bit non-committedly. "Do you have a comprehensive business plan with you?"

Todd and Carlitos exchanged worried glances. "Um, we're putting the final touches on it," Todd said. "It's not quite ready for primetime."

"Alright, let me know when it's done. It's good not to rush these things. You have to cram a lot into them, you know. Data, projections, market analysis."

"Yes. The market analysis," Carlitos said unsteadily. "We're still working on that part."

Megan knew they were clueless. "Well?" she asked Rex, "What would you say are the most important components of a really good business plan?"

"Jeez, where to begin?" Rex sighed. "There's the Mission Statement, of course. Give me the big idea. Why do you matter? Why do you even want to *exist*?"

"Well," Maureen said. "That sounds a bit harsh."

"When people ask other people for their money, the people being asked tend to be that way," Rex said. "I'm sure you've seen *Shark Tank*."

"Of course," Maureen said. "But I thought we were family."

"We are. Which makes those questions even more important. Lending to family can be, well, problematic."

"So, what else do you look for?" Megan asked, desperate to move along.

"A Product/Service Summary, Market Opportunity Summary, a Traction Summary…"

"Traction?" Todd asked.

"Yeah. You need to highlight some of your biggest achievements to date, and tell me how they would build the foundation for your future success."

"That's what I thought," Todd said.

"Then there's all the usual stuff. Market overview, product description, revenue and operating models, marketing and sales strategy, cash-flow statement, analysis of the competition, customer definition and acquisition, an annotated description of your complete management team, and your total funding and financials."

"Right," Todd said. "Financials."

This channel needed changing, Megan realized. "I have an announcement!" she said. "We've settled on a name. It wasn't easy."

"We almost made it to Cordelia, my grandmother's name, until that whole idea fell apart," Rex frowned.

"I liked it," Megan said. "But in the end, I thought it was a bit too Elizabethan. We all know how *King Lear* ended."

"So…?" Todd said, literally on the edge of his seat.

"Yeah! *So?*" Maureen asked.

"We're naming her after you, mom. Maureen."

"Oh my God!" she cried. "I can't believe it! Really?"

"Really," Rex said. "I just hope the kid gets here before we change our mind. Again."

"I love it!" It was Todd. "Maureen Bainbridge. If that's not a classic movie-star name, I don't know what is. I can see her playing Shia LaBeouf's daughter one day, in a heartfelt drama about a struggling family."

"No!" Carlitos said. "Jake Gyllenhaal. Even better."

"Deal. Get me central casting!"

The next afternoon, Megan's water broke, two days earlier than expected, and she went into labor. She was calm, but Rex was a mess, instantly devolving into a whimpering heap of helplessness. Maureen took over, as though she had grown up on Fifth Avenue. "Todd, tell Dimitri to bring around the car. Carlitos, have Gabriella come in right away and help Megan get up and get dressed. And Rex, go have a really big glass of bourbon and sit down. You look seasick. I'll call the hospital. Now, battle-stations, everyone!"

Baby Maureen was born six pounds, ten ounces, at precisely 8:00PM. Rex's self-appointed task had been to video the miracle. But he was still queasy, and now shaking like a paint mixer at True Value. He pulled out his iPhone, fumbled to hit play, and then, as the baby's head began emerging, passed out stone cold. The phone flew through the air and onto Megan's heaving chest. As the others went to help Rex, Megan cried "Oh fuck it," picked the thing up, pointed it at her vagina, and proceeded to record the great blessing herself.

"It's something we can tell our grandkids," she laughed later.

Megan was quickly back on her feet. She mostly wanted to play with Maureen, but she needed some adult time, too. Brigit took her for her first dinner out, an Indian place on Lexington in the Twenties, in "Curry Hill," and Beverly insisted on hosting a tea party celebration for the newborn, only this time, she said, "the cakes will be miniature, and of the non-fulminant variety."

The little gathering went reasonably well, until talk turned to "the help," in this case, a governess.

"What are you going with?" Jackie asked. "West Indian, or Scandinavian? There's Irish, too, I suppose. But they always end up sleeping with the husbands. Trust me."

The ladies gasped at Jackie's let-slip admission. Nobody had heard this before. Jackie looked around frantically, muttering at her own indiscretion. "Oops," she stammered. "Never mind."

"But Megan," Beverly said, "you still haven't answered the question."

"I'm going with no one. No governess, no nanny. *Je suis* the au pair."

"You can't be serious!" Jenna demanded, semi-scandalized. "What, you're going to push the damn stroller around the park, all by yourself?"

"What if anyone sees you?" Beverly said in alarm. "What will they say?"

"They'll probably say I am a deeply devoted parent. Who loves her baby girl very much. People push strollers all the time back in Michigan. It's no big whoop."

"Well I think it's sweet," Jackie said, in a futile attempt, perhaps, to fill the departed Martha's "nice" shoes. "A bit chilly this time of year, but such is a mother's love!"

"Why thank you," Megan said.

"You're welcome. Say, you and Rex are coming to my big opening this Saturday, right?"

"We wouldn't miss it," Megan said, simultaneously praying for any legitimate excuse to blow it off.

As these things go, the opening of Green Acres, "A Farm-to-Table Emporium," really wasn't that awful, despite the crowded conditions, the straw bales everywhere, and the country-western band Jackie hired to tie in with the farm theme, Virgil and the Virginians. It was all "a bit *Hee Haw*," most people concurred behind her back.

267

As Jamal Dix later noted, the VIP list, apart from regulars like Beverly, Wanda, the Bainbridges, Thaddeus Pepper (and his latest squeeze, soap opera vixen Veronica LaSalle), included Joe Scarborough ("a friend of the family's"), Dennis Rodman, Peggy Noonan, the CFO of Yahoo, Hugh Jackman's personal trainer, the actress who plays Flo on the Progressive Insurance commercials, Ralph Lauren's niece and "somebody-or-other" from *The Book of Mormon.*

Megan was surprised but happy to see Tony there, with his cocoa-butter eyes and gleaming smile. "One of the bartenders called in sick. On opening night. Can you believe that crap?" he said. "So the chef here asked my uncle if I could fill in. It's actually pretty fun. You wouldn't believe how many of these people order triples."

"Yes," Megan said, "I would."

"So, how's the baby girl?"

"I can't believe how much I love her. It's crazy magic."

"I get it. Let me know if I can ever do anything to help out. I'm pretty crazy about that little bunny myself."

Jackie had seated Megan at a prominent table, next to Celia. Rex, meanwhile, had asked to eat next to Scarborough, who was interested in some tungsten holdings Rex was managing in Uzbekistan.

Megan was relieved to be with Celia, her only real female friend left in town, apart from Brigit, who was conspicuously not invited.

"How's life in the birdcage?" Celia asked. "Gilded much?"

"It's a fucking trip. every moment of it. These people."

268

"You know, Megan. If you wanted to write about your experiences, it might be of interest to *Wow!* Everyone wants to devour the comic foibles of our most celebrated citizens."

"I could never, Celia! You know that. Much as I might want to, my persona would instantly become non-grata."

"Well, it's just something to keep under your hat," Celia said. "Just in case the time ever comes. Which of course I hope it won't."

Between the first course - "Wood-fired Woodstock pork belly and toasted chestnuts, with a peach-cherry chutney from Underwood Farms of Hudson Valley" ($23.50, but on-the-house tonight, naturally) and the main course of "Amish-bred game hens from Lancaster County, raised exclusively on wild dandelions and organic grubs, with Long Island duck pate under candied Jersey persimmons, and roasted South Bronx community garden hothouse Brussel sprouts in a hollandaise drizzle, ($52.00)". Tony approached the table.

"Megan?" he asked rather formally, but with an expression of good-humored eagerness. "Might I have a word with you?"

"Sure. What's up?"

"In private, if you don't mind. I think you'll like this. You're not gonna believe what Jackie is up to."

"You see?" Celia whispered conspiratorially. "You, my friend, have inside sources. Roll with it."

Megan excused herself and followed Tony to the hallway outside the unisex restrooms. "I'm on my break," he said. "And I just went out back. For a smoke."

"You *smoke?*" Megan looked a bit crestfallen.

"Sometimes, but that's not important right now. When I put out the cigarette, I didn't know where to toss the butt. So I opened the dumpster lid, and...."

"And?"

"And I found this." Tony pulled a crumpled wad of cellophane from his apron pocket. On it was a label, with the blue-white-and-gold logo of Perdue Chicken. Tony grinned at Megan. "There's a whole bunch of them."

"Oh my God! You're kidding me! What a total fraud! Not that I'm surprised." And then, "There must be more stuff like this in the dumpster. Got time to go have a look with me?"

"Yes. But not much," Tony said, looking at his watch.

They snuck out back, cell phones alit, and peered inside the trash. It was filled with boxes, jars and cans of wholesale restaurant supply-chain products. The "Woodstock" pork bellies were actually from crates of Oscar Mayer Smoked Bacon Bits ("No artificial flavors!" the label assured). The peach-cherry chutney had apparently sprung from liter-sized jars of Smucker's, the Brussel sprouts were Green Giant, and the "hollandaise drizzle" was ladled out of five-gallon buckets manufactured by Knorr Foods/Unilever USA.

They snapped photos of everything. "Hey Tony," Megan whispered. "This is our little secret. For now. Okay?"

"As if you had to ask. This is leverage. I love leverage."

Now shivering in the mid-winter night, they went back in. Megan sat down next to Celia, who leaned over and whispered, "I hope it was good."

"It was. You have no idea. But you might want to skip the hollandaise."

A few days later, Celia called Megan with big news. "I've had a new job offer, and I don't see how I can't take it," she said.

"Celia! That's amazing! I'm so happy for you! Where?"

"At Tatler. They need a new executive editor."

"What's Tatler?"

"You know, that poofy English rag that caters to what's left of the aristocracy over there."

"Over there?"

"In London, of course. I leave in two weeks. The salary is ridiculous."

"Oh no! Please! You can't leave me in this madhouse."

"I'll miss you Megan. Really. But you never know. I might need some good freelancers back here in Manhattan. Can I keep you in my virtual Rolodex?"

"I hope you will. I'm happy for you. But I'm also really bummed. For me."

The following weeks settled into something of a routine: Baby yoga with Maureen, working from home on new Safe Harbor initiatives, sitting for interviews and photo shoots with media arranged by Claudia Bing, Wanda's publicist, trying to help Todd and Carlitos with edits to their business plan, and the occasional night out with Rex, before the obligatory 2AM feeding and diaper change.

By mid-March, it was warm enough to start taking Maureen to the park in her Swiss-engineered *kinderwagen*, a gift from Jackie. Megan adored these moments, and often stopped to sit down and chat with other new moms, exchanging parenting tips and good-natured grievances.

One particularly sunny morning, they went out, happily greeting Tony on the way. They entered the park and began walking west. Then, quite unexpectedly, droopy clouds gathered in the sky as a north wind tore straight down the Hudson. Megan only had a light jacket, and Maureen was twitchy in the chill. They needed to go back for more cover.

"Rex?" she shouted, entering the foyer. "Suddenly it's freezing out there! We need some wraps." Silence. "Rex? Where are you, honey?" She walked down the main hallway, Maureen cradled in her arms. "Rex?"

And then she heard the panting.

"Fuck," whispered Megan, who looked at the baby, put a finger over her lips, and said, "Sorry. Mommy said a bad word." She peered into the master bedroom, where Rex was sitting on the edge of the bed, his head turned skyward, eyes closed, his burnt-umber wool trousers dropped to his ankles on the floor, where Gabriella was kneeling, bobbing her head up and down.

Megan cleared her throat, loudly. "You two," she declared calmly, "are trash." She turned and ran back down the hallway.

It happened just as Rex was coming. He pulled out of Gabriela's mouth, shoved her aside and leapt to his feet, without noticing the viscous filament of semen dangling below.

"Honey! Wait! I can explain!" Rex cried as he ran after Megan, instantly realizing how totally stupid that sounded. He wobbled down the hallway like a giant penguin, his pants still around his ankles like shackles. Megan was out the door before a gob of Rex's spooge plopped onto the floor, causing him to slip on the polished marble tile, smack his forehead on a bronze bust of Sir Edmund Hillary, and tumble like a rag doll.

Chapter 17

~ "ⱺⱷⱺ" ~

A Not-So-Merry Megan

Megan exited the elevator and tore out of the lobby, not even looking at Tony this time. Shit, she thought, I forgot our coats. Her head reeling – how could he be such a creep? – and tears streaming down her face, she hurried toward Madison, where there was a warm and cozy little Hungarian place, with great coffee and killer pastry. "I need pastry," she said to Maureen.

Megan sat morosely at a corner table, trembling in shock. Even the *Somlói Galuska*, made of cocoa and walnut sponge cake, with chocolate, vanilla and rum-orange sauce, smothered in freshly whipped cream, did little to calm her. As she began crying again, she noticed other patrons looking at her. What are you staring at? She wanted to blurt out. *What*? Never seen a woman eating pastry while her husband's getting a blowjob from the maid a block away in his penthouse?

Instead, she called Brigit.

"Megan! What is it? You sound horrible."

"That's because I am."

"Oh God, What happened? What did he do?"

"Rex? How did you know that?"

"Unlucky guess, I guess."

Megan explained the whole sorry tale.

"What a royal asswipe!" Brigit said. "That fucking cocksucker!"

"Well, in this case, cocksuck*ee*," Megan said, trying to laugh, without success. Listen, Brigit? Can you come get us? I feel so helpless right now."

"Of course. I'll tell Jamal there's a family emergency. Cuz you're family, honey, and this is an emergency."

About fifteen minutes later, Brigit walked in the café door, ran to Megan's table and hugged her wildly, rocking her back and forth like a baby lamb. "I'm so sorry." she said.

"Me too. Hey, can we come stay with you for a little bit, until I can clear my head and figure everything out?"

"I have to ask Bill. He'll say yes. I'll make sure. But you'll need some things. C'mon, I'll go over there with you. If Rex shows his shitty-assed face, I'll punch it to hamburger."

Back at the building, there were three TV News vans, an EMS truck and two NYPD squad cars out front. Megan spotted Tony, standing by the door, looking pale.

"What happened?" Megan asked.

"I don't know how to tell you this."

"What do you mean?"

"Word in the building is that he somehow tripped and fell, and hit his head on a statue," Tony said as paramedics rolled out a covered body on a gurney. "There're some detectives upstairs. I think they want to talk to you."

She went up with Brigit, swimming through a daze. The police were kind and respectful. "We found some semen on the floor where he fell, ma'am" one of them said. "We think he slipped on it. But we need to get our forensics team in here first."

Megan told them everything she knew. "He got up to chase after me, but I had no idea what had happened next."

"Thank you, Mrs. Bainbridge," the detective said. "Here's my card. Please stay in touch. We may have more questions for you at some point."

"Questions? I already told you everything I know."

"Well, until we determine the exact cause of death, and eliminate any kind of foul play."

"Foul play! Are you fucking kidding me? What am I? A suspect?"

"Megan," Brigit said, grabbing her friend's arm. "He was a prick and you caught him getting a hummer. They have to consider everything. So you might watch the tone."

"Tone!? My cheating asshole of a husband slipped on his own jizz and is now dead, and the cops think I did it, and you're worried about *tone?*"

"You're a person of interest, that's all," the detective said. "Right now, we think it was an accident. We just need to make sure."

Megan grabbed some clothes and baby things, and they Ubered up to Brigit's place. Bill was there, bonging, the smoke so thick you could barely discern his bloodshot eyes from across the room.

"Christ, Bill." Brigit yelled. "Baby on board. Air this place out. Now."

Bill went to open a window and switched on the fan, as Megan stepped into the cat-pee hallway with Maureen to wait. A few minutes later, Brigit came out.

"Coast is clear," she said. "There's actual oxygen in the apartment now. But it's freezing." They went into the bedroom and closed the door. "How are you holding up, honey?"

"How do you *think*? Shit, Brigit. What a stupid question." Megan began trembling uncontrollably, as if freezing. Brigit noted that the room was warming up quickly.

"It's not cold," Megan said. "I just feel achy all over my body, like I rolled down an asphalt hill in a bikini. And I'm so damn tired. I could sleep till summer. What is wrong with me? This makes morning sickness seem like a mild case of the sniffles."

"Emotional shock," Brigit said. "I'm so sorry about all this. What a royally fucked up day."

Megan laughed loudly. "When I write my memoir, that will be the title: "What a Royally Fucked Up Day – How I Lost My Husband, Twice, in the Course of an Hour." Brigit decided it was best to just *be* with her friend. Words would come later. Megan rested her head on Brigit's shoulder, let two tears drop from her eyes, and passed out.

Later, Brigit returned with some tea. "Meg's?" she whispered. No luck. Brigit gently shook Megan's arm. Megan sat upright like a cadaver in a cheap horror film and let loose a piercing scream. Bill tore into the room. Maureen, sleeping in a bassinet on the bed, began wailing. Megan, rattled and flustered, looked at her surroundings with heaving breaths.

"My husband is *dead*! He's fucking dead, the fucking mother fucker."

Brigit sat down and threw her arms around Megan. "It's okay. You get to be sad and mad and raging at the world. Let it out. I know how much it must hurt."

Megan picked up Maureen. Eventually, both of them calmed down, though Megan's trembling had returned. "It's just so weird. I mean, I'm not surprised he cheated on me, and yet I'm furious about it. And even though I'm furious, I'm so sad. I'm going to miss him so much. It doesn't make any sense."

"Of course it does. It's so much harder when your partner dies and there are unresolved issues. Some people spend the rest of their lives playing the scene over and over in their head, to make it end in the fairytale fashion they were cheated out of."

"Some fairytale. From the Brothers Grimm. Rated X." Megan paused a moment. "But what you said; it's true. Infidelity is a hard issue to resolve, and I never got the chance. I don't know what would've happened, but I'd like to think I wouldn't have left Rex. It'd be rocky for a while, and I would always have to worry about repeat performances. But I think we'd work it through, don't you?" Brigit nodded.

"And that's what makes this so ridiculously unfathomable. Now, I'll never know." Megan closed her eyes and took another deep breath. "I'm going to stay here tonight, but tomorrow I'd like to go back home. It will be weird. And lonely. But we'll be better off there."

"Of course, honey, we'll take you over and get you settled."

Megan woke up with blurry eyes and a crushing headache. Maureen was crying and wanted her morning feeding. They went into the kitchen, where Brigit and Bill were having eggs, toast and coffee. Megan was not hungry.

"It's all over the news: *The Times, CBS This Morning, Fox & Friends*. And Jamal, of course," Brigit said, handing Megan The *Post*.

"I don't think I can." Megan sat down. "Not before coffee anyway. I knew this was coming. He's been calling and texting, but I'm not answering."

"You really need to read it," Brigit said.

————————————————————

THE GLEANER
"A Death in the Family"
By Jamal Dix – February 25, 2019

This is without question the saddest piece of news I have written in quite some time, though I'm sure you already know.
Yesterday afternoon, an accident was reported at the Fifth Avenue penthouse of Rexford Bainbridge, III. His wife, Megan, was out with their newborn, Maureen, and not home at the time. Instead, the 9/11 call came from one of Rex's housekeepers. Apparently, he had slipped on a polished marble tile in the Grand Hallway, hit his head on a bronze statue, and tumbled to the floor.
The exact cause of death has not been determined, but my police sources

inform me that a corner of his forehead had been crushed in. He'd lost a lot of blood.

Rex, a figure well known to readers of this column for his wealth, looks, youthful glamor, laudable philanthropy and beautiful rags-to-riches bride, was pronounced dead at the scene, according to a brief EMS dispatch issued last night.

"We are devastated beyond recognition," Rex's downstairs neighbor Beverly Gansevoort-Stein told me. "I knew him since he was a little boy, for goodness sake. He used to come down and play with my daughter. He was like a son to me, a constant companion, a closest confidant. And he was a hell of a lot of fun. Rex made people smile. New York just won't be the same without him."

Indeed.

As for the poor young widow, she is not returning my calls and texts. But who can blame her? Married just six months ago – and suddenly with an infant daughter to raise alone – she has other things on her mind. One expects they will be well taken care of by the estate. I wish them both nothing but the best.

Megan looked up from the page. "Well, so far; not so bad," she said.

"Keep reading," Brigit said glumly.

But this is where things get a little, well, icky.

The Gleaner has obtained a copy of the NYPD Report. The accident happened at 12:47 PM, just before the 9/11 call was placed. EMS techs arrived at 12:55 PM. Rex was unconscious, and was pronounced dead at 1:13 PM, after several attempts to stop the bleeding and revive him with CPR.

Megan Bainbridge told the police that she had arrived at the apartment just minutes before the tragedy occurred. She said it had grown cold in the park and she had returned home for warmer clothing. And that's when she heard noises in the master bedroom.

Rex was sitting on the bed, pants around his ankles. A maid was in front of him, on her knees, in flagrante delicto. *I won't say what she was doing, exactly, but the name Monica comes to mind.*

Megan, rightly outraged and shell-shocked, ran out of the apartment with the baby in her arms. Rex got up to chase her, without fully removing his trousers. And that's how it happened. Foul play, at this point, is not suspected, I am told.

No word about funeral arrangements yet, but there will be no lack of mourners, even with this rather salacious twist.

It gives me no joy to report such an inglorious detail. But you were going to find out anyway. People have many weaknesses. This is one of them, especially in this town, it seems. Even so, bad deeds and horrible judgment do not, in my mind, outstrip all the good that was Rexford Bainbridge.

"Oh my God! The police told Jamal all this?"

"No," Brigit said. "You told them. They put it in their report. And those are public record."

"I assumed that information would be kept confidential."

"Don't you ever watch *any* cop shows?" Bill asked.

"I watch PBS. And Rachel. Fuck, Bridge. What do I do now? I'm going to be pitied – *and* the laughing stock of the town – at the same time. I don't think I can handle it."

"Honey, most New Yorkers are more sophisticated than that. Everyone knows it does not reflect badly on a woman. It doesn't make the guy look that great, but they tend to get away with it, especially in the higher circles. I mean, it's practically expected."

"At least Jamal left out the semen part. That was nice."

"Yeah, but it's still in the report," Brigit said.

When they returned to Megan's place, it was overflowing with flowers and handwritten notes of condolence. The expressions of grief and sympathy were genuine. As Brigit had predicted, not one even obliquely referenced oral sex. Megan had forgotten that deep down, somewhere, most New Yorkers, even the richest ones, harbored an actual soul.

Megan was pleased to see Tony there, helping Ramon set vases of flowers on any free surface available. Gabriela had vanished, with neither note nor trace. "I never liked her. None of us did," Ramon said. "We had a little expression around here for her: She's such an asshole that, when other assholes look at her, they say, 'now *there's* an asshole!'"

Megan cracked up. It felt good to laugh. "Thank you for that, Ramon," she said. "It's a bit out of character for you, but it's really funny."

After they settled in, Duchamp prepared a late lunch of grilled cheddar-and-tomato sandwiches and a heaping platter of onion rings for *les femmes américaines*.

"What now?" Brigit asked. "Especially the funeral. And the will."

"I'm sure the ladies want to plan the services. At this point, I'm too exhausted to even think about it. As for the will, Rex's lawyer texted me earlier. Everything needs to go into probate. He said it might take longer than usual."

"Why?

"Something about back taxes. And litigation. My mind is so muddled right now."

That night at the apartment, the first since Rex died, was haunting. After

Brigit and Bill left, Megan had never felt so alone. For the first time since arriving in New York, she seriously considered going home.

Two days later, Devonshire called. "We need to discuss the probate. I'd like to come over. Are you free at two?"

Whatever it was, it wasn't good. Megan waited nervously for the doorbell to ring, which it did precisely at two. They went into the salon, where Ramon brought tea and warm brioche with whipped butter and jam.

"It's my mid-afternoon comfort food," Megan said with a nervous smile. "I have a feeling it's going to come in handy. How bad is it, Mr. Devonshire?"

"Please. Call me Barton, or Bart. Now, as executor of the will, I must deliver some bleak news. You see, Rexford had been dealing with a number of financial challenges."

"Challenges? As in plural?"

"We've managed to keep it out of the papers. Your husband was under investigation for tax fraud. Apparently, he kept two sets of books, something we never knew, until we found the actual ledgers in his safe deposit account."

"You went in there? Without my knowledge?"

"It was stipulated in his will." Devonshire handed her a copy of the document. Megan realized she had never seen it before. "IRS placed a lien on the estate for back taxes, fines, penalties and interest. Quite a bit. If he were still alive, he might be facing prison time."

"My God. So, how much are we talking?"

"Twenty-seven million and change. It will be direct-deposited into the U.S.

Treasury as soon as probate ends."

"But there's still plenty left over."

"There is. Except..."

"Now what?"

Devonshire explained that Rex was "overextended" in several investment schemes, especially the startups. When he couldn't raise the capital he needed from individuals, he began borrowing from a number of banks. "Chinese, mostly. Now that he's gone, they want it back."

"And how much will that be?"

"Maybe another fifteen or twenty. They're filing a claim against the estate, which will be taken out after probate." He paused a moment and frowned. "There's been one other development, and it's troubling. It might involve criminal activity."

"By Rex?"

"I'm afraid so. About a year ago, he began meeting at his home office with some oligarchs from Ukraine with close ties to its Mini-Putin dictator, Petro Poroshenko, and the best mafioso thugs in Kiev. A very unsavory bunch. I warned him to head for the hills."

"Those creeps. They were here, a lot. I *knew* something was up. Something not good."

Rex wanted to start a U.S. company that would import Ukrainian steel, at a discount to make up for Trump's tariffs. The Ukrainians would essentially underwrite their own attempt to increase U.S. market share. But Rex needed a blessing from Kiev. And money.

"The Ukrainians kicked in seven million, but it all belly-flopped, a victim of official corruption over there, and the Trump Administration's apparent loathing of all things Ukrainian over here. The import permits weren't, let's say, processed promptly. I don't know why Rex didn't see it coming."

"But how is that criminal? It was a bad business deal. That's not a felony."

"No. But money laundering is."

"What?"

"Three months ago, the FBI opened an investigation. They suspect the Ukrainians had blackmailed Rexford into creating a shell company in Delaware, where Central Asian drug money could be funneled. It was either that, or he, you, and the unborn baby would probably cease to exist. I understand that the feds were monitoring his emails and texts."

"But...even if they have evidence, you can't prosecute a dead man."

"True. But if the government believes any of his assets were gained by or *used in* the commission of a crime, it can seize them. Now, there's one more thing. We discovered that Rexford's parents set up a trust fund, for any future grandchildren."

"That's amazing!" Megan said, her eyes lighting up for the first time.

"Well, it would be, if those Swiss villagers hadn't gotten their greedy hands on it. You know, after that night at Lake Lucerne."

Megan took a bite of brioche and sipped some tea, trying to process everything. She stared at the lawyer. "Why didn't Rex tell me any of this?"

"He was adamant that you not find out."

"But why?"

"I imagine he didn't want to stress you, especially when you were pregnant."

Megan again felt torn. She was furious that Rex had been so reckless, without saying a word. But damn, he was trying to protect her. "Tell me, where is this money supposed to come from?"

"Huge swaths of investments will be liquidated. The lion's share is with Stroganoff. I urged Rexford to diversify, but that Russian was making him a forty-percent annual return. It will take a while to sort it out."

"What do I do in the meantime?"

"About what?"

"About living, Bart."

"All accounts and credit cards are frozen. You'll have to live off your own assets, for now."

"My *assets*?" Megan laughed. "Everything was in his name! All I have is my checking account. With a few hundred dollars. I haven't exactly been working, you know."

"We'll figure it out. You won't starve. There's just one other matter: funeral expenses."

"How do I pull that off?"

"They're covered." Rex held a $50,000 life insurance policy, and his will stipulated that it be spent on "final expenses," the lawyer explained. Rex didn't want anyone else to be burdened with such matters.

"So, there's nothing there for me - for now."

"My hands are tied." Megan escorted Devonshire to the door. "Why don't you just *borrow* money from your family? It seems rather obvious to me."

"That's not going to happen," Megan said.

"Really? That cheap? Huh."

She broke into tears. "No. That poor."

"I see. Tell you what. Fly them here for the funeral, and we'll list it as an expense."

After he left, Megan went to inform the staff, gently, that they were being dismissed. They could stay as long as needed, but she couldn't pay for salaries or food. She grew teary as she hugged Ramon, and then Duchamp. "I'm going to miss you, sweet Dominique," she said. "And your cooking. *Très beaucoup.*"

Megan barely got out of bed the next two days, ignoring calls and texts from the ladies, the media and actual well-wishers. She spoke only to Brigit, Celia, so far away in London, and, of course, her mom, Todd and Carlitos, who were arranging to swap shifts at work to come to the funeral.

The funeral. Megan had no idea where to begin. She could confer with Beverly, Wanda and the others, but she didn't have the stamina to handle their comically pompous bullshit and unyieldingly demanding "tastes." Megan wanted straight-to-the point simplicity and solemn dignity. She would not turn this into the highest-profile, most celebrity-packed and glitzily catered event of the season. No, the ladies were *right* out.

Megan needed a funeral director. But who? Brigit was clueless, and even Celia offered scant counsel. "All the people I know in New York are under forty, and still very much with a pulse," she said. "What about Jamal? He knows everybody."

At first, Megan scoffed. Why should she speak to that little shit-weasel? But she knew there was no one else to ask. "I have the perfect guy," he told her. "Frederick Montague, of Montague and Pierce. They're masters at sending people off in understated style."

The next day, Frederick, a tall sapling of a gentleman in his sixties, with gaunt cheeks, grey eyes and matching vintage three-piece suit, came over for lunch. Megan's family had arrived that morning to help make decisions. Todd and Carlitos prepared Sicilian pizza and caesar salad, because, according to Todd, "it's tasty, simple…and cheap." Megan served at the dining room table, where Anderson Cooper had once cracked everyone up with his fart jokes. That seemed like lifetimes ago. And in some ways, it was.

"Mr. Devonshire has provided us with instructions that Mr. Bainbridge left behind," Frederick said. "There aren't many, so it's up to us to fill in the blanks."

Rex wanted the service to be at Saint Thomas, which came as no surprise, with Canon Arthur Chadwick presiding. What did startle everyone was his stipulation that there be no members of the working media inside, save for invited guests in that profession. "According to Mr. Devonshire," Frederick explained, "Mr. Bainbridge had become rather wary of live media coverage, given the cake incident and all."

Rex wanted to be buried in The Bronx's monumental Woodlawn Cemetery, where his parents and WASPy ancestral family were interred. For music at the reception, he'd requested a string quartet to play selected sonatas from Haydn and Beethoven. For the actual funeral, however, he wanted something decidedly more contemporary.

"Mr. Bainbridge decreed that three specific songs be performed live at his church service," Frederick continued. "They are, 'Wake Me Up Before You Go-Go,' by Wham!, 'Another One Bites The Dust,' by Queen, and the Pet Shop Boys' 'What Have I Done To Deserve This?' Forgive my indiscretion, but I guess it's true what they said about him? In the papers?"

"That he had a wicked sense of humor?" Megan asked. "Yeah, he was a regular riot, our Rexford. A nonstop laugh-track."

"Why those songs?" Carlitos asked. "Do you know?"

"Apparently, they were emblematic anthems from his days as a club kid, which Mr. Brainbridge liked to call the Ecstasy Years. Now, there's one more thing, he wanted someone well-known to perform, and he provided a list of his top-five choices, in order, beginning with Lady Gaga."

"Holy cow," Todd said. "Do you know how to contact her, Megs?"

Megan said the star had sent her white orchids and a condolence card. The note was very moving. And, she included her email, in case she could be of any help. "How gracious was that? I think she meant it. So who knows? Stranger things have happened. Trust me."

"I've booked Saint Thomas for Tuesday at ten, and the Canon is available," Frederick said. "What about food, for the reception?"

"I thought it would be nice to have my staff prepare it, along with Todd and Carlitos here, for a fee. It would be better than some stuffy Madison Avenue caterer. And cheaper."

"Fine. Which leads us to costs. We're working with fifty thousand, correct?"

"Well, forty-nine," Megan said. "We already paid for their airfare."

"It will be tight. The better plots at Woodlawn, in the Bainbridge family's section, begin around twenty thousand; or nearly half our budget. And, Canon Chadwick's Suggested Contribution is not cheap."

After Frederick left, there was a knock at the door. It was Beverly and Wanda, who pushed their way in, trailed by Jackie and Jenna.

"What's this?" Megan asked. "An intervention by the concern-troll brigade? Because, how creepy."

"You wouldn't respond to our calls or texts," Beverly said as she barreled toward the salon and plopped down on a divan, folding her arms tightly.

"It was quite rude of you, sweetie," Wanda added. "What choice did you leave us, really?"

"I left you the choice of leaving me the hell alone. You know, like I wanted."

"That would have been entirely out of the question," Beverly said. "We care, you see."

"You are, after all, the talk of the entire town!" Jenna said. "Not to mention half of LA, and the better parts of London."

"A victim of his own ejaculate." Jackie added. "They're calling it the blowjob heard round the world."

"Ladies! Where are your manners?" Beverly said. "A man is dead. Very, very dead! And he was our friend."

"Yeah," Jenna said. "A friend who would be with us today, if not for the fellatio part."

"You must miss him ever so terribly, regardless. And we are so sorry," Wanda said, walking over to Megan and giving her arm a gentle squeeze. "Though it was a terribly unfortunate little detail, that. Everyone says so."

"Well you tell *everyone* that Rex was a fucking prick for what he did."

"We can't do that," Beverly said. "We loved Rexford. We still do."

"He had style. He had grace. He had money, all over the place," Jackie sighed, looking at Megan. "At least you'll be inheriting one of those things. It should go a long way. Back in Itchylandy, or wherever."

"Go perform a sexual act on yourself, Jackie," Megan glowered. "Preferably in hell."

"Well, money or not, this whole bloody affair just *sucks*," Wanda said. And then: "Oh Christ, did I say that?"

"Yes. You did," Megan said, with a look that suggested a thousand flying daggers. "You know Wanda, you should pick up some mouthwash on the way home. Because after that, it's going to taste like foot."

Wanda roared with laughter. "Well *played!*"

"Anyway, I don't need any of your condolences. Which is a good thing, because I doubt they were the motivation for your little sojourn up here anyway," Megan said. "I'll get through this without your alleged help. I'm tough. I've survived this city for a year. And any crocodile tears you want to shed, save them for the funeral."

"Yes, regarding that," Beverly said. "What are we doing?"

"*We*, Beverly?"

"Of course, dear! We have so many ideas. Some of them quite brilliant, if you ask me."

"Getting the horse-drawn carriages to the cemetery was mine!" Jenna said.

"To the Bronx?" Megan asked. "That might tie up traffic."

"And I'm inviting Mike Bloomberg to deliver the eulogy," Jackie said. "He went to school with my father. I'm sure we can book him."

"Rex loathed that man," Megan said. "You guys are batting a thousand. Look. Everything is set. The funeral director was just here and I'm in extremely good hands. You will receive invitations for everything. Funeral, burial, reception. Rex would have wanted it that way. Even if I don't."

"How wonderfully frank of you, dear," Beverly said.

"Grieving widows are allowed. Or so I'm told. Especially when their husband died while cheating on them."

"Look," Beverly said, "I know what you're going through. When Mr. Stein passed, I was crushed like a bug. But we had our issues, too. I had a lot to forgive him for. Many, *many* martinis later, I managed to pull it off."

"So, just get liquored up, and stay that way?"

"As long as the vodka is imported, yes." Beverly asked who was handling the guest lists and invitations, noting that she still had the entire database of addresses from the wedding. "Let us carve out at least that piece of it, will you?"

Megan relented. "To be honest, it would really take a load off. And Wanda, no puns this time please."

"I wasn't intending any. But you must admit, that one just oozes possibilities, doesn't it?"

Todd and Carlitos entered the room to see if Megan was ready to discuss the menu. "Guys, I believe you know this little posse: Beverly, Wanda, Jackie and Jenna," she said.

"Yes. We remember you," Carlitos said with a sarcastic grin. "We remember that you did not like the chicken in Coca-Cola. And we remember that you are not very nice ladies."

Megan let rip a loud chuckle. "And you all know our chefs from that night, my brother Todd and his partner Carlitos?"

"Hello boys," Beverly said, pouting.

"One can only hope that the chicken won't be making a repeat performance at the reception," Wanda said. "It won't. Will it?"

"You know, we weren't going to," Todd said. "But now that you bring it up, I think we will. So, 'yes.' Yes is the answer to that particular question."

Megan laughed again. "If you'll excuse me, ladies, I have a reception to plan. Oh, and a superstar to email."

"Do tell!" Beverly said as Megan led her out by the arm.

"You'll find out on Tuesday. Maybe. In the meantime, I just wanted to make you envious. It will bring me great comfort at this terrible time."

Megan returned to the dining room where her mom, carrying Maureen, had joined Todd and Carlitos.

"*Pollo en Coca-Cola.* They hate it, so of course I love it," Megan said as she sat down. "Perfect. What else you guys got that they might hate? And by the way Carlitos, your takedown of those alleged ladies was epic."

"They have some nerve walking around with their rich white noses in the air," he said. "People like that need to be cut down a few notches. Back in my village near Puebla, we have a saying: '*El karma es una chingada, solo si tu eres otra.*'"

"What does that mean?" Maureen asked.

"Roughly translated, I believe it means 'Karma's a bitch, only if you're one, too.'" Megan said. "Am I right?"

"*Si, mi hermana.*"

"It's perfect. Now, what else are we serving?"

Aside from the Mexican chicken, served warm in chafing dishes, there would be a straightforward cold buffet, starting with asparagus wrapped in Italian prosciutto, crudité and toasted Lebanese flatbread with a Greek yogurt-garlic-cucumber dip, and a few platters of imported French cheeses and sausages with baguette slices, plus fried Burmese dumplings, curried yellow potato samosas with spicy cilantro dip, giant bowls of tropical fruit salad, wilted spinach salad with braised ichiban eggplant in a Japanese lime, soy, rice vinegar dressing, orzo salad with seasoned prawns, kalamata olives and fresh Danish feta, and a carving table with angus sirloin in a horseradish crust, brisket simmered slowly overnight in dark Belgian beer, and free-range roast turkey in a guajillo chile glaze.

"And for dessert, lots of little pastries stuffed with fruit, custard, chocolate mousse and what not," Todd added.

"That is dazzling, you guys. Rex would have loved it: American, but not too American."

"What does that even *mean?*" Maureen asked.

"It's a New York thing. Once you cross the river, you're not back in the homeland anymore. Not entirely. You now have one foot in the rest of the world. And you eat accordingly."

Megan rose. "You guys have full run of the kitchen. The staff will be paid to help, and even Duchamp will be at your disposal. Just don't let her snob you into upgrading anything."

Megan picked up Maureen and walked into the study, where she grabbed her iPad and Gaga's card, and began typing.

Dear Ms. Germanotta – Or do you prefer Ms. Gaga? I really wasn't sure.

First, I wish to thank you sincerely for the wonderful flowers and beautiful note you sent at the passing of my dear husband Rexford. He worshiped you, as do I. Your talent is overwhelming. And, your presence at our wedding transformed a magical affair into a fantastical one, so thank you for that as well.

I hope you don't find me impertinent by asking this, but I am fulfilling the final wishes of my beloved. In his will, he requested that three pop ballads be performed live at his funeral, which will be held this Tuesday at Saint Thomas Church at 10:00 am. He also left behind a list of five singers he wanted, in order of preference, and you were, of course, at the top of it.

If you would rather not perform, which I would completely understand, we would, of course, be beyond honored if you could still attend. An invitation is going out today.

Wishing you love and light,

Megan Bainbridge

Megan was wiped out. She brought Maureen back to her mom's lap, went into the bedroom and fell asleep for three hours.

By the time she woke up, the star had responded.

Dearest, Sweetest Megan,

I think our planets have aligned. I had a studio rehearsal scheduled for that morning, but my lead guitarist is out sick. I would be honored to sing. Rex was quite a guy. And he was always very good to me, even back in the early days, when others weren't so much. You must miss him terribly. Meanwhile, I'm dying to know what the three songs are. I will ask my manager to have a grand piano delivered to the church first thing Tuesday morning. Now, please don't forget to send along the playlist.

Lovingly yours,

Gaga

Chapter 18

The Bells of Saint Thomas

Everything went according to schedule, according to plan, and according to the surprising military-style precision of Frederick and his crew. They arranged for an armed private security detail to keep crashers and reporters out of the service, managed to snag four NYPD officers to guard the front door at Megan's building, and even got the Mayor to briefly shut down one lane of the FDR Drive, to allow the funeral procession, projected to be about thirty vehicles, to swiftly make its way up to the Bronx for burial.

For Megan, the service was beyond surreal. Same church. Same guests. Same Canon and boys' choir. Even the same damn paparazzi out on the sidewalk. The only thing missing was the groom – and the happiness.

It was almost impossible to believe that terrifying, exhilarating day had only been seven months before.

Megan sat up front with Maureen and her family, a few of Rex's cousins (whom she barely knew), Brigit and Bill, Celia, who had flown in from London, and several dignitaries including de Blasio and his wife, *The New York Times* Managing Editor Chester Mansfield, Brent Ashby from the Stock Exchange, Anderson Cooper, Gaga (ever the quintessential professional, she had arranged with Frederick to show up at eight with her own tech crew for rehearsal and soundcheck) and right there on the aisle for all to see, Anna Wintour, in her impenetrable dark glasses.

On the other side in front sat Beverly, who refused to look even a few feet away, where her nemesis was sitting (Celia had suggested the devilish seating arrangement to Megan, who loved the idea), her daughter Hillary, Wanda and Trevor, Jackie and Jonathan, Jenna and her date, Hector San Martin, a rising Univision *telenovela* idol and good friend of Thaddeus Pepper's soap-star girlfriend, Veronica LaSalle, both of whom were also in the front pew.

Megan had decided not to speak. She hadn't worked out her inner eulogy yet, so how could she possibly deliver one in public?

The homily, of course, was given by Canon Chadwick, who knew Rex since he was born. The kindly, slightly fey old man told some corny, rather odd stories about Rex's affluent upbringing. "He loved playing *Miami Vice* with his friends, for instance, and even got his mom to order little white suits, a la Don Johnson," he recalled to awkward, smattered sniggering. "Oh, how cute and tough they all looked! In their matching linen slacks and jackets over pastel t-shirts, with their little slip-on loafers and no socks."

Other speakers included Beverly, who had to halt three times while sobbing, the President of the NRDC, who reverently dubbed Rex "A Patron Saint of the Planet," and Dr. Thaddeus M. Pepper, who proved against all odds that only he, even at the most somber of events, could come across as nothing less than a steaming pile of shit-headedness.

"We all loved Rex. And I think we can agree, he was a great guy. Except for when he was a douche. But even then, he was *our* douche," Thad said to abject silence. "Ooh, tough crowd." He went on to talk about Rex's dating prowess, and the gay rumors. "My how the ladies lined up for him, even knowing they might not ever get laid. Old Rex and I always had a good laugh about that one. Because, he was actually very pro-muff."

Thankfully, the lights dimmed, revealing a spotlight on the grand piano. Even for Lady Gaga, it was a roof-raising performance. She camped it up for the Wham! song like a 1980's MTV trooper, surprising everyone by signaling for three young men in black tights to come out and dance around her, all while doing yo-yo tricks.

For her version of "Another One Bites The Dust," the superstar's musical brilliance sparkled like polished silver. She magically conjured those notorious bass lines from the lower keys of her piano, and howled the increasingly urgent lyrics into the mic in a way that would have dazzled even the great Freddy Mercury himself.

And then came the finale. Mild gasps were heard as Gaga rose from the piano bench. "This one would be much better a capella, I realized," she said. It was perhaps the most mesmerizing, stunningly mournful rendition of that already haunting ballad, "What Have I Done To Deserve This," ever performed.

When Gaga got to the chorus, the part that Dusty Springfield so famously sang, she walked over to Megan and gazed at her sweetly:

Since you went away, I've been hanging around, I've been wondering why I'm feeling down. You went away, it should make me feel better, but I don't know, oh. How'm I gonna get through?

Megan smiled back, but that line engulfed her mind. You went away, it should make me feel better, she thought. Lady Gaga knows exactly what I'm going through.

The burial afterward was brief and bitterly cold, with two feet of fresh snow on the ground and gusts hurtling straight down from Quebec, dropping the wind chill to minus five. It was so cold, Megan had to leave Maureen in the heated limousine with the driver.

Arriving back home on Fifth Avenue, Megan, the baby, her mom, the boys, Brigit, Bill and Celia climbed out of the limo and hurried through the frigid air into the warmth and brightness of the lobby at 1080. Megan saw Tony and signaled for the others to take the elevator without her.

"You hangin' in there?" he asked.

"I'm not sure, to be honest. This whole thing has just been so fucking weird. Is it okay to say that?"

"Megan, after all you've been through, it's okay to say any little thing that pops into your mind – totally unfiltered. Enjoy it while you can, though, 'cuz these people won't put up with it for very long." He smiled at her. "For now, consider this your own personal open-season on swearing, saying crazy things, and best of all, insulting people."

"I'm tired, Tony."

"I bet."

"And now I have 120 hungry people coming over. Several of whom I wish would be suddenly devoured by wolves before they got here."

"You want any help? I get off early."

"That's so sweet. Tell you what. When your shift ends, change into your civies and join us. But as my guest, not my footman. Deal?"

300

"Of course, Lady Megan." Tony tipped his Soviet-style hat and bowed politely. "And a most wonderful deal it is."

Upstairs, the penthouse was filled with the homey scent of roasting meats and root vegetables. Megan had thirty minutes before guests started arriving. She went to the kitchen to check on everything. Todd, Carlitos and Madame Duchamp were circling around each other with the efficiency of a finely tuned glockenspiel. She watched in astonishment as they deftly put the finishing flourishes on dish after mouthwatering dish, which were then promptly ferried out to the buffet tables by Ramon and the housekeepers. The aroma of fresh-brewed French roast mingled with the rich buttery smell of Danish pastry, as if from the ovens of Valhalla.

Megan went into her bedroom, fed the baby, and lay down, silently crying as she thought about the Pet Shop Boys and their gorgeous, prophetic song.

The reception was an undeniable hit. The food was "scrumptious," as Rex might say. The chicken in Coca-Cola, in particular, was extremely popular. Three full chafing dishes were quickly devoured, "with great gusto," as Carlitos made sure to point out to Beverly and Wanda. The liquor proved more than adequate, the string quartet hit all the right doleful notes, and smatterings of laughter were heard around the house as people recalled their favorite, meaning funniest and raunchiest, stories about Rex.

Megan knew she had to mingle, as much as she hated the very idea. Moving around the room, she took in endless hugs, kisses (real ones, mostly) and torrents of condolence. She was very moved by it all. "Everyone thought the service was perfect," Brent Ashby said. "Gaga was simply sublime," Celia assured her. Megan was especially touched when Jamal Dix hugged her softly, and she felt a few warm tears fall on her bare shoulder.

Even the ladies were cordial.

"We must get together soon, just us girls," Beverly said, clasping Megan's hand between hers. "I'll arrange a little luncheon. Nothing fancy. You let me know when you're ready, okay?" Megan wanted to answer: "How about the day after never?" But instead, she chose to just nod respectfully.

Megan needed a break. She quietly walked over to a corner sofa in the salon, sat down and closed her eyes for a moment.

"Can I get you anything?" It was a young woman's voice. Megan opened her eyes, but did not instantly recognize her.

"It's Hillary. Beverly's daughter? I met you at the wedding reception, but I was just one of the hordes. Now, how about a drink?"

"Double Kettle One, please. You're an angel. Thank you."

Hillary returned with two full glasses and sat down. "First of all," she said, "I want you to know how really, truly sorry I am about Rex. He was like a big brother to me. We used to get into hellish trouble all the time, especially during the Ecstasy Years. I still wonder how we didn't end up in boarding school. Or jail. The legal bills alone were astronomical."

"I heard. Must've been a blast."

"You have no idea." Hillary smiled. "Listen, Megan. I really admire you. I always have, from afar. The way you navigated this looney-tunes world of ours. With good humor, I hear, and aplomb. I love aplomb. Everyone does."

"That means a lot to me."

"And there's another thing I love: Anyone who can cut mother down to size. According to my sources, Martha and Dexter mostly, you're really good at that. As she herself might say, '*touche*, darling.'"

Megan let out a bitter laugh. "Your mom has been a thorn in my paw since the day we collided, I will give you that. But we've somehow managed to navigate each other's troubled waters, for the most part. After all, both our boats are still floating."

"Well, sail on with caution. I know for a fact she'd love to sink your battleship."

"After what I've been through, it might be a relief to abandon ship."

Hillary regarded Megan with a look of respect. "You know, I think we could be friends. We share a lot in common. Same age, more or less. A deep love for Rex, despite his many glaring flaws. And a shared distaste for Mumsy Dearest. Here's my card. Come have dinner with me sometime. Downtown. Where the blood is not so bloody blue, the margaritas are strong, and none of the men would be caught dead in Brooks Brothers."

"That'd be wonderful, Hillary. I'd like that very much."

Megan got back up to mingle, when she ran into Tony. "Having fun?" she asked.

"Am I supposed to be? That word doesn't seem like the right fit. But the food is killer. Listen, are you going to be okay here, after everyone leaves?"

"I think so. Although my family flies back tonight, and most of the staff are leaving soon."

"So, you'll be left up here? All alone? In this ginormous apartment?" Megan nodded. "Well, not if I can help it. Why don't I stay for a while? We could pile on the couch later, eat leftovers and binge on Netflix. Something funny would be good. You like Monty Python?"

"You have no idea."

Gradually, the guests began slipping away. They lined up to say farewell to Megan, who was stationed at the foyer doorway. One of the last to leave was Alexi Stroganoff.

"Megan," he said. "Rex was like a son to me, and you like daughter. I never had daughter. Always wanted one. Please. Promise me this one thing: If you ever need anything at all, you call me. Yes? I will always be there."

"Thank you, Alexi."

He planted an avuncular kiss on her forehead. "Again. Anything. For instance, you want Wanda Covington gone? And this time, I don't mean deportation."

Megan laughed. "I'll let you know."

The only ones left, besides Tony, were Maureen and the boys. They gathered in the foyer with their luggage, to say goodbye. A barrage of hugs, kisses and tears were exchanged.

"Listen you guys. As you know, right now the entire money thing is in limbo. Probate. And there are claims against the estate. It'll take some time to sort it out, as much as three months. But then I will be, you know, filthy rich. And you will, too. Mom, you'll get a fine new house, all your own. Todd and Carlitos, start planning your business."

"For reals?" Todd asked.

"Yes, little brother. For reals."

"Megan! I don't know what to say!" Maureen cried.

"Say thanks, Mom. You deserve this."

"But what about you?" Carlitos asked. "What are your plans?"

"I have a lot to think about. I have no idea, yet. Maybe I'll move back home. Maybe I'll stay here. And if I do, why don't you all come to live with me? Penthouse life can be very exhilarating."

Maureen scoffed. "After what the wretched people in this city have done to you? I wouldn't live here for all the wings at Planet Wings."

"Well, we would," Todd said. "We can cook, and babysit, and go shopping. All the time."

"Wouldn't that be fun? I'll be here. At least for the time being. As long as I have a carved plaster ceiling over my head."

After they left, Megan and Tony joined the rest of the staff to clean the place up. When the last round of dishes was done and all the leftover food divided up for the staff, with some reserved for Megan and Tony's TV dinner, the two went into the salon for their Monty Python marathon.

Tears of hilarity quickly streamed down their faces as they roared at the medieval antics flying from the screen during *Monty Python and the Holy Grail*. Just when the Knights Who Say "Ni!" were demanding their shrubbery in exchange for safe passage, and Megan was thinking what a perfect distraction this was, her phone rang.

"Crap." Megan got up. "Who on earth is bothering me now? The party's over, people!"

"You want me to pause it?"

"Thanks," Megan said, looking at the phone. The caller ID said "M Bradbury."

"Hello? Martha? Is that really you?"

"Oh dear, sweet Megan," Martha said, fighting back tears. "Can you forgive me? I wanted to be there today. For you. But everything is still just too raw. I couldn't face that crowd. It would have been unbearable. And I realized, I would've been a horrible distraction."

"I'm so glad to hear from you, Martha. I miss you something awful."

"I miss you too. I'm sorry I skipped town without saying goodbye. That was very lowbrow of me."

"Don't be silly. The important thing is that you reached out. I've been trying to find you, you know. You hide yourself very well. Where are you?"

Martha was back outside Boulder, where she had bought a 15-acre farm, secluded in the woods outside town. "Only I'm raising chickens. Not hemp. And I never go outside without my bear repellent."

Megan filled Martha in on all that had happened since New Year's Eve – the rather hilarious self-photographed birth of Maureen, the financial woes, Rex's infidelity and self-inflicted annihilation, the funeral, Gaga, and the successful reception orchestrated by Todd and Carlitos. "You were missed today," she said.

"Well, maybe by you. But not everyone. So far, seven *former* friends have filed suit against me. For gross negligence, emotional and physical distress, plus exterminator fees, dry cleaning and hotel bills. It could wipe me out, Megan. I'm scared."

"Assholes."

"Yep. Speaking of which, one of them is our own Thaddeus Pepper."

"Jesus. That guy is such post-consumer waste," Megan said. "When it comes to the human race, he's losing. Besides, you never had bedbugs before. It seems odd they would suddenly appear that night, at your party."

"Well, it's funny you mention that. My attorneys are looking into it. The building manager sent in a professional exterminator, and he said the only place any bedbugs were found was in the cloakroom. Nowhere else. Not in my bedroom. Not in my bed. I was never bitten, by the way."

"You think someone brought them in?"

"That's the working theory right now."

"Oh good lord, some member of this uppity circle is walking around with bedbugs in their coat, inadvertently infecting the finer closets of the Upper East Side?"

"Can you believe it?" Martha said. She paused, and then, "Unless..."

"Unless what?"

"Unless someone brought them in...on purpose."

"But who would do such a thing? And why?"

"Simple. For revenge. And I think I may know who it might be." Martha told Megan all about the Safe Harbor coup, and how Jackie ended up as chair, instead of Wanda. "I cast the tie-breaking vote against her, despite her crude attempt to blackmail me out of it."

"What do you mean, blackmail?"

"She found out that you forced Jackie to pay for my party. She threatened to spread it around town, to humiliate me. But at that point, I just didn't care. Bitch deserved it."

Megan laughed. "Why Martha Bradbury! I do believe that mountain air is doing you a world of good."

"The weird thing is, I found out that Wanda had been using my exterminator. I mean, he kept her place bedbug-free. Right? So why wouldn't the same be true for my apartment?"

"It *is* odd," Megan said, looking over at Tony, who was now cooing with Maureen in her bassinet. On the screen, the frozen face of a Knight Who Says "Ni!" sneered with snooty English disdain. "Who was your exterminator?"

"Juan Carlos. I don't know his last name. But he's the uncle of my former maid, Rosalinda."

"Ah yes, how is she? She was always so lovely."

"Good question. I hear she works for Beverly now, the poor thing. So, your guess is as good as mine."

"Give me some time," Megan said. "But my spidey sense tells me there are some dots to connect here. I'll be in touch, for sure. Okay? Love you... Bye!"

Megan walked over to the sofa and picked up Maureen, as Tony clicked the frozen knight back to life. "Good news?" he asked.

"Not exactly. But very interesting news. One more item to put in my files."

"You have files?"

"I think I do. First of all, I have trash, literally, on Jackie, thanks to you. And now, I'm on the scent of a most diabolical plot, hatched by none other than everyone's favorite Britch.

"Britch?"

"British bitch. I'm trying it out."

"Might need some work," Tony smiled. "So, what about Wanda? What did she do now?"

"That was Martha Bradbury, calling from Colorado. I'm sure you heard about her big New Year's party."

"Every doorman in New York heard about it. We still talk about it. But what does that have to do with Wanda?"

"You can keep a secret, right?"

"Megan. I'm your friend. Besides, who'm I gonna tell?"

"I think Wanda planted the bedbugs in Martha's cloakroom. Her motivation against Martha is complicated. But I'm pretty sure she did it. I intend to find out."

"Holy shit."

"I know. Like I said, files. You never know when they might come in handy."

When *The Holy Grail* finished, they got up and grabbed some carved turkey, orzo salad and a juicy bottle of Napa Valley cab from the kitchen, then returned to watch their mutually agreed-upon second-favorite Python flick, *Life of Brian*.

The last thing Megan remembered before falling dead asleep was Terry Jones, as Brian's put-upon mother, yelling at her son's followers gathered beneath the window of their crumbling home: "'E's not the Messiah, 'e's a very naughty boy! Now go away!"

Chapter 19

Going Down?

Megan did little in the week following the funeral. She was drained physically and emotionally, and depressed. The outside world tried to barge in on her self-imposed sanctuary, but to no avail. Emails from the ladies went ignored. Several entreaties from Jamal, pleading for an interview, were not answered. Even Devonshire had no luck getting through, despite some rather urgent news in the money laundering case against Rex.

On the nights that Bill and Brigit did not drop by with take-out, Tony would come over. They were both addicted to *The Handmaid's Tale*, and would stay up late racing through each soul-crushing episode.

"Just one more," Megan said once, at two-thirty in the morning.

"That's what my family used to say on Christmas Eve," Tony said. "We were each allowed to open one present. But that was never enough. before we knew it, there was virtually nothing left to open the next morning. It was kind of depressing."

"So is this show," Megan said. "Your analogy is perfect."

She took in Tony's profile as he watched TV. The rush of jet-black hair, that Roman nose, hooked like an eagle's in a way that might make other men look ugly, the taut jawline, the lush, full lips and those long feathery eyelashes. She would kill for lashes like that.

Tony's tight gray t-shirt revealed perfectly rounded pecs, flat stomach, and well-developed biceps. But what was this? On his sensuous neck, normally hidden from his shirt collars at work, was a wide scar, with the unmistakable rivets of stitches.

"What happened there?" she said, pointing. "You look like you were in a knife-fight."

"It wasn't a knife," was all that he said.

Violent scar aside, Megan thought him quite the package. All this, and smart, funny and kind, to boot. He even smells nice. If I weren't a recent widow... Megan quickly escorted that thought out of her mind. No sex. Not now. Probably never. Why ruin a perfectly good friendship by fucking?

Tony noticed Megan staring at him and grinned his dazzling grin. That's when she realized it: he wanted it. Much more than she did, which was not at all. He should be so lucky, she tried to tell herself.

The next morning, at seven, her phone rang incessantly. She looked at the screen: Brigit.

"Are you awake Megs?"

"I wasn't. And I'd rather not be. What's up?"

312

"Go to *The Times* website. It's the third story from the top."

"Oh God. What now? Is this about Rex? Is it about *me?*"

"No. Not directly. Read it, then call me later."

"Investment manager with ties to mafia indicted on federal fraud charges."

Notorious financier and Russian immigrant Alexi Ivonovich Stroganoff, with alleged ties to Russian organized crime figures, was indicted by a federal grand jury in Manhattan yesterday for bilking hundreds of millions of dollars out of wealthy investors in New York and beyond, along with 11 other counts of money laundering, wire fraud, bank fraud, obstruction of justice and criminal mischief.

The charges were filed by the federal attorney for the U.S. District Court of the Southern District of New York.

Prosecutors, who allege that Mr. Stroganoff had embezzled a total of $540 million from his clients, stated in court papers that he was "the new Bernard Madoff – only much more dangerous."

Mr. Stroganoff reportedly spends time between New York and Moscow and has ties to several Russian oligarchs and, the government alleges, crime-syndicate bosses affiliated with President Vladimir Putin. He pleaded not guilty. Over the objections of chief defense counsel, Sasha K. Steinhoff, District Court Judge Omar Bashara ordered Mr. Stroganoff held without bond at the Metropolitan Correctional Facility on Park Row.

The first hearing is scheduled in two weeks in federal court in Lower Manhattan.

Megan was no financial whiz-kid, but she knew what "the new Bernard Madoff" meant. Alexi was running a giant Ponzi scheme and Rex, as one of his biggest investors, was likely one of his biggest victims. She called Brigit back.

"Damn," Megan said.

"I know. Damn."

"Am I broke, Bridge?"

"You need to get hold of your attorney. Right now. Some people lost their entire fortunes with Madoff. This could be really, really bad."

When Megan hung up, she dialed Devonshire. It went right to voicemail. And then the intercom buzzer sounded.

"There are some people here to see you, ma'am." It was Carlton, the morning doorman. "A Mr. Barton Devonshire and an associate of his, Ms. Katie Collins."

This was serious, if Bart was dropping by, unannounced. "Please send them up," she said, before shooting into the bedroom to throw on something respectable.

The attorney's face told Megan everything she needed to know.

In jarring contrast, however, Katie Collins seemed downright giddy. The odd demeanor of the largish woman in her late twenties — with her girlish smile, suspiciously sunny disposition and garrulous Irish accent as thick as the head of a just-drawn Guinness — could best be described as "injudicious," especially given the circumstances.

314

"Megan, this is Ms. Katie Collins," Devonshire said.

"Well hello there!" Katie chirped, jutting out her hand for a good shake. "How's the form?"

"The what?"

"Ms. Collins was recently transferred from our Dublin office. She means, 'how's it going?'"

"Oh. I'm afraid not too well, Ms. Collins. I wouldn't know where to begin."

"Well, I heard everything?" Like many Dubliners her age, Katie Collins used an abundance of upspeak. "And I'm sorry that life went all arseways on you?"

Megan had to laugh. "Is that what the Irish call it? Because it totally fits. Ms. Collins."

"Oh *please*. Katie." She gazed intently into the foyer, and all the plush riches that lay beyond, with the look of a delighted child entering a bouncy castle. "I can't believe your gaff? Bloody hell it's deadly, i'n'it?'"

Megan looked to Devonshire for help. "Your house is very cool," he translated.

"Thank you Katie. I think. Now Bart, what's this all about?"

He drew a deep breath. "You saw *The Times*, I assume?" Megan nodded. "Well, that."

"Come into the salon and sit down. I'll get us some coffee."

"That'd be grand!" Katie said. "Could I use your jacks?"

Again, Megan looked at the lawyer, who was equally clueless.

"Oh right! America." Katie said. "I mean, the bathroom?"

"Down that hall," Megan said, already looking exhausted. "Second door on your right."

Once they were settled, Megan turned to Bart. "How bad is it, what can I do, and am I about to be chucked out on the street?"

He and Katie exchanged fidgety glances. "Here's the thing. Rexford's account with Stroganoff, on paper, was worth more than sixty-five million. Of course, much of that was merely phantom earnings. His actual investment came to about thirty million."

"So technically, he only ripped us off for that."

"From the government's perspective, yes."

"And how much will I get back?"

"It's very hard to know." With Madoff, the feds doggedly pursued restitution because the case was so high-profile and the amounts so astronomical: about twenty billion dollars. Funds came from seized assets, and clients who had actually profited. But it wasn't enough, and it took a decade.

"This case, I'm afraid, is much more garden variety: five hundred and forty million. In most Ponzi schemes, recovery rates range from five to thirty percent, though many victims don't get a dime. And it takes forever."

"So, that's sixty-five million that I thought I had, but don't."

"Well, you can't count on any of it to settle claims against the estate."

"And how much are those?"

"Between IRS and the banks, upwards of fifty million."

Katie whistled in disbelief. "My," she said. "That's quite a rake of spon-doolicks."

Megan, in near panic, glared at Barton. "So I'm left with nothing." His look affirmed the worst. Everything would have to be liquidated: About forty million in bank accounts, IRA's, stocks and bonds, the combined value of his companies, the villa in Mallorca and the penthouse, with their contents.

"And that's where I come in." Katie said. "On contents?"

"Ms. Collins is one of our auditors. Her team will be arriving shortly to take full inventory of everything to appraise its total value."

"It's savage craic, really." Katie said. "You know, a whole *quare* of fun?"

"You have fun rummaging through other people's things?"

"Who doesn't? I simply live for foostering around a flat. I mean, all that artwork? Those fab collections? The rare furnishings and oriental carpets? Not to mention the china, crystal…and silver. That's my favorite part." She lifted a solid-silver candelabra from the table and fondled it, virtually drooling.

"Is that really necessary?" Megan said. "So soon?"

"We also need to catalogue every piece of clothing worth more than three hundred dollars," Bart said. "And then there's the jewelry."

"What about it?"

"It goes into escrow, now. We're allowed to preserve something. To cover the legal costs."

Megan instinctively twisted the large diamond ring on her finger.

"Including that," Katie said, looking lustily at Megan's left hand. "She's a beaut, that one."

"My engagement ring? You must be kidding me. Bart?"

"I wish I were," Devonshire frowned. "Please, give it to Ms. Collins."

"Go on. Give it a lash," Katie said, holding out her hand. "Atta a good lass.".

Megan took off the ring, kissed it, and handed it over, tears welling in her eyes.

"Aye, come to mama, me sweets!"

"Ms. Collins! You are upsetting my client and I must ask you to stop at once. Your behavior is atrocious. We talked about this."

"Oh dear, that *is* a bit of a fret? I'm so sorry, I'm really acting the maggot, amn't I?"

"Yep," Megan said. "Maggot." And who the hell says "amn't," anyway, she thought,

"Must be the coffee talking," Katie said. "It's strong in New York. If I have any more, I fear I'll be wired to the moon!"

"I think," Megan said, dry as melba toast, "you're already there. Bart, how long do I have? To stay here."

"Until probate ends. We'll do everything possible to stall. That should buy you three months. Maybe four."

"And how do we get by?"

"There should be about four-fifty in the safe. We'll cover maintenance and related costs. If you need a loan, for groceries, let me know."

About a half-hour later, the young inventory team, three men and two women, invaded the home, armed with clipboards, cameras and calculators.

"Hello, *Katie*," one staffer, Naomi, said, looking like she wanted to turn and flee. "We didn't know you'd be on this job. How lucky for us."

"Ain't it grand?"

"Yeah right, grand. Totally grand."

"Let's not keep larking on, then, shall we? Let's inventory! It's time to suck some diesel."

Megan heard Naomi whispering to a coworker. "Has she been hitting the Jameson's again? What does that even fucking *mean*?"

"I think she wants us to get to work," the guy answered. "Who knew the Irish could be so annoying."

"Right? I thought that was the job of the French," Naomi snickered. "Hey Justin, wanna do the master bedroom with me?"

Megan couldn't bear any more of the incursion. She picked up Maureen, dressed her warmly, threw on a coat and went downstairs. It's not that she wanted to go anywhere. She didn't. What she really wanted was to see Tony.

Her look alarmed him.

"Megan. What happened?" Atypical silence. Megan realized she couldn't even think about everything, let alone explain it to somebody else. She should've stayed upstairs and not bothered him.

Megan burst into tears. "We're totally broke."

Tony knew better than to ask how. He threw his arms around Megan and the baby, and kissed them each on the cheek. "I'm about to go on break. How about coffee?"

"Can we go to that Hungarian place?" Megan said mid-sniffle. "They have killer pastry."

"I know. The best this side of Buda — *or* Pest. Let's scram."

They walked through the arctic cold to the café, its windows steamy with warm breath and fatty chicken broth spiked with paprika. They chose a corner table in the rear, near the kitchen and its fabulous smells. Megan sighed as she stirred her coffee.

"You know, at Rex's funeral, Lady Gaga sang 'What Have I Done To Deserve This?' Now I can't help but think that the Pet Shop Boys wrote that song just for me. Seriously, Tony. What *have* I done? Why has all of this happened? Why is life puking all over me?"

Tony reached across the table and softly took her hand in his. It felt strong, and good. She told him all that had happened.

"Geeze, Megan. I had no idea. About the money problems, I mean. And the legal stuff. Yikkity-yikes."

Megan blew her nose. "I should've told you. But it's not something you just walk around saying. 'Hi, I'm Megan. My dead husband was a cheat, a fool, and a felon, And now I'm worth exactly zero dollars and zero cents. I got literally nuthin'.'"

"That's not true! You got beautiful little Maureen here. And me."

"That's very sweet. But I don't exactly *have* you. We're friends."

"Yeah," Tony said with a hard lump of disappointment. "That's what I meant."

"At least I can shelter in place for a few months. That'll allow me to figure out what I'm going to do."

An older Eastern European woman with the blasé eyes of the post-Communist era brought over the pastries. "So. What *are* you going to do?" Tony asked.

"My family will insist I move home, of course. But do I really want that? If you think *Handmaid's* is depressing, Ypsilanti makes Gilead look like Munchkin Land. Besides, they had to move into a tiny one-bedroom. The guys sleep on a fold-out in the living room. Where are they going to fit a mother and her baby? It's mathematically impossible."

"What about your friends, uptown?"

"Brigit and Bill? Again, no room at the inn. And way too much ganja smoke. Maureen would grow up to look like Sean Penn."

What Megan needed was work. Tony asked what kind.

"Journalism, of course," she said. "But no more of these piddly little online blogs that pay you in hamster feed. I need some big, juicy feature stories that can be sold to newspapers and magazines. You know, the kind that still print.

On paper."

"Any ideas?"

"Files, my friend." Megan smiled. "Now, those handmaids are expecting us tonight. At seven. I'm making spaghetti."

When Megan returned upstairs, the inventory team was still scouring the household for valuables. Devonshire had left, but Katie Collins remained, seated at the dining-room table, gushing ecstatically at every *objet d'art*, sculpture and painting brought to her by team members. Megan stood quietly in the hallway, out of sight, eavesdropping on the auditor's unbridled merriment.

"What have we *here*? A small oil-on-canvas by Frida Kahlo?" she heard Katie yelp. "Still Life With Avocado. That's mega. Naomi, did you know that the Aztec word for avocado is *ahuácatl*? It means testicle, because of the shape. Remember that next time you're smashing one on some toast."

Oh brother, Megan thought. And then:

"Well, blow me down with a French kiss." There was frantic typing on a keyboard. "According to the Googs, this is an 18th-Century, eighteen-karat yellow-gold snuff box and watch designed by Barnabé Sageret and leading Parisian clockmaker Charles Dutertre!?To find such a precious *objet* by two renowned craftsmen is rare. Like hen's teeth. It's bang on. It'll fetch us quite a lot of dosh."

Us? Megan thought. Rex had bought that for her in Bora Bora. This was too much.

"You bitch!" Megan cried, coming around the corner. "That was a special gift from my husband. He bought it at a little antique store in Tahiti. On our honeymoon. So you can drop the drooling. That's mine."

"I didn't see you there, love," Katie said. "Were you earwigging on me? Besides, I believe you mean it *was* yours. No longer, alas. With any luck, you can go visit it at a museum somewhere. Have you ever been to Dusseldorf? They love this stuff there."

Megan turned and went into the study, closed the door, and called her family and Celia to deliver the news. She decided not to bother Martha. With the bedbug lawsuits and all, she had enough troubles of her own.

As Megan predicted, her mom, Todd and Carlitos said she should come home. "You can stay with us for a while," her mom said, "until you find a little place of your own nearby."

"Mom, I don't have any money for a little place of my own. Hell, I don't think I could even swing the airfare. And I'm not putting Maureen through an eighteen-hour Greyhound. For now, I have food to eat and a place to stay. A palace, actually. Things could be worse. It's not as though I have to drink the sea.'"

"The what?"

"Never mind. It's just that, fortunately, I don't have to rush any decisions."

Over the next few days, Megan began planning her reentry into journalism. She was convinced that an expose on the unspeakable misdeeds of four leading New York society matrons would not only fetch a hefty fee, the whole thing would be immensely gratifying to investigate and write. Megan had Jackie in the bag already, so that was done. And now she was close on the high heels of Wanda. There must be some way to link the Britch to the cloakroom caper.

But what about the other two? Surely someone as old and preposterous as Beverly harbored a dark secret or two, though Megan had no idea how to go about unearthing them. As for Jenna, she was so vacuous, it was hard to imagine her being crafty enough to get into any kind of real trouble. Still, one could hope.

Such investigations took time. She needed some other ideas that could be written, published, and paid for more quickly. Perhaps she should swallow her pride and throw herself at the not-so tender mercies of Jamal. She would need some ideas to pitch him first. Megan made a mental note to sit down with Brigit soon, for some creative brainstorming.

Gossip, of course, is only written about famous people. Megan had met several in the past year, but she hardly felt like snitching on Gaga, or Enrique Iglesias, or Anderson Cooper. Chevy Chase, maybe. But that would mean bothering poor Martha. No, what Megan needed was someone famous, to whom she had access, and about whom she would not hesitate to malign, short of actual defamation, of course.

And then it came to her.

"Alexi Ivonovich Stroganoff," Megan said out loud. "That asshole owes me big time." After all, the last thing he said to her was, "If I can ever be of any assistance." Well, the greatest assistance he could offer her, at this point, was to grant her a measly interview. She went online to find contact information for his lawyer, Sasha K. Steinhoff, and sent her a request via email, mentioning her own personal connection to Stroganoff, and his solemn promise on the day that Rex was buried.

Megan was staggered when, a few hours later, the lawyer wrote back.

> *Dear Ms. Bainbridge. I contacted my client just now, and against my strongest advice and counsel, he said he will speak with you. I will send*

you all of the Federal Bureau of Prisons paperwork you must fill out before making a formal request for a visit. It is quite extensive, especially for a working member of the media. And because he is an "unconvicted person," federal law requires that you first get permission from the District Court, which is handled through the U.S. Attorney's Office. I can help you with that. The whole process takes about two weeks. Good luck, and congratulations. It is, as they say, quite a big "get."

Best, Sasha K. Steinhoff, Attorney at Law

Millstein, Steinhoff & Associates, New York

Megan let out a squeal so loud it woke up Maureen. She ran to coddle the girl, then picked her up and danced her around the room in wide circles. "Mommy's going to be a famous journalist!" she sang as Maureen giggled wildly. "Yes she *is*! Mommy's luck is changing!

After a few more spins, Megan called Brigit to give her the great news. "Jamal is going to flip! Don't you think?"

"I don't know. Financial crimes are not really his thing. And there's no sex involved."

"But this is huge!"

"I agree Megan. It's fabulous, actually. But it's too important for *The Gleaner*. This isn't gossip. It's hard news. And pretty big news at that. Stroganoff will be in the headlines for weeks to come, at least here in New York."

"And?"

"This seems much more *Timesy* to me. Here's what you do. Reach out to Chester Mansfield over there. He knows you. He was just at your house for

Christ's sake. Pitch it to him. I bet you anything he'll bite."

"*The Times*? Oh my God! You do know that's the holy grail for every journalist on planet Earth, right? My mom's going to explode."

"I know, Megs. I'm in the biz. And I'm not above saying that I'm jealous. But also proud. Very, very proud. Look, I gotta go, but good luck. By the way, Bill and I can't make it over tonight. He's come down with a bad cough. It's probably something bong-induced, but I don't want to risk it, with Maureen and all. Love you."

Megan steeled herself for making the big phone call. She was stunned when Mansfield's assistant patched her right through. His tone was both respectful and solicitous. She told him all about Stroganoff and the time she had spent with him – including tracking down her attempted rapist in Coney Island – and how she was now a destitute widow because of his greed and callous disregard. And, he was willing to talk.

"Well, that *is* a most unusual pitch," Chester told her. "But typically speaking, it would be unethical, unthinkable, really, for a news reporter to interview someone who had caused them such harm. Objectivity would be questionable, if not impossible."

Megan let out a little sigh of defeat. "Of course. I hadn't really thought about that."

"But there is a way around it. We wouldn't cover it in the news section. But we could publish it in the *Sunday Magazine*. Much more room for subjectivity there. And the idea of a crime victim confronting her victimizer is a compelling one. I'm thinking maybe an eight-hundred-word intro, followed by a straight-up Q&A, about another two thousand words or so. How's that sound?"

"That… that sounds wonderful, Chester. Thank you. If you don't mind my asking, how much would the fee be for something like that?"

"Two dollars a word. Your contract would be for fifty-six hundred. Mind you, I still need to run this by the editors over there. But they usually like my ideas. Hopefully I can get a contract out to you shortly."

"Great. Just one more question. How quickly does *The Times* pay?

"One week after publication. Now, please keep me posted on your prison paperwork. And thank you."

Megan didn't know who to tell first. But of course, it was Tony. She ran out to the hall and rang for the elevator. Going down, it stopped one floor below. "Ruh-roh," Megan whispered to Maureen. "Bad juju a comin', Mommy fears."

Sure enough, it was Beverly, with Wanda and Jackie. This was going to be a long ride down.

"Megan, my poor dear. You must be beside yourself. First Rex, and now that inglorious Russian," Beverly said, placing a few gentle fingers under Megan's chin, like a sweet fairy godmother. "The whole thing is just so dreadful. Everyone lost a bundle."

"*Everyone?*" Wanda scowled. And then she turned to Megan. "It seems that our dear Beverly here got out, as you Yanks like to say, while the gettin' was good. So fortunate of her, don't you think? Trevor and I, alas, were not quite so lucky."

"Us either," Jackie said. "How much did you get taken for, Megan?"

"None of your goddamn business."

"Ouch," Jackie said. "That much. So, what now? Back to Stony-Patch Farm, or whatever Midwestern hell you came from?"

"Again. Business. Speaking of hell. Where's your little Mini-Me?"

"If you must know, Jenna's in Sao Paulo."

"What for?"

Wanda guffawed. "Let's just say she went there for work. Lots of it."

"Megan dear," Beverly changed the subject. "Please join us for lunch, or cocktails, or *whatever*, as soon as you feel up to it. We are, after all, still neighbors."

"Silly me," Megan said. "And I thought we were friends. Thanks Bev. I'll get back to you."

Mercifully, the elevator glided to a halt and the doors opened onto the lobby. "So long ladies," Megan said. "Enjoy your outing. Or whatever."

"Ta-ta!" Beverly answered, blowing the falsest kiss ever known to humankind. "And take care of that sweet baby. My goodness isn't she the cutest thing? Like a little Munchkin."

Megan looked over at Tony, standing behind the desk, and laughed. "Gilead!" she mouthed to him. When they left, she walked over.

"I hope you're free tonight, because I've got something to celebrate. And I'm going to buy some real food, too. You like grilled tuna steaks? Stuffed artichokes? What about crab dip?"

"That sounds amazing. What's the occasion?" Megan filled him in. Tony beamed at her with unmasked pride.

"And, it pays almost six thousand dollars. That, my friend, is move-in money. It looks like my run of lousy luck has run its course. So, tonight?"

"Geeze, I wish I'd known. I just agreed to work extra hours, until midnight. One of our guys called in sick."

Megan frowned. "But you'll get overtime for it, right?"

"Yes. It's in the manual." Tony smiled at her. "Can we celebrate tomorrow?"

Megan returned to the penthouse and spent the afternoon Googling Alexi Stroganoff. His past was even shadier than she realized. After emigrating from the Soviet Union, in 1986, he quickly came under federal investigation for his ties to leading figures of the Brighton Beach-based *Banda Vorav* (literally, "Gang of Thieves"), which specialized in extortion, financial fraud, illicit gambling, the occasional kidnapping, and smuggling contraband black caviar from the Caspian Sea. In 1989, he was indicted on a number of racketeering charges, which were later dropped, under mysterious circumstances. The office of the U.S. Attorney for the Eastern District of New York had declined to comment on the matter.

After Bill Clinton's election in 1992 and the ensuing boom years, Stroganoff apparently went legit. He took his millions in ill-begotten gains and got in on the hedge-fund craze, which really took off along with the stock market. He did so well so fast, he bought a massive oceanfront mansion in the exclusive, privately-owned Seagate section of Brooklyn, on the far-western tip of Coney Island. People noticed. Important people. Several of them privately began letting him invest considerable chunks of their wealth. Among his first clients were Rex's parents, Rexford and Florence Bainbridge, Herbert H. Stein, Beverly's late husband, plus Leona Helmsley, Imelda Marcos and Donald Trump. Word got around town fast.

Megan tapped off the iPad, satisfied with her research and proposed line of questioning. She looked at the prison-visitor papers that Sasha Steinhoff had sent over. Included among the many federal forms and endless pages of rules, were a Criminal History Check Authorization (Form BP-A0880), and a Media Representative's Agreement (Form BP-S232.014), which contained this ominous clause: "I recognize a visit to a prison presents certain hazards, and I agree to assume all ordinary and usual risks to my personal safety inherent in a visit to an institution of this type."

My God, she thought, I'm actually going to the slammer, aren't I?

Megan put Maureen to sleep, turned on the baby cam, and had pumpkin soup and a simple salad in the kitchen. Except for the night after Rex died, it was her first evening home alone. She did not like it. Normally, there would be eight people in the house, talking, or at least making noise as they went about their duties: A vacuum; a blender; a phone call; the clanking of copper pots in Duchamp's kitchen. Even the sound of two people arguing would be a welcome relief from the vast, empty silence that filled every crevice of the penthouse.

She had a hard time sleeping that night. Maureen was colicky and crying, and Megan's mind would not stop talking to her. It raced from Rex, to Stroganoff, to picturing her byline in *The Times*, to Tony, to Maureen and inevitably, back to Rex. Megan cried every time she thought of him. She missed him so much. She desperately wanted to tell him about her big new assignment, her investigations into Jackie and Wanda (he would have been appalled) and of course, the sheer amazement of watching Lady Gaga perform at his funeral.

"You would have fucking loved that," she said into the dark.

But of course, his many misdeeds also stormed through her mind, as if on a loop. The blowjob. The semen-slip. The IRS. Bad business deals and vengeful Chinese banks. And then, the money laundering. For the Ukrainian mafia, of all things. Then again, Rex had risked getting caught and sent to prison rather than putting his family in harm's way. It seemed really weird to think about, but Rex was actually a hero.

Megan was still in love with her husband.

The next night, Tony came over for the promised meal.

"I've been looking online for a place to live," Megan said. "It's obscene. Who wants to spend half their income or *more* on rent? I have a feeling I might end up back in the Midwest, where the food is bland, the people are civil, and apartments are affordable. If I hit it rich, I'll move back here. Maybe."

"I wouldn't want to see you go," Tony said, his face etched with genuine sadness.

"Well, I still have a few months to decide, thank God. And who knows? Maybe there's a job in New York somewhere for me. What about you, Tony? What are your dreams?"

"I want to go to cooking school. To be a chef. Not in a restaurant. I've seen firsthand how that ages people. But maybe a personal chef, like my uncle. Only, not for someone like Beverly. I think someone who doesn't scare little children would be nice."

"A definite prerequisite. Talk about aging someone. Can you imagine?"

"I don't have to. Uncle Jack bitches about her all the time."

Later, despite their solemn vow not to, Megan and Tony tore through the rest of the second season of *The Handmaid's Tale*. It would be a while before Season III began. They would have to find a new addiction for the time being.

It was late. Well past midnight. "Megan?" Tony asked, stretching and yawning. "Do you mind if I sleep here? The Q Train's a bitch at this hour."

Megan had to think about it. She noticed Tony staring at her, and not in a friend who just-wants-to-crash way. "In a guest room, right?" she asked.

Tony looked like he was in pain. "Well, that's not exactly what I had planned." He started walking toward her, a sexy smile now plastered across his face. As he neared, all she could see were those full red lips.

"You had something *planned*? Wasn't that a bit presumptuous? Because it's not what I had planned. At all. Tony, my husband has only been dead for ten days. Jesus Christ. No."

Just as he was about to kiss her, Megan cried out: "What part of 'no' don't you fucking understand?" She pushed him away forcefully with two palms to the chest, like Elaine Benes does on *Seinfeld* while shouting "Get *out!*"

She pushed too hard. Tony flew about three feet back and landed with a loud thud to the head against the polished marble floor. Megan was horrified to see he was just steps away from the bust of Edmund Hillary – a piece that had been of exceptionally avaricious interest to Katie Collins.

"Oh my God! Tony! Are you okay? I am so sorry." She helped him off the floor. "I guess I don't know my own strength."

"I'll live. But you might want to get better acquainted with that strength of yours. The better to control it by."

"I feel awful."

"I'm sure you do. Um, under the circumstances, I think it's better if I go face the music. And the Q Train. Alone. Good night, Megan."

Chapter 20

West to East Orange – And Back

A few days later, there was a thunderous pounding at the door. Megan, consumed with alarm, came tearing out of the bedroom. "Who is it?" she shouted over the noise.

"Federal Marshalls!" A man's voice bellowed. "U.S. Department of Justice. Open the door Mrs. Bainbridge. Now."

Megan looked through the peephole. There were men outside, some in uniform. "Can you show me ID, please?" One of them held up a federal badge. Megan let them in.

"What is going on?" she demanded. A man handed her some papers.

"I'm Special Agent Maalouf. We're here to seize this property under the Civil Asset Forfeiture Statute of the U.S. Federal Code."

Megan looked at the guy, a striking young man of Middle Eastern origin and accent, well-groomed and impeccably dressed in a charcoal business suit and black Harrys of London loafers. Despite her fear, she couldn't help but think: Who knew federal agents could be so well put together?

"Seize?" she said "What do you mean, seize?"

"Take. Possess." said the dashing agent in the expensive shoes. "The government has reason to believe that these premises were used in the commission of multiple felonies, including wire fraud and money laundering. Under the law, it is ripe for seizure."

"But how? Why? This doesn't make any sense." Megan's heart was racing. "My husband was never even charged with a crime, let alone convicted of one."

"That's why it's called *civil* asset forfeiture. We can take the property without any charges ever being brought. Whether the owner is living or dead. No offense, Mrs. Bainbridge."

"Can I call my attorney?"

He said Megan could, but warned her there was nothing Devonshire could do. Soon, the federal government would petition for the forfeiture of the property, at which time it would become an asset of the United States. It would then be sold, with proceeds going back to the Justice Department.

"You have the right to contest the forfeiture. But it takes a long time, the legal bills are astronomical, and your chances of prevailing are slim. Again, I'm sorry."

"But I can stay here in the meantime. Right?"

"I'm afraid not. The documents I just handed you include an order for all occupants of the apartment to be removed immediately. Then the place will be sealed. You can take a reasonable amount of personal belongings with you."

"Wait. You said 'immediately?'"

"Yes," the officer said. "You have thirty minutes. We'll station two men inside, to make sure nothing of value is removed.

Megan was shaking. Her head was foggy. She froze in confusion.

"Thirty minutes," the agent said sternly. Suddenly he didn't seem so attractive any more. Megan packed up some things. She then went to the safe and retrieved the remaining cash, just over $350, which she hid in some socks.

Swearing in shock and fighting back tears, Megan put Maureen in her stroller and, towing a large roll-aboard bag behind her, headed for the door, where the agent was waiting for her.

"Goodbye, Mrs. Bainbridge," he said. Megan stopped and turned around for one more moment of relived memories. Some great; some really, truly shitty. But the view *was* spectacular. That part was impossible to argue. The reservoir looked particularly tranquil and, today, a dazzling deep blue.

"Mrs. Bainbridge? It's time."

A loud gurgling arose from Maureen's stomach. "Uh-oh," Megan said.

The baby coughed, spat, and then leaned over the stroller's edge to vomit — all over Special Agent Maalouf's three-hundred-fifty-dollar English leather shoes.

"Oopsie daisy!" Megan said. "Well, you know what they say: Where there's babies, there's puke-covered loafers. Sorry about that. Goodbye, sir. And, thanks for your service. Ain't America *grand?*"

Mercifully, the elevator did not stop on the way down. Tony was behind the desk, brooding, bearing all the signs of unfulfilled sexual desire and bruised male ego. A dose of morning sunshine he was not.

"Hello," he said flatly. "What's up with the luggage?"

Megan was tempted to tell his pouty little self to go to hell and then rush out the door. But to where? She looked outside. It was starting to snow again. She froze in place. She started to tremble violently. Suddenly, she was terrified. Of everything.

Tony's stone face melted and he came over to her. She told him everything. He brought their things into the office, got Megan some coffee and sat down with her. This time, he didn't hold her hand. "I must've been on break when they arrived. I had no idea."

"I can't believe this."

"Me either, Megan. I mean, what the hell? They can just swoop in and take everything without charging anyone with a crime? What is this, North Korea?"

They sat together in silence as Megan cradled her daughter and sipped some coffee. "Where do we go?" she asked, finally. "What do we do?"

"Well that's easy. You come stay with me."

"And your three roommates? In a five-hundred-square-foot, two-bedroom apartment in Flushing? All six of us? That's very sweet. Really. But you know it's not going to work."

Megan realized that, among the leading people in her life – her family, Brigit and Bill, and now Tony — space was the rarest commodity of all. She literally had nowhere to go.

"What about an AirBnB?" Tony said. "Out by me, people rent rooms for forty, even thirty bucks a night."

"I don't want to bring a baby into an apartment full of strangers. It just doesn't feel right. Plus, she's been crying at night. People find that annoying. Especially when sleeping."

"So. You going home?"

"I can't even afford it right now. Not the airfare. Not a new apartment. And I told you about my family's situation. Sardine City. Plus, I want to stay. At least until the Stroganoff interview. That could really help launch my career, no matter where I end up."

There was an aging desktop computer in the office. "Can you get me online?" Megan asked. "I want to look at affordable hotels. It's stopgap, I realize. But it'll have to do, until I can clear my mind out and actually think. Because, that's not really happening right now."

There was virtually nothing under sixty-five a night, even the dumpiest dumps. Looking a bit further afield, Megan found a motel in East Orange, New Jersey, the Bergen Arms, about an hour away by public transit, for thirty-nine.

"I don't know," Tony said. "That's a pretty shady area. East Orange is the worst Orange."

"I grew up on the outskirts of Detroit. I think I can handle it."

Tony was getting off in an hour and insisted on taking them there. "We'll get an Uber. My treat. I'll take the train home from there."

It wasn't clear if the Bergen Arms had actually seen better days, but if it had, they were a long time gone. With its faded beige stucco, peeling brown trim, smudged windows and broken neon sign that blinked "Berge Ams," it made the Bates Motel look like the Walforf.

"No. Nope. I'm not letting you stay here. And that's final," Tony said as they pulled up.

"How patriarchal of you, talking to a grown woman like that," Megan replied. "I thought you were more enlightened."

The owner would not let Tony carry their stuff to the room. "This is not a sex motel," he scolded. "You want that, you go over to Newark."

It may not have been a sex motel, but there sure was a lot of sex going on. Megan pressed the flimsy pillow over her head, in a vain attempt to shut out the thumping racket coming from both next door and upstairs. At one point, she was certain she caught a whiff of the acrid smell of crack cocaine. And then, at exactly three thirty, someone let out a blood-curdling scream, followed by a thud, and then silence.

Megan woke up sweating the next morning. The place was even more ghastly in daylight, if possible, with its stained walls, dripping rusty faucet and cobwebs forming between the folds of the clanking metal radiator. At least the heat is on, she thought.

This wasn't going to work. Megan needed help. But who would rescue the destitute single mother of a newborn baby?

"Well DUH!" she said out loud to Maureen. "Why didn't I think of this sooner? You wanna go live at Safe Harbor House for a while? Do you? *Yes?* So does mommy!"

It was the perfect temporary solution. Megan knew the place well, all safe and clean as it was. She knew the clients, the staff, the volunteers and, for better or worse, the board. What's more, she could give a class on the basics of nonfiction writing, for the older kids. Why, she could even help them publish a little in-house newsletter, *Heard 'Round The Harbor*, or some-such. And, she could take advantage of the free childcare program, allowing her to go out, do some reporting, and maybe even find a job.

At this point, it was more feasible than Ypsilanti, and so much better than this shithole.

Megan took a deep breath and called Beverly. She methodically laid out the grim details of her situation, to general silence on the other end. She then brought up staying at Safe Harbor, "only until I can get back on my feet."

At last, Beverly said something. "Megan, I am so sorry to hear all this. I had no idea. You lost everything? Really?"

"Yes, Beverly. To be honest, I wouldn't be calling you if I hadn't. I really need help. Maureen too. Right now. Please?"

"You see, the thing is, we are filled to capacity. With a waiting list of more than fifteen mothers. It just wouldn't be proper protocol to let you jump the line. And I'm quite sure the board would oppose it. Trust me."

Megan began to cry.

"Now, now. Let's just think here. Let's be creative. There must be some place you can go." A pause. "Why, I've *got* it!"

"You do?" Megan asked. "Because, I gotta tell you. I'm all ears."

"You and Maureen shall come live with me, of course."

"With you? Why would you do that?"

"I need the help."

"Help, Beverly? What sort of help?"

"You'd be part of my household staff, of course."

"So, you want me to be your maid."

"Goodness no! You're not Salvadoran. I won't have you scrubbing toilets or anything like that. But I could see you taking on duties such as coordinating my appointments and charity work. Like a social secretary, of sorts. Or helping Dexter with entertaining, household orders, deliveries, floral arrangements and general management. And yes, perhaps some light housework as well, when needed. Dusting, ironing. Things like that."

"So, your maid."

"It's the best I can offer, Megan. Under the circumstances, you should take it. I pay nine dollars an hour. It includes room and board. I can let you and the child stay in my little back office. We can make it very cozy for you. And, I will cover her well-baby visits, as a bonus."

Megan looked around her tiny, filthy room, and at Maureen, oblivious to the squalor. Fleeing to Safe Harbor had been one thing. But working for Beverly? And living there? How perfectly nauseating, she thought.

On the other hand, and there always was one, it would only be for a month or so, until Megan could cash the *Times* check. She winced: "Do I have to wear a uniform?"

"No. Not every day. On occasion, perhaps. During parties and such."

Megan struggled to complete the mental calculus. Pro. Con. Pro. Con. On the one hand, this. On the other hand, damn. *That.*

"I would need evenings and weekends off," she said after a pause. "To pursue other work."

"That's fine."

"And I'll need a babysitter for those times. Tony."

"The young doorman downstairs?"

"Yes. Otherwise, no deal."

"Alright. Have it your way. Just please, do not tell anybody about that. You know how people in this building talk."

Megan grudgingly thanked Beverly and hung up. She decided not to tell Tony. She wanted to surprise him.

"Are you sure?" He asked when they came back later that morning. "I mean, c'mon. You're going to arrange luncheons for these broads, who obviously hate you and always have, and then *serve* it to them on a platter? In a black dress and little white apron?"

"Wow, Tony. When you put it that way. What a buzzkill." Megan grew lost in thought. "Look, it's only for a while, and I learned long ago how to handle Beverly Gansevoort-Stein and her little platoon of vipers. Besides, I'm here. And I'm hungry."

"Alright. I'll buzz Mrs. G and tell her you guys are downstairs. Can I see you later?"

"I don't know. I have no idea what my hours will be. Or if I'm even starting today. I suspect there's a lot of instruction in my near future."

"I bet there's a manual."

"I bet so, too. Listen, I asked Beverly if you could babysit for Megan on certain nights and weekends when I'm out. Reporting stories, that is. I didn't tell her that part."

"Why not?"

"Because hopefully, before too long, she'll be in one of them. So. You'll do it?"

"Babysit? Are you kidding? I'm crazy about that kid. She's a little Munchkin, you know."

Megan entered the elevator and punched the 28th floor. She was tempted to go to the top, but knew that all she would find was a sealed entrance. And heartache. She rang at Beverly's oaken doors and waited, thinking of the time she stood at that very spot, a nervous young woman from Ypsilanti on a very big date, bearing nothing but a simple smile and a dozen cheap carnations from the Korean deli.

The door opened. It was Isabel, the diminutive, pleasant housekeeper from Mexico, who had forged a bond with Beverly's personal maid, the long-suffering Margarita.

"*Buenos dias,*" Megan said. "*Yo soy Megan.*"

"You speak Spanish," Isabel said in near-perfect American English. "We'll have to remember that the next time we gossip with you nearby. Just kidding!

342

Here, we only gossip about the *senora* and her *loca* friends. It's so easy. I just don't understand what they mean by that term, 'American Exceptionalism.' I sure don't see any around here. Now. please come in. I'll tell the boss lady you've arrived."

"I think I'm going to like you, Isabel."

"I know. Everyone does. It's amazing what you can find out about people that way."

"I'll have to remember that."

"Yes. You will. If you ever need information, I'm a font."

Megan stood in the formal entryway, looking around at her new "home." She had never fully appreciated how, compared to the sleek and sexy penthouse upstairs, this place was so fussy and cluttered, like grandma's house.

After a while, Beverly, acting as though she were Lady Cora of Downton, breezed down the hall to greet Megan, hands outstretched.

"I'm so very glad you're here. Let's get you settled in your room, and then we can take some tea. Backstage, of course. I'll introduce you to everyone. Margarita! Please show Mrs. Bainbridge and her daughter to their quarters."

"Right this way, Mrs. Bainbridge."

"No," Megan protested. "Call me Megan. *Por favor.*"

The room was small but, as Beverly had promised, cozy. The computers and office furniture had been removed, replaced by a flouncy featherbed with royal-blue comforter, an antique wooden cradle, two easy chairs, a coffee table, a desk and chair, several lovely lamps, a mini-fridge and a small walnut armoire. There was also a television: Megan and Tony's late-night bingeing rituals, she was happy to see, could continue uninterrupted.

Isabel popped her head in the doorway. "Okay Megan. Showtime."

She placed Maureen in her cradle and set up the baby-cam, linked to an app on her phone. She grabbed a pad and pen and followed Isabel "backstage," whatever the hell that was.

The entire crew was waiting in the kitchen, at the staff dining table, where tea was being poured. "Now Megan," Beverly began. "I believe you know our House Manager, Mr. Dexter." Megan nodded respectfully. "You shall report to him, mostly, except for when you're working directly under my supervision. And I believe you've seen the girls on your prior visits, Maria Eugenia, the head housekeeper, sweet little Isabel, and Margarita, who sometimes gets a bit confused. You'll learn to work around it. We all have."

"Very nice to see you again," Megan said to them.

"Now, I'm not sure if you've met Rosalinda, our newest. She used to work with Martha until, well, that night. And when Martha got out of Dodge, so to speak. I acquired her. I have no real regrets, so far."

Megan waved at the pretty young maid and smiled. This was the person she wanted to befriend the most.

"We've met, actually." Megan said. "Several times, when I was visiting Martha. I've spoken to her, by the way. Martha. She sends her regards."

"Isn't that lovely?" Beverly said, without bothering, Megan noted, to ask after Martha's well-being. "And last but certainly not least, this is our indispensable Chef. Driver has the day off. You'll meet him another time."

"Heya Megan," Chef said. "It's Gillespie, actually. Jack Gillespie. Ya know, I think my nephew has the hots for you."

Megan laughed. "I'm fond of him, as well."

"Tony? The *doorman*? The one who will be babysitting?" Beverly interjected with a scandalized face. "You didn't mention that part, Megan."

"You didn't ask. But a deal's a deal, right Beverly?"

Beverly cleared her throat. "I prefer that the help refer to me as 'Missus' or 'Madame.' You may also call me Mrs. Gansevoort-Stein, though I realize that's quite a mouthful."

"Yeah, no. That's not gonna happen, *Beverly*." The maids giggled until Dexter cut them off with a stern look and audible *tsk-tsk*. "Because that, I did not sign up for."

"We'll discuss it later," Beverly said. "Now, Mr. Dexter will give you a thorough tour of the house and its inner workings. We're like a well-oiled machine around here, and all it takes is one wrench of a rotten employee to jam up the gears. So please, be careful out there."

"Oil," Megan said, jotting on her notepad. "Gears. Okay, got it. Beverly."

Madame ignored the slight. "Dexter, please get a copy of the House Bible and give it to Megan to study."

"I'm not very religious," Megan said.

"It's not a real bible, silly girl. That's my name for our manual." Hah! Megan thought. She could not wait to tell Tony. "Now, after your tour, come down here for some lunch with the staff and then you can have the afternoon off, if you like, to rest in your room. This evening, before dinner, you and I will go over your duties."

"Am I free after that?" Megan wanted to know. Beverly nodded.

As instructed, Megan appeared in the salon at five-thirty. Beverly was seated in a large, comfortable English wingback, circa 1865, lined with pillows and covered in emerald-green silk – a "gift" to herself during a spring sojourn to Cornwall. On the tea table in front of her was a large purple envelope. Beverly motioned for Megan to sit down across from her, on a polished wood Windsor chair with its rock-hard seat and spindly back. The message could not be clearer.

"Welcome back to the salon, Megan. Of course, this is the only time you will actually be sitting in here. You know. Going forward." Megan stared directly at her new boss in silence.

"I see," Beverly said. "You don't seem very happy to be here. Or appreciative." More silence. Beverly called for Margarita. "It's cocktail hour," she said, pointing at her Serpenti Tubogas watch by Bulgari. "Look, Megan. If you're going to stay here, we're going to have to get along. And to get along, you're going to have to speak. Especially when spoken to."

Megan thought of the strict doorman rules in other buildings that Tony had told her about. She shuddered.

"Yes, Mrs. Gansevoort-Stein," she found herself saying bitterly, much like the lead handmaid Offred ("Of Fred") does when responding to Mrs. Waterford, the icy Wife in whose house Offred is forced to live.

Oh my God, Megan said to herself. I am henceforth to be known as "Ofbeverly."

346

Beverly looked surprised "So, you changed your tune? You're going with Mrs. Gansevoort-Stein after all?"

"No." Megan shook her head. "That was the only time you will actually be hearing me say it. You know. Going forward."

Well, this is turning out to be rockier than I thought, Beverly told herself. But I'll break her in. Just wait. It will be a project. I could use a new project.

"Did you settle in okay?" Beverly asked.

"Yes, thank you. It's very nice."

"And how was the tour?"

"Long and complicated, to be honest. But Dexter was very patient with me. I think he likes me. Or pities me. Or something."

"And the bible?"

"Very…comprehensive. I shall endeavor to study it. Religiously."

"Wonderful!" Beverly clasped her hands together theatrically, as if being presented with a favorite treat. She picked up the purple envelope and handed it to Megan.

"Here's a rundown of your official duties and your schedule for the month of March. Typically, your hours are nine to six weekdays, but some evenings you'll be expected to stay on, especially for large gatherings when we are short of hands. There will be some weekend work, too, as you will see. But I will try to respect your desire to have those off. I don't pay overtime."

Margarita returned with a tray, set down a single martini glass on the tea table, and walked away. "Cheers," Beverly said, lifting her cocktail and smirking. "Oh my, this is good." Megan could have slapped her right there.

Madame went on to explain that Megan would have breaks to check on the baby, and that she herself would do the same on occasion, "because that's probably as close as I'll ever get to becoming a Grandmother. I just don't see Hillary as the mothering type."

Megan opened the envelope. On one page was a list of "Duty Categories" with details on the exact duties entailed under each category. The other pages were weekly calendars, broken into hourly allotments. It was all color coded, so that the activities on the list matched the colors of those on the schedule. Yellow meant "Invitations, Scheduling & Correspondence," blue was for "Household Planning and Purchasing w/Dexter," green meant "Important Meals, Parties & Other Entertaining," pink stood for "Wardrobe & Jewelry Maintenance," and red meant "Reserve for Light Housekeeping & Sundry Related Activities."

"Wanda and I came up with this system a while ago. She thinks it's quite genius, and I agree," Beverly said, beaming with self-satisfaction.

"So, which colors do I have to wear a uniform for?"

"Just the green ones. When you'll be serving. And red, during housekeeping."

"I see a lot of that here, Beverly. Much more than I was led to believe."

"But a deal is a deal, like you said. Right? And, the social season perks up in March, and my poor girls have been overtaxed lately. Since I doubt you'll be staying long, I thought I'd give them time off while you're around."

"That's very socially responsible."

"I try. And, as promised, there isn't *any* toilet cleaning on here, you'll note.

That would've been color-coded brown. Which reminds me, I've decided to give Margarita tomorrow off, so you'll be reporting to me. Eight sharp in my suite upstairs. Dexter will slip a "To Be Completed Today" list under your door overnight. I think you're about the same size as Margarita, so the uniform should be no problem."

"Uniform? Really?"

"Of course. These are red hours. Now, off you go. Staff supper is served at six. Backstage."

"If you don't mind," Megan said. "I think I'll have dinner in my room. With Maureen."

"That's allowed. Just don't make a mess. Remember, don't be a wrench in the gears!"

Megan practically ran back to her room. She wanted to see the baby, of course. But oddly, she also wanted to see Tony. Yes, she was still upset about his clumsy attempt at seduction. But it had been a really weird two days. And now she was, well, *here*. She needed a friend. And some vodka.

Megan called the front desk. "Tony! They have a manual! Can you believe that?"

"Told ya. So. How was your day?"

"Like one of those really bad dreams that, when you wake up, you thank the lord. Or whoever. Listen. You want to come up for a while tonight? I was thinking we could order Chinese. I have *Fleabag* cued up on Amazon."

"Perfect."

"Text me when you're at the door and I'll quietly let you in. No reason to upset Madame on the first night," Megan said. "Oh, and Tony? Can you pick up some Kettle One?"

For the first time in two days, Megan was able to relax. She sat with Tony and ate Kung Pao chicken and spicy sesame noodles, glued to the racy British comedy. Despite the copious copulation on screen, nothing close to that was going to happen in this little room.

"Megan," Tony said. "About the other night. I was a dick."

"That's because you *have* a dick. I can't control my strength. You can't control your boner. So we're even."

"It's just that…well, it's hard. No! Wait! I meant difficult." Tony laughed at his own goof-up, but Megan did not seem that amused.

"Look, Tony. I like you a lot. And you're cute as a baby seal. I'm not saying it will never happen. I'm just saying not any time soon. Okay?"

Tony went home at 10:30.

Chapter 21

Are You Being Served?

The late-winter sun poured directly down East 87th Street and smack into Megan's face. Damn, she thought getting up, don't rich people know about blinds? It was 7:30. Just enough time to feed and bathe Maureen and herself, and then get upstairs to Beverly. As promised, a hand-written note was tucked under the door.

Good Morning Ms. Megan,

I wish to personally welcome you to your first official day working on our team. We all feel most fortunate to have you on board, and hope to make your stay here as free of sturm-und-drang as possible – though it certainly cannot always be avoided, I fear. Mrs. Gansevoort-Stein, it will come as no surprise, can be, shall we say, a bit taxing. So much so that one wants to set one's hair on fire every now and again. But one refrains, in the name of "service" – and those bloody gears she keeps droning on about.

At any rate, as you know, today you will be working upstairs with Madame. You

351

are expected to perform the following duties:

8:00 am – Deliver double latte, The New York Times and croissant with quince preserves to room.

8:10 am – Run bath at precisely 97 degrees Fahrenheit – use of digital thermometer is imperative.

8:15 am – Lay out cosmetics and European skin-care products on vanity, as per instructions in enclosed appendix.

8:25 am - Retrieve breakfast tray from room.

8:30 am – Help Madame select outfit for day. Slate, Bone and Rust are the preferred colors for March

8:45 am – Assist Madame with any dressing requirements she may have. If asked, help with hair and makeup. Discourage overuse of mascara.

9:00 am - 12:00 noon – Dust and vacuum entire upstairs suite, adjoining sitting rooms, Cinema Lounge and Facebooking Room.

Noon – Staff lunch: Tuna melt with chips; iced tea; banana. Backstage.

1:00 pm – Madame's private luncheon with Mrs. Covington in the Dining Room. Pour wine and serve appetizer, bisque, salad, sorbet course, main course and dessert. Set out petit fours and tea on credenza. DO NOT, under any circumstances, loiter while they dine.

2:30 pm – Pick up party dresses at dry cleaners, and three bottles of Domaine de la Mordoree, 2009 Chateauneuf-du-Pape La Plume du Peintre at Madison Cellars. See appendix for addresses and accounts information.

3:00 pm – Feed, brush and play with Walter Mitty.

3:45 pm – Polishing of the jewelry, part one. (Maria Eugenia will instruct you your first time).

5:00 pm – Serve cocktails in Salon.

5:30 pm – "Day In Review" with Madame. Backstage.

6:00 pm – Off duty.

You will find a freshly laundered uniform outside your door. I do hope it fits. If not, Maria Eugenia can make some last-minute alterations.

On a rather personal note, and please do not think me too forward, I wish you all the luck in the world, now and in future. I have followed your travails closely. We all have on staff. We know you are one of us. We are on your side.

Respectfully yours,

Dexter

"Who the hell is Walter Mitty?" Megan said aloud. She opened the door and, sure enough, there was the uniform: black dress with white apron. "At least I don't have to wear a stupid little hat. I'll count my blessings."

Still, Megan felt humiliated, which was, after all, Beverly's point. The last time she was in this house, not that long ago, she was wearing Givenchy. She wished she still had the opulent silver-and-topaz brooch that Rex bought her in Anguilla. But Ms. Cooper had fairly swooped down and snatched it from her hands.

What could she wear, to put Beverly in her place? And then it came to her.

She unzipped a suitcase pocket and pulled it out: A large button that said *WARREN 2020 – Restore The Middle Class. (She has a plan for that).*

It was better than any brooch. This will make her go positively apeshit, Megan thought. She dressed and went to the kitchen, where Beverly's breakfast and a neatly folded copy of *The Times* were waiting on a teak tray. She headed upstairs and knocked on the bedroom door. Beverly was in a silk dressing gown, on the bed, cradling a small animal with mean-looking teeth. Beside her was a form of some kind, and a pen.

"Right on time. Good. I'd like you to meet my ferret. Walter Mitty." Beverly nuzzled the creature with her face. "Walties? Say hello to Megan. I'm afraid we're stuck with her for a while."

"Good morning, Mr. Mitty. Hello, *Bev.* Here's your breakfast. I'll set it right here."

"What's that you have on?"

"This?" Megan pointed to the button. "It says 'Restore The Middle Class,' which is rather ironic, since that's where I started. And now it's something I aspire to."

"How ghastly for you. But Elizabeth Warren? Are you kidding me? Yeah, right. She's going to tax *my* wealth. I've never heard such nonsense."

"You don't want a woman president?"

"We tried that already, didn't we? And look how well it turned out. Besides, Hillary was hardly a Communist. And she didn't look like a librarian at an all-girls school in Vermont. And that voice! She always sounds like she's about to break down in tears."

"She's got my vote."

"So. You're a Communist."

"No, Beverly. I'm a humanist. Ask me how."

"Whatever you are, remove that thing at once. I will not have the help walking around with Bolshevik propaganda."

"Free speech, Beverly. First Amendment and all that."

"Take it off."

"No."

Beverly was flummoxed. Nobody *ever* used that word in her presence, unless she asked if she looked fat in a particular garment. "Very well. Just don't wear it when we have company. I'd never hear the end of it. Now, one other thing before we start. Sign this." Megan walked over and grabbed the paper and pen. "It's a nondisclosure agreement. NDA. Perfectly standard. I mean, we can't have people telling tales out of school, can we? Especially people who want to make a name for themselves. In the media."

Megan read the conditions. "Ferrets are illegal in New York?"

"Terribly. Now sign."

"Why are they illegal?"

"It was that abominable Mr. Giuliani's doing. Something about rabies. And little kids. So absurd."

"Fine." Megan signed. "And don't worry. I won't fink on your mink."

"Ferret. Remember: Ferrets are for cuddles. Minks are for stoles. Now, go run my bath. Ninety-seven. On the dot. You don't want to turn me into bouillon."

When she was all done and dressed, at nine sharp, Beverly critiqued Megan's first "Morning Session" with her.

"You had a good go of things, I suppose. Though the cremes were not in the precise order prescribed. And I think I need more mascara. But we can discuss it all at the Day In Review. Now, I'll see you at lunch. Well, *my* lunch."

The doorbell rang at one o'clock. "Megan!" It was Beverly, of course, crowing from somewhere in the house. Megan was with Rosalinda in the kitchen, finishing up her banana. They had bonded over tuna melts, and Megan felt confident she could extract more bedbug evidence soon.

"Why can't she answer the damn door?" Megan asked.

Rosalinda rolled her eyes. "What do you think? Diamonds are to socialites as doors are to maids. You are expected to love it."

Wanda's face went rice-white when she saw Megan, in uniform, open the door. Clearly, she had no idea.

"Is this some sort of daft joke, Megan? Because, sweetie. Halloween is not for another nine months."

"I just wanted to see that exact look on your face." It was Beverly, standing a few feet behind Megan, smirking. "That expression alone made it worth keeping quiet. Which, believe me, I struggled to do."

"What in the blazes are you babbling on about, woman? Keep what quiet? What's going on?"

"Oh, I'm a crafty one. You are *not* going to believe it. Come to the Salon. I'll fill you in all about her."

"I'm standing right here, you know," Megan said.

"Yes, but why? Wine, please."

A few minutes later, Megan carried the wine and appetizers — broiled Maine mussels with Pernod sauce, crushed Jersey greenhouse tomatoes, and wild golden chanterelles culled from the beech forests of Lower Transylvania – into the Salon.

"Megan," Beverly said, pointing at the Warren button and nodding toward Wanda. "Company."

Megan laughed. "Her? She's not company. Wanda's here all the time, devouring Chef's cuisine for free. She's not a guest. She's an almswoman."

"At least I'm not a maid," Wanda said. "In that *uniform*. Bloody hell."

Despite Dexter's admonishments against "loitering" (also Found in Book Four, Chapter VII of the House Bible), Megan lingered by the door, just for a moment.

"There's a federal seal on the apartment upstairs, Wanda. You can go see for yourself. It's all just too scandalous. Our dear Rexford, rest his soul, apparently landed into a roiling sea of trouble with those Ukrainian gangsters. I can't imagine how he let such a mistake happen."

"Perhaps he was distracted. You know, by that *thing*." Wanda suddenly noticed Megan by the door. "Why Megan. How church-mousey of you. Perched there so quietly."

"There's not much to say, Wanda. After that."

"Well, your entire, sad little situation is just so terribly *stupid*, isn't it?" Wanda replied. "I mean, you're like Lily Bart in *The House of Mirth*. No rich husband, and off to the dusty rooming house you go. Only, her fall from grace took two years. Yours was, what? Ten days? Two weeks tops?"

"My house is not dusty." Beverly said.

"You know what I mean, sweetie."

"It's funny you should mention Edith Wharton," Megan said. "I studied her a lot in college. Even wrote a paper about her. I'll never forget one scholar's quote about that book. 'It exposes an irresponsible, grasping and morally corrupt upper class.' Isn't that perfect?"

As she left, Megan turned and said, "Oh, and Wanda? Perhaps you should maybe *ix-nay* on the *itch-bay* a bit. It's so very played. Everyone says so."

Having put Her Royal Pain-in-the-Arse in her place, Megan proceeded with the rest of her day at work. The Walter Mitty portion turned out to be surprisingly delightful.

Ferrets are cute, cuddly, curious and very, very naughty, Megan quickly learned. Way too smart for their own or anyone else's good, they get into everything. And they love to steal. They also stink. Males are musty, Megan discovered while cleaning Mitty's cage and litter box, as per the instructions in Dexter's appendix.

Later, as she was polishing Madame's astonishing collection of jewelry, part one, the little land mammal came tearing out from under a divan and leapt atop the vanity. He paused at Beverly's iPad and sniffed. Clearly curious, he began tapping the screen with his claws. When the light blinked on he jumped back in surprise. Megan let out a laugh. Still, Walter Mitty persisted. He kept tapping the screen.

Megan gasped in astonishment as she heard a phone ringing on the other end. Somehow, he had managed to speed-dial somebody.

"Hello, Royal Bangkok Restaurant. Is that you, Mrs. Gansevort-Stein?" a woman's voice with a Southeast Asian accent said. Walter Mitty froze, stared at the screen curiously, and sniffed.

"Hello? Mrs. Gansevoort-Stein? Do you have a cold? Yes? Okay. We'll send over your regular order, and put it on the account. Feel better!"

Twenty minutes later, Dexter walked in, carrying a stapled paper bag. "Megan," he said. "Did you order Yam Pla Dook Foo for Madame? It's her favorite guilty pleasure, aside from *Property Brothers*."

"Of course not! Why?"

"Well someone did. Apparently, there's a prankster amongst us."

Megan looked at Walter Mitty. "Maybe he did it."

"That's very droll. Normally, this would be the first matter of business at The Day In Review. But it's been canceled. Madame has developed a headache and will take to her room. So you may leave."

"What a pity," Megan said with a false grin. "On all counts." She wasn't certain, but she thought she detected the corners of Dexter's mouth rise ever so slightly.

Chapter 22

Best Served Cold

The next morning, Megan made a point of sitting next to Rosalinda at breakfast. Eventually, talk turned to her ex-boss, poor Martha, and her unfortunate sudden departure from town. "You know," Megan said after the others had left. "Martha has lawyers looking into the whole bedbug thing. We think they were planted."

Rosalinda looked at her in shock. "How did you know?"

"I didn't. Until I saw that look on your face. Rosalinda, is there something you want to tell me? Does it involve Juan Carlos? Did he come over before the New Year's Eve party?"

Rosalinda broke down in tears. "I'm sworn to secrecy. Please!"

"If Wanda did something terrible, she needs to be held to account. Just think of poor Martha. People are suing her! Any information you have would be extremely helpful."

Rosalinda paused for a deep breath. "That witch blackmailed him. She threatened to call immigration if he didn't do it. Her maid, my cousin Lucia, told me all about it."

"Do you think I could speak with him?"

"I don't know. He's back in Mexico. He couldn't take New Yorkers and their shit anymore. I think they call it 'self-deportation.'"

"Please find out if I can call him. And ask if he'd sign a sworn statement?"

"He will. If I ask him. Just leave Lucia out of it? All she did was translate." Both women smiled. Wanda's ass, Megan knew, now belonged to her.

It wasn't the only item that Megan would add to her burgeoning files that day.

At three o'clock, as she waited backstage for an accounts-payable meeting with Dexter, her phone rang. Caller ID said it was Beverly. "Yes?" Megan said with a sigh. Silence. "Hello?" Nothing. Must be a pocket dial, she thought.

And then she heard it: Sniffing. This was no pocket dial. This was a ferret dial.

There were voices in the background – Beverly, and Margarita, talking about Jenna, of all things. "My friend Sofia cannot stand working for her," Margarita said. "She's *muy mala.*"

"You don't say. How so?"

"Well, for one, she turned in Lorna and Lupe, Mr. Rex's maids, to ICE. At the wedding."

"However do you know this?"

"I heard Miss Jenna talking on the phone. She was very proud of herself. Something about clout. Her family knows people who work for Trump."

"But why would she do such a thing?"

"Simple. She hates Megan. Wanted to ruin her big day."

"Well I think it's appalling. We have an unspoken code. You simply do not rat out the staff of a friend. Or even an enemy. It just isn't done. Full stop."

"Please! Don't say anything. It would get Sofia in trouble."

"I won't. Not yet anyway. Though it may be useful… in the future."

Just then, Dexter walked in. Megan hung up. She already had plenty to go on. Three down, she thought, one to go. The big one.

A few days later, Tony turned up at the door, in uniform. Megan answered.

"Package for you, miss. Just delivered." He grinned and handed her a manilla envelope. "It's marked 'United States District Court for the Southern District of New York.' Is there something you're not telling me? Is your last name actually Gambino?"

Megan laughed as she opened it: some official papers and a letter from the Court, granting permission to interview Stroganoff at the Metropolitan Correctional Facility downtown. It was scheduled for Saturday, for one hour, at two o'clock.

"No. But I *am* going to prison. Stroganoff. It's on. This Saturday. My big proverbial break."

Tony instinctively gave her a giant, prolonged hug. But she didn't mind. She was ecstatic over the news. And besides, he really did smell good.

"Can you babysit?"

"Of course! And then, let's celebrate. I'll take you out to dinner that night. Somewhere kid-friendly. And no hanky-panky. At least not on my part."

Megan said he had a date. Then she went to her room to call Chester Mansfield. "That's excellent," the editor said. "Assuming you get the goods, and he wouldn't agree to speak with you if he didn't have something to say, if you can get it done by, say, Wednesday, the Magazine will run it on Sunday."

Megan's heart rate spiked. This was all so *real*. "Great. Just one other thing. I need to file a Freedom Of Information Act request. With the Department of Homeland Security." Chester asked why, and Megan told him the deportation story. She said she was trying to develop it as part of a larger expose. And, she noted, Jenna did a really shitty thing.

"I want to see any communications between DHS officials and Jenna Forsythe. But I'm not sure how responsive they will be to a lowly freelancer."

"You want me to do it?

"Would you?"

"I shouldn't. But I will. Send me the details, exactly what you're looking for. The narrower the better. It's a fairly innocuous request. I don't see anything tying it up."

"Oh my God Chester. You're the best."

"Please tell my wife that. Take care, Megan. And have fun in jail. That place is a literal dungeon. One inmate who had been in Guantanamo said MCC is a thousand times worse."

Megan hung up. Her mind was spinning. There was so much going on up there, it was hard to keep track. She decided to call Martha, regarding the Wanda files.

"I got the receipts," Megan said. Wanda had sent Martha's *own* exterminator over on New Year's Eve to infest the cloakroom. Rosalinda confirmed he was there, while they were out at lunch. "I'm going to interview Juan Carlos, who's back in Mexico. And get a sworn affidavit. Tell your lawyers. They may want to speak with him, too."

"That wretched woman!" Martha said. "She ruined my goddamned life, and for what? Petty spite over a stupid chairmanship. I really do hope there's a hell, because..."

"At least you can get those lawsuits dismissed. So long, Dr. Pepper."

"I suppose. But I can never get my good name back. Fuck it. I'm taking that stuck-up Brit to court. She's not only going to pay for my enormous legal bills, she's going to pay for what she did to me. They won't be calling me 'The Nice One' anymore by the time I'm finished with her."

"You go girleen! Way to grow a pair."

"Megan, I just can't thank you enough. You're an ace investigator. And, when I win in court, even if it takes years, you'll get a chunk of the award. You deserve it."

Just overhead from Megan, ensconced in the boudoir with Walter Mitty, Beverly was on another call, with the bedbug villainess herself.

"You are not going to believe this," Wanda said. "But you *are* going to love it."

"You're moving back to the UK, dear?"

"You'll regret that remark, Beverly, when you hear what I've done for you."

"I doubt it. But go on."

"I've got the ring."

"What do you mean? Are we in some sort of le Carre novel, now?"

"Shut up and listen. I was poking around to acquire more precious jewels from fallen socialites, you know, like I do, and I came across the most fabulous opportunity. I happen to know Barton Devonshire, Rex's lawyer. He told me the firm was allowed to keep Megan's jewelry to cover legal bills. So, I snatched it up, at a ridiculous discount. Retail is sixty-five thousand. I paid forty-three."

"And?"

"*And?* Why, it's yours, silly. I'll let you have it at cost. For the cause. Of humiliating our dear Megan, that is."

"But what would I do with it? I wouldn't wear the thing."

"Why not? Or, just leave it in your jewelry box. Let her find it during polishing duties. The message will be abundantly clear."

"You are evil," Beverly said. "I *like* evil."

On Saturday after lunch backstage (cold chicken, iceberg salad, banana) Megan got ready for Stroganoff. She took the train downtown and walked across a deserted, windswept Foley Square to the notorious jail, whose nameworthy inmates had included the Ponzi schemer extraordinaire himself, Mr. Madoff.

After clearing security and being escorted by an armed guard to the Visiting Room, Megan sat down, got out her questions and recorder, and waited for Federal Inmate #943667-154. He had aged a decade, she thought. Alexi Stroganoff gave her a boyish shrug and a sad, affectionate smile as he sat down. For a millisecond, she almost felt sorry for him.

Megan kept her demeanor on the cold-businesslike setting. "We only have an hour," she said, switching on the recorder.

"You're in luck. I will tell you all. I have nothing to lose," he said. Megan asked why. "On Monday, I enter plea deal. They have all the goods on me. Even my lawyer says don't fight. So I don't. Maybe this way, I don't die in prison. But maybe I do. Life is funny like that."

They began with his youth, spent in a dreary suburb west of Moscow with no trees and endless rows of concrete blockhouses, where "everyone spied on everyone else." His father was a mid-level functionary at the Ministry of Cellulose-Paper Industry, his neighborhood and school reserved strictly for Communist Party Members. The indoctrination was endless. Young Alexi worked his way up through various Soviet Youth groups, including the "Little Octobrists," the Vladimir Lenin All-Union Pioneer Organization, and finally, the All-Union Leninist Young Communist League, better known as *Komsomol*.

"Deep down, I hated Marxism-Leninism" he said. "We couldn't even have Levi's."

"So that's why you came here? For the jeans?"

"Of course not. I come for same reason as everybody. Money. That, and I really like hamburgers. And Doris Day movies. Is cliché, I know. What can I say?"

"We do have so much to offer the world," Megan smiled, for the first time.

After briefly and somewhat vaguely running through his Brighton Beach years, Alexi turned to his hedge fund business and "the troubles," as he called them. He said it began innocently enough. But then, more clients were cashing in than he had expected, and he came up short. That's when he started juggling. Until it was too late.

"I was borrowing from Peter to pay Paul," he said.

"No, Alexi. You were stealing from Peter. And from us. I don't have a dime. And now I'm working for Beverly. Thank you very much."

His face looked like a Siberian snow drift. "I had no idea. I am very sorry. It won't probably make you feel better, but they will come after the earnings she made from me. Close to four million. Maybe one day, you end up with some."

"But don't you think it's odd that she cashed out, and no one else did?"

"She had her suspicions about me. Correct ones."

"And she didn't tell anyone? Her friends? Rex? The authorities?"

"*Nyet.* She wanted to. But she was under, let's say, pressure."

"You threatened her?"

"No comment. By the way, others will have to give back money too. Including

Russian President."

"Putin?"

"No. Other Russian President. Trump." Alexi explained how businessman Trump had invested early on, turning about thirty-million in holdings into seventy-five million. And then he got out. "Probably only good business deal he did. Only now, he'll have to pay back forty-five million." Megan asked if Trump knew about the Ponzi scheme.

"I have no idea. His lawyer, Mr. Cohen, that bucket of human sewer-sludge, maybe did. He was chummy with the Brighton Beach boys. They knew. But what happens in Brighton, stays in Brighton. Usually."

"Thank you, Alexi. We have five more minutes. Anything else?"

"Just this. I have secret for you. About Beverly. She was in Cuba after revolution. Very good *friends* with Castro."

Megan literally gasped. "No way!"

"*Da*. Way."

"How do you know this?"

"My uncle was a bigwig in the KGB. Stationed in Havana in the sixties. There are photos. Documents. Cables. File cabinets full. Moscow was very curious to know who this young American was. Is all in files. My uncle will email everything to you from St. Petersburg. By the way, her real name is not Beverly. Or Gansevoort. She is Kitty. Kitty Kaczkowski. From Hackensack."

"She's a Jersey girl? That's a hoot. So how long did she stay for, and why did she leave?"

"Eight months. Then Castro put her on a plane. To Mexico City. After the abortion."

"You mean...?"

"*Da.* Premier Fidel's love child."

Megan laughed so hard, she drew a stout shushing from a nearby guard. "And she calls *me* a Communist." She asked what happened after Mexico.

"KGB mostly lost interest. Nobody really knows how she changed name or made it back to States. The Americans were aware of her, through spies in Havana. They wanted her. To make example of. Could have charged her with aiding and abetting. Treason. Still could. But it is doubtful. She's lucky, because there's no statute of limitations. And of course, they shoot you for it."

"Well, that would've made my life easier, at least. Still, I'd love to know how she made it back into the country, undetected."

"Ask her girlfriend. Who went to Cuba with her."

"And that would be...?" Megan readied her pen and pad.

"Now, she goes by Babs McGee. She lives in Poughkeepsie. Runs bakery. Keeps very quiet. This is all we know."

"Babs McGee? Sounds like an Irish dive bar in the East Village.

Alexi chuckled. "I know. The KGB said so too. They have better humor than people think."

The guard motioned for Megan to go. "Alexi," she said, shaking his hand across the partitioned table, "you ruined my life, but you gave me one hell of a story. Two, actually. So thanks. And goodbye."

"Is okay," he smiled. "I owe you. Lots."

It was great to be back out in fresh air, despite the chill. Megan dialed Tony. "Hey! Wanna go on a field trip?" she said. "Poughkeepsie. There's a train in fifty minutes. Bundle up the baby and meet me at Grand Central, by the clock.

At the station, Megan filled Tony in on the interview, and Beverly's hilarious past, as she tapped the words *bakery Poughkeepsie babs mcgee,* into her phone. "Aha!" she said. "This must be the place: McGee's Bake Shop – Fine Soda Bread and Other Irish Delicacies. Four-and-a-half stars on Yelp. Not bad."

The Metro North ride, with its unobstructed wintertime views of the Hudson, was spectacular. It was a bright afternoon, with sunlight glinting off little wind-tossed waves eddying in the steel-gray river. It felt wonderful to escape the city, even for a few hours. They stared out the window as they passed Gilded Age mansions and historic river towns with quaint names like Croton-Harmon, Manitou, Garrison and New Hamburg. Poughkeepsie, at the end of the line, was more, well, Poughkeepsie. Once considered the Queen of the Hudson, it was now neither beautiful nor ugly. It was among the few Hudson Valley towns not to take off flying. Nearly everywhere up and down the river had become as croissant-and-latte as Beverly's breakfast. But the city retained its post-industrial, hardscrabble character, which made it sort of charming, in its own Poughkeepsie way.

The Irish bakery was on Delafield Street, in the northwest corner of town called, ironically, "Little Italy." The wind had begun whipping up off the Hudson, and it was delightful to step inside and be embraced by the warm yeasty smell of oven-fresh bread. The woman at the counter looked about Beverly's age, with defiant green eyes and red hair piled atop her head like tomato-infused linguine. She was neither pleasant nor unpleasant. Just like

Poughkeepsie, Megan thought. "Bab's McGee?" she inquired, smiling.

"Yes," was all that came out.

"Um, my name's Megan…" She hesitated, knowing that people here read the city papers. *"O'Riley.* This is my friend Tony Milano, and this is my little pumpkin, Maureen."

"Hello. Are you here for bread?" Tony said he'd take two loaves, and ordered two coffees. "She's not the most talkative one," he whispered as Babs fetched the drinks.

"Why do I feel like you folks are not just here for bread?" Babs asked. "What do you want?"

"Fine. If you want to get down to business, we're here to talk to you," Megan said. "About Kitty Kaczkowski."

Babs looked as if they were about to faint. She heaved and coughed. She plopped down on a stool. "You're from the government, aren't you? You guys finally caught up with me, fifty-four years later. So much for the almighty Deep State. You *suck* at your job."

"That's not my job," Megan said.

"Then what is?"

"I'm a maid. For Beverly Gansevoort-Stein."

Babs grunted. "The wicked bitch of the Eastside."

"Exactly. But I'm also a journalist. I'm doing an expose on Beverly and her so-called friends. I have questions."

"Hah!" Babs roared, suddenly smiling like an old pal. "Goody. Fire away."

Megan told her everything she'd found out. "I'd like to know two things. I won't use your name. First, why did you go to Cuba?"

"We were stupid, silly girls. Hippies before our time," Babs said with a whimsical look. "We were rebellious and anti establishment. We hated America, and the war. We wanted adventure and we wanted to taste real revolution. Besides, Fidel and Che were totally hot. We went for the Communism, but came home with just scabies."

"Right. Home. How did you get back into the country?"

"Oh, that. We heard they were looking for us at JFK, Port of Miami, Mexican border crossings. We were scared as rats in a box."

"What happened?"

"It turned out that Kitty's cousin was a Congressman from Trenton. Her parents were furious at her, as were mine at me. We'd told everybody we were doing a year abroad in Mexico. We even pre-wrote postcards and had a friend in Mexico City drop them in the mail every so often. Nobody caught on. Until we called them. Panicking."

"And the cousin?" Tony asked.

"He pulled God-knows-what kind of strings at the US Embassy down there. I think he bribed someone. I'm sure he did. Anyway, a week later, we had new passports, new identities. We didn't pick the names. I have no idea who did. But I like mine. Better than hers, for sure. Then we flew to Montreal, caught a bus to the border, and walked right into New York State."

"Do you remember the Congressman's name?" Megan asked.

"How could I forget? Representative Benjamin Crook. Republican of New Jersey."

They finished their coffee, thanked Babs, and headed back to the train. Megan was beaming. Beverly's secret was the best secret of all. Megan's files were almost complete. Just a loose end or two, but this mission was practically accomplished. Damn, she thought. I'm good.

"I have the perfect place for tonight," Tony said. Megan was beat, and so was Maureen. But Tony's eager-beaver look said it all: They had to go. "It's farm-to-table. But not like Jackie's place. It's for people who make under a half-million a year."

"We certainly qualify," Megan said. "Speaking of Green Acres, I've been thinking. I now have solid evidence against all four ladies. And the secrets they keep! My God. But I'm worried about the Jackie part. We were there a while ago. What if she's cleaned up her act?"

"You wanna go back?"

"I can't. But you can. Didn't she ask you to pick up some hours?"

"Yes, but..."

"Uh oh. But what?"

"I can't do it. And I shouldn't've done it before. The cook there is my uncle's best friend, for Christ's sake. I already feel very Benedict Arnold-y. Don't make me be a traitor twice."

"But Tony. I'm calling Jamal Dix soon, to tell him I've collected solid proof of wrongdoing by these four. I need an update on Jackie. If I'm wrong, she could sue me. But no. You gotta protect your uncle's *friend?*"

"Best friend. In my world, that's like family. I'm sorry Megan."

She was furious. "I can't do this." Megan grabbed Maureen and moved to another car. When she stepped out on the platform at Grand Central, he was nowhere to be seen.

Over the next few days, still miffed at Tony, Megan tried to focus on her interview. She had to edit the Q&A down to the assigned words, and write the intro. It was harder than she thought. But she got it done. It was scheduled for Sunday.

On Wednesday morning, quite unexpectedly, Hillary Stein called. "I heard about Stroganoff," she said. "How fabulous is that? *Times*, baby! Good for you."

"How did you find out?" Megan asked. She wondered if Hillary knew about Cuba.

"I follow Isabel on Twitter, to collect dirt on mother. I guess you mentioned it to her? She's very proud of you, you know. I won't say anything. Listen, now that you're writing for *The Times*, I have a scoop. About Pepper."

"What about him?"

Hillary explained that a friend was Pepper's patient. He'd fallen behind in paying for treatment, and Thaddeus was threatening to drop him. But the good doctor proffered an alternative solution. "That fucking creep runs what he calls a 'boutique' porn studio on the side, in Hoboken. It specializes in B&D," she said. "My friend, let's call him 'Brian', says he was forced into it against his will. Other patients, too. Would you like to speak with him?"

"Of course. My God. He really is the devil." As disgusted as she was, Megan could not believe her good fortune: Four Evil Queens, and now the Prince of

Darkness, himself. Dr. Fucking Pepper. This was going to be one hell of an article.

That afternoon Megan was back on ferret-and-polishing duty, part two. This comprised Madame's "major collection," her best, brightest and most ridiculously expensive trinkets. Walter Mitty bounced around the room like a pinball.

And then she saw her ring.

The floodwaters of memory opened uncontrollably. Megan pictured Rex on his knee, with the Tiffany box, and Enrique Iglesias swooning nearby. She fondly remembered wearing it proudly at her wedding, and in Bora Bora. When crazy Katie Collins swooped into her nostalgia, the memories shut themselves off.

"Beverly," she said. "You are a monster."

Megan was shaking, dizzy. She got up to splash cold water on her face in the bathroom and catch her breath. When she returned and sat down, the ring was gone.

Mitty.

Panic would be a mild description of her reaction. That ring could be anywhere by now, under the mattress, stuffed away in some shoes, hidden in a little cranny. Megan didn't know where to start. She entered the cavernous closet and, methodically, began rifling through things.

"Looking for something?" It was Beverly. Megan let out a piercing yelp and dropped a hatbox. She told her boss what happened. "How did you get my ring anyway?" she asked. "Was it Wanda?"

"None of your business. And I don't believe your little ruse for a second. I think you stole it. For spite and money. And now, you're trying to frame my poor ferret. How pathetic."

Megan had enough. "Fuck you, Beverly. I wouldn't steal it and I didn't. How can you think such a thing?"

"All maids steal. From me at least. Now. Cough it up." She held out one palm. "Otherwise, I'll call the police."

"No, you won't. Because, ferret."

"Oh yes I will. Because, NDA."

"Hmmm…Go to jail, or get sued by Beverly? So sue me already."

Beverly growled like a bobcat. "Well, he did swipe my favorite Mont Blanc once, so I guess it's possible. It turned up in the lingerie. Two weeks later. I'll give you four hours. Then I'll speak with my attorney, to discuss law-enforcement options."

Megan continued the frantic search. It seemed hopeless. And then, Walter Mitty let out a most exaggerated belch. She stared at him. "Oh, no," she said. "You didn't." She picked up her phone and Googled *can i give my ferret x-lax?* The short answer was no. Canned pumpkin was the recommended method. Once an hour, until the ferret poops.

Megan ran down to the kitchen. "Hey Jack! We got any canned pumpkin?"

He frowned. "Nope. No cans allowed in this household. But I do have some leftover cream of pumpkin soup. Would that help?"

"It wouldn't hurt, thanks." She went back to the bedroom. To her relief, Walter

Mitty loved the stuff. "Good boy," she said. "Now please. *Poopie?*" Megan continued her foostering around, as Katie Collins would say. An hour went by. Nothing. More soup for Walter. A second hour, and then a third. Still nothing. But shortly after his next serving, he scrambled to the litter box.

"And…we have feces?" Megan said in Katie Collins's Dublin brogue. "Ain't that *grand?*" Ferret scat, she knew, looks like a smaller version of the human variety. But not this time. What came out was more like melting orange sherbet. It smelled like Halloween, gone terribly wrong. But beneath all that sticky viscosity shone the unmistakable glimmer of a precious gem. Megan grabbed some tissues, crossed herself, and dove in. Fighting back vomit, she ran to the bathroom and opened the faucet, not noticing the small orange smudge on her apron.

It was five o'clock. Time for the Day in Review. Megan dried off the ring, put Mitty in his cage, and ran down to join everyone backstage. She sat next to Beverly and dramatically placed the ring in front of her.

"Where was it?"

"He ate it," Megan whispered. "I gave him pumpkin. It came out. He's resting quietly."

After reviewing each employee's performance that day (Megan "really went the extra mile," it was noted, without explanation) Madame turned to the imminent Gala Dinner, a one-year anniversary celebration and thousand-dollar-a-plate fundraiser for Safe Harbor House, scheduled for Saturday. Beverly reviewed the guest list. It was everyone Megan would've expected, though she was shocked to hear that the ladies had given two comps to Thaddeus, "in recognition of his wonderful volunteer clinical work there. Especially with the children."

"You let him work with *children?*" Megan gasped.

"How utterly out of your place to ask. But yes. Why?"

"Never mind. You'll find out."

Beverly went through the menu, timing and staff duties. Megan was assigned to the Formal Dining Room for the entire evening. Madame was about to adjourn when Megan raised her hand. "What is it now?" Beverly asked.

"What are you doing for cocktails?"

"The usual. Martinis and such. Why?"

"I was thinking it might be fun to mix things up a little." Megan stared directly into Beverly's sorry soul. "Maybe something tropical. You know, like mojitos. Or *Cuba Libres?*"

Beverly's face puzzled up. "Dismissed, everybody," is all she said.

As Megan rose, Isabel pointed at her stained apron. "What's that?"

Megan looked down. "Oh! Oh, that's…" She peered at Beverly, who mouthed the words "No ferret!" "That's pumpkin soup. Chef gave me some, and I must've spilled it."

"Well," Isabel said. "It smells awful."

That night, Megan arranged to meet with Hillary and "Brian" at a dark, quiet bar downtown on St. Marks. He was a gawky dark-headed guy of about twenty, with an overly long neck, frightened eyes behind wireframe rims and a nervous twitch. Not exactly, Megan thought, porn material. He told her how he had fallen behind in payments. How Pepper had at first gently offered the work, "as an option…something to mull over." But as the bills piled up, the doctor pressed harder, even threatening to call a collection agency.

"So I relented," Brian said. "Fortunately, he had me use a disguise. After one forty-minute scene, my debt was wiped out."

"I'll need documentation," Megan cautioned. "Otherwise, it's your word against his."

Brian glanced at Hillary, as if looking for approval. She nodded grimly. "Show her."

Brian tapped around his phone until a video appeared. "Presenting, my big star turn," he said. *"Sick Puppies On Parade."* The scene depicted a thin young man, presumably Brian, hands bound behind his back, wearing only a spiked collar, leash and a Schnauzer mask with a large hole in the mouth area. He was on his knees, pleasuring a clearly much older man, who had on a St. Bernard mask, panting phlegmatically and brandishing a whip. Megan winced and looked away.

"I know," Brian said. "Even esthetically speaking, it's pretty bad. And I'm not even gay. At least there was no anal. And, like my gay friends say: 'What's the difference between a straight guy and a gay guy? A six-pack of beer.' Only in my case, it was a fifth of Smirnoff."

"Oh my God. Brian. Or whoever. I'm so sorry. Just one thing, how do we prove that's you?"

"Simple." He held up the phone again. Megan braced herself and looked. "See that tattoo? On my ass?" Megan nodded. Brian handed the phone to Hillary and said, "shoot this." He quickly lowered his pants to reveal the same tattoo: Popeye, with a can of spinach and bulging bicep. "Long story," Brian said. Hillary snapped the shot

"Can you email me that? And a screenshot from the film. Of Popeye?" Megan asked. "Now, you said there were others. Will they talk?" Brain said maybe.

Megan asked why they didn't go to the authorities.

"We haven't decided. We all signed releases, so I'm not sure it's a crime. For now, we think the media is the best way to begin. Besides, we'd rather sue him, than send him to jail."

Megan laughed. "Well, the DA might have another opinion. I don't know if coercion is a crime, but extortion is."

The following day, two critical communications popped into Megan's inbox. The first was from Chester Mansfield, with an attached file containing FOIA-acquired rounds of emails between Jenna and the deputy assistant director of U.S. Immigration and Customs Enforcement, "concerning two illegal aliens working for Rexford Bainbridge, III at 1080 Fifth Avenue, NY, NY 10128."

Jackpot.

The second was even better. It was from St. Petersburg. It contained absolutely everything, including a grainy photo of a shirtless Fidel and bikini-clad Kitty, wading through the water at Playa Varadero, holding hands. If you looked closely, you could see the little bulge in her belly.

That evening, Megan took Maureen out for some air while she could: One final, early-spring snowstorm was expected. Tony was on duty. They regarded each other cautiously.

"Tony, I'm so sorry. That was very rude of me. On the train. I was only thinking of myself. Maybe I'm a bit too involved with this story."

"Megan. The thing is, I wasn't thinking about *you*. Only this friend of my uncle, who I don't even know that well and, frankly, he's kind of a chump. A bit racist. Besides, he's just as wrong as Jackie. Fuck him, and his reputation." He handed her a folder. "Forgive me?" Inside were photos of the dumpster, in all its inglorious Perdue and Green Giant splendor. He'd even held a copy of yesterday's *Post*, showing the date, off to one side.

"I tended some bar last night," he said. "I just emailed those to you, too."

Megan ran around the desk to hug him. And then, to her total surprise, she kissed him. On the lips. Hard. "Hey," she said. "Come up and watch some TV tonight. Oh, and, Tony. You got a toothbrush?"

His sensational smile, sweet but randy, burst out all over. "I'll pick one up," he said.

Megan went upstairs, called Jamal and gave him the elevator pitch.

"Jesus, Joseph and Dalilah!" He said. "So. Let's recap: Jenna turned in your maids; Jackie is pawning off Perdue as Amish; Wanda staged the bedbug scandal; Pepper's a felon, a very creepy felon; and our dear Mrs. Gansevoort-Stein is a former communist named Kitty who used to fuck Fidel? Hah!-Hah!-Hah!"

"Yep," Megan said. "So?"

"So, yes! Great work. Just dot those I's and cross those T's. Three times over. This has to be rock solid. Like Ryan Gosling's abs."

"I've got the goods, Jamal. Trust me. Just be sure to make it to dinner. There will be an unannounced *presentation*. And then the handoff to you. How much will I get for this?"

"Let me think about it. It will be the full front-page cover, of course, with a jump of two or three more pages. Probably around two grand. Maybe a bit more."

"Awesome. See you Saturday."

Megan was actually jittery before Tony arrived that evening after his shift. She hadn't felt this way since that first night in Anguilla. With Rex. Tony got there at eight, holding up a bag from the local diner, and a toothbrush. They settled in to watch their agreed-upon choice, *Curb Your Enthusiasm.*

After a few acerbic episodes, Megan snuggled up to Tony. For the first time, she rubbed her hand over his rippled stomach. He kissed her sweetly. "I have something to tell you. There's a dinner party here this Saturday. And I'm serving. But more than just the chateaubriand. I'm pulling the curtain back on the whole lot of them. Then I'm leaving."

Tony looked crushed. "You mean, back to…?"

"Yes. We go Saturday. After dinner." She paused a moment. "Look, why don't you come with me? Between *The Times*, the *Post*, and what little I've saved up here, that's almost nine thousand. That's new-life money in Michigan."

"Leave? Here?"

"Yes, Tony. Leave. But with me, and Maureen. Cooking schools are much cheaper out there. And Todd and Carlitos are starting a catering company, out of home, for now. You can be part of that. It's a wonderful opportunity."

"But I got friends and family here. Work. I dunno. Can I think about it? I can't just up and skip town by Saturday."

Megan smiled. "Of course. And, it's a two-hour flight, if you ever change your mind."

They got undressed and climbed into the feather bed. Tony felt smooth and warm. Everything about sex with him was the opposite of Rex. Rex had been a raging bull, always in a bit of a hurry. Tony was soft and slow in his approach, lingering gently with his lush lips along her stomach, on her neck and around her nipples. Where Rex would jam his tongue in her mouth, Tony used little flicks and swirls that were almost ticklish, but highly erogenous. Rex always assumed that oral sex was in the offing, Tony asked solicitously, cautiously. There was just nothing forceful about him in bed, and Megan loved that. It was the most relaxed sex she'd ever had. And Tony's cock, while beautiful, was considerably more manageable than the monster that hung between her husband's legs. She climaxed four times that night. A record.

Friday was quiet at 1080. Madame was spending the day antiquing with Wanda in Bucks County, where they would overnight at a little spa outside New Hope. The snowstorm had picked up strength and now the stuff was coming down hard, obscuring the park views. It made the day feel cozy indoors. Megan passed most of it doing light housekeeping and helping Dexter and Maria Eugenia manage orders and deliveries for the gala dinner. She was also assigned to ferret-sit for an hour, with all gems securely locked down, naturally.

Megan and Tony spent their second night together, her last night in New York, in her quarters. Megan knew she would miss her friend, now with benefits. Really good ones. Besides that, he'd been there for her throughout the insanity of the past few weeks. Leaving would be hard. But she just couldn't afford to live here. And like the exterminator Juan Carlos, she had had it with most New Yorkers. It was time to self-deport. JetBlue, she thought, take me away.

They both had the daytime off on Saturday. As Tony drank coffee, watched the NBA game and played with Maureen, Megan spent the late morning loading up the lap-top he'd brought over. She quietly marveled at her files, now complete and exquisitely catalogued. Each document, diplomatic cable, photograph, email, hotel receipt, sworn affidavit, and interview transcript was arranged according to defendant. Only, this was not going to be a trial.

This was going to be a massacre.

They spent the afternoon shopping for baby things, eating at a vegan place, Faceless Foods, Megan wanted to try, and taking one last stroll through the winter-wonderland park, where they stopped to watch kids sled down a hill, squealing wildly, something that delighted Maureen to no end.

"Megan," Tony said. "I'm coming up after dinner. To help you with your things and ride with you to the airport."

"Even better, come before dinner. That's when the fun begins."

Back at Beverly's, Madame was in a state. "We were practically snowbound at that damn spa!" she complained to Dexter, as if it were his doing. "What else could we do but go downstairs and order the Corinthian Body Polish and Gunkan Nori Seaweed Wrap Detox? And dear God, the antiquing was abysmal. When the hell did Bucks County go all maple-and-chintz? Everything was depressingly Dolly Parton."

The doorbell began ringing at seven, as guests arrived and cocktails were poured. Court was now in session.

As she expected, reactions to seeing Megan, hands clasped, in uniform, waiting quietly in the Formal Dining Room, were mixed. Most of the men, Brent Ashby from the Stock Exchange, Chester Mansfield, Trevor Covington, Jonathan Farquharson, Jamal, and the guys from P&G, looked sorry for her, embarrassed, even.

But Thaddeus Pepper, his soap-star gal Veronica LaSalle, and that contemptable quartet of hoochie-mammas either regarded Megan with curious disdain, like some freakshow act at a back-highway carnival, or ignored her altogether, like an invisible one.

Dinner was announced at eight and everyone took their seats. As the first course was served, lobster *en croûte* with braised endive and *crème de Cognac*, Madame clanked an empty wine glass. "I believe a toast is in order everyone! Just imagine. One year of saving mommies and their precious babies. And none of it could have happened without you. Or, well, me, of course."

Wanda squawked. "She just can't help herself, can she? God knows we tried."

Beverly ignored her. "And what a whirlwind year it was! My goodness, exploding cakes and worldwide headlines, Anderson Cooper and the unyielding generosity of Procter & Gamble." Polite applause all around. "But as with any year, unspeakable things happened as well. I'm referring, of course, to the tragic passing of Rexford Bainbridge, our generous benefactor, beloved friend, and my upstairs neighbor." She lifted a glass. "To Rexford."

After the hear-hears had died down, Jamal spoke up. "Aren't you forgetting someone, Beverly?" He nodded toward Megan.

"I assure you," she replied, "I am not."

"Well then, I have a toast, too. To Rex's dear widow, Megan, a friend and, now I can say with confidence, a colleague. You see, Megan here has made the big leagues." He held up a copy of the *New York Times Magazine*, which had just hit the stands. There were loud gasps.

"*Stroganoff?*" Wanda said. "What in God's name is that larcenous reptile doing on the cover?"

"Cover? Really?" Megan ran over to Jamal and grabbed the magazine. "Holy moly. You put it on the cover, Chester? I can't believe it!"

"It was something of a fourth-quarter decision," the editor explained. "But your piece was so compelling, they went for it. I wanted to surprise you."

"Let me see that," Beverly snapped, holding out her hand. It was passed down the table, left-to-right, as etiquette dictated. "How Stroganoff Busted Me: The Rise and Fall of a Charlatan," she read. "By *Megan Bainbridge*? What is this? When did you speak to him? What did he tell you?"

"It's my ticket out of here. Last Saturday. And you'll find out."

"Damn," Jamal marveled. "I may have to pay you more. Landing two covers in a week."

"What are you talking about, Mr. Dix?" said Beverly, who was now adopting the appearance of a cornered wombat.

"Megan's been a busy, busy girl," he chuckled. "Like she said, you'll find out."

Megan cleared her throat. "Now, I have an announcement. And a few things to say."

"You do *not* speak unless spoken too!"

"Sure, Bev. That horse is so far out of the barn, it's halfway to California by now. This is my last night here. I'm leaving. This job, this house, this city. And best of all, you."

"Do you *promise*?" Jackie blurted out.

"Oh my God!" It was Jenna and her lightly-stretched-canvas face, fresh from Brazil. "My life coach, Tenzin the Tibetan, predicted this on his I Chingy thing. Those Asians are so good at mysticism. I can't wait to tell him!"

"Are you really leaving us, sweetie?" Wanda picked up the tickled-pink theme. Megan nodded. "Why, it rather puts one in mind of Oscar Wilde. What was that quote? Oh, right: 'Some cause happiness wherever they go, others, whenever they go.'"

Tony entered the room. In one hand was a suitcase, in the other, he held up a blue-and-white boarding pass that said *JetBlue.* Megan almost fell over with happiness.

"What's that doorman doing here?" Beverly said.

"He's taking me...or us?" Tony nodded, "to LaGuardia. But first, I hope you like slideshows. I have a power-point." She set the laptop on a tall side table, for all to see.

Beverly rumbled. "Young lady, I don't know what underhanded mischief you're up to, but you are to cease. This instant."

"Watch, listen and learn, Bev. Oh, and shut up while you're at it." She flicked on the computer. "This, my friends, is the sordid tale of five exceptionally naughty New Yorkers. I hereby charge them with various crimes - against the state, against humanity, against any sense of common decency. Each of them, in their own special way, is a rapscallion. Or to use the vernacular, an asshole."

As she spoke, Megan looked around the table. She could tell, no one knew precisely what was coming. Several looked petrified. "Let's begin with you, Jenna, shall we?"

"What about me?"

"You reported our maids, Lorna and Lupe, to ICE and had them rounded up on our wedding day. At Saint Thomas Church. Very Christian of you."

"I did no such thing!"

"Oh, but you did. I overheard Margarita telling Beverly how you had bragged about it to friends, about your clout and your White House connections."

"You spied on me?" Beverly said.

"There's a difference between spying…and overhearing. You see, your ferret likes to make calls."

"Megan!"

"That's right everyone. Beverly here owns a highly unlawful pet. Walter Mitty, who has a keen affinity for iPads. He calls people. Thai restaurants. Me. That's how I overheard."

"You have no proof!" Jenna said, now shaking.

"No, Jenna? I figured you'd never heard of FOIA, the Freedom of Information Act. It's remarkable what the government will turn over, if you just ask. I give you Exhibit A." The string of emails between Jenna and DHS/ICE appeared on the screen. "They speak for themselves. According to Beverly, Jenna violated a sacred code of high-society honor: Don't ICE the help. And this wasn't some misguided act of Trumpian patriotism. She did it simply because she doesn't like me."

Jenna ran from the table in tears, leaving the others to blink in stony silence.

"Buh-bye Jen-Jen," Megan smiled. Tony was trying hard not to crack up, she noticed.

"So, who's on deck? Ah yes, our resident restaurateur, Mrs. Jacqueline Farquharson. Now, has anyone ever noticed how her braised, organic, Lancaster County chicken is just a little too plump? That's because it's not from the Amish. Not even the Mennonites. It's from Frank Perdue. That's right, Jackie charges fifty bucks for a buck-fifty breast. Meanwhile, the farm-to-table-fresh veggies are frozen Green Giant, and the hollandaise comes literally in buckets, courtesy of Knorr Foods/Unilever USA."

"You lie!" Jackie leapt up, inelegantly wadding her napkin on her plate. "I'll sue you!"

"No. You won't. Though the New York State consumer affairs people might sue *you*. I have already sent them, the Attorney General, the USDA, and for good measure, the Better Business Bureau Exhibits B and C. You can see the labels for yourself, in the dumpster. One set of photos was taken on opening night, the other...when was that Tony?"

"Wednesday."

"Why you little snot-weasel!" Jackie curled a lip at Tony. "And after I gave you work."

"Maybe so. But at least my garbage isn't newsworthy, Mrs. Farquharson."

Megan loved that. "Moving on. Our next case is going to be fun. Yes, I'm talking to you, Wanda Covington."

"For fuck's sake. Bugger off and leave me out of this barmy circus."

"But Wanda, you're practically in center ring. Or shall I say, center *cloakroom*? You see, everyone, New Year's Eve at Martha Bradbury's, when so many came home itching with bedbugs, was not poor Martha's fault." She pointed at Wanda. "It's the Brit what done it."

"What utter tosh. You've gone right off your trolly, haven't you?"

"I give you exhibits D, E and F. First is the roll-call from the last Safe Harbor board meeting. As you see, Wanda ran against Jackie to replace Beverly. The tie-breaking vote was Martha. We know how that turned out. Hence, we have a motive: bald-faced revenge. The next two exhibits are my interview transcript with, and sworn affidavit by, Martha's exterminator. Wanda blackmailed him with deportation to infest Martha's cloakroom. Now we have means. Finally, she sent him over when she knew we would be taking Martha out to lunch. Rosalinda confirmed this. Opportunity. I rest my case. Utter tosh, it is not."

The entire table turned and glared at Wanda, who seemed to be shrinking in her chair.

"Penny for your haughts, *Wanda*," Megan said.

Thaddeus stood up. "You lousy British skank! Do you have any idea how long it took me to get rid of those things? I even brought them to my fucking office!"

"Martha is moving to have all lawsuits against her, including yours, Dr. Pepper, dismissed. I advise you to refile…" Megan looked at Wanda, "*elsewhere*. And Wanda? Martha's amassed a battery of high-powered attorneys, who now have this evidence. That Rocky Mountain Hemp Widow is loaded for bear. I suggest you lawyer up, too, lady. Tout-suite."

Megan turned to Pepper. "As for you, good doctor, be grateful your bedbug problems are over, because things are about to get extremely more itchy for you." He sat down and glared at her, half in fury, half in terror. "Now, what Jenna, Jackie and Wanda did was terrible. Unforgivable. But not criminal. You, however, may have the word "felon" in your near future.

Megan explained the whole *Sick Puppies on Parade* situation as delicately and non-graphically as possible, then put the next three exhibits on screen: the transcript with "Brian," the Popeye tattoo from the screensaver, and a

390

carefully cropped pic of his butt. She looked at Beverly. "Still want to have him volunteering with the children?"

Megan said other victims were ready to step forward, to file civil suits. "I suggested they consult with Rex's lawyer, Barton Devonshire. That man's a human shark. You know him Wanda. He hired a crazy Irishwoman to appropriate and appraise my engagement ring, which he then sold to you, which you passed on to Beverly, and which then passed through the GI tract of Walter Mitty. What a long, strange trip it's had. Meanwhile, Thad, the Manhattan DA wants to speak with you. I imagine your parole officer is probably in the tenth grade right about now."

Thaddeus stood up again, this time wobbly and askew. He took in the looks of horror flying his way. A rush of blood coursed through him. "B'but...," he mumbled weakly. Pepper turned avocado green and put his hand on his stomach. And then he fainted, forward, slamming onto the solid-oak dining table with a deafening *bang!* The impact toppled two glasses of specially ordered, unoaked Alsatian Gewürztraminer and sent his creamy lobster *en croûte* whizzing into the face of Veronica LaSalle, who let out a high-pitched screech.

Dr. Pepper quickly came to. "Sorry about that. Damn, what was *in* that sauce?" he tried to say nonchalantly. "Anyway, what I was going to say is they signed releases. So, I'm good." He staggered off to the bathroom to clean up, conspicuously unassisted.

After an eternity of silence, Beverly spoke at last. "You said five, Megan."

"I did, Bev. What's interesting about this last case is the victimless nature of the crime. The first four perps screwed people in awful ways. But you didn't. Your transgression was fairly harmless, though the Johnson and Nixon administrations didn't see it that way. Before they gave up looking for you."

"For me? You're insane."

"Am I? *Kitty?*" Beverly did not say a word. She didn't move.

"I didn't include this in my *Times* article, but Stroganoff told me many colorful stories about our Beverly, or as she was once known, Kitty Kaczkowski." Megan related the entire jaw-dropping Cuba story while clicking from one exhibit to another, from K to X, including her interview with Babs McGee. The Castro-on-the-beach photo and abortion records caused particular stir.

"What do you *want?*" Beverly hissed.

"I don't want anything. Not from any of you. Though I'd accept an apology. But what I'm going to *do*, is publish this. That's where Jamal comes in." Megan pulled a thumb-drive from the laptop and tossed it to the columnist. "Catch," she said. "And Godspeed."

Jamal slipped the thing into his breast pocket and bolted for the door. "Get him!" yelped Thad, who had, surprisingly, returned to the table. "Get that fucking thumb-drive!" He jumped up, knocking P&G's Vanessa Yoon down to the Persian carpet. Wanda and Jackie chased after him, but Jamal was already in the elevator before they reached the door.

Beverly's place emptied out quickly, with a thousand-dollars-worth of uneaten chateaubriand taking up all that counterspace. Chef was miffed, and Dexter beside himself. Tony helped Megan gather her things. When they finished, she went backstage to say goodbye to everyone. Tears were shed. Before she left, Megan went upstairs and knocked. No answer. She slipped inside to find Beverly slumped at the vanity staring in the mirror, hair down and makeup removed, looking older than dirt. Mitty was sniffing in his cage.

"Goodbye, Beverly."

Madame sat motionless, her back to Megan. "You'll get through this. You're strong. By the way, Jamal swore to me, not one word about Walter Mitty. So don't worry, the ferret stays in the picture." Beverly got up and fetched her beloved pet. She buried her face in his warm flank and sobbed like she had not sobbed since Mr. Stein passed away.

"Oh, and Babs McGee sends her regards. Sort of." Megan turned and left.

"What have I done to deserve this?" Beverly wailed. But then, she suddenly thought of every transgression that she and the ladies had lobbed against Megan with such merry abandon, right from that first night at Piazza San Marco. Megan wasn't a bad person, really. Why had they ganged up on her like that? She was no witch, yet this had been mass hysteria. They had run her through a crucible of nonstop humiliation and scorn. They were the new villagers of Salem. The four had been implacably brutal, to the point of shoving that ring in the poor girl's face. It was depravity unbuckled.

And then, Beverly Gansevoort-Stein brightened. *The ring.* I'm never going to wear that thing. Especially now. Besides, it *is* hers. She retrieved it from its box and sprinted to the window. Megan and Tony were down in the street, loading stuff into a taxi, where Maureen was waiting in her safety seat.

"*Yoo-hoo!* Up here!" she cried. They looked up. "Megan! Catch!"

Megan watched the metal object tumble through the snowy night, just like her first night in the city, also snowing and also on Fifth Avenue, though much further north, when Bongload Bill's keyring carved a tiny chunk from her forehead. "Tony!" she grabbed him. "Get back!"

Thwonk.

The ring disappeared into the snow, just as a heavy plow roared past, hurtling a three-foot berm of dirty road slush on top. Beverly watched anxiously from above as Tony ran inside for a shovel. It took a while, but they found it. Megan looked up. She could barely make out Beverly, waving goodbye, before shutting the window and disappearing into the dark.

They climbed in the cab, snuggling in the back, as they rumbled down the fabled avenue. Megan rested her head on Tony's shoulder, put the ring on, and smiled.

"Imagine," she said, "this very expensive piece of jewelry once popped out of a ferret's ass. It's something we can tell our grand kids one day. Ain't life *grand?*"

Manufactured by Amazon.ca
Bolton, ON

20320804R00223